JESSICA JUDE

# Joker's Endgame

*Copyright © 2026 by Jessica Jude*

*All rights reserved. No part of this publication may be reproduced, stored, or transmitted in any form or by any means, electronic, mechanical, photocopying, recording, scanning, or otherwise without written permission from the publisher. It is illegal to copy this book, post it to a website, or distribute it by any other means without permission.*

*This novel is entirely a work of fiction. The names, characters, and incidents portrayed in it are the work of the author's imagination. Any resemblance to actual persons, living or dead, events, or localities is entirely coincidental.*

*First edition*

*ISBN: 979-8-9906231-6-3*

*This book was professionally typeset on Reedsy. Find out more at reedsy.com*

*To everyone who's had to claw, scrape, or fight their way to survival
—you're worth fighting for.*

# Contents

| | | |
|---|---|---|
| | Author's Note | iv |
| 1 | "Hit Me With Your Best Shot" - Pat Benatar | 1 |
| 2 | "CANCELLED!" - Taylor Swift | 10 |
| 3 | "Cleopatra" - Nova Twins | 16 |
| 4 | "illicit affairs" - Taylor Swift | 24 |
| 5 | "Queen" - Loren Gray | 30 |
| 6 | "Father Figure" - Taylor Swift | 37 |
| 7 | "I Like Me Better" - Lauv | 42 |
| 8 | "Anti-Hero" - Taylor Swift | 46 |
| 9 | "Actually Romantic" - Taylor Swift | 52 |
| 10 | "Electric Touch" - Taylor Swift ft. Fall Out Boy | 60 |
| 11 | "Eldest Daughter" - Taylor Swift | 66 |
| 12 | "Treacherous" - Taylor Swift | 73 |
| 13 | "Bad Habits" - Ed Sheeran | 80 |
| 14 | "Blank Space" - Taylor Swift | 90 |
| 15 | "When Did You Get Hot?" - Sabrina Carpenter | 97 |
| 16 | "These Arms of Mine" - Otis Redding | 108 |
| 17 | "Dirty Little Secret" - The All American Rejects | 114 |
| 18 | "Fire Up the Night" - New Medicine | 125 |
| 19 | "Getaway Car" - Taylor Swift | 130 |
| 20 | "Sick Little Games" - All Time Low | 141 |
| 21 | "That's So True" - Gracie Abrams | 145 |
| 22 | "Better Than Revenge" - Taylor Swift | 149 |
| 23 | "Bad" - The Cab | 158 |

| | | |
|---|---|---|
| 24 | "The Fate of Ophelia" - Taylor Swift | 163 |
| 25 | "Maneater" - Nelly Furtado | 171 |
| 26 | "A Love Like War" - All Time Low ft. Vic Fuentes | 177 |
| 27 | "R U Mine?" - Arctic Monkeys | 185 |
| 28 | "Bring Me to Life" - Evanescence | 192 |
| 29 | "No I'm not in Love" - Tate McRae | 195 |
| 30 | "The Archer" - Taylor Swift | 201 |
| 31 | "cowboy like me" - Taylor Swift | 210 |
| 32 | "Rebel Girl" - Bikini Kill | 218 |
| 33 | "End Game" - Taylor Swift ft. Ed Sheeran, Future | 221 |
| 34 | "Call It What You Want" - Taylor Swift | 227 |
| 35 | "Nothing's Gonna Hurt You Baby" - Cigarettes After Sex | 236 |
| 36 | "us." - Gracie Abrams ft. Taylor Swift | 246 |
| 37 | "Mr. Brightside" - The Killers | 257 |
| 38 | "Misery Business" - Paramore | 264 |
| 39 | "Out of the Woods" - Taylor Swift | 271 |
| 40 | "Paper Crown" - Alec Benjamin | 280 |
| 41 | "if u think i'm pretty" - Artemas | 286 |
| 42 | "Jump Then Fall" - Taylor Swift | 291 |
| 43 | "Colour My Heart" - Charlotte OC | 296 |
| 44 | "Control" - Halsey | 301 |
| 45 | "You're Losing Me" - Taylor Swift | 307 |
| 46 | "Burn Me Beautiful" - Shadow Beloved | 314 |
| 47 | "Haunted" - Taylor Swift | 323 |
| 48 | "Ruin" - Shawn Mendes | 332 |
| 49 | "The Way I Loved You" - Taylor Swift | 337 |
| 50 | "exile" - Taylor Swift ft. Bon Iver | 345 |
| 51 | "The Scientist" - Coldplay | 355 |
| 52 | "champagne problems" - Taylor Swift | 361 |
| 53 | "I Hate That It's True" - Dean Lewis | 367 |

| | | |
|---|---|---|
| 54 | "Cold As You" - Taylor Swift | 375 |
| 55 | "The Black Dog" - Taylor Swift | 382 |
| 56 | "end game" - Cat Burns | 389 |
| 57 | "The Great War" - Taylor Swift | 395 |
| 58 | "Clarity" - Zedd ft. Foxes | 406 |
| 59 | "You Are in Love" - Taylor Swift | 413 |
| *Up Next . . .* | | 423 |
| *Acknowledgments* | | 424 |
| *Also by Jessica Jude* | | 426 |
| *About the Author* | | 427 |
| *Discussion Questions* | | 428 |

# Author's Note

Wesbourne is a fictional island country set in the middle of the Atlantic Ocean between North America and Europe. It is ruled by a queen, and you can read about her story in Thrones We Steal. While the country is a fantasy concocted in the playground of my mind, all of my books are contemporary and take place in the modern world.

This book is the fourth and final book in a series, and while they can be read alone, I recommend starting with Book 1, Ace of Betrayal, for the full reading experience.

The following book contains mature content and potential triggers, including: sexual abuse of child (off-page), marital affair (not between MMCs but involving FMC), car accident (off-page), coma, verbal / emotional abuse, language, and explicit sexual content. It is not intended for readers under 18. If you prefer to keep the door closed, you may want to skip chapters 4, 15, 16, 17, 18, 19, 27, 30, tiny bit at the end of 33, 34, and 58 (yeah, this one's spicy).

Each chapter is named after a song that fits its vibe. (Yes, Taylor and I practically wrote it together.) Access the entire playlist on Spotify by going to jessicajude.com/joker-playlist

And finally, I am not responsible for any damages inflicted upon books or reading devices by the consumption of this book.

xoxo Jess

# 1

## "Hit Me With Your Best Shot" - Pat Benatar

*Maeve*

There are few things in life worse than waiting, but I'll tell you one of them. *Waiting with Pierce St. James.* The man is absolutely maddening.

Take right now, for instance. I'm pacing, but he's on the couch in his living room, the one facing the large window with the panoramic view. The lights of the city are nearly hidden by the storm clouds rolling in. You might see him and think there's nothing particularly obnoxious about the way he's sitting there, but you'd be missing all the little details.

He has an ankle propped on his knee and an arm draped across the back of the sleek modern sofa, settled in as though he's relaxed, when I think it's safe to say "relaxed" is not an appropriate adjective to describe either of us right now. Which makes his posture a lie.

Then there's his face. It's not exactly a bad face, not what you'd call ugly. Sharp cheekbones and jawline, pouty mouth, symmetrical. It's passable, okay?

Fine, it's definitely in the top 1 percent of attractive faces in the country. Or it would be if not for those eyes. Dark brown, nearly black, and spaced the proper distance from his nose, it's not the eyes themselves that are the problem. It's what he does with them.

I spin on my heel in front of the window, and sure enough, he's watching me. Those stupid eyes travel the length of me—and listen, I know I look good tonight, but the way they linger over every inch of my body makes my muscles tighten.

Smoothing my hands over my long-sleeve dark floral-print minidress, I continue stalking the living room, ignoring him. A tiny huff comes from the sofa, like he's scoffing at me, and it takes every single ounce of willpower I have not to march over and smack that smirk right off his face.

The man is a menace, a godforsaken outright smudge on humanity. The only thing more shocking than the fact that I am stuck in the same room with him—*alone*—is the fact that we were friends up until this past year.

I *know*. You're wondering how I could've possibly been friends with a guy like him. Trust me, it has been the cause of countless sleepless nights. It bothers me that I didn't notice it before, not because I have regrets from the past twelve years, but because I'm afraid it means my skill at reading people is slipping.

If Pierce and I could have been friends for nearly half my life and I didn't recognize the signs, what other things am I missing? The thought is terrifying.

Movement from the other side of the room snags in the corner of my eye, and I turn on instinct. Pierce has gotten up and is removing his jacket. The man practically lives in custom suits—not something I typically have a problem with, but lately, everything about him makes my blood boil. Doesn't he own a pair of slacks?

Muscles ripple under his shirt as he tosses the jacket over the back of the couch. My mouth goes dry before I realize what I'm doing. I jerk my eyes back where they belong—the far end of the room—and resume my pacing.

I don't need to look to feel that infuriating smirk being cast in my direction.

When I reach the end of the room and turn around, I glance at the clock above the mantel. Pierce and I have been out here for nearly forty minutes. If the rest of them don't invite us into the game room soon, I'm going to snap. Why the hell is it taking this long to put together a stupid challenge?

"If they are in there playing poker," I mutter under my breath, "so help me god."

Pierce lifts his chin, and I realize I've spoken out loud. Fuck. I had no intention of being the first to cut through the silence filling this room like smoke. As if the man needs another reason to gloat.

"What will you do if they are?" he says, now that I've broken the silent treatment and nonverbally declared him the winner in our little standoff. He's perched on the arm of the sofa, just begging to be knocked over.

I briefly consider ignoring him, but do you know how hard it is to go forty minutes without speaking? God, I've been getting lightheaded with the backlog. "None of your goddamn business," I snap.

His eyebrows do this subtle upward flick, as though I've amused him, and you know what? He can go fuck himself.

"Actually," he says, standing and immediately shifting the energy in the room, "since this is my flat, I have a vested interest in knowing whether you plan to torch it to the ground to spite our friends."

I roll my eyes to let him know he doesn't ruffle me, even though my palms have become as clammy as a dead body's. "Don't be an imbecile."

This time his brows move up an entire inch. He shoves his hands into his pockets. "Me? The imbecile?" He takes a step toward me, and I instinctively take a matching one backward. "I'm not the one with a vintage hot-air balloon in my basement."

Tension radiates from my jaw to my head. I force a single deep breath in through my nose, out through my mouth, the way my yoga teacher is always blathering on about. It doesn't help, which confirms my suspicions that she doesn't know what she's talking about. "I wouldn't have that stupid balloon if you hadn't brought in that bloody shell bidder."

Once again, the corner of Pierce's mouth lifts into that ridiculous smirk that I swear will get him killed one of these days. My hands twitch with desire to do the honors.

"And yet, we agreed on the shell bidder," he says.

"For the thousandth time, we did not!" I say, my voice rising several decibels higher than I intended. I bring it back down to a normal range. "The plan all along was for me to drive up the bidding."

He shakes his head as though I'm a clueless child and he's humoring me. "Have you considered that you might be dealing with early onset dementia?"

My nostrils flare as I intensify the glare I have leveled at him. "I do *not* have dementia."

Forehead creasing with mock concern, he tsks and shakes his head. "And yet you own a hot-air balloon." Leaning in closer, he lowers his voice, and I catch a whiff of his cologne—sharp, smooth, a little spicy. "One you paid an obscene amount of money for."

"Because your bidder wouldn't back down!" I say.

Several months ago, we attended a charity auction with the express purpose of exacting revenge on Deirdre Cox. The bitch scammed both of our companies and dragged the name of our joint project, HavenNet, through the mud while pocketing hefty consulting and licensing fees from the people we were trying to help. She is scum of the earth, and I'd like nothing more than to etch my name on her back with the heel of my favorite pair of Louboutins.

You could argue that she's brilliant to have been able to pull off something like that, but I would like to point out that she didn't immediately flee the country after her little scheme. If she were truly smart, she would have taken her millions of stolen money and retreated to a tiny desert island somewhere, where the rest of the world never has to look at her mousy face again.

Instead, she decided to stick around to try to win some old, moldy hot-air balloon. The same one I ended up with, thanks to the bastard standing in front of me.

"Have you taken your maiden voyage yet?" Pierce asks, snapping me out of my fantasy of hunting Deirdre down and forcing bits of torn fabric from her precious balloon down her throat.

"Actually," I say, through a smile that feels more like a grimace, "I thought I'd save those honors for you."

His eyes narrow. "How thoughtful. But I'd prefer not to plummet to my death."

"How *would* you prefer to die?" I inject extra sugar into my voice. "I'm sure I could arrange something."

A flicker of amusement crosses his face before vanishing without a trace. "You couldn't kill me."

I let out a sharp laugh. "Is that a challenge?"

"Sure." He shrugs, hands still in his pockets. Those gray dress pants hang from his hips in a way I'm sure some people would describe as sexy, a subset of society of which I am not a member. "Hit me with your best shot."

"Gross," I say. "You did not just quote Britney Spears at me." Running my hands along the spearpoint collar of my dress, I double-check that it's still lying exactly as it should. I drag the black string tie through my fingers, then tighten the bow ever so slightly. It never hurts to look perfect.

Pierce is still studying me with an unflinching gaze, his eyes resting just below my chin. A tiny quirk of his lips has me reaching back to my collar, even though I just checked it.

"What would you prefer?" His voice has lowered and now sounds almost . . . sultry.

I repress a shudder. "I'd prefer you keep your mouth shut. Things were better before you spoke."

"Ah," he says, then looks down at the floor in a show of faux humility.

I brace myself for the next words from his mouth.

"So then you'd prefer I not tell you that we've made some tweaks to the budget?"

My head rears back a fraction of an inch. "You did what?"

He shrugs, nonchalant, then pulls his hands from his pockets and begins rolling up the sleeves of his white shirt, still in pristine condition despite being worn all day. Or maybe he comes home from work every evening and changes into a new suit. How would I know?

"You said you prefer my silence."

I grind my molars together and force my eyes to stay on his face, not on the way his fingers are dexterously folding his sleeves into perfect photoshoot-ready rolls. "Tell me what you did."

He tugs his mouth to the side and sucks air between his teeth like he's wincing, the bastard. "I wish I could, but—"

I close the distance between us, my heels clicking on the hardwood floor, the sound like gunshots. "This is a joint project."

"And yet you seem to have forgotten the meaning of *teamwork*." He finishes with his shirt and leans down until our noses are only inches apart.

I steel myself to keep from backing away. I cannot lose face now, no matter how badly I want to put distance between us. "We do not have the funding to go any higher—"

"Who said anything about going higher?"

"The only thing you've managed to do so far is increase our costs."

His brows arch upward. "Is that right? What about providing the tech? The team? The entire project is Luminara's—"

"But you don't have the contacts to get it into the countries that need it," I cut in. "Hence, the Wilson Foundation owns you."

A muscle in his jaw twitches, and I mentally pat myself on the back for causing him to break, even if it was just for a millisecond. "No one owns me."

I bite back a smile and cross my arms over my chest. Our verbal firing is finally shifting in my favor. "Really? Wasn't that Cinderella you were on the phone with earlier?"

"Her name is Amara."

"I don't care what her name is. She's nothing but a carbon copy of the last twenty-five women you've dated."

He rolls his eyes and takes a step backward. "What does this have to do with anything?"

"Nothing," I say. "Just that I've never seen you take a phone call from your girlfriend with other people around."

"It was an emergency." His eyes flash a warning, which I proceed to ignore.

I inspect my fresh and immaculate manicure—tiny red roses hand-painted on a bed of onyx. "I'm just saying it appears both the Foundation and Amanda have your balls in their pockets."

He moves so quickly I nearly miss it. One second he's standing a foot away, glaring at me. The next he's so close there's nothing but a hairsbreadth between our bodies, close enough that I can feel the heat of him through my clothes. His face is bent so near to mine that were I to raise my chin a fraction of an inch, my lips would brush against his. Disgusting.

"You're mistaken if you think for one second I will be owned by anyone or anything," he says in a whisper that feels as loaded as a gun to the temple.

I swallow, and his eyes flick down to my throat. He doesn't even bother to correct me about his girlfriend's name.

"Are we clear?" he asks.

A loud clap of thunder punctuates his words and reverberates through the entire flat. I jump, the involuntary movement forcing our bodies to brush against each other, and time stands still.

I've touched Pierce before. Obviously I have. We've been in the same friend group since we were fourteen. We even kissed during one particularly lame birthday party, but that was so many centuries ago, I'm not even sure he remembers it. I've certainly done my best to scrub it from my memory.

This, though. This is different. Accidental, for one thing. Not a hug and peck on the cheek goodbye. Not fingers brushing as he hands me a drink. Not sitting on his lap when there isn't enough room in the car for everyone to have a seat.

I am not a believer in sparks. I'm a grown woman with a career and the ability to make stupid creatures shrink back when they see me coming, for god's sake. So I'm not saying there are sparks as my chest makes contact with his, but I'm also not saying there isn't *something*. Because there is definitely something. It's enough of a something that I find my eyes focused on his mouth as I move away. It's the slowest motion in the world, as though I'm waist-deep in a vat of peanut butter.

He has a nice mouth, I'll say that much. Don't care much for what comes out of it most times, but the shape of it is just right. Big pillowy lips, not thin like some guys'. There's a dip in the center of the upper one, a neat little cupid's bow. His chin is shaded by a light amount of stubble that only seems to accentuate the lines of his face.

*I bet he's a good kisser.*

I blink in surprise. My mouth falls open of its own accord, because where the hell did that thought come from? His eyes track the motion, and now we're both staring at each other's lips.

Neither of us moves; neither of us says anything. We're stuck in this trance that I don't know how we got into in the first place. There is so much electricity coursing in this little space that I'm suddenly scared to touch a metal surface.

"Maeve—" he says in a raspy voice that sounds as though he's been screaming all night, but before he can finish his thought, the door of the game room opens.

"We're ready," Lux calls.

# 2

## "CANCELLED!" - Taylor Swift

*Pierce*

This night was doomed the minute Walker suggested a challenge between Maeve and me. Seriously, what was she thinking? I know we need to do something to end this feud between us, but to force one of us to leave our friend group is maniacal. Not that that was Walker's idea. Oh no, that one was courtesy of Maeve herself, the little psycho.

I follow her to where Lux is standing at the door, welcoming me into my own game room. In front of me, Maeve's dress swishes back and forth around her hips, and I can't help wondering what would have happened if Lux hadn't come out when she did. There was some serious tension between us, and I don't think it was all venomous. I'd love to know what Maeve might do if I backed her into a situation and forced her to let her guard down.

The gang's all here, sitting around the poker table like a board of executioners waiting to dole out capital punishment. Lux flits back to her seat next to Slate, and he immediately clamps a hand on her leg. Doesn't like to let her out of his sight for long, that one. I'm just relieved she's no longer with the scumbag who was hurting her. He's nicely tucked away in federal prison after we set him up to go down as the city's most notorious drug dealer.

The room is dimly lit by the chandelier hanging over the table, but it's bright enough to see that my housekeeper forgot to dust one of the cubicles on the wall holding my miniature slot machines. I'm going to have to talk to the cleaning company. Again. As I move to take one of the empty seats at the table, I straighten one of the machines that wasn't lined up correctly. Whatever happened to using a measuring tape when arranging things?

Maeve and I sit next to each other, but she has positioned herself as far from me as possible without climbing into Walker's lap. Walker herself looks slightly amused by this, and her eyes flick to me in a silent question. *What did you do?*

It's not what I did. It's what I didn't do. I should've given in to Maeve back at the auction when we tried to take down Deirdre. The plan was to run Deirdre's bidding on the hot-air balloon up to a ridiculous sum while Lux drained her accounts. Temporarily, of course. We'd never be stupid enough to actually steal the money. It was only meant to be long enough for her check to bounce, so the auction house would cause a scene trying to get their money for the antique balloon.

You know all the rest. How I hired a shell bidder because that's what we agreed on, while Maeve thought the plan was for her to be the opposing bidder. To tell you the honest truth, I don't remember what the plan actually was. It's just as likely that I was wrong as it is that she was. But did I have the foresight to just admit that?

No. Like a complete idiot, I fought her over it, insisted I was right and she was wrong. Now we're stuck at this table with our hands at each other's throats, waiting for our friends to tell us how to fight for the right to their friendship.

Rhett is sitting directly across the table from me, wearing a hot-pink shirt, silver chains visible where it hangs open. He waggles his brows at me, then smacks the table. "Shall we get this shitstorm started?"

Beside him, his fiancé, Saylor, rolls her eyes. She's the newest addition to our group, and I don't know her well, but from what I've seen, she's good for him. Keeps him grounded. I really hope it works out for them and that I'll be around long enough to witness it.

Slate shifts in his seat, his gaze flicking between Maeve and me. "Here's the plan. The two of you will complete a series of challenges between now and October."

October? It's only January. I'm not sure whether I'm frustrated or relieved that we have nearly a year of this before us. Maeve makes no secret of how she feels, however.

"That's ten months away." She leans her arms on the baize-covered table and pins Slate with an angry gaze.

He ignores her, just continues with his speech. Why he's been chosen as their spokesperson is easy enough to guess. Without Maeve or me to lead, he's the next obvious choice. Big guy with a commanding presence who doesn't take bullshit from anyone. The muscles in his arms bulge against the tight fabric of his black T-shirt, evidence that you don't want to cross him. "The winner will be announced at Heath and Walker's wedding in October. The loser agrees to leave the group."

Maeve straightens in her chair. Even though she's put a space between us the size of a refrigerator, I can feel the tension emanating from her body. She doesn't like this any more than I do, and this woman *feeds* on stuff like this. Must not be too confident in her ability to win, then. Unusual for sure.

"How will the winner be determined?" she asks.

I bite back a smile. Already trying to mastermind her way to the top.

"The six of us will determine the winner of each challenge," Slate says. "The person with the most wins by the wedding also wins the game."

I glance at Heath and Walker, curious how they feel about their wedding being used as a stage for this ridiculous plan, but neither of them looks particularly agitated by it. Heath leans back in his chair, hands tucked into the pockets of his sky-blue hoodie. Walker is sandwiched between him and Maeve, and she looks more anxious for our sakes than her own as she fiddles with the necklace at her throat.

I clap my hands together, ready to get this over with. "Sounds good. What's the first challenge?"

Lux clears her throat and pulls out her phone. She's wearing a soft white sweater that accentuates the glow in her cheeks. She reads from her screen. "You will take turns being each other's assistants for twenty-four hours. Whoever cracks first loses."

I can feel my brows pulling together. "It took you nearly an hour to come up with *that*?"

"Easy," Slate growls, clearly not liking the way I'm talking to his girl. "We were planning all of them."

Maeve has perked up, back ramrod straight. Gone is her uncertainty from before. In its place is a look I know all too well. So help me god, she is already plotting exactly how to take me down.

I am so fucked.

The easiest thing to do now would be to forfeit. I don't have the time or bandwidth to prance around the entire city at Maeve's beck and call, let alone complete whatever other stupid challenges this crew has cooked up for us. I'm the CEO of the largest tech company in the nation. Granted, Wesbourne isn't a huge country, but Luminara Tech is known worldwide for its innovative and sustainable solutions.

I should toss my metaphorical hand of cards onto the table, tell everyone it was good knowing them, but I'm out. I don't need to deal with this shit. We're all adults, but we're playing games like teenagers.

It's what I should do. But it's not what I'm going to do. These are my friends. We've been close since our first year of high school, when we plotted the takedown of the teacher who accused us of cheating. It wasn't our best or cleanest revenge plot, but we got the job done with stripper posters and a phone number stolen from school records.

These guys are my family. I would do anything for them, even though the thought of pulling out of the challenge for the sake of my sanity over the next year is tempting.

Maeve is certainly not going to let it go. She's like a dog with a bone when it comes to stuff like this. She'll stay in if it kills her—she won't allow herself to back down. Comes from her family, that shit. A deep-seated need to control and to win, no matter the cost.

Can't say I don't struggle with a bit of it myself, if I'm being honest.

I regret not giving into Maeve at the auction even more now. If I had done it then, it never would've escalated to this. She would have gloated for several weeks, but then it would've been over. So why the hell didn't I?

Because there's something about fighting with her. There. I admitted it. I like fighting with her over stupid shit. I enjoy our arguments. I particularly like the way her face and neck turn red, like the sun when it crests the horizon in the morning. Everything's suddenly illuminated.

It's like an addiction, our fights. I just can't seem to stop. I can tell the second her feathers get ruffled, and the words to push her over the edge always find their way into my brain. They're out of my mouth before I can stop them.

I don't want to *be* with her. Obviously that would be hell on earth. The woman is a maddening combination of cunning brilliance and take-no-prisoners ruthlessness, a fucking panther. She never slows down, never stops, hardly takes time to catch her breath before she's off again, either changing or ruining the world in a single day.

It's not that I think she would be bad in bed. Oh, no. If there's one thing I'm certain of, it's that Maeve Wilson is a firecracker between the sheets. With that kind of drive and tenacity? I've been imagining what it would be like to fuck her ever since I was fourteen and figured out how to roll on a condom.

She's stunningly gorgeous too, with those dark eyes that are always sparkling with some devious plan. Her tiny frame barely reaches my shoulder but packs just the right amount of softness in all the right places, and her hips move in a sultry way even though I know she's not trying. It's just her Italian roots coming through.

She's magnetic, intoxicating, enigmatic. She's also fully off-limits. For obvious reasons and then some.

She would demand more from me than I could ever give. Maeve Wilson wouldn't be content with a man's body and money. She'd demand his heart too. And that's one line I'll never cross, not even for her.

"Any questions?" Lux asks, looking between Maeve and me.

I toss a glance in Maeve's direction, and she turns to me with a devilish smile.

"Nope," she says, her bright red lips stretching even wider over her white teeth.

She doesn't need to say anything else. I can read her body language better than a book. The words are there, written all over her in permanent marker.

*Prepare to die.*

# 3

## "Cleopatra" - Nova Twins

*Maeve*

"Would you watch where you're going?" I sidestep to avoid colliding with a man who decided that blocking the path of a woman carrying two drinks was a good idea. It's absolutely ridiculous the way pedestrians behave these days. I'd be safer walking through four lanes of traffic with my coffee order.

I ride the elevator to the fifth floor of the Wilson Foundation's headquarters, where all of the executive suites are. Ever since the fiasco of HavenNet, our joint project with Luminara Tech, I've been spending more time here. Someone has to do damage control.

Several first-year interns are clustered outside the doors of the lift when they open. They immediately stop giggling and step back when they see me. I give them each a hard look. What are they even doing up here? They should be down on the first floor, filing something.

I approach Mrs. Rodriguez's desk, and she smiles at me. She's been the executive receptionist since I was a toddler. I hand her one of the coffees—nonfat latte with two pumps of cinnamon syrup—and she beams as though this isn't our tradition. Every morning I come in, I make sure to pick up her favorite drink.

"It's so good to see you, Miss Wilson," she says. I wonder if she knows she's the only person who will think or say that to me today.

"You too, Mrs. Rodriguez. How's Howie?"

She sets her coffee down and pulls her phone from her cardigan pocket so she can show me a picture of her French bulldog. We chat about his recovery from surgery and how expensive vet care is these days, not that I would know. I make a mental note to invent a reason to give her a bonus and hope she knows she's the one bright spot in my workweek.

When I was little, I'd sometimes accompany my father to the office. As the oldest child in our family, it was deemed essential that I learn the ropes from a young age. The most important thing I learned at four years old was that Mrs. Rodriguez stocked the best candy in her desk drawers, and she always slipped me a handful whenever my dad wasn't looking.

Behind me, the lift chimes its arrival, and I glance over my shoulder to see my father exiting it. Out of habit, I straighten as I turn to face him. Oliver Wilson III has that effect on people. My mother says he "commands a room." He commands a whole lot more than that.

Mrs. Rodriguez does her best to scoot her chair back and stand as he approaches the desk. She's getting too old for this job—heck, she was already old when I was a kid—but she is an invaluable asset to our company, if only for that smile she gives everyone, even my diabolical sperm donor. I stand between them in case he sees fit to take out his ever-surly attitude on her.

He doesn't even glance in her direction, however. Instead, his eyes focus on me for several seconds before he swipes the coffee cup from my hand. "Thanks, sweetheart. I didn't realize you knew I was coming in this morning." He heads for the conference room where most of our board meetings are held.

I clear my throat and follow him. "I didn't. What a pleasant surprise." You get really good at lying through your teeth in the Wilson family.

"I thought I'd pop in for the meeting, see how you're getting on without your old man here to oversee everything." He halts in the doorway and turns around.

I come to a quick stop before bumping into him, then watch in horror as he lifts my drink to his lips. I know exactly what will come next.

"What in the bloody name of god is this?" He looks at the cup as though it has physically assaulted him.

"That was actually my coffee," I say hesitantly. More specifically, it's an extra-large almond milk cappuccino with a 3:2 ratio of foam to milk, a split shot—half decaf, half single-origin espresso—a full pump of lavender syrup, a half pump of rose-cardamom syrup, and a half pump of Madagascar vanilla syrup.

"Who drinks this garbage?" He gives the cup one more disdainful look, then tosses it in the rubbish bin.

There's no point in answering. The question was purely hypothetical. He walks into the board room and takes the seat at the head of the table.

I take a deep breath and steel myself for the next two hours.

\* \* \*

Fifteen minutes later, everyone has gathered, except for the senior liaison from Luminara Tech. Their compliance officer and public affairs director are already seated at the table, and my team is getting antsy. We don't have all day.

I scan my list of invitees, looking for the name of the person we're missing. I've just spotted it—Tao Chen—when someone speaks from the doorway.

"Sorry I'm late," he says, taking the last empty chair. Only it's not Mr. Chen. It's Pierce.

I stare at him a beat too long. "Mr. Chen?"

He winces, but it's as fake as my nails. "Food poisoning. I'm filling in."

He expects me to believe that the CEO himself is filling in for the senior liaison? I wasn't born yesterday. I can think of only one reason why Pierce would be here, and it's to sabotage my plan to give HavenNet a rebrand before launch.

I narrow my eyes. "Let's begin, then."

He holds my gaze, those stupid eyes catching mine like bloody magnets. I can read the challenge in them. He thinks he can destroy me, but if he believes that, he has gravely underestimated Maeve Wilson.

I fight the sinking sensation that my entire day has been tanked by his arrival by reminding myself that, in a few short months, he'll be out of my life for good and I'll never have to look at that ridiculous jawline again. I'll simply pretend he's as significant as the rubbish I narrowly avoided on the street this morning. Annoying, disgusting, but ultimately inconsequential.

It's a good plan. A brilliant plan, actually. Except that, only minutes into my presentation, I can already tell it won't be enough.

"Transparency is the way to go," Pierce says.

I take a deep breath through my nose, my nostrils flaring slightly. "We need to distance ourselves from the havoc that Deirdre wreaked." The woman took our program—the one that was supposed to be provided free of charge to the countries that need it most—and charged them for it before we even realized what was happening.

"People value honesty," he says, eyes still fixed on mine.

My father grunts from the head of the table. He hasn't said a word yet, but he's cleared his throat enough times to have given an entire speech. He doesn't believe in using his words when a simple cough will accomplish the same thing.

"We can't afford to be associated with her," I insist, not meeting my father's eyes. He wants me to wrap up this disagreement and take charge, but what the hell am I supposed to do when our partner's CEO refuses to accept my plan?

Pierce leans forward. "We can't afford to wait any longer. Those people need our tech today, not a year from now."

HavenNet is a global humanitarian project that delivers rapid-response technology to disaster zones and refugee camps. The system includes solar-powered Luminara tablets, real-time translation apps, and drone-based signal relays that help displaced people connect with emergency services, reunite with loved ones, and access aid faster.

"If we don't rebrand, the project will never be accepted, not after the scandal she created," I say. How much longer is he going to push back on this? We must salvage the reputation of the initiative above all else. Otherwise, we limit the amount of good we'll be able to do before we even start.

My father shifts in his chair, and I know this isn't looking good. Under normal circumstances, I'd be able to handle Pierce and this meeting just fine. But with my dad sitting in, not to mention the tension from last night's poker game, I'm finding it hard to maintain a calm presence.

We continue in the same vein for the next hour, and by the end of it, Pierce has managed to push back against all of my plans for a rebrand and make his own ideas sound like a symphony orchestra next to my street violinist. Is it possible he knew my father was going to be here when he chose to attend this particular meeting? I wouldn't put it past him, the bastard.

My father slaps his palms on the table and pushes to his feet. "I think that's enough for today." He dismisses the meeting without another word, his actions themselves words enough.

Everyone gets up from their seats, relief evident in the way they laugh and make small talk on their way out the door. Hardly any of them weighed in during the meeting, and I realize in hindsight how ridiculous it must have looked for Pierce and me to be at each other's throats the entire time.

I begin gathering my things and my pride. After this, I'm going to need an afternoon at the spa. The knots in my back feel the size of boulders. I stand up, and that's when I realize that I'm not alone in the room.

Pierce is leaning against the far wall, one ankle crossed in front of the other. His suit today is navy blue, and he's wearing a light-blue shirt underneath it. He's skipped a tie and instead left his top two buttons undone. During the meeting, he put on a pair of the most obnoxious black-framed glasses—the kind some women go completely feral over—and has yet to take them off.

I shoot him a glare as I swipe my stack of folders into my arms. "I cannot believe you." He doesn't answer, so I continue. "You would actually rather see the entire project go down in flames than wait long enough to give HavenNet the start it deserves."

I move around the table, intent on leaving without another word, but the cocky way he's standing there—arms crossed, watching me—heats my blood to the boiling point. "You know as well as I do that it's better to get out in front of these problems before they can escalate," I add. "So why did you combat me on every single thing? You know I'm right."

He blinks but doesn't move. If anything, he looks even more at ease than he did at first. "Are you done?"

I shoot him the dirtiest glare I can muster, really dig down in the basement of my soul for an old Halloween mask I can use. Then I push past him toward the door.

"I know what your problem is," he says to my retreating back.

My feet stop before reaching the door. I turn and slam my folders onto the table, then cross my arms over my chest and tighten my glare. "Oh yeah? And what's my problem, Pierce?"

His eyes narrow as he takes me in. I'm wearing a tweed skirt suit over a black polka-dot silk blouse with a tie in the same fabric. I look fucking fantastic, so let him look all he wants.

He slowly drags his gaze back up and settles it on my face. "You haven't been laid in a long time."

I scoff to cover the sudden heat billowing in my core. How dare he? No, seriously, how dare he? "I have a boyfriend. I get laid *plenty*." I emphasize the last word even though it's not true, because this prick needs to understand that he doesn't know everything.

"Let me rephrase." Pierce finally pushes away from the wall, then comes to stand mere inches from me, mimicking our pose from last night—him towering over me, me looking up at him. It's nothing but a power play, and you know what? Fuck him.

He leans in even closer, and I catch a whiff of bergamot. He smells like a fifteen-thousand-dollar Italian suit, which I suspect is what he's wearing. His voice drops, smooth as whiskey, his tone hushed like we're sharing secrets. "You haven't been *properly* laid in a long time."

I bark out a laugh that sounds too forced. "What would you know about how often or how well I get laid?" I'll humor him, but only because the other alternative is to strangle him, and that would not look good for HavenNet.

He shrugs but doesn't back away. "I recognize the signs."

My mind immediately whirls, trying to figure out what signs he could possibly be referring to, but then I remind myself that Pierce St. James is a weasel and is only trying to mess with my head. "Fuck you."

A tiny smile makes the corners of his eyes crinkle. "If you ever want to, just say the word."

"Ew." I wrinkle my nose. "I'd rather impale myself on a spike, thank you."

"Mine's open for business." He drops a significant gaze to his pants. "You're disgusting."

Something happens to his eyes then. They go kind of soft, and for a second I wonder if I've hurt his feelings, but the smile is still in place, so probably not. Besides, the man is a St. James. You'd need a fucking lorry to hurt them.

"Well," he says, his voice as soft as caramel, "whenever you're ready to be laid by a man who actually knows what he's doing, you know where I live."

# 4

## "illicit affairs" - Taylor Swift

*Maeve*

    I don't think it's possible for this day to get any worse, and I'm not even exaggerating. After that atrocious meeting, I sent one of the interns to get me another coffee. I even wrote out my entire order on a piece of stationery and told her to just give it to the barista, and yet somehow she still managed to screw it up. It's not even a complicated order. How hard is it to remember rose-cardamom syrup? I forced the coffee down but missed that flavor profile the entire time. I should have sent her back, but I didn't want to come across as a bitch. People are so sensitive these days.

    Then one of our high-priority donors threatened to pull funding after a miscommunication issue, and I spent two hours on the phone with different representatives before finally being able to talk to a decision-maker. Even my name didn't grant me immediate access, and that definitely stung.

    I'm not thinking about what Pierce said. Of course I'm not. The guy doesn't deserve real estate in my head. Probably not in anyone's, but definitely not in mine. His arrogance is completely astounding.

    *You haven't been laid properly.*

Damn him. Damn him for implying that my life is anything less than perfect. I have a terrific boyfriend, one who certainly knows his way around the bedroom. And yes, there's the small issue of him still being stuck in his stupid marriage, but that certainly doesn't affect his performance. It may make seeing each other more difficult, but that just means we have to get creative.

In the women's restroom, I inspect my reflection in the mirror. The face that peers back at me is flawless. Smooth, creamy skin in the perfect shade—not too pale and definitely not fried in the sun. I've never understood the American fascination with skin that looks like chicken that's been left in the broiler too long.

After touching up my lipstick, it looks perfect as well. Crimson, as always. I was just at the salon yesterday, so my hair looks fantastic. Soft black with brown undertones, the right amount of shine, and a good amount of volume, although after being stuck at work all day, that's starting to wane.

I give my strands a fluff, but I can't find a single thing about my appearance that would give Pierce the impression that I'm not getting enough sex. It's more than likely he made it up to mess with me, but what if he didn't? If there's even the slightest possibility he's right, I need to do something about it before he can use it against me.

I wave to Mrs. Rodriguez on my way to the lift while trying to remember when I last saw Preston. Obviously he was at the masquerade ball this weekend, but he was with his mousy wife, so it's not like we could even talk.

The last time he came over must have been nearly a month ago, when he faked a business trip and spent two whole nights with me. A month without sex isn't that bad, right? People go much longer than that in the military. And what about astronauts? Heck, monks and nuns go their entire lives without sex.

Maybe it's not ideal, but it works. Preston and I are good for each other, and he's working on getting a divorce. Soon all of this will be behind us, and we can have sex once a week like normal people.

Still, on the off chance that my complexion has changed in response to a month of abstinence and Pierce somehow noticed it, I pull out my phone and text Preston. I can't just call him, unfortunately, because I never know when he's with her. But he has a second phone he keeps hidden just for me.

*Can I see you later? xx*

Even just sending the message and knowing that I've taken charge of the situation makes me feel better. Screw Pierce for thinking he could win this challenge by eroding my foundation. He's going to have a much harder fight on his hands than that.

\*\*\*

It takes Preston hours to respond and say he's on his way. I'm working on my plans for the HavenNet rebrand when my phone chimes. There are still so many details to get sorted, and that's if I can convince the rest of the team that this is the direction we should be heading in. And if Pierce St. James stays the hell out of it.

Preston arrives twenty minutes later, wearing a gray cashmere sweater and dark slacks, his wavy brown hair pushed back from his forehead. He's tall—not as tall as Pierce or Heath, but taller than me by quite a long shot. Although with me being five foot one, most people are.

"Sorry it took me so long," he says, and leans down to peck me on the lips. "I had to wait for Janie to fall asleep."

I fight the urge to frown and force a smile instead. I don't love how often he brings her up—*Janie*—but whatever. I can deal with it. We've been together for nearly a year. What's a few more months?

"I've missed you," I say, then wonder if that's even true. I hadn't thought about seeing him until Pierce made me question my love life.

It doesn't take us long to lose the clothes and get into bed. The nice thing about sex with Preston is that he's very predictable. I've dated guys who wanted to mix things up, have sex in the living room—can you even imagine?—or in positions other than missionary. Maybe that's one of the reasons Preston and I get on so well. We're both content to keep things simple between us. I don't make demands of him he can't deliver, and in exchange, he is happy to go along with whatever I want.

If only the rest of the world could be as obliging. I think about that disaster of a meeting earlier today as Preston rolls my nipples between his fingers. Why did my father choose this morning to show his face? The man comes into the office roughly once a month, preferring to seclude himself in his home office or on the golf course instead. I can only imagine how family dinner will go this week. God, stab me with a fork now.

Preston moves between my legs, eager to finish. You're probably wondering why we're even together if not for really hot affair sex. I'll be the first to admit, I'm a bit of a pillow princess. I've never had much of a desire for sex. It just feels like a necessary part of life.

Preston and I met just over a year ago at one of the Wilson Foundation's annual galas. His wife was home sick that night, lest you think I preyed on a married man. We found ourselves both catching some fresh air on the veranda and got started talking about Audrey Hepburn movies. He's almost as big of a fan as I am.

One thing led to another. We didn't do anything that night but talk—I'm not that easy—but by the time we said our goodbyes, I couldn't believe I'd had such an invigorating conversation with a man. Maybe it's the fact that he's nearly fifteen years my senior. Males under the age of thirty seem to care about only a handful of things: sex, sports, and cars. I don't give a damn about any of them, so to find an attractive man willing to discuss films and culture and topics that actually matter was a refreshing change. We started sleeping together several months later, after he told me his marriage was over.

He enters me slowly, watching my face for signs of discomfort. I smile up at him to show him I'm fine, even though I'm not as ready down there as I could be. He starts thrusting, slower than usual, and I wonder if he had sex with her earlier tonight. I was definitely under the impression that things between them were over before the two of us got together, and by the time I learned the truth, we were already in too deep.

Don't tell my friends that, though. They would use the opportunity to proclaim that they tried to warn me, that they knew all along Preston wasn't actually going to leave his wife for me. And that's where they'd be wrong, because he will. Do I wish he'd left her a year ago? Obviously. But that's neither here nor there.

If I can't find a way to annihilate Pierce in this challenge, none of us will even stay friends long enough for them to see that I was the one who was right about Preston. I must find a way to take Pierce down. I cannot imagine life without our weekly poker nights or flying to Japan at a moment's notice. Even Rhett's bullshit would be missed.

Do you know the best way to take someone down? Discover their weakness, of course. The problem with Pierce is that he keeps his cards very close to his chest. It makes uncovering his Achilles' heel hard, but not impossible. I already have a few possibilities in mind.

Preston's grunts become more rapid as he nears his climax. That's my cue. I meet each of his thrusts with a moan of my own, allowing them to grow longer and louder. I wait two seconds into his orgasm to fake my own.

I know what you're thinking, and you shouldn't. I don't always fake it. Preston has given me plenty of orgasms, okay? All of them were quite nice. But do you know how much energy it takes to climax? I just don't have it in me tonight, and I don't want Preston thinking he didn't do a good job. He's quite good at it, really. So the best thing for everyone is for me to fake it on occasion.

He pulls out, a satisfied smile on his face—see? I did a good deed—then goes to the bathroom to dispose of the condom. I roll out of bed to put my pajamas on as my phone vibrates from the nightstand. Tugging on my underwear, I glance at the screen.

At the sight of Pierce's name, my heart picks up speed. What does he want? It's already after midnight. Maybe there's been an emergency? As soon as the thought enters my mind, I dismiss it. Pierce wouldn't text me if something bad happened; he'd call. I know him well enough to know that much. The guy might be a jerk, but at least he's a predictable jerk.

So then why is my heart racing through my chest like my dad's horses on the track?

# 5

## "Queen" - Loren Gray

**Pierce**

I stare at my phone, the message still unread. It's been five minutes. Why the fuck isn't she texting me back? I know for a fact Maeve doesn't go to bed before 1 a.m.

Then it hits me. What if she's with him? That dipshit, Preston Ansley. He's been stringing her along for the better part of a year, pretending he's going to divorce his wife, but everyone knows it will be a cold day in hell before he leaves the heiress of one of the largest oil empires in the country.

I reread my message. *Is tomorrow a good day to start the challenge?*

Regret creeps in, and I frown. There's nothing wrong with what I said, but the feeling is there all the same. I'm about to toss my phone aside and go to bed when the three dots appear, showing that she's responding. I settle back into my chair, my heart picking up speed as I wait.

**Maeve**: *Autocorrect: Is tomorrow a good day to die?*

**Me**: *I wasn't aware you planned to die tomorrow. What should I wear to the funeral?*

**Maeve**: *Since you'll be the one in the casket, I suggest something that* *makes your skin less . . . sallow. A catsuit, perhaps?*

The corner of my mouth twitches.

**Me**: *Do you have one I can borrow?*

Shit. Am I flirting with her? Time for damage control.

**Me**: *I thought I could go first doing the assistant shit.*

**Maeve**: *So you DO intend on dying tomorrow. Why would you go first?*

**Me**: *Because I'm a gentleman.*

**Maeve**: *If you were a gentleman, you would've admitted the truth by now.*

I pause to consider. I could end this whole thing by telling everyone I was wrong, that the agreement was for Maeve to run up the bidding on the hot-air balloon. So why can't I? Is it pride holding me back? Or something else?

**Me**: *Which truth? That you need to relax?*

The dots appear on my screen again, and I picture her typing away furiously, eyebrows drawn together in anger. The thought makes my smile grow wider.

**Maeve**: *Tomorrow. 9 am. Wilson Foundation HQ.*

* * *

If Maeve thinks I'll be easy to break, she's in for a surprise. Instead of showing up at nine, I'm already in her office when she gets there at 8:45. The look on her face is worth every single second I spent waiting.

"What are you doing here?" she asks, setting her purse down rather violently. "I said 9 a.m."

"I know." I slowly straighten from where I've been leaning against her desk. "But a good assistant always shows up early."

She gives me a withering look. "A good assistant does what they're told. I'll be docking points for that."

"Ahh." I wag an admonishing finger at her. "But you're not the one keeping score."

Her nostrils flare as she moves around the desk to take a seat on the other side. She's dressed in a black twill jacket cardigan thing with buttons down the front and a matching skirt, both of which I would very much like to divest her of. I could bend her over the desk and have her begging for me within seconds.

"I hope you're wearing good shoes," she says, breaking through my thoughts like a hammer through glass. "Because you've got a busy day ahead of you."

"Perfect. I could use the workout."

Her eyes flick up from her planner for just a second, checking out my midsection, before quickly returning to a list I can't make out. I'm pretty sure she knows it was a joke—I haven't missed my daily gym session for the past six years—but I could swear there was the tiniest hint of curiosity on her face. Interesting.

"Your first task is to make copies," she says, not looking up, as though I actually am an assistant, not one of her oldest friends. Although "friends" may not be the right term for us anymore.

I hold out my hand. "If you just give me the list, I can tackle everything without bothering you."

Slowly, she lifts her head to give me the wickedest smile in the history of mankind. "No, no." She flicks the planner shut, and the sound echoes through the room. Then, like a cat satisfied with the meal she just made of a songbird, she leans back in her chair. "You'll report back to me after each and every task so I can ensure you did a good job and give you your next assignment."

I resist the urge to roll my eyes. Instead, I prop my hands on the edge of the desk and lean toward her. "And will one of my tasks be helping you relax?"

It has the desired effect. Her face goes crimson, nearly matching her lipstick, and she sits up so fast the chair lets out a loud crack. "I expect you to be done in fifteen minutes." She pushes a large stack of files toward me.

"That's ridiculous." It will easily take half an hour to copy everything.

She gives me a smug smile before turning to her computer. "Then you're welcome to forfeit."

And so begins the day from hell.

\* \* \*

My dad would be appalled if he could see me right now, standing at a copy machine, interns all around, making copies like I'm fresh out of uni and don't have any strings to pull at the company.

After looking at some of this stuff, I'm pretty sure Maeve doesn't actually need copies of it. She just gave me the most humiliating task she could think of. I'd be worried scrubbing toilets is next, but I'm not confident Maeve even realizes there are people who clean them. She probably assumes they never get dirty.

I've been chief executive officer at Luminara Tech for four years. When I graduated from Oxford, my dad said it was time for me to take over. And before you think it was just a handout, I had already been proving myself for years. I've been on the board since I was eighteen, and I've played a role in some way, shape, or form since I was in prep school.

Since the company's creation, the plan has always been for Luminara to be my first acquisition. My parents are both still investors and members of the board, but for all intents and purposes, she is mine. Eventually, I'll take over the rest of the St. James companies—Vireon Systems, our ultra-secure encrypted cloud storage and the backbone of all the rest of the companies; Solena Earth and Axis Bloom, my mother's two "green luxury" passion projects focused on eco-friendly environmental design; and Mirae Press, our digital arm, which shapes the narrative around climate and technology. I'm an investor in all of them, in addition to curating a sizable real-estate portfolio of properties all over the city.

And yet, here I am, listening to the drone of the machine as it scans page after page. Fortunately, this particular challenge will only last twenty-four hours, because I'm already dreading whatever else Maeve has in store for me.

It takes twenty-eight minutes to make all the copies and return to Maeve's office. I knock on her door, and when there is no answer, I push it open. She's sitting at her desk, glaring at her computer screen. She startles when she sees me.

"All done." I drop the stack of papers on her desk.

She frowns, then swipes her arm and dumps them into the rubbish bin at the end.

I bite the inside of my cheek and nod. "What next, then?"

"Get my coffee," she orders.

I snap my fingers. "Be right on that. Where is it?"

Some of the life returns to her eyes. "At the shop, I'm assuming." She says the words slowly, as though I need time to absorb them fully.

"You placed an order already?"

A smile that some might mistake as sweet spreads across her lips—bright red lips just begging to be bitten. "Of course not. That's the job of an assistant."

I press a fist to my mouth. "And I'm just supposed to know how you like your coffee?"

"Any good assistant would keep track of such things."

I want to point out that it would be unreasonable to expect that of anyone on their first day, but I'm not dealing with a reasonable person. "Fucking terrific."

Tightening my hands into balls, I head to the coffee shop across the street. I ought to give Maeve something better to do with her mouth than talk. I could take her in that chair and drive every thought from her mind but me.

"Good morning." I smile at the perky blond behind the register, and her face brightens.

She straightens her spine and returns my smile with a blinding one of her own. "What can I get for you?" she says, her voice at least an octave higher than what must be her normal.

I lean over the counter like I'm about to share a secret with her. "There's a girl who comes in here, about this tall"—with my hand, I indicate a height just below my shoulder—"black hair, red lips, looks like she eats small children for breakfast?"

The barista's face falls, either because she thinks I'm describing my girlfriend and or because Maeve terrifies her like she does the rest of the city's inhabitants. Maybe both. She swallows, then gives a tiny nod. "I know who you mean."

My instincts have paid off. "Do you happen to know her usual coffee order?" I give her my most encouraging grin, as though she and I are in cahoots together. "I really don't want to die today."

Realization dawns in her eyes, and a small smile reappears on her face. "It's a very complicated one. We have it written down so we don't get it wrong."

"Ahh," I say, nodding. "Very smart." I toss in a wink for good measure and am satisfied to see the blush staining her cheeks.

"I'll get it ready for you." She turns away quickly, ponytail swishing.

She's cute. Not exactly my type, though, even if I was single. Good-looking enough, but I tend to date women from my own circles. Makes things a lot easier. Date someone who doesn't come from money, and they start thinking it means a future together. At first they balk at you paying for anything, but it usually doesn't take long for entitlement to sink its teeth in. I've tried it, and each time it ended after only a few weeks.

The barista hands me the cup containing Maeve's coffee. "I hope this helps." That's definitely hope in her eyes, and it's not for my well-being. I recognize eagerness when I see it.

"Thanks," I say. "You saved my life." I reward her with another tiny wink, and she turns a lovely shade of pink.

My hand is already on the door handle when something occurs to me. I return to the counter, and the blond perks up, probably thinking I'm back to ask her out. Instead, I hold up the cup, all traces of camaraderie wiped from my face. "I just want to confirm, this was made with dairy-free milk, right?"

She nods. "Almond milk, yes."

"Perfect." The last thing I need is for Maeve to get sick from ingesting lactose.

As I return to the office and ride the lift up to the fifth floor where my dictator awaits, I'm not thinking about the cute girl at the coffee shop. I'm not even thinking about my girlfriend. I'm thinking about a black-haired vixen and the look of shock that'll cross her face when she realizes I got her coffee order right.

# 6

# "Father Figure" - Taylor Swift

*Maeve*

I've sent Pierce off to fetch my coffee like a hound. I'm confident he'll bungle this one. There's no way in hell he knows Madagascar vanilla syrup even exists.

Sending him to make those copies was genius on my part. I only wish I had been present to watch him squirm in front of all the interns, probably wondering if they knew he's the CEO of one of our biggest partners.

My office door swings open, and I look up, expecting to see Pierce holding a paper cup from the espresso machine downstairs, because it's the only coffee he could have acquired this quickly. But it's not Pierce. It's my father.

I immediately stand as he pushes his way into the room and shuts the door behind him. Every muscle in my body tightens, waiting for the first blow. Not physically, of course. God, what kind of man do you think he is? Not the kind to hit his children, at least not with his fists.

But the look on his face tells me right away this isn't going to be a friendly visit—specifically, the way he mashes his mouth into a tight line. Not that any of his visits typically are, but this one in particular seems to have the distinct purpose of setting me to rights.

Lord Wilson is a big man. His suits are made of only the finest fabrics and tailored to hide his stomach. He's not huge, but he's definitely put on weight in the last ten years, which only makes him seem more gigantic, thanks to his six-foot-four frame. His dark hair is streaked with white, and his skin is perpetually brown from spending his days on the golf course.

He stops in front of my desk, arms crossed over his massive chest. Genetics did not work in my favor, because I seem to have inherited nothing from him but his ruthlessness. And now, in the presence of the scariest person in my life, it has all but disappeared.

"What was that bullshit yesterday?" he says, his voice definitely loud enough to be heard in the corridor, despite the closed door.

I tuck my lips between my teeth and shake my head. "You'll need to be more specific."

His eyes flash a warning. "The meeting with Luminara. It was a complete shitshow."

Something you should know about my father: his favorite word is *shit*. Uses it every chance he gets.

"I'm not sure why they're insisting on going ahead without rebranding—"

"Because it makes more sense!" He smacks the desk with his palm. "We don't have time for a rebrand."

"But I—"

He points a threatening finger at my face. "Have you forgotten that you represent the Wilson name everywhere you go?"

"Of course not," I say.

"If you can't uphold our image behind closed doors, how the fuck do you expect to be able to do it in public?" Spittle flies from his mouth and lands on his outstretched arm.

I shake my head and drop my eyes. "I'm sorry. It won't happen again."

"No, it most certainly won't, or you may be looking at a new job."

It's an empty threat. At least I hope it is. It's not like either of my siblings could do even half the job I've done since joining the foundation right out of uni. Vivienne couldn't possibly care less about what she calls "a tax shelter with a god complex." And Bash—well, he's Bash. I'm not sure he's even aware of what we do here. He'd burn it to the ground within a week and smile the entire time.

"I'll see to it that we come to an agreement soon." I don't know how, since I'm still not willing to give in to Pierce on this one. HavenNet *does* need a rebrand before launching—of that I'm certain. But if it means appeasing my father, I might need to consider a compromise, much as I loathe the word. It's not winning if neither person gets their way. It's just a double loss, and trust me, knowing the other person didn't get what they wanted doesn't make it any easier to swallow.

My father leans over the desk, extended finger only a few inches from my face. "You will have any conversations with Luminara's reps out of earshot of anyone else. Do you understand?"

I swallow and nod, then edge away slightly to put a little more distance between us.

"We cannot risk this family's reputation because you have a thing for a man who doesn't want you."

My good-girl facade shatters as it hits the floor. "*What?*"

He shifts his weight back and lowers his hand. "You're upset because St. James isn't interested in dating you, but you can't bring that shit into the light."

My mouth hangs open for several seconds before I regain my voice. "I assure you, sir, that is *not* what this is." Does he actually believe what he's saying? Worse, does anyone else? Nausea churns in my stomach. I might actually be sick.

"I don't really care what it is, as long as you act like you deserve the name Wilson."

"Trust me, this is strictly about HavenNet." Pining after Pierce? Gross. Besides, I have a boyfriend. Not one my parents are aware of, but is this seriously what my father thinks of me? That I would sacrifice the project over a man?

"See to it that it remains that way," he barks. "And do whatever they want. It's not worth fumbling the entire deal because your ego got in the way."

By now, my hackles are well and fully raised. I don't care about staying on my dad's good side anymore. "This is not about my ego. A rebrand is crucial if we want to retain support."

He shakes his head, disgust lining his face. "You wouldn't know what's crucial if it smacked you between the eyes."

I bury the pain, not willing to let him add to his running tally. "I've spent a lot of time going over the reports—"

"Screw the reports," he says. "Scrap the plan and go with whatever they want. Understood?"

Before I can respond, the office door opens and Pierce enters. He takes in my father and flashes him a huge smile. "Mr. Wilson," he says, extending his hand. "It's good to see you again so soon."

My father relaxes into that easygoing personality he uses with people he deems to be "above" him in the social hierarchy. The St. James family is worth billions. In fact, Pierce himself might be worth that much, not that I've ever bothered to find out.

"I was just telling Maeve that I think your plan to move ahead as quickly as possible is the way to go," my father says, shaking Pierce's hand.

"Actually,"—Pierce darts a quick glance at me—"I've had some time to consider everything, and I think a rebrand is the best option for the project."

# 7

## "I Like Me Better" - Lauv

*Pierce*

I hear their raised voices as soon as I step off the lift. Maeve's I know well enough, but it takes me a few seconds to realize it's her father she's arguing with. Their words become distinct as I approach her office.

Call me a dog who doesn't like anyone else playing with his toys, but no one gets to talk to Maeve like that. I open the door and am immediately met with Lord Wilson's bulk. The man is a bloody giant. Next to him, his daughter looks like Tinkerbell.

I fake enthusiasm at seeing him, because the man has an ego the size of Wesbourne Palace, but angle my body so I'm between him and Maeve. "I think a rebrand is the best option for the project." I don't look at her as I say this, but I can feel her surprise.

The lord's smile grows even wider and takes on a knowing glint. "Now, mate, you don't need to say that just to keep her happy." He gestures toward Maeve as though she's nothing more than a yapping terrier. "She might not be thrilled about it, but she'll do what you tell her to."

My fist tingles with the need to punch this guy directly between the eyes, to watch the lights flicker in them as he struggles to maintain a grip on consciousness. "Actually, I value Maeve's opinion. She's incredibly smart and talented," I say instead.

He laughs, and the sound is so loud, I hear Maeve start behind me. "Believe me, I know. She's my daughter, after all. But you and I both know she has a hard time admitting when she's wrong." He tosses Maeve a smile, like he just paid her a compliment, before continuing. "But she's promised to cooperate."

God, I want to smother this guy. I place my hand on his burly chest and pat it a few times. "Don't worry. I thrive under patriarchal oppression."

Lord Wilson doesn't have words immediately, and I'll admit, it's a nice change. Finally, he sputters something about the two of us working something out and excuses himself. Only after the door clicks shut behind him do I turn to Maeve.

"Your coffee, ma'am." I hand her the cup.

Her brows are knitted together as she takes it from me. "Did you mean that?"

"Which part?"

"About the rebrand."

I sniff a laugh and cross my arms. "Of course not. I was just helping you save face."

An unamused look settles on her face as she takes a sip of her drink. "Asshole." Then she blinks a few times and stares at the cup in her hands. "What is this?"

Shit. Is it possible there are two dark-haired hellcats who frequent that shop and scare its patrons? "Your coffee, as requested," I say.

The frown settles itself on her face again, kicks back in an armchair, and turns on the television. "How do you know how I take my coffee?"

I wink at her, knowing it will aggravate her even more. "What kind of assistant would I be if I spilled all my secrets?"

"You're about to be a dead one if you don't tell me." She sniffs the coffee. "Did you put anthrax in here?"

I snap my fingers. "Darn, now I'll have to come up with a different backup plan. I assumed the cow's milk would do the job."

Her eyes grow wide as she lowers the cup to the desk. "Did you—?"

It's the fear in those depths that gets me. "No, of course not." I soften my tone and shake my head. "You know I wouldn't do that."

The concern wrinkling her forehead tells me she doesn't know this, which only compounds the sick feeling in my chest faster than the interest on my offshore accounts.

"I wouldn't," I say again, praying this time she believes it. I would rather get caught in a street fight than actually hurt her.

She nods but doesn't pick up the coffee again. "Ready for your next task?"

"As I'll ever be, Your Highness."

She cuts me a glare, but there's a gleam sparkling in those dark eyes. "Great. Then you can go get rid of that stupid hot-air balloon."

\* \* \*

If Maeve thinks taking her shopping is the key to breaking me, she doesn't realize how many girlfriends I've escorted to these exact stores. The chairs outside the changing rooms are practically conformed to my shape. Still, there's a night-and-day difference between being with a woman who hates your guts and one who wants to jump your bones. Not that I'd be opposed to getting it on in one of the fitting rooms, but I hardly think that's what Maeve had in mind when she ordered me to accompany her.

We've been here since early afternoon, after she had me running all over creation to do her bidding this morning, which included instructions for disposing of the giant hot-air balloon filling a storage room in her basement. But what she doesn't know won't kill her.

While she was trying on the first dress, I told the shop assistant to put whatever Maeve wants on my card. There's something satisfying about buying shit for a woman. Their faces light up, and they get all gooey-eyed, as though they weren't expecting that exact thing. It's a great way to prime the pump for later, so to speak, although I'm under no impression it will have that effect here.

I glance down at the shopping bags surrounding my feet. When Maeve discovered that I'd already paid for everything at the first store, she simply blinked at the clerk a few times before waltzing out the door. She's been snatching things up left and right ever since. If she thinks she can reach my limit by maxing out my cards, she severely underestimates the size of my bank account.

She also underestimates how much fun I'm having buying things for her, but that's just one more thing I have no intention of her discovering.

# 8

## "Anti-Hero" - Taylor Swift

*Maeve*

I glare at my reflection in the changing room mirror. This dress is atrocious. It looked great on the rack, but now that I've put it on, I look like overcooked pasta. Absolutely disgusting. I take it off and thrust it outside. There's a three-second delay before Pierce takes it from my hand.

"What's wrong with this one?" he asks.

"Nothing, if you're Sydney Sweeney." I shut the door before he can get any ideas.

"Sydney Sweeney is hot as hell."

I turn the knob and stick my head outside. "She's also blond. I, on the other hand"—I grab a fistful of my black, ultra-straight hair—"am not."

Retreating back into the fitting room, I reach for the last of the gowns I picked out. Hopefully this one will work, because I'm about to reach my limit with Pierce. Not that he's being super annoying at the moment—quite the opposite, actually, which is weird—but because I can't stop replaying the scene with my father from earlier.

What in the world prompted Pierce to say that I'm smart and

talented? Personally, I prefer "brilliant," but it's a start. Neither of these things are news to anyone, but for him to verbalize them was a surprise. What I can't figure out is if he said them to mess with me, or even worse, if he actually meant them.

I wonder if Pierce would have said what he did if he knew it might jeopardize his "golden boy" status with my dad. Lord Wilson likes people because of what they can do for him, and he's always liked Pierce. He views the St. James family as close friends—although I doubt they feel the same—and Pierce as the son he never had. He has a son, mind you, but Bash is as different from Pierce as a carnival is from a royal ball.

While HavenNet might be our biggest project with a St. James corporation to date, it's not like we haven't helped each other over the years. They've been one of our biggest donors, naturally, and so my father thinks we're in each other's pockets.

But for Pierce to defend me to him? That was a risky move on his part. There's no telling what my father will do now, but I'm sure I will bear the brunt of it regardless. If there's one thing a Wilson can't handle, it's an attack on their pride.

I shimmy the plum off-the-shoulder fitted floor-length gown over my hips. I had the perfect outfit already chosen for tonight's charity dinner, but I heard a rumor this morning that Celine Di Laurentis is going to be wearing the same design. The audacity.

So here I am, trying on dresses mere hours before the event, with Pierce St. James waiting for me outside and pretending to be completely fine with the situation. I'll admit, I was shocked when the shop assistant told me he had already paid for everything, but I think I did a good job hiding it. I've never had a man buy me clothes before, not because they haven't offered but because I've always declined.

If Pierce had asked, I'm not sure what I would have said. Part of me would like to take him for every penny he has—not that even I could rack up a bill high enough to drain his accounts—but another part of me doesn't want him to think he has any power over me.

Lucky for me, I didn't have to make that decision, because he didn't ask; he just did it. It causes a weird feeling in my chest, one I don't have words for, because I've never experienced it before.

But what am I doing, still thinking about all of this? I have a dress to find and an assistant to boss around. I only have Pierce for seventeen more hours, and I'm going to need to get creative if I want to crack him before then. If I can get him to forfeit this challenge, it's an automatic win for me without having to do any heinous tasks. God knows what he would come up with.

I tug at the zipper of the gown, but it's in the back (stupid) and not the side (why?). I can only get it up so far before my arms refuse to go any higher. If this were a normal shopping trip, I'd simply ask the shop assistant to help me with it. But I've brought my own assistant, and this feels like a good task for him.

Sticking my head out of the fitting room again, I look for Pierce, half expecting him to have abandoned his duties already. Instead, he's sitting in the same chair as before, phone pressed to his ear. His eyes catch mine instantly, a tiny frown creasing his brow. He ends the call before I can say a word, then stands and walks toward me.

I turn around so I don't have to look at those ridiculous eyes any longer. Holding my hair away from my neck, I say, "I can't reach the zipper."

Without a word, he grips the dress in one hand and the pull in the other. Before I can stop him, he's unzipped it the entire way.

I gasp as the cool shop air hits my lower back. "Up, not down, you idiot," I hiss, hoping there's no one around. But Pierce is more than enough shield from the rest of the store, so even if there is, they can't see a thing.

I hear him smirk. I know you're thinking you can't hear someone smirking, but have you ever seen Pierce St. James smirk? Then you know what I'm talking about. There's a sound to it. Maybe a fully internal one, but it's there all the same.

It takes him much longer to get the zipper up than down, and I know what he's doing, the bloody bastard. He's taking in a full view of my back, the lack of bra, the smoothness of my creamy skin. It's nothing the whole of Wesbourne hasn't seen before—hello? Backless dresses?—but it still makes me feel as though there are a million tiny ants crawling over my entire body. Sounds unpleasant, but I'm not sure that's quite the word for it. Anxiety inducing, maybe?

Once he's done me up, I move in front of the mirror, turning so I can inspect the gown from different angles. It's not the best I've ever worn, but it'll do. I catch a glimpse of Pierce in the glass. He's watching me, and there's this expression on his face I can't place. I frown as I try to discern what he's thinking. His eyes have gone soft, the lines on his forehead smoothed out.

"Well?" I say. "What do you think?"

His gaze snags on mine in the reflection. "Perfect."

"I meant the dress."

He watches me for a few more beats. "I didn't."

*　*　*

Tonight's event features a dinner, followed by a bridge tournament, and if you're thinking that it must be one of the most boring fundraisers on the Wilson Foundation's annual calendar, you're right. If you're also thinking it's mostly attended by the city's oldest and wealthiest citizens, I might have to call you Einstein.

This year promises to be much more entertaining for all persons attending, though. Particularly for those who identify as female. The idea came to me this morning, after Pierce left to get my coffee—I still need to know how he knew what to order—and before my father barged into my office.

Contrary to popular belief, I don't keep a running list of ways to make people's lives miserable. They usually just come in a flash of inspiration. As I sip my champagne, I take note of everyone's reactions. The plan was for Pierce to spend the evening escorting patrons to their seats. As stoic as he is, and as good looking as most people consider him—with the exception of yours truly—I assumed it would be entertaining for the ladies and absolutely hideous for him. After all, the CEO of Luminara Tech acting as an usher? It's positively snort-worthy.

However, things are not shaping up quite the way I anticipated. The women are certainly having the time of their lives. But instead of looking miserable, Pierce looks fucking . . . delighted. *Delighted.*

I watch as he walks slowly, escorting a lady who looks as old as my great-grandmother to her seat. My nan wouldn't be beaming up at him as though she planned to snack on him later, though. Pierce laughs at something the woman says, and I imagine the flirtatious conversation they're having. Positively disgusting.

Dame Adelaide Mansfield, one of our long-time donors, sidles up next to me. "Where have you been hiding this one?" she says. "They'll never be satisfied again."

We both glance at the long line of elderly women who are waiting on Pierce to take them to their seats. There are other ushers, but hardly anyone will accept their help, preferring instead to wait three times as long for the man of the hour.

"I think it's time for him to go back to his hidey-hole," I mutter.

When he comes to escort the next guest, I grab his arm and tug him aside. He's wearing a dark gray tuxedo and a matching bow tie. His muscles feel as hard as rock through his sleeve, and I quickly let go.

"What are you doing?" I hiss under my breath, even though everyone in attendance wears a hearing aid.

"What do you mean?" he says. "I'm helping these women to their seats like you told me to."

"I didn't tell you to flirt with them."

Shaking his head, he laughs. "I'm just being friendly. You should try it sometime." Then he fucking winks at me.

"Betty White over there is practically eye-fucking you as we speak."

He looks over at the ladies waiting their turn like kids at an amusement park. "Hmm. She looks less flexible than I prefer, but I bet she's great with her mouth."

I cough out a gasp, but by the time I have a retort ready, he's already gone.

# 9

## "Actually Romantic" - Taylor Swift

*Maeve*

When my alarm goes off at 3 a.m., I spend exactly five seconds cursing myself for this ridiculous plan before switching on the bedside lamp and grabbing my phone. A Wilson doesn't quit, doesn't give up, and doesn't lose. I can sleep when I'm dead.

I tap Pierce's name on my screen. It takes six rings for him to finally pick up, but when he does, his voice sounds tight and concerned. "What's wrong?"

I experience a single second of guilt before pushing it aside. "Good morning to you, too."

His sigh fills the phone. "What do you want, Maeve?"

"Since you're still my assistant for another six hours, I need you to pick up some things for me and bring them over."

He clears his throat, and I wonder if he's put his glasses on or if he's still lying in bed in the dark. "In the middle of the night?"

"That's correct. Unless you'd like to let everyone know that you're dropping out?"

"What do you need?" The iron in his tone is unmistakable.

I bite back a smile so he doesn't hear it in my voice. "Tampons."

"Tampons," he repeats.

"Yes, but they need to be a very specific kind. You'll probably want to write this down."

There's a brief pause, then: "Naturally."

"I need the Cora Organic Compact line, and they must be fragrance-free and chlorine-free. Look for the brown-and-purple box. It will say 'biodegradable' and 'paper-wrapped.'"

"Got it," he says.

I wonder briefly at that before adding one more thing. "Make sure you get heavy flow. Two boxes, please."

While I wait for Pierce to arrive with the feminine care products I hope are embarrassing him in the checkout line right now, I fix myself a mug of tea and pore over the HavenNet plans once more. I know what you're thinking. How am I going to go back to sleep after focusing on this for an hour? I probably won't. Like I said, I can sleep when I'm dead.

When the doorbell finally rings, I've nearly forgotten why I'm up in the first place. I cinch the belt of my satin dressing gown a little tighter and answer the door.

Pierce is standing on my doorstep, holding several shopping bags. He has on a light gray crewneck sweatshirt, black joggers, white trainers, and those infuriating glasses, as I suspected. Inclining his head, he gives me a measured look. "As requested."

I reach to take them, but he doesn't hand them over. At my frown, he gestures with his chin. "Tell me where you want them."

The furrows in my brow grow deeper as I move aside to let him in. "Just . . . anywhere."

He brushes past me and into the house. I've lived here for two years, and I can count the number of times Pierce has been inside on one hand. Nevertheless, he moves to the kitchen as if he lives here.

"Thank you," I say. It comes out stilted. "That's all I needed." Now that he's here and his presence is filling every crevice of my home, I feel a little stupid for dragging him out of bed in the middle of the night.

"I'll just heat this up for you first," he says, keeping his back to me while fishing something from one of the bags. The muscles under his sweater ripple. He takes a container to the microwave and pops it in.

"What is that?" I ask.

He looks at me for the first time since coming inside. "Soup. I thought it might help you feel better." While the microwave runs, he returns to the bags he left on the counter. "I also grabbed some aspirin, chocolate, and a heat pack. I assumed you had one already, but just in case." He removes said items, along with two large boxes of organic tampons.

Keeping my arms folded over my chest, I stare at his haul. "Do this a lot?"

He shrugs, then grabs the soup when the microwave pings. "Occasionally." Fishing a spoon from the silverware drawer—which he located on the first try—he gives me a look. "Never at three in the morning, though."

I imagine him strolling the aisles of the supermarket, looking for the right feminine products. It was meant to be humiliating, but he doesn't seem affected in the least. In fact, he seems rather proud of himself. Cocky, even.

Tucking both boxes under my arm, I give him a sugary smile. "My housekeeper will be so grateful for these. Thank you again."

The lines around his eyes tighten ever so slightly. "Your housekeeper."

"Yep." I set the cartons down near the back door with a flourish. "I'll make sure she knows you were the one who got them for her."

The silence between us grows loud and thick. Finally, after an entire century passes with the two of us staring at each other across the room—something we've gotten quite good at lately—Pierce sniffs and sticks his tongue in the side of his cheek. "You're not on your period, are you?" he deadpans.

"Nope," I say cheerily. "And when I am, I use a menstrual cup. But this"—I gesture to the items on the counter—"is really quite impressive."

He folds his arms across his chest, and I don't know whether it's the fact that 90 percent of the time I've seen him he's worn a jacket or if I've just honestly never noticed that he is an actual warm-blooded male with ridiculously high testosterone levels, but mother of god, have you *seen* his biceps? His sweatshirt does little to hide the bulk there.

His silence prompts me to fill it. "But anyway, it was really over the top of you to bring all of this. I'll make sure to let the others know how helpful you've been. Quite stellar, really. Maybe not enough to win the challenge, but it's the effort that counts."

Most people would take that as a not-so-subtle social cue to leave, right? But the man just keeps standing there, staring at me, as though he's waiting for something. I don't have a clue what it is. I just admitted to luring him here under false pretenses after dragging him around as my slave all day. What else does he want? An apology? Fat ch—

"Well played." His voice cuts through the air, making the hair on the backs of my arms stand up. "But you should know something."

My mouth goes as dry as a good vintage cab sauv, and I swallow as he steps closer. I force my feet to stay planted on the French terracotta tiles, because I will not allow Pierce St. James to see me flinch.

When he's a breath away, close enough that his scent wafts under my nose—not cologne, but toothpaste and soap—he leans in. The man really has a propensity to use his height to his advantage, and it's starting to piss me off, but I hold my ground.

"And what's that?" I say, because he cannot think he scares me in any way, shape, or form.

He ducks his head so that his lips are hovering right above my ear and whispers, "You're not the only one who intends to ace this challenge."

\* \* \*

After Pierce leaves, I wait an hour before calling again, just long enough for him to get back to bed and hopefully fall asleep. But when he answers, he sounds anything but tired. In fact, he sounds out of breath.

"Yes, Panther?" he says.

"Sorry, this isn't your girlfriend calling."

A sharp laugh cracks through the phone. "Trust me, I do not call Amara a wildcat."

A twinge of something unpleasant rolls through me at the sound of her name. "What are you doing?"

"I'm at the gym, Maeve." The way he enunciates my name hints at irritation hunkering just below the surface of his voice, like soldiers in a bunker. "What do you need?"

I picture him panting from exertion, his body a sweaty mess of hard muscles and strong tendons. I clear my throat and those thoughts. "Wilson Foundation. 8 a.m. sharp. If you're late—"

"I'll be there."

He hangs up, and I'm left staring at the phone in my hand.

Three hours later, he waltzes onto the fifth floor as though he owns the place. You'd never be able to tell the man only got a few hours of sleep or that I was the person responsible for those lost hours.

He flashes me a brilliant smile as he spots me across the reception.

"Looking stunning today, Maeve."

I immediately glance down at my outfit, looking for bathroom tissue stuck to my shoe or an undone zipper, but I can't find anything out of place. My short-sleeve red-and-white Dior minidress is flawless, as are my stockings and velvet-bow pumps. Shooting him a glare, I snap, "Conference room." Without waiting for a reply, I turn and march toward it.

When I reach the doorway, I look to see if he's following, but he's bent over Mrs. Rodriguez's desk, that same stupid smile on his face. He hands her a bag from Cafe de Olla, and the way she practically glows back at him when she pulls out the croissant makes me see red for a few seconds.

Everyone knows those croissants are the best, okay? Her face has every right to light up like that at the thought of eating one. But spoiling her is *my* job. I've never brought her a croissant, and Pierce doing so now, after only knowing her a handful of months, is making me look bad.

He leans forward to say something else, then they both turn to glance in my direction, knowing smiles on their faces. I suck in a breath through my nose and spin on my heel into the room.

Several staff members have already gathered around the big conference table, and when I enter, their chatter immediately stops. I don't know why. It's not like I'm a dictator or something. They get to talk, for god's sake.

Pierce walks in seconds after I've taken a seat. He greets everyone with a smile as he approaches me. I keep my eyes narrowed to let him know that under no circumstances will I be tolerating shenanigans this morning. He must have truly underestimated my desire to win this thing if he thinks he stands a fighting chance.

It's absolutely infuriating how good he looks after so little sleep. I'm suddenly insanely curious to know if he visits the spa. How dare there be no bags or dark circles under his eyes when I spent half an hour covering them on my own face? He looks refreshed, wearing a dark suit and navy-blue tie. When his eyes come to rest on me, his expression is impossible to read.

He stops behind my chair and sets a small box on the table in front of me. "Good morning," he murmurs in my ear.

I steel my jaw against the goosebumps racing up my spine. My eyes refuse my orders not to look at the box and instead immediately seek out the label. It's another croissant from Cafe de Olla, this one with a green "gluten-free" sticker on the package.

"What would you have me do?" he asks, voice still brushing against the hair at the nape of my neck. He could have run his fingers over that same area, and it would have felt no less intimate.

I shift in my seat, putting distance between us. Pointing to the chair to my right at the head of the table, I say, "You're leading the staff meeting."

He doesn't say anything, but there are several beats of silence, which I presume he is using to process this information. But then he takes the seat and smiles at the whole table, which has been accumulating more attendees over the past few minutes.

My fingers ache to tear into the croissant—I didn't have breakfast this morning—but I deny them the pleasure. Not only will I absolutely not eat in front of my staff, but I will not give Pierce the satisfaction of knowing how badly I want it. Besides, watching him fumble this meeting will give me much more satisfaction than a bunch of butter and carbs.

But as time progresses, I realize I have greatly underestimated my opponent. Not only did he have zero preparation, but he doesn't even know these people, and yet he is doing a smashing job leading. Instead of working from an agenda, he allows each person to share about any issues or struggles they are having in their department.

It's unorthodox and completely uncalled for, but I have to admit, it appears to have its benefits.

As the hour winds down and we've collected a list of issues that need to be addressed, I remind myself that Pierce is the enemy here. No matter how good he might be at leading a staff meeting—and really, the awe I experienced probably had more to do with my empty stomach than anything actually impressive on his part—he needs to be taken down. I cannot afford to lose this challenge and the only real friends I have.

Annoyingly, every staff member takes the time to thank Pierce afterward. Some of them even slap him on the back like he's a mate, and I catch more than a few suggestive glances thrown his way, although he seems oblivious to those.

After the room has cleared of everyone but the two of us, I can feel his gaze on me and pretend to be busy with my phone.

"It's 9 a.m.," he says.

"It is." I put my device down on the table and meet his eyes.

He's standing near the door, hands in his pockets, looking like a damn *L'Uomo Vogue* model. "So I'll be off, then."

I nod and purse my lips. "Don't let the door hit you on the way out."

As he turns and walks out, I tell myself the tiny catch in my chest is from lack of sustenance, nothing else.

# 10

## "Electric Touch" - Taylor Swift ft. Fall Out Boy

*Maeve*

My heels click on the glossy tile floor as I head to the elevator. The only thing on my agenda at the office today was the staff meeting, which Pierce already handled, and the longer I think about it, the more convinced I become that he fumbled it. How can you expect to get anything done if you just let people talk about their problems the whole time?

Shifting my purse higher on my shoulder, I press the down button. Footsteps sound behind me, but I don't turn to look, just inwardly sigh at having to share the lift. Is it too much to ask for a little peace and quiet occasionally? God. Maybe if I'm fast enough—

The doors open with a ding, and I step on, then quickly smash the button for the lobby. But before the elevator can close, Pierce jogs in.

I frown up at him. "I thought you left."

"Forgot my phone on the table," he says, wiggling it back and forth.

I ignore him and face the front, grateful we only have five floors to descend. His scent is filling the car and making it hard to think about my plans for the rest of the day. There's no way he's always smelled this good. I would have noticed. I notice everything. If one of my best friends smelled like an expensive fuck, trust me, I would have noticed.

"So, did you try it?" His voice is low and rumbly, like a train on the tracks.

"Did I try what?" I scowl, because I can't help it and because he deserves it.

He scoffs under his breath. "Evidently not."

"What are you talking about?" I say, pushing the emergency stop button before I can think better of it. It's time we dealt with this, once and for all. The elevator comes to a grinding halt, rocking us both where we stand.

Confusion flickers across Pierce's face, quickly chased away by amusement. His arms are crossed over his chest, and he's leaning against the back wall. One foot is propped up behind him, revealing a herringbone-patterned sock. He looks impossibly relaxed, like he has nowhere to be and nothing to do. "Sex," he says. It comes out so easily, as though we're talking about the weather. "Did you have sex, then?"

My mouth drops open. How dare he ask me that? "That is the furthest thing from your business—"

"It obviously didn't work."

I want to beat the smirk off him so badly my hands twitch. "How would you know?"

"Because you're still wound as tightly as a vegan at a barbecue."

White spots flash across my vision, and I briefly wonder what the chances are that I would be the prime suspect if Pierce St. James suffered a suspicious death in an elevator. "I am not wound tightly," I hiss.

He leans forward and pokes my arm with a single finger. I gasp and jump backward, swatting at his hand. He chuckles. "Yes, you are."

"Because I'm due for a visit to the spa," I sputter, the sensation of his touch still tingling on my skin.

"Sex is faster and way more fun."

I sniff. "Then you're not visiting the right spa."

A slow, sexy grin—not sexy, I didn't mean sexy. More like smarmy—stretches across his face like a cat before a nap. "Or maybe, just maybe," he says, dragging it out, because he likes the sound of his own voice or because he knows the exact effect it's having on me—which is none at all, if we're being honest here—"it's because you're not doing it with the right person."

I imagine my face looks the way it would if I had stepped in dog poo. "Sounds like you think you could do better."

His chuckle is deep and dirty, ejaculating through my bloodstream. "Oh, I *know* I could."

Have you ever had one of those times right before you actually truly fall asleep when you feel like you're falling? There's this weird sensation of time halting, but then you realize too suddenly that you're plummeting to the ground. It's the scariest sensation in the world—death waiting to claim you—but then you blink awake and realize the whole thing was just a dream.

This feels a little like that. One minute I'm furious at Pierce for implying he knows anything—anything at all—about my life. The next I'm reeling, absolutely reeling, from what he said. It's like it takes my brain a full minute to process everything that has just transpired.

I'm positive that had he reached out and grabbed me, it would have affected me less than those five words. It wasn't even the words themselves. It was the way he said them. *Oh, I* know *I could*. Such certainty. Such confidence.

And this whole time I'm staggering for breath, do you know what the man is doing? He's just standing there watching me, arms still folded. Waiting for me to say something.

## "ELECTRIC TOUCH" - TAYLOR SWIFT FT. FALL OUT BOY

My heart is pounding as though I've raced up the entire five flights of stairs. My skin feels clammy and is covered in goosebumps. There are a million things I could say, that I want to say, but I settle on: "I am done having this—"

He doesn't let me finish. He pushes off the wall toward me, too fast for me to react. Then his hand is on my waist, pressing me against the wall, the other wrapping around my throat.

I can't breathe.

He hovers over me, his breath coming as hard as mine, and our eyes connect with an intensity they never have before. Have his always had a dozen shades of brown in them, or is that a trick of the light? His hand scoots upward and clasps both of my wrists, then pins them above my head.

I am completely at his mercy, and we both know it. The scary part is, there isn't a single part of me that wants to escape.

He inclines his head, and I know what's coming, but I am unprepared for it.

His lips touch mine, and that's it. We're over. Done. Complete. Our era as separate entities has come to a close, not nicely wrapped up with a bow and a few souvenirs, but with a crash, like a plane hitting water and plummeting below its surface. Fatal wreckage everywhere you look, because this fusing of us together means that everything that came before was wrong.

If this is right, then all the rest was wrong.

He tastes like sweet peppermint, better than any candy I've ever tasted. If I had to pick a flavor to taste for the rest of my life, I'd choose this one.

I've already told you how perfect his lips are, but that was just their appearance. They are even softer than they look. They nip at my mouth, barking orders without a word, chastising me when I don't cooperate quickly enough.

And teeth. Holy fuck, the man uses teeth like I've never experienced before. He bites my lips, my tongue, anything that gets in his way.

He still has one hand wrapped around my throat—not nearly enough to mess with my airway, but enough to signal his power. If he wanted to, he could end me right here, and I'm not sure I'd object.

As he kisses me until I'm completely chafed from his stubble and my lipstick is far beyond redemption, a single thought becomes crystal clear.

He was right. I'm confident now that he was entirely right, much as it pains me to admit it. There is no doubt in my mind that this man could chase away every single demon keeping me from fully relaxing.

His grip on my wrists tightens, and a tiny whimper slips past my lips as he changes the angle of the kiss. An answering growl comes from his throat. The sound raises my libido to its breaking point, and I press up against him. He meets the movement by grinding against me even harder.

All I can think is, what would it feel like to have this man's hands and mouth on my entire body?

"Fuck, Maeve," he says, and it comes out strangled, making me wonder if I somehow did that to him.

He drops my arms slowly back to my sides and removes his fingers from around my neck. A single step backward is all it takes to separate our bodies, but it will take much more than that to separate us now that we've been joined in this way.

He reaches for the emergency brake, and then we're descending again, almost as though nothing has happened. The lift dings, alerting us right before the doors whoosh open. Pierce doesn't say a word, just gives me one final look before walking into the foyer and then out through the exit.

"ELECTRIC TOUCH" - TAYLOR SWIFT FT. FALL OUT BOY

 I lift a shaky hand to my smudged lipstick, a single thought swirling through my brain.
 *What the fuck just happened?*

# 11

## "Eldest Daughter" - Taylor Swift

*Maeve*

It's Friday night, and I know what you're thinking. *Oh yay, let's hit a club or fly to Madrid for the weekend.* Except you're not a Wilson, so you don't understand the importance of family dinners. We don't have them every single week, especially not while the twins are at school, but when my mother issues an invitation to one, you'd better be canceling any plans you have, even if they include a visit to Wesbourne Palace.

If I'm ever forced to choose between my parents and Queen Celia, you'd better believe I'll be choosing them, because not even the monarch herself can inspire the level of fear in a person that either of my parents can.

Actually, I rather like the queen. She's ambitious, determined, and dynamic. If we were after the same things in life, I'd hate her, but since we're not, I'm perfectly content admiring her. Not to mention snagging Prince Henry? Job well done, girl. That man is *fine*.

I walk up the front steps of Kenswick House and ring the bell. My parents have lived at this address in the Hills since before I was born, but whether this place can be called a home is debatable. Would you call a mausoleum homey? The place I grew up in—four stories of white stone framed by massive marble pillars and locked behind tall wrought iron gates—is as formidable as the people who live here.

My mother opens the door wearing a sleeveless ivory silk dress and a fresh blowout. Caterina Wilson comes from an aristocratic Italian family, if that wasn't already obvious from her high cheekbones, olive coloring, and jet-black hair. She gives my outfit—Valentino bow-embellished black-and-white-checked tweed minidress under a black double-breasted cashmere peacoat—a cursory glance, then makes a show of checking behind me for a guest.

"Yes, Mother. I'm alone," I say, walking past her into the house.

The hall is open all the way to the roof, a balcony on each of the three stories overlooking it, making you feel as if you've just stepped into a luxury hotel, not someone's residence. Of course, that could also be because of the lack of personal touches around.

After hanging my coat in the closet, I follow my mum to the dining room, where a hundred-year-old chandelier drips from the ceiling, highlighting the huge table that can easily hold twenty people but has only been set for five. At my father's bark, we all take our seats without a word—or rather, four of us do.

Dinner is served promptly at seven thirty, something my brother is acutely aware of—how could he not be, growing up in this family?—and yet his empty chair screams louder than a ringing phone during a funeral.

My father notices Sebastian's absence but pretends not to. I toss my sister a questioning glance, but she simply flicks her brows upward and sips her wine. Either their twin homing beacons are malfunctioning at the moment, or she's not willing to sell Bash out.

They both head back to uni on Monday after a six-week holiday, which means I'll be forced to endure these atrocious dinners alone. Don't you just envy my life?

"How high did you school today?" my father asks Vivienne as he cuts into his perfectly seared rib eye steak.

She tucks her long dark hair behind her ear before answering him in an even tone. "Three feet."

His fork clatters against his plate, and his face turns the same shade as his crimson tie. "Why? You know she can do more than that."

To my sister's credit, his words appear to roll right off her. Viv has been on a horse since she was five—we all have—but she's the only one of the three Wilson children with the grace and discipline necessary to make it in the sport of show jumping. However, our father has never met something he couldn't criticize.

Viv spears another bite of truffle-infused potatoes. "Because unlike you, she has boundaries."

Before the two of them can get into it about the merits of pushing a horse past its limits, the dining room doors open with a clatter. I don't need to look to know who has just arrived, but I do anyway, because that's just the kind of person my brother is. He doesn't enter a room; he sets it on fire.

You may not know him yet, but you will—trust me on that. Sebastian Wilson is destined for a life in the tabloids. I'm not sure if he does it to infuriate our father or if he simply considers that a bonus, but from the grin spreading across his face as he glances around the table, it's obvious he doesn't feel the slightest remorse for his tardiness or his rude appearance.

Is it mean of me to say that I'm glad to see him, though? Not because I'm eager to be in my brother's presence, but because it will take the focus off me for once. And with everything that's happened this week, it would be really nice to not have my father breathing down my neck tonight, too.

"Sorry I'm late." Bash rounds the table to where my mother is sitting, then leans down and presses a loud kiss to her cheek.

She places her hand on his face, holding him to her. After Bash releases her and takes the last seat at the table, she says, "Sebastian. So nice of you to join us."

"Got caught in traffic," he says, winking at Vivienne.

I roll my eyes. He's not fooling anyone, but we're all happy to let him think he is. By "traffic" he means street racing, although I doubt my father would deign to call it anything other than "reckless behavior that is a disrespect to your upbringing."

Something else you should know about Oliver Wilson—everything is about him, and every mistake you make can be construed as disrespecting him, his family, or his legacy. Consider yourself warned.

"Where's your dinner jacket?" he snaps now, looking at Bash as though he's walked in covered in horse manure.

Bash looks down at his black-and-white Balenciaga T-shirt and winces. "Fuck. Must have left it in the car."

Mum gives him what I'm sure is meant to be an admonishing look, but it loses its effectiveness by the time it reaches him. She has a soft spot for him the size of the Atlantic. "Language, Bash."

I slice another bite of steak and pop it into my mouth. My family might be dysfunctional, but at least they're doing a great job keeping my mind off that kiss. That stupid bloody kiss that hasn't given me a moment's peace, not even when I'm sleeping. Last night I dreamt— Well, I'm not telling you what I dreamt, because it was inappropriate and you don't need to know.

I've had enough time and distance from the event itself to properly analyze it, and the conclusion I've come to is this: the reason I keep hyperfixating on Pierce and the kiss is twofold. One, HavenNet. If we weren't forced to work together so closely on something so important, this would be a non-issue. Two, the challenge. Fighting over our friends sounds stupid and childish, I know. But how am I supposed to back out now? I can't just let him claim our group and push me out.

Which means I'm stuck in purgatory for the foreseeable future. The best thing to do is to find a way to relax. If I can manage that, I can stop envisioning stripping the clothes off one of my oldest—former—friends.

"So, Maeve," Bash says, a wicked gleam in his eye I don't care for, "I heard Pierce was your date the other night." He keeps his eyes locked on mine as he chugs his wine.

I also do not appreciate being used as a means of diverting our father's attention, and Bash knows it. But my brother is one of the most selfish people you'll ever encounter, so you can't really expect much else. I tighten my glare. "It wasn't a date. He was assisting."

"Whatever you say, sister dear." He holds up his glass, and one of the servers waiting in the shadows refills it.

My mother clears her throat, and my stomach clenches. Both of my parents are exceptional at communicating without words. Throat clearing is a favorite tool in both of their arsenals, which is how I know exactly what's coming next.

"Perhaps—"

"No, Mother." I hold up my hand before she can finish her thought. "There is absolutely nothing between Pierce and me. Besides, he has a girlfriend." Maybe if I say it enough times, my brain will finally get the hint.

She raises one perfectly arched brow. "I was only going to say, perhaps it's time you find someone and make a commitment."

I close my eyes for a brief second before forcing a smile. "Sure. I'll get right on that." Of course, none of them know about Preston. My dad would have a coronary if he knew I was seeing a married man. God, the scandal it would cause. That would be his one and only concern. How would it reflect on the Wilson name?

So I plaster a fake smile on my face and pretend I don't have a boyfriend who is currently with his wife, and whom I haven't thought much about these past two days because my former best friend kissed me in an elevator while we were having a row, and I haven't been able to stop thinking about it ever since and I don't know what kind of person it makes me that my body wants another go the way it wants oxygen.

\* \* \*

Over the weekend, I try everything. The spa, naturally—you really should get the La Mer Signature Facial the next time you're there; it's exquisite—a three-hour massage, an Audrey Hepburn movie marathon, and shopping with Lux. That last one I only did because she invited me and I thought it might help. But have you ever shopped with Lux Colombia-Clarke? God, it only heightened my anxiety, and I remembered immediately why I prefer to shop alone. The only exception was when I went with Pierce. It was rather nice to have someone to hold my bags and tell me I looked stunning, even if I know he was only saying it to gain points in the challenge.

By Sunday night, I don't feel any less stressed. I can't fall asleep, my thoughts go all hazy when I try to focus on anything work-related, and there's a jitteriness running through my veins as though I'm on Adderall. I popped a Valium earlier, but it only made me tired.

I pull my phone from the bedside table, and it slips from my grasp and lands on the floor. Stifling a very loud "fuck," I get out of bed and retrieve it. I send a text to Preston, asking if there's any way he can come over tonight. I need that orgasm. Besides, he kind of owes me one or two.

His reply comes several minutes later. *I can't tonight. So sorry. xx*

I toss the phone onto the bed beside me. Don't ever date a married guy, okay?

    Reaching into the drawer of my nightstand, I find my vibrator. It's been a hot minute since I've used it, but if Pierce is right, maybe it's time to dust it off a little more often. Thinking of him makes me think of the kiss, and by the time I have my panties pulled down, my need for a lubricant has greatly decreased.

# 12

## "Treacherous" - Taylor Swift

*Pierce*

We're getting too old for this. Purple lights are strobing throughout the club, and velvet sofas line the walls. Lush plants dot the room and hang from the open rafters. It's a swanky place, but most people in the crowd appear to be in their early twenties.

"Anyone else think we may have aged out of this scene?" I say, taking my drink from the bartender.

Rhett claps a hand on my shoulder. "Nah, mate. But maybe if you didn't dress like a forty-year-old man, you'd get a little more action." He flicks a finger against my dress shirt before leading Saylor to the dance floor.

I glance down at my clothes. Slacks, button-down, belt, shoes. I'm not even wearing a tie. What is his problem?

"Don't listen to him," Heath says. "Someone needs to be the dad."

Walker socks him in the stomach with her elbow.

My eyes find their way to Maeve, something that happens way too often these days. She's wearing a dark strapless minidress with a sweetheart neckline and chandelier earrings. (Before you ask, yes I know what those are. I have a girlfriend.) It's been over a week since

I kissed Maeve in the bloody lift, and I can't stop thinking about it. It's like a scab you can't stop picking.

And before you ask, yeah I remember that I have a girlfriend. I shouldn't have kissed Maeve. It was a shit thing to do, but it's done. I'm not going to tell Amara about it, because it would only hurt her, and for what purpose? There's nothing going on between Maeve and me. I would never cheat.

Let's just say Maeve has always fascinated me. She talks a big game, but I'm convinced that underneath all that bravado, she's actually a scared little puppy. I only caught a glimpse of it during that kiss, but it was enough to confirm my suspicions.

All of our friends have coupled up and are on the dance floor, even Heath and Walker. Somehow I missed him convincing her to dance. Maeve is still leaning against the bar, nursing her French 75 and looking everywhere but at me. She hasn't made eye contact with me since the elevator. I know, because I can't keep my eyes off her.

In what I really hope is a smooth move, I sidle up next to her, close enough that she can hear me over the music, but not close enough to scare her away. It seemed like the perfect distance in my mind, but she still shifts farther from me.

Goddamn it, this woman.

I close the distance between us, because fuck it. Leaning down, I say into her ear, "Dance with me."

She pretends not to hear me, just takes another sip of her drink, but the small tick in her jaw gives her away.

"Come on, Maeve. Say yes."

She whirls on me so quickly, I nearly spill my Negroni. "You know very well I'm not a club dancer."

"It's not like we have anything else to do." I keep my eyes on her as I lift my glass to my lips.

"Then maybe you should have brought your girlfriend to keep you entertained."

I never bring my girlfriends when we hang out, and she knows this. "Still haven't been laid, have you?" I say, shaking my head.

The sharp intake of air through her nose makes her nostrils flare, and honestly, that's enough for me tonight. Just that tiny reaction scratches the itch I had to make her feel something. But at the same time, it also peels back the lid on my desire to watch her explode.

I don't get the chance, however, because she moves into the crowd, leaving me at the bar to watch her retreating form sparkle as the lights catch her dress. Why the fuck does she have to be so beautiful?

By the time I've ordered a second drink, Maeve has finished her cocktail at the other end of the lounge. But before I can ask the bartender to make her another, this random bloke approaches her. I can't hear what they're saying, but she hops off her barstool and follows him to the dance floor.

The fucking balls on this guy. Maeve isn't exactly approachable under the best of circumstances, but tonight? Tonight she's dressed to kill.

Tonight I have the strange urge to kill as well. The energy thrumming through my veins is not from the DJ's pounding music or the alcohol in my blood. It's definitely from a desire to annihilate the guy dancing with her.

Sipping my drink, I watch them. Couldn't tell you what the wanker looks like, though, because she has my full attention. She looks ill at ease out there, because she's right—club dancing isn't really her thing. But put her in a ballroom, and prepare to be amazed.

Someone lets out a low whistle, and I turn to find Rhett next to me at the bar, Heath on his other side. Rhett nods toward Maeve and the mystery guy. "Maeve's dancing? What's next? Cats doing the tango?"

I shake my head and take another drink. "No fucking clue."

Heath leans over the counter. "I rather thought the two of you might . . ."

Frowning, I look up. Do they know something they shouldn't? "Might what?"

"Dance." He shrugs and lifts his beer bottle to his lips.

"I tried," I say. "She turned me down."

"She turned you down, mate? What the fuck?" Rhett says.

My eyes move back to the dance floor, because apparently I can't go more than thirty seconds without getting a fix. Why does her rejection sting so badly? Maeve turns down everything suggested to her. You tell her how good the smoked salmon is, and she'll intentionally order the duck, then the next time she goes without you, she'll get the salmon. Doesn't believe in unearned satisfaction, that one, even if it's just a suggestion of what to order at a restaurant. I'm guessing that comes from her jackass of a father.

"That bloke looks like he's having more fun than she is," Heath says, nodding toward Maeve and her wannabe suiter. He's right. The guy has his hands on her waist, and they keep sliding lower. Maeve looks less than thrilled about the arrangement, but she's the one who agreed to dance with him. Definitely doesn't need me to rescue her.

"Maybe you should try again," Rhett says, nursing his drink. "She looks like she might say yes this time."

I shoot him a glare. I have no interest in being turned down again, especially not while all of our friends are watching.

Rhett's brows shoot up. "I'm kidding, mate. Forget I mentioned it."

I swing my gaze back to Maeve and the fucking asswipe she said yes to, but they've disappeared. Pushing off from the bar, I scan the sea of heads. She better not be thinking about leaving with him.

Next thing I know, I'm getting jostled by the people on the dance floor. I move to the last place I saw them, but they're no longer there. My heart rate is going about twice its normal speed when I finally spot them at the edge of the room.

Maeve has her arms slung around his neck, but she doesn't exactly look happy. Not that that's unusual. If you ever see Maeve looking happy, call an ambulance. She's probably overdosed on something.

I cut through the swaying bodies between us. When I reach them, I clap a hand on the guy's shoulder. He turns in surprise. A mixture of confusion and irritation spreads across Maeve's face when she sees me.

"My turn," I say, keeping my eyes locked on hers.

The wanker doesn't put up much of a fight, which is lucky for him, because I'm not opposed to pounding him into the pavement outside if I need to. He slinks off, and Maeve scowls at me. "I was ready to quit anyway."

"Too bad." I grab her arms and wrap them around my neck.

She bristles and pulls some of the hair at the nape.

I yank her close to me. If she wants to play, I'm more than ready for the game. The feeling of her against me—god, how do I explain it? Have you ever touched a live wire? It's a little like that. The shock of it runs through my whole body until I can taste the electricity, smell the smoke. Her waist fits in my hands like it was made to be there. She's as cold as an ice cube, but if the heat between us continues, she'll thaw in no time.

Our faces are close together—there's no other option with this many people—and I can smell her perfume. Can't place it, though. I haven't smelled it on anyone but her, cool and electric like iced champagne but also like silk sheets warmed by the sun. I breathe in deeper to get a better whiff.

Another couple bumps into us, sending Maeve further into my embrace. I'm not mad about the contact, but she looks pissed. She removes her arms from my neck, where they have been hanging with all the enthusiasm of a dead fish. "I'm done," she says. She moves to walk away, but I grab her hand.

She turns back in surprise, but rather than explain, I lead her toward the side door, the red neon sign above it guiding me through the sea of people.

We push outside, and the cold night air feels good on my flushed skin. But it's still winter, so she'll quickly get chilly in that dress, I remind myself.

"What are we doing out here?" she snaps once the sound of the club has been muffled by the door closing.

"You owe me a conversation."

She barks out a laugh. "I owe you nothing."

I cross my arms and lean back against the exterior wall of the club. "I could use your help on Monday afternoon."

The surprise that skitters across her face is satisfying in a primal way. I love nothing more than keeping her on her toes. "With what?" The edge in her voice could cut a vein.

"As my assistant. Unless you're having second thoughts?"

"Of course not." She tilts her chin up. "I'll be there."

"Perfect," I say. "May want to rest up this weekend. I intend to fill every minute of those twenty-four hours."

Her glare sends laser beams into my gut. "Nothing I can't handle."

"I guess we'll see about that." I shrug and make a mental note to come up with things for her to do. I'm not sure I thought we'd make it this far into the challenge. I think I was secretly hoping she'd call it off long before now. But who the fuck am I kidding? Maeve Wilson doesn't quit.

"Prepare to lose," she says, a wicked smile curving up the corners of her mouth, "because I certainly don't intend to."

"Is that right?" I let my eyes travel the length of her, pretending to be considering something, but in reality just feasting on the look of her.

Have I already mentioned how gorgeous she is? Raven-black hair just brushing her shoulders, tight little body with curves in all the right place, bloodred lips that taste even better than they look—thank god I got to experience that—and sharp eyes that will cut you if you meet them for too long.

She grows more uncomfortable the longer I look, which only makes me increase the intensity of my gaze. She's not going to bring up the kiss; I know she's not. In her mind, by ignoring it, she can pretend it didn't happen. But I'm dying to know if she's thought about it as much as I have. I need to know I wasn't the only one who lost sleep replaying it in my mind.

If it were up to her, we'd continue dodging the issue until we're dead.

"You know," I muse, "I'm done with this shit."

"Terrific. That makes two of us." She moves to go back inside.

"Not what I meant," I growl, pressing my hand against the door before she can open it fully. "You've been ignoring me."

She blinks up at me, those huge dark eyes tinkering with my very soul. "This may come as a shock, but not everything is about you."

I lean down until she's only inches from my face. "Maybe not, but it sure as hell is about that kiss."

"That kiss was nothing," she snaps.

"That kiss was everything," I say, keeping my eyes peeled for any flicker of emotion. "Don't tell me you haven't thought about it."

She sniffs, nose in the air. "I haven't." But then there it is. The sign I've been waiting for. Her eyes drop to my lips for a millisecond before meeting my gaze again. In that split second, I can read the hesitation in her expression.

I toss back my head and let out a loud, very relieved laugh.

She crosses her arms and glares at me. "What's so funny?"

I let my smile rest fully on my face, a dog lying in the sunshine after a long winter. "You're a terrible liar."

# 13

## "Bad Habits" - Ed Sheeran

*Maeve*

I've dressed for the occasion: black turtleneck, black twill skirt with gold trim, and knee-high black boots. As I step off the lift on the twenty-first floor of Luminara Tech, I'm wondering if the boots are overkill, but the second I spot Pierce through his open office door and watch the way his eyes travel up and down my body, pausing an extra beat on my shoes, I know they were the perfect choice.

My satisfaction is hampered by the fact that he seems to have been on the same wavelength as me this morning. Black suit, unbuttoned black shirt, no tie, and black-framed sexy glasses. Bastard.

"Funeral today?" I ask, placing my palms on the edge of his desk.

He pulls off the glasses and leans back in his chair, using the opportunity to scan the length of me again. "I could ask you the same thing."

I shrug demurely. "You never know when someone might accidentally die."

The corners of his eyes pinch together ever so slightly—I almost miss it—but when he turns his face away, I know he's trying to hide his amusement. "I hope you're ready for a day of slave labor."

If he thinks he can intimidate me, he's in for a surprise. I have every intention of slaying whatever tasks he sets before me. "Bring it on."

"I think the phrase you're looking for is 'hit me with your best shot.'" He punctuates this with the world's cockiest smile. It's a nice smile objectively, or would be without the gigantic dose of arrogance he infuses it with. Bright white teeth, all perfectly aligned, full lips with that damned Cupid's bow, curving just so in all the right places.

It takes zero imagination to remember exactly what that mouth felt like on mine, those teeth pressing into my bottom lip, tasting me like a sampler platter at Del Lucca's. I still haven't been able to shake the flavor of him, and it's been nearly two weeks. This challenge is going to mess with my head in the worst way. I'm beginning to wonder if it would have been smarter to simply bow out entirely, tuck my tail between my legs, and put as much distance between me and Pierce St. James as possible.

But it's too late for that now. I'm here, and this means war. I straighten my shoulders and fix him with an unblinking gaze. "If that phrase ever leaves my lips, consider it permission to kill me."

"With pleasure." He sits upright and leans across the desk until he's way too close for comfort, but I can't very well back up now and let him think he intimidates me. "Your first task is to handle all incoming calls and text messages."

I open my mouth, but no words present themselves. I was expecting him to stick me in a basement with a thousand boxes of files and tell me to sort them alphabetically in the dark. "How will I know what to say?" I ask.

He slides his phone from his pocket and holds it out. "You can ask me."

Gingerly, I accept it, being careful not to touch him in the process. This seems to amuse him as well, judging by the way the corners of his mouth are quirking. The phone is warm from being pressed against his body, and I can't tell if what I feel is repulsion or fascination. Maybe a little of both?

"So I'm just supposed to sit here, waiting for someone to call or text you, then ask you how to reply?"

He gets to his feet and rounds the desk. "Nope. You're coming with me to a meeting." Leaning around me to reach a file on his desk he definitely could have grabbed while he was still sitting behind it, he adds, "And taking notes."

I nod and accept the file from him. "Got it."

"Last chance to back out." He ducks to catch my eyes.

"Game on."

Instead of responding, he just grins and heads to the door, holding it open for me to walk through. He leads the way to a conference room down the hall. There are people already seated around the table, and I can't help but notice the way they react when Pierce walks in. Backs straighten, eyes lift, smiles hover.

"Good morning," he says.

Everyone responds with a clear "good morning," congeniality present on their faces.

Pierce pulls out a chair for me, and I sit, hiding my surprise when he takes the one right beside me rather than the one at the head of the table. He leads the meeting much the same way he led the one at the Wilson Foundation—with efficiency, while also ensuring everyone feels seen and heard.

I do my best to take notes—he never told me what he wanted exactly—but I'm not used to writing by hand much these days, so not only is my handwriting sloppy in places where I hurried (annoying), but I keep getting distracted by Pierce's presence next to me.

I know what you're thinking, and yes, we've sat next to each other plenty of times before. But those times we hadn't just had the hottest kiss of my life in an elevator. Despite what I told him outside the club, I haven't been able to stop thinking about it, and having his body brush against me every five minutes is not helping it stay out of my mind.

It's as though his essence is another entire person in the room. I'm hyperaware of every movement he makes, every shift in his position, even the scent of him every time I inhale. I can't relax, because the second I do, our bodies will touch, and I'm doing my bloody best to avoid that at all costs.

By the time the meeting is over, I have a stiff neck and am in the beginning stages of carpal tunnel. "Here," I say, thrusting the small spiral notebook at Pierce once we're out in the hall. "I took as many as I could." I bite my tongue to prevent the rest of what I really want to say from spilling out.

He glances down, then slides his hand over mine to take the notepad from me—completely unnecessary, by the way. He could easily have grabbed it without any physical contact at all.

My face burns at the sensual way his fingers rest over mine for a beat too long before letting go. Snatching my hand away, I badly want to make a sharp retort, challenge be damned, but before I can, his phone buzzes in the pocket of my skirt. I pull it out and glance at the screen, but it's locked.

I hold it up so he can see. "How am I supposed to handle your phone if I can't even get inside?"

He gives me a nonplussed look and rattles off his code.

I blink. I didn't expect him to actually give me access to what could potentially be his deepest, darkest web of shame and secrets. Heck, I don't even know Preston's password, and we've been dating for a year.

Instead of waiting to see what I do, he heads back to his office. "We're leaving in five minutes," he calls over his shoulder.

I glance up from the treasure trove at my fingertips. "Leaving?"

"The rest of your tasks will take place at my flat."

I snap my jaw shut and follow him into the room. "Why? What could you possibly have for me to do at home?" Oh god, he's not going to make me do something gross like laundry, is he? "Don't you have a housekeeper?"

He doesn't bother looking at me, just continues whatever he's doing on the computer. "I do."

"So then—"

His chair swivels around so fast, my words cut off midsentence. "If you'd rather bail, I'm sure—"

"Nope," I say, sitting down in one of the chairs near his desk. "I can't wait to see what your sweet disposition has in store for me." My syrupy smile is literally hurting my mouth, and by the look on his face, I think he knows it.

While he finishes at his desk, I open the text he's just received. It's from an unsaved number with no previous exchanges. *I'm free tonight if you are.*

The message is punctuated by a kissing winky emoji—my least favorite. I briefly consider asking Pierce how he'd prefer I respond but decide I can handle this one myself. A devious smile tugs at my lips, and I glance up to make sure he hasn't seen. He's still absorbed in his screen, so I type out a quick reply.

*My place at 10.*

\* \* \*

By the time we leave Luminara, it's started to rain, the air cold. Pierce has a car waiting for us outside, but there's a short walk to the street from the glass skyscraper that houses the country's leading tech firm. He opens an umbrella and holds it over my head as we both dash toward the waiting black Mercedes.

## "BAD HABITS" - ED SHEERAN

I slide in first, and he follows after shaking off the umbrella. As the door closes, I'm struck by the intimacy of sharing a back seat with someone. The air feels charged with electricity. I do my best to put as much space between us as I can, but Pierce is not a small man, and his presence is even bigger than his physical body. I hug my side of the car, but he still manages to encroach on my personal bubble with his intoxicating scent and warmth.

Fortunately, the Atlantis is only a few blocks from Luminara. As we ride the lift up to Pierce's flat, I pretend to be absorbed in something on my phone, because the last thing I need is for him to think I'm thinking about what happened the last time we shared an elevator, which I'm definitely not. I can feel his eyes on me, though, so I'm not entirely sure he isn't thinking that anyway.

He escorts me into his flat, and I realize I've never been inside it during the day. I'm here nearly every week for poker night, but it feels different with the afternoon sun streaming in through the huge windows and without the chatter of everyone else in the next room.

"Do you want something to drink?" he asks, moving into the sleek kitchen.

I frown. "Are you planning to lace it with barbiturates?"

He lets out a sharp laugh. "Naturally." Coming back into the foyer, he hands me a glass of ice water with lime.

I take it gratefully—we won't be discussing how he knows how I take my water—and wait for him to deliver my orders.

He gets right to it. "Your first task is to help me choose an outfit for my date tonight."

After choking on my drink, I follow him toward what is presumably his bedroom. Let's get one thing straight. That is not jealousy curling up in my stomach like a cat on a windowsill. The man has a girlfriend. I am under no illusion that our kiss in the elevator was anything more than the result of heightened emotions, close proximity, and a grave lack of judgment on his part. (Not mine, because I was taken completely by surprise.)

If he's taking his girlfriend out tonight, it's no skin off my back. In fact, I'm relieved. Hopefully he's gotten over his ridiculous idea that that kiss meant anything to anybody in any universe.

We walk into his bedroom, and I'm hit with the scent of him. It fills the air like smoke, seeping into my pores until I'm pretty sure that when I leave this place, I'll still be oozing him. If I thought sharing a small space with him was bad, this is torture. Or bliss, depending on how you look at it. If you're into bergamot, cognac, coffee, and men who eye-fuck you from across the room and expect you to thank them for it, then you'd probably like it.

He leads the way into his walk-in closet, which is, as expected, full of suits.

"Do you own anything other than jackets?" I say, glancing around.

He gives me an amused smirk and gestures toward the shelves holding cashmere sweaters, all neatly folded and organized by color. The whole thing really is a masterpiece. I can't find a single shade out of place.

"Great." I clap my hands together and begin sorting through the clothes as quickly as I can, but Pierce is leaning against the opposite side of the closet, watching me, and it makes me fumble more than one hanger. "Pretty sure I can handle this if you have things you need to do," I say under my breath.

"I don't," he says.

"Terrific," I mutter.

"What was that?" He pushes off from the wall and moves closer. "Was that a complaint?"

I shoot him an appalled look. "Absolutely not. I was simply remarking on how much fun I'm having." Running my hand over the coats lined up in front of me, I add, "I've never touched this much

## "BAD HABITS" - ED SHEERAN

Italian wool in my life. It's really something."

He now props his shoulder against the wall nearest me. "I'm glad my closet entertains you."

While he probably thinks I was kidding about having fun, if I'm being honest, this isn't too bad. At least he's not asking me to run a washing machine, or god forbid, scrub dinnerware. And I rather enjoy the feel of his clothes. They're made of the finest fabrics, and they smell . . . well, we've already discussed how they smell.

I'm scanning the drawers of his accessories when I spot it. I pull a half-familiar red scarf from behind the rows of gray and black ones and hold it out to him. "Is this mine?"

His face still wears a look of indifference as he glances at it. "Don't think so."

"I'm almost positive it is," I say, fumbling for the tag. "Mine was a vintage Prada cashmere wool blend."

"Why would your scarf be in my closet?" he asks.

I find the tag and show it to him. "My question exactly."

His eyebrows flick upward, but he still looks bored. "You must have left it here, and my housekeeper thought it was mine."

I frown and tuck it into my handbag, then return to the task of finding his outfit for tonight. I finally decide on a custom-made light gray suit, light blue shirt, and a navy tie with a small weave pattern.

That settled, he takes me to the game room where I spend most of my Tuesday evenings. "I need you to create a detailed inventory list of my slot machine collection," he says.

I turn and stare at him with a cocked brow. "Come again?"

He tosses me a wink and heads back to the door. "You'll find everything you need to know from Sotheby's."

Once he leaves, I stare at the wall of mini slot machines in front of me. Each one is nestled into a cube and lit with a red glow light. I've seen them a million times before, but never really paid much attention. There must be over fifty of them.

It feels weird to be in here without everyone else. I send Walker and Lux a photo of the wall and ask whether the slot machine collection should have been a sign to us all that Pierce is secretly a psychopath. And then I get started.

I've just hung up after my two-hour phone call with Sotheby's when Pierce walks back into the room. His hair is still damp from his shower, and his ever-present stubble has nearly disappeared from his jaw. A tiny sniff of the air tells me he's applied a fresh layer of cologne and I'm better off breathing through my mouth.

"All done?" he asks, arms crossed.

"Documented, photographed, and cross-referenced for future ease," I say. "I just emailed you the file."

"You're a genius."

"I know." I stand right in front of him and frown at his outfit. "This isn't right."

He smooths a hand over his chest. "What's wrong with it?"

"The tie isn't the right pattern." I shake my head and motion for him to follow me.

In the closet, I find another navy tie, this time with a herringbone design. "Much more suitable," I say, holding it up. "See the subtle hints of gray?"

He grunts in reply, then stands completely still while I remove the first tie from his neck. It doesn't occur to me what I'm doing until he swallows and I see his Adam's apple bobbing.

Fuck, we are really close. My body is brushing the front of his, and I have to stand on my tiptoes to be able to reach properly, making me press into him even more any time I start to lose my balance.

His hands reach out and grip my waist, keeping me from toppling into him as I make the last adjustments to the new tie. My face has never felt so hot before, not even when Rhett told me I couldn't eat that stupid chili pepper and I felt the need to prove him wrong.

Being this close to Pierce and him touching me makes my fingers fumble much more than they should, which only delays the process. My brain has decided the only things worthy of my attention right now are the way he is holding my waist and the heat of his body against mine. I'm still breathing through my mouth, so at least I don't have his scent messing with my head as well.

Finally, the new tie is on, and I let out a long sigh of relief as I lower back to the floor and take a step backward. "Better," I say.

The corner of his mouth lifts as though he understands my double meaning. "Thank you," he says, and clears his throat. "You're free to go. Unless you'd rather wash some plates and cutlery?"

I hold up my hands. "Not at all."

A full grin takes over his face then. "There aren't any anyway," he whispers.

He walks me to the front door, and I expect to feel elation at being released from any further duties. Instead, there's this strange swirling in my stomach. It carries a faint trace of nausea with it, which is weird. Almost like an impending doom.

"Thanks again," he says, opening the door for me.

"Have a fantastic time." I smile, thinking about the unexpected visitor he'll be receiving at ten tonight. I step out into the corridor, the sick feeling growing with every passing second.

"Maeve," Pierce calls when I'm halfway to the lift.

I turn back to find him still in the doorway of his flat.

"Try to relax tonight." Then he winks and steps back inside.

Irritation joins the nausea in my belly. One thing is for sure: I won't be doing any relaxing tonight.

## 14

## "Blank Space" - Taylor Swift

*Maeve*

The thought comes while I'm on my second glass of wine. It's Friday night, and I've just returned from dinner with my parents—a nightmare, but that was to be expected. My father lambasted me for a good fifteen minutes about the deal with Luminara Tech still being in limbo.

That was followed by my mother chiding me relentlessly throughout the rest of the meal for everything I do that drives men away. Want to hear all of my atrocious personality traits? I don't smile enough. I'm too angry. I'm too uptight. I'm not soft enough. I don't slow down long enough for anyone to approach me. I frown too often. I say too much. I don't say enough. I could continue, but I'm sure you're as bored as I am.

As far as either of my parents are concerned, I'm the furthest thing from the daughter they wish they had. And I'm starting to wonder if maybe they're right about me.

It's been eating at me ever since poker night on Tuesday. They declared Pierce the winner of the stupid assistant challenge. Can you believe it? They said it was a close call, but since I sent Lux and

"BLANK SPACE" - TAYLOR SWIFT

Walker a text essentially calling Pierce a psychopath, they labeled it a complaint.

So I'm labeling them the worst friends in the world for 1) snitching on me for the text, and 2) siding with said psychopath. The guy has an entire showcase of collectible slot machines. There's got to be at least a little something wrong with his head, don't you think?

I could blame my decision on the wine, even though I haven't drunk any more than usual. I could blame it on my parents making me lose my bloody sanity, but in reality, this was just a normal Friday night.

And before you judge me for what I'm about to do, you should know that I have explored every other reasonable solution. I wouldn't be standing out here if I hadn't. Nothing has helped. This is quite literally my last option. I'm not exactly hopeful it will help, but I figure if my world's going down in smoke anyway, a little more fuel on the fire can't hurt. At least the blaze will be more dramatic.

So, before I can talk myself out of this for the fifth time, I lift my hand and knock on Pierce's door.

\* \* \*

I half expect him not to be home. It is Friday night, after all, and he has a girlfriend. Normal guys would be out having dinner. Although it's a little late to still be eating. It was eleven when I left my house, which means it must be nearly half past now, thanks to my sitting in the parking garage for a good fifteen minutes before finding the courage to come up here.

And then it occurs to me that, if by some miracle he actually happens to be home, he's probably with *her*. I slap my hand over my mouth, horrified that of all the excuses I used to talk myself out of this, that was the only one that *didn't* occur to me.

I'm slinking back to the lift when the door to Pierce's flat opens.

"Maeve?"

I turn around, certain I must look like a child who just got caught with their hand in the cookie jar. (Not that I would know—my mother doesn't believe in cookies.)

"What are you doing here?" Pierce asks, leaning against the doorframe. He's wearing dark pants and a white shirt. The sexy glasses are nowhere in sight, thank god.

"I, uh—" I wince and squeeze my eyes shut, hoping this is just a wine-induced dream. "Are you alone?"

He runs his fingers over his jawline. "If I say yes, will you try to kill me while there are no witnesses?"

"I thought about it," I say, "but I'm actually here for an unrelated reason."

"A reason unrelated to my death. How intriguing. Do go on."

I gesture to the gulf of empty space between us. "I'm here to do this thing."

"Do what thing?"

"Don't pretend you don't know," I snap. "It was your idea."

He sniffs and readjusts his position. "Which idea? I have a lot of good ones."

We're still standing six feet apart, and I'm terrified someone will come out and overhear us, so I take several steps closer. "Don't make me say it."

He lowers his voice until it's practically a purr. "You're going to have to if you want me to know what you're talking about."

I breathe my frustration out through my nose. "You said if I ever needed someone to help me . . . *relax*, you would . . . you know." God, that might be the most mortifying string of words I've ever had to utter.

This whole time I thought he was playing me, but I can see the realization wash over his face as he puts the pieces together.

"Maeve Allegra Wilson," he says, running his tongue over his bottom lip and managing to dampen my brand-new lace underwear as he does so. "Are you propositioning me for sex?"

Rolling my eyes, I cross my arms over my chest. "You don't have to put it that way."

He scans me from head to toe, slowly and with a touch of amusement. "I thought you had a boyfriend."

"We're not exclusive," I say. "Obviously."

He arches a single brow.

"He has a *wife*."

His chin tilts upward in a silent *ah* as he considers me. My palms grow sweatier the longer he stares. What is he waiting for? If he's going to turn me down, I'd rather he just get it over with. But maybe that's the point. He intends to play with his food before he eats it.

Finally, he pushes the door open and inclines his head. "Come in."

It feels a little like the fox inviting Henny Penny into his cave, but I cross the threshold anyway. If I'm Henny Penny, I'm confident enough in my ability to get the fox into the cooking pot if it all goes to hell.

Pierce closes the door behind me, and the click as it latches into place jolts through me. Everything is screaming at me to run, but that would be admitting that this was a bad idea in the first place. Wilsons aren't known for having bad ideas, and I don't see a reason to start that rumor now. Although I have to confess, this is the most uptight I've felt since the first time I was in the same room as Preston and his wife after we started seeing each other.

As far as relaxation techniques go, I'll have to put this one at the bottom of the list.

Pierce is still standing at the door, watching me. Cool sexuality ripples off him, and I don't know how I've never noticed it before. The man personifies sex. The outline of thick muscles is visible through his sleeves, and his steady gaze sends a signal to my core that this man is probably quite good in the bedroom.

"Well?" I say, eager to get this over with. "Shall I undress?"

He ducks his head to hide his smile, but I see it anyway. Great, so we're back to me amusing him.

"No, you don't need to undress."

I gape at him. "Are you planning to do this fully clothed?" That isn't something I'm comfortable with. I've never tried it, but it sounds abhorrent.

"Can we slow down?" he asks, running a hand through his hair. "I need to make a call first."

"Sure, I'll just get some water." Mortified, I head to the kitchen. God, he must think I'm some kind of sex fiend, ready to jump his bones the second we're alone. I skip the water and head straight for the wine. The glasses I had earlier were hours ago and are no longer deadening anything. And if I'm actually going to crawl into Pierce St. James's bed, I'm going to need something to take the edge off.

I turn around, wine in hand, to find Pierce staring at me from the kitchen doorway. Startling, I nearly slosh liquid over the rim of my glass. "Ready?" I ask.

"Not yet. She didn't answer."

My eyes dart back and forth, trying to put the pieces together. "Who's she?"

"Amara."

I widen my eyes. "Isn't that your—?"

"My girlfriend, yes."

I set my goblet down before I drop it. "I'm sorry, are you saying you're going to tell your girlfriend that you're about to have sex with me?"

Closing his eyes, he breathes out a laugh. "No, Maeve. I'm planning to break up with her."

"Wait." I hold up my hand to stop whatever trainwreck is about to happen. "This doesn't mean anything. We do this one time, but that's it. Nothing happens after this. We're not going to be exclusive. We're not going to be anything after this."

He nods as though he understands. "I know, but she and I are."

"I thought you wanted to do this. It was your idea." My heart rate is twice what it was when I walked in, and that's saying something.

"I do want to. Believe me." He wiggles his phone in the air. "Hence the breakup."

"You're going to break up with your girlfriend to have sex with me one time?" My boyfriend can't even leave his wife for me, and it's been over a year.

"I'm pretty sure we'll do it more than once," he says, then tosses me a wink.

I stand there speechless as he holds the phone to his ear, eyes locked on mine.

"Hey, Amara." His tone is soft, and I have a fleeting thought: if this is his bedroom voice, will he use it on me in a few minutes?

My face grows hot.

He keeps holding my gaze. "Listen, this just isn't working out." The guy doesn't even leave the room, just breaks up with his girlfriend while I'm standing here like a bloody idiot.

A few seconds pass while she is presumably saying something, but from the way Pierce's gaze is traversing my face, you wouldn't be able to tell that anyone else has his attention.

"Yeah, I'm sorry," he says. "If it makes you feel better, it would've happened sooner or later anyway."

I can verify that this is, in fact, the truth. I've never seen him with the same woman for more than three months. Maybe I should be worried that there's something wrong with him, but since we're not going to be dating anyway, it's of no concern to me.

He pauses for Amara's response, then winces. A second later, he pulls the phone from his ear and pockets it.

"I take it that didn't reassure her," I say, catastrophically nervous now that there is nothing between us.

"It did not." Something shifts in his eyes, turning them more predatory.

"You couldn't have thought it would." I don't know why I feel the need to point this out, but there's a tremor in my hands that makes me want to buy time.

He shrugs. "Didn't really think about it."

"Why not? She's your girlfriend."

"Was." He reaches for a bottle of whiskey on the shelf above my head. "And I didn't think about it because my mind was full of something else."

My mouth goes dry as I watch him pour a glass. "And what was that?"

Pierce raises the tumbler to his mouth but doesn't take a drink. "Considering how I want to fuck you for the first time." Then he tosses the whole thing back in one go.

# 15

## "When Did You Get Hot?" - Sabrina Carpenter

*Maeve*

Please tell me a symptom of cardiac arrest is not your heart pounding so loudly against the sides of your chest cavity that the neighbors in the flat next door can hear it in spite of what I'm certain are soundproof walls.

I wipe my sweaty hands on my dress, not at all sure what comes next. Pierce might have been thinking about this moment, but I haven't. At least not in terms of specific actions. I assumed it would follow much the same process as with the other men I've slept with—we go to the bedroom, take off our clothes, get under the blankets, and have sex.

Something about the look on Pierce's face tells me this is not what he has in mind. And that terrifies me.

He sets his empty glass on the counter, his movements slow and calculated. My blood responds by surging so forcefully through my veins, I'm in danger of bursting something. I'm sure my face must be flaming red by now.

I clear my throat, needing to cut through this weird sexual energy surrounding us. "Ready whenever you are."

The corner of his mouth twitches with a smile. "I am aware of that, yes."

I give him a "then what are we waiting for?" look.

He closes his eyes and shakes his head. "You're not going to relax until we're in the bedroom, are you?"

Now might not be the best time to tell him that I'm not sure I'll relax even once we're in there, but I play along, gesturing overhead. "The bright lights just don't do it for me."

"Let's go, then." He leads the way out of the kitchen and down the corridor. If I had known when I was here a few days ago that I'd be back so soon, we could have simply done it then, gotten it over with, and saved ourselves a bunch of time.

His bedroom is lit softly by several table lamps, and it smells exactly the way I remember. This time I allow myself to drink in big gulps of the Pierce-scented air. It's practically foreplay.

In the center of the room is a massive bed covered with deep-charcoal linens. He has a surprising number of pillows on it for a bachelor, but I suppose that's the work of his interior designer. It looks very luxurious, masculine, and comfy as hell.

Once again, I jump when the door shuts. Pierce walks farther into the room, rolling up his sleeves as he goes. The sight instantly makes my pulse quicken. As the fabric moves higher up his arms, defined muscles that were only hinted at before come to light.

I don't know what I was thinking. This was a terrible idea. It seemed doable out in the kitchen, but in here—in his bedroom, for god's sake—the thought of him touching me, pushing inside me, is almost more than I can handle. Not because I don't want it, but because it scares the life out of me.

I can't do this after all. I move toward the door. Before I can open it, however, he's right there, holding it shut, his hand pressed flat against the smooth wood. "Where are you going?"

"I—I can't do this," I whisper, transfixed by the veins bulging in his hands.

He ducks his head so we're eye to eye. "You and I both know you wouldn't be here if you hadn't explored every other option first. Which means you need my help."

I swallow, and it's as loud as a jackhammer.

As if sensing how truly terrified I am, he slips one hand under my jaw and into my hair. "There's nothing to be scared of, Maeve."

And then his lips are on mine, and it all comes flooding back to me—why I considered this idea long enough for it to blossom into the only possible option. The taste of him—exquisite. The scent of him being branded into my nostrils—intoxicating. The feeling of his hands on my face—luxurious. He is life and breath and oxygen. He is a delectable dessert, a strong glass of whiskey, a warm bubble bath. He is everything I've ever wanted and everything I've been too afraid to hope for. He is—

He breaks off the kiss and murmurs against my lips, "Still want to leave?"

I mumble something incomprehensible as I shake my head, eager for him to keep kissing me.

But he doesn't, the bastard. Instead, he pulls back, shattering all of those embarrassing thoughts I was having into thousands of shards. He reaches for my dangling diamond earrings and removes them smoothly, as though it's something he's done many times before. "Don't want these to get caught in your hair."

It's a thoughtful gesture, which is the perfect reminder of how treacherous the ground I'm standing on is. "We should set some ground rules," I say.

Sighing, he places the earrings on the nightstand. "Will there be a slideshow presentation too, or—?"

I narrow my eyes and reach for the zipper of my dress. "No, but I wouldn't be opposed to a contract being drawn up."

"Since you've made it clear this will be a one-time thing, I'm afraid it's a little late for that." Taking the zipper from me, he pulls it down much more slowly than I would have done, but at least we're finally getting somewhere. Goosebumps chase the touch of his fingers down my spine.

"Rule number one: no one finds out," I say.

He carefully peels my dress over my shoulders and lets it drop onto the floor. As he takes me in, standing here in nothing but my bra and panties, the look that crosses his face is one I can't place—part awe, part anguish, maybe? It's one I've never seen on a man before, except maybe at a wedding when the groom saw his bride for the first time, which is a ridiculous comparison, I know.

"Rule number two," I say, because someone needs to break the tension, "we never mention it again."

"Mmm," he murmurs as he toys with my bra strap. "Permission to renegotiate."

I frown up at him. "Whatever for?"

"I fully intend to remind you of this moment as many times as possible."

"Hence the rule."

He doesn't argue it further, but he doesn't agree either. His fingers reach for the buttons of his shirt, and I watch in fascination as he starts to undo them. "I have one. No less than two orgasms," he says.

I bark out a laugh. Is he serious? "I don't think so."

"Nonnegotiable."

"Are you referring to one for each of us or . . ."

His brow furrows. "Of course not. I meant two for you."

"That's . . . generous, but—"

"Like I said," he growls, "nonnegotiable."

Fucking terrific. That means I'll have to fake the first one, and now this whole thing will take twice as long. "Fine," I grind out. At this rate, the sun will be up before I leave.

He studies me, a puzzled look on his face. "Why do I get the feeling you don't want to be here?"

I undo the clasp of my bra and discard it on the floor. "Because I don't."

His fingers fumble over a button as he stares at my bare chest. "Do you not enjoy sex? Or is it the idea of sex with me in particular that you find repulsive?"

Shrugging, I rest my hands on my hips, ready for him to finish undressing so we can get started. "While I wouldn't say sleeping with my nemesis is on my bucket list, I typically find sex to be quite nice."

"Quite nice?" His voice is lined with amused disbelief.

"Yes. Pleasant. Pleasurable."

He blinks several times before responding. The man looks genuinely surprised. "Is that what you think? That sex with me will be 'quite nice'?"

Why is he making this so difficult? "I had hoped." God, is that too much to ask? How does he expect me to relax otherwise?

His eyes squint, and my heart skips a beat at the look in them. "I'll show you 'quite nice,'" he mutters under his breath. Then he finally—blessedly—strips off his shirt.

Irrational anger blooms in my chest. "Why have you been wearing shirts all this time?" I cross my arms and ogle him. He looks like a Greek god come to life, flesh covering marble perfection.

He smirks, pleased with himself. And don't you dare tell him I said this, but he should be. The man is *exquisite*. "You've seen me without a shirt before."

I shake my head, unable to tear my eyes from the masterpiece before me. Everywhere I look is hard muscle and bronze skin. "No, I haven't." I would have remembered this.

His mouth hitches even higher on the left side. "Maeve, we've gone swimming together a thousand times."

His words are enough to snap me out of the trance I'm in. "Yeah, but I wasn't thinking about you as a snack then."

He wipes away a smile with his hand. I'm glad I'm once again providing him with entertainment, because god knows I don't seem to be good for much else tonight.

Capturing my wrist in his fingers, he peppers kisses from my palm down to my elbow. I remind myself to breathe. His lips feel like angel's wings charged with electricity. As they travel up my arm, my blood pressure spikes even higher. If he thinks this is relaxing, he's got a few things to learn.

Speaking of things to learn, now is probably a good time to warn him. "Just so you know, it's difficult for me to climax," I say.

He lifts his head and stares at me as though there's a glitch in his mental processing.

"It's not a big deal." I place my hands on his chest, and holy cow, the man runs hot. "It's a me problem, not a you problem."

A low growl slips past his lips as he grabs my waist and yanks me against him. "You're mistaken if you think for one second that you climaxing is not my problem."

His mouth meets mine in a rough kiss that has me struggling for breath. One of his hands is planted on the small of my back, keeping our bodies pressed together. The other clamps around my neck as he devours me.

It's like something has snapped in him. He walks me backward, my lips still captive to his, until the backs of my knees hit the bed. Satisfied that I'm not going anywhere, he finally releases me, and I take in a jagged lungful of air. He doesn't pause, just crouches in front of me and tugs my lace panties down my legs, leaving them pooled at my ankles.

I've always been confident about my body, but with his face right *there*, it's hard not to feel a little insecure, to wonder if he appreciates my wax job or if my scent will be off-putting to him.

I needn't have worried. He closes the distance between us and buries his face in me. A tiny gasp sneaks past my lips as his stubble scratches across sensitive nerves. He grabs my ass and tugs me even closer. The heat from his mouth scorches my skin.

I fight the urge to press against him, to ride his face, but when I feel the warmth of his tongue between my folds, I have no choice. I lose all sense of reason as he fucks me with his mouth, torturing my clit with long, heavy strokes. He slides one of his hands from my ass and brings it around to join his mouth.

I gasp again when he slides a finger inside and can't resist looking down at where he is feasting on me in a way no one ever has before. My legs are growing weaker the longer I stand here, and just when I think I'll combust, he adds a second finger to the first. White-hot pleasure shoots through me at the sensation of being thoroughly filled.

As though he can tell I'm on the verge of collapse, Pierce lifts his head and eases his fingers out. At the pressure of his hand on my ankle, I lift one foot at a time so he can remove my underwear. Slowly straightening up, he says, "God, you're fucking delicious."

My breath catches in my throat.

"I could eat you all night and still not get my fill." There's a low rumble in his voice that wasn't there earlier. "But I have other plans for you as well. Get on the bed," he orders, and my pulse jumps.

I do as directed, scooting up to the headboard. At least here I know what's coming next.

Pierce takes his pants off in less than three seconds, and then he joins me, crawling between my legs like a predator.

My teeth sink into my bottom lip as he approaches, a hungry look on his face. I have to do something, or I'll pass out from high blood pressure. I open the drawer in the bedside table and fumble inside.

"What are you doing?" he asks, sitting back on his heels, leaving that mouth-watering physique on display. (And I'm happy to report his thighs are just as defined as the rest of him.)

"Getting a condom," I say.

He scowls at me. "I'll handle the condom."

My fingers close around a foil packet, and I toss it at him. "Great. Where's the lube?"

That frown has yet to disappear from his face. "We won't be needing it."

I prop myself up on my elbows and return his expression. "What are you talking about?"

He reaches down and slips two fingers inside me, making my whole body shudder. "I prefer to create my own lubrication." He holds up his hand, his fingers glistening in the dim light. "And if that doesn't work, there's always this." Lowering his head, he uses his mouth on me again, and it's all I can do not to cry out.

Is this what he meant by being properly fucked? Because I've already experienced more pleasure tonight than during any sex in the past, and he hasn't even entered me yet.

Pulling back, he looks at me, his expression dark. "Now, are you ready to let me handle things?"

I nod meekly, which might be the first time in my life that's ever happened.

Pierce keeps his eyes on me as he strips off the black boxer briefs he's wearing, and good god, I've never seen a more glorious sight than the very large, very erect, very pink penis in front of me. Within seconds, the condom is rolled on, and he's poised above me.

He drags a hand over my stomach, and immediately, goosebumps cover my skin. Smiling, he leans down to press a kiss to my navel. Then he uses both hands to spread my thighs apart, giving him access to the most vulnerable part of me.

I swallow loudly as he stares down at me. His face is unreadable, and that makes me nervous. Finally, as though he can't resist one more taste, he drops back down and sucks on me again, harder this time. A cry slips past my teeth, and I feel the rumble of his chuckle echo through my bones.

All too soon, he's up on his knees again, wiping his mouth with the back of his hand. He reaches for me and pulls me up until I'm straddling him. I brace myself as he positions his cock at my entrance. Do I tell him or let him discover it on his own? Because confident as he may be, there's no way I'll be climaxing in this position.

I don't have time to decide, because the next second he's thrusting inside me, and my eyes are rolling back in my head. Wrapping my arms around his neck, I collapse against him. He clamps his hands on my waist and pulls me down onto him again and again. The angle makes him hit parts of me that have never been touched before.

His breathing picks up speed as his thrusts become more rapid. "Shit," he mutters, and eases up. He must be close, which means it's time to do my part.

I throw my head back and moan, riding him harder as my breasts bounce. After ten seconds, I slow down and rest my head on his shoulder, pretending to pant.

He pulls out of me abruptly and sits back, leaving me to plop on my ass. "What the fuck was that?"

I lift my brows in confusion and lean back on my elbows. "What was what?"

His eyes narrow into dangerous-looking slits. "Did you—" He pauses. "Did you just *fake* an orgasm?"

"I—" Fuck. "I might have?"

He ducks his head, making him look even more menacing. "That may convince the weasel you're seeing, but it sure as hell doesn't fool me."

My heart is pounding so fast it stands a fighting chance of beating one of my father's horses in the next derby. I scoot back several inches. "How can you . . . tell?"

Slowly, Pierce starts to crawl over me. "You don't think I'll feel the walls of your pussy squeezing me when you come?" He pushes me down with one hand. "Besides, when I make you climax, you'll be a lot louder than that."

He's fully on top of me now, and I'd be lying if I said I wasn't a little scared. But I'm also turned on. *Very* turned on. I can't remember the last time that happened.

He reaches between us and pinches my clit, making me nearly bow off the bed. A devious smile lifts his lips. "That's for trying to fake your first orgasm. I suggest not doing so again, unless you're ready to face the consequences."

I give him a smug smile I don't at all feel. "I'll take my chances."

He glowers down at me. "You're going to climax this time."

"You can't know that," I say, desperate to hold on to whatever scrap of control I have left.

He chuckles, deep and dirty, as if he knows a joke I don't. "Oh, but I do."

And then he enters me with a single deep thrust, filling me so full I think I feel him in my stomach. He pulls back and repeats the motion, and I'm flown to a new level of heaven I didn't know existed.

"Eyes on me."

His voice startles me, and I open my eyes. I didn't even realize I had closed them.

As I meet his gaze, he murmurs, "Good girl."

A blaze of desire streaks up through my core. I've never looked at a man while having sex with him before, and it's completely unnerving. His eyes are locked on mine, refusing to let me look away. Our bodies are rocking together, but I'm hardly even aware of that, entranced as I am by his face.

Then I feel it. It's been building for a while, but I didn't want to raise my hopes in case it ended up being less of a deluge and more of a sprinkle. I didn't realize it would be an absolute thunderstorm.

My orgasm shudders through my body, pleasure in every single nerve ending. I'm sure I make some noise, but I can't tell you what it is, because that would require awareness I simply don't have at the moment. As I fly higher and higher, there's only one thought in my mind.

*How will anything else ever live up to this?*

# 16

## "These Arms of Mine" - Otis Redding

*Pierce*

You know how they say time slows right before death, like the time-space continuum is at play? Where time passes differently for people in different states of motion? This feels a little like that. Like God Himself has reached down to stop the clock, to force time to slow, like a gentle nudge to take note of something beautiful happening.

Because holy fuck. I've seen a lot of really cool shit in my life—Victoria Falls, the Great Barrier Reef, Ha Long Bay, the aurora borealis. But none of them—and hear me when I say this—*none of them* compare to watching Maeve Wilson come apart in my arms.

She's mindfuckingly beautiful at the worst of times, and she would hate me for remembering this, but I've seen her at her worst. The time some wanker broke her heart at school. The time her dad made a public spectacle of her at her own graduation party. The time the tabloids spread a nasty pregnancy rumor and I found her crying in the bathroom.

But when she's at her best . . . You'd better hope you have your armor on, because not only will just looking at her break your heart, but she'll tear it to shreds too, if she catches you doing it.

I don't know what this condition qualifies as. Maybe some kind of angelic visitation? I've never seen her like this, and I suddenly hope with every fiber of my being that no one else has either. Back arched, hair strewn across my pillow, fists clenched in the sheets, mouth open in ecstasy.

And then she screams my name.

I grunt and fall on top of her, unable to hold it back any longer, not if she's going to call for me at her peak. My cock pulses inside her, and it's fucking amazing, of course, but I'd trade it all just to watch her again.

When we've both finished, I don't pull out right away, just prop myself up on my elbows so I can stare down at her. Her cheeks are flushed, and several strands of dark hair are stuck to her temple. She doesn't smile, but her eyelids are at half-mast, as though she's nearly asleep.

"That was . . ." she murmurs before trailing off.

"Fucking incredible." I brush my lips across her clavicle. "The next one will be even better."

Her eyes fly open, clamping onto mine with a sudden fierceness. "What do you mean, next?"

I brush the hair from her face. "We agreed on two orgasms."

"We did no such thing." She tries to sit up, but I'm on top of her, inside her, and much bigger than her, so she's not going anywhere.

"As long as it's been for you, you're going to need more than one to fully relax," I point out, trailing a finger between her tits.

She frowns as she ponders this. "I'm not a two-orgasm girl."

I sniff a laugh. "Pretty sure I can handle it."

"What are you talking about?"

"Your orgasms are my responsibility. You don't need to worry about it."

Her brows furrow even more, until they're nearly touching in the center of her forehead. "You're presuming far too much."

"I meant tonight," I say, nibbling at her neck.

"Oh." She relaxes back into the pillow.

I won't tell her that if I only get her for one night, I fully intend to give her as many orgasms as we have time for. My flat is pretty big, and there are hundreds of surfaces we can explore. My cock is already stiffening again at the thought.

Shifting off her and taking care of the condom, I consider my options. "Let's debase the poker table."

Her eyes nearly bulge out of her head. "Please tell me you're joking."

"I'm not." I give her a hand to help her up. "Imagine Tuesday nights, everyone playing without a clue what happened there."

She glowers at me. "I was."

I wait a few beats to see if she's messing with me, but when her expression doesn't change, I decide to change tactics. "Okay, how about the shower?"

"Standing up? Are you insane?"

"What's wrong with standing?"

She climbs out of bed, grabs my shirt from the floor, and slips it on. "I can't do it."

As uptight as she is, I'm not too surprised, but she is grossly underestimating my abilities. "The kitchen counter, then."

Buttoning my shirt—don't know why, because it's coming off again within seconds—Maeve says, "We're not in a movie. No one actually does that."

I laugh abruptly as I yank her toward me. "Hate to break it to you, but yes they do."

She frowns up at me. "Well, I don't."

A heavy sigh works its way from my chest. "Fine. You pick the spot."

Glancing sideways, she shrugs. "The bed."

"We just did."

"And it was good." Dear god, she's completely serious. "You know what they say about a good thing."

"Pick something else."

"I don't want to," she says, the imp.

Something occurs to me then, a niggling suspicion that I'm not sure what to do with. "Have you ever had sex anywhere besides in bed?" I hedge, slightly worried she'll slap me for the insinuation.

Instead, she pulls out of my arms and fiddles with the buttons on the shirt again. "I don't understand why you'd want to do it anywhere else when the most comfortable place is available."

"You haven't, have you?"

Her eyes flash as she looks up. "If you want me to climax again, it will have to be in bed. Missionary."

While I don't hate the thought—and my cock certainly doesn't, considering its already erect position—I'm determined to take her somewhere new. "We'll see about that."

She crosses her arms over her chest, practically swimming in my shirt. "I can't relax outside of a bed, okay? It's hard enough the way it is."

I reach for her and pull her close, needing to breathe in her goddamn scent again. "I told you not to worry about that."

She's stiff in my arms, and I rub my hand over her back. "I don't know how to not worry," she says quietly.

"Just trust me," I murmur into her hair. She feels and smells so good, I'm scrambling to find a way to keep her here forever. "If I say you're going to have two orgasms, you're going to have two."

She grows even more rigid. "I don't like being told what to do."

"I know." I chuckle. "But that wasn't a directive for you."

I can't see her face, and I'm dying to know what she's thinking. How has a woman this beautiful taken full responsibilities for her own orgasms up until now? I'd like to tear the head off every bastard she's been with before me, for more reasons than one.

If she thinks the only place she can relax enough to climax is in a bed, I have one mission tonight, and it's to prove her wrong. It might take some time, but that only means I'll get her longer, and I'm sure not going to object to that.

\* \* \*

I decide to take her on the floor. While it's not as soft as the bed, it's not too much of a stretch. She balks at first, but I kiss her into submission. I leave my shirt on her so the carpet doesn't give her rug burn.

She's not wrong about the relaxing thing, though. I can feel the tension emanating from her in waves. After several seconds of consideration, I plant a kiss on her lips and tell her I'll be right back. Then I jog to the closet and return with a tie.

She objects, of course, but I expected no less.

"To help you relax," I tell her. I tie it around her head, adjusting the knot so she's comfortable. After checking to make sure she can't see anything, I begin massaging her body. I feel her muscles start to slowly loosen as I knead the knots out.

After half an hour, she's finally limp on the floor, her pussy wet as I gently work my way over every inch of her. Her mouth opens on a gasp as I spread her legs and enter her quickly. She's so slick and tight, it takes everything in me not to spill my load immediately.

She moans, moving her head from side to side as I thrust into her again and again. Then I feel her tighten around me and know she's close. I reach down and press her clit with my thumb. She arches her back, allowing me to drive in deeper.

I continue rubbing her until her climax breaks, and it's somehow even more breathtaking than the first time. My own orgasm hits, but I barely notice it, entranced as I am by watching her fall apart. How has she managed to be a million times better than in my fantasies of this?

She stays on the floor for a few minutes afterward, recovering, but as soon as a tiny amount of energy returns, she's up and putting her clothes back on. I know what's coming, but I'm not prepared for it. I should be, but I'm not.

Within five minutes, she's out the door, thanking me for a good time. I half expect to find a Venmo payment waiting for me on my phone. Instead, I hear the ding of the elevator arriving and feel a strange pinch in my chest as I look around my empty flat.

This was our arrangement, so why the fuck do I suddenly feel like shit?

# 17

## "Dirty Little Secret" - The All American Rejects

*Maeve*

Today feels like the day that refuses to end. I've handled no less than four donor fiascos and spent an hour on a conference call I wasn't needed on at all, thanks to my lovely father dominating the entire conversation. Now I have to lead a HavenNet meeting with staff from both the Wilson Foundation and Luminara Tech that I'm completely unprepared for.

Part of it is due to my schedule, which is currently overflowing, but a larger part is due to a certain decision that was made last Friday night. A decision that will go down in the books as the worst one I've ever made and may single-handedly cause my destruction.

Who sleeps with their friends? Especially friends they can no longer tolerate being in the same room as? I think we're going to have to go with the plausible excuse that my brain grew legs, walked out of my head, and left me to fend for myself for the night. I cannot think of any other explanation for having sex with Pierce. Not once, but twice.

*God.* I will never forgive myself as long as I live.

By some miracle, I haven't seen Pierce since then. As soon as the aftereffects of my duo of orgasms wore off, I slunk away from his flat like some kind of high-priced call girl. Yes, I'm fully aware that I've hit rock bottom. We're blaming it on some kind of mental breakdown, remember?

I told the others I caught a virus to get out of flying to Tokyo with them for the weekend, which peeves me to no end, because it's been ages since I've had good *unagi no kabayaki*. My only consolation is that Pierce probably wondered the whole time if he'd catch whatever I came down with. But I'll probably never know if he was tormented or not, since I have no intention of talking to the man ever again if I can help it, challenge be damned.

Shifting the files in my arms, I round the corner to the elevator and stop short. Pierce is leaning over Mrs. Rodriguez's desk, laughing with my favorite receptionist. She is making moon eyes up at him.

I hate them both.

Three and a half days. That's how long it's been since I've seen him. In that time, I've used my vibrator no less than six times. Before you read into that, I'm ovulating right now, which always makes me hornier. Nothing to do with Pierce St. James.

His light gray suit and white shirt look as crisp as if he's just pulled them from that spacious closet. I don't need to be next to him to imagine their luxurious scent. His dark brown hair is styled impeccably as always—close shave on the sides, longer on top—and there's just a hint of stubble coating his jaw, which I can still vividly feel scraping across my skin. The thought makes my face heat.

As if he senses my blush, he turns to look over his shoulder, spotting me. I narrow my eyes, just in case he thinks I'm pleased to see him, and march to the lift.

"Don't you have a company to run?" I say as I walk past him. I don't know why he's always finding reasons to show up at the Wilson

Foundation. That sensation racing up my spine—irritation, okay? Nothing else.

"Several of them, actually." He catches up to me in one ridiculously long stride and enters the elevator before the doors can close.

"Then why are you here?" God help me if I get stuck in here with him again.

"For the meeting, what else?" His glibness is positively nauseating. Does he think I'm an idiot?

"How was Tokyo?" I say as the car descends.

Pierce shrugs. "Could've been better."

I turn with a look of faux concern. "Oh no! Don't tell me you got sick too."

"You're going to have to try harder than that."

Keeping my eyes on the lift doors, I refuse to give him the satisfaction of an answer. That, and I have no idea what he's talking about.

The elevator dings, and right before it opens, I hiss, "We're not having sex again."

He matches me stride for stride as I head to the large conference room on the ground floor. We've just rounded the corner when he smacks my ass. "We'll see about that," he says in my ear, squeezing before removing his hand.

I stop so fast, he doesn't even realize it right away and keeps going. "How dare you?" I say as quietly as my rage will let me. There may not be as many offices down here, but there are still plenty of people who move up and down these corridors.

He considers me with his hands in his pockets, not a single trace of remorse on his face. "I don't know what you're talking about. I'm just trying to get to my meeting on time." He glances at the Rolex on his wrist. "In fact, I should be going." Tossing a wink at me, he turns on his heel and walks away.

I'd report him to HR if I thought it would do any good. Well, that and if my panties weren't suddenly so damp I'm debating slipping into the restroom to remove them before the meeting. But he's right about the time, so I just follow him to the conference room.

Pierce is already seated as far as possible from my own seat, thank god. It isn't until I'm five minutes into the agenda that I realize sitting at opposite ends of the table puts us in each other's direct line of sight.

I start out by ignoring him, but my eyes keep straying despite my best efforts to look at anyone but him. At this rate, I'm going to cause severe strain. It appears he doesn't have a care in the world, reclining in his chair and clicking his pen on and off. It's absolutely infuriating.

The way his eyes flicker across my silk blouse tells me he's not listening to a single word being said. He's undoing each of my buttons in his mind and envisioning exactly what he would do once he'd divested me of my top. My traitorous nipples react as if he's brushed his thumbs across them, and that heated gaze doesn't feel much different.

I squirm in my seat, praying to anyone listening that nothing leaks through my skirt. God, I would die an early death if that were to happen.

We had sex. Big deal. It was once. Well, twice, if we're being technical. If he thinks it's happening again, he is about to be sorely disappointed.

This meeting has to be the longest in the history of mankind. I've never been so anxious to leave a room before. So anxious, in fact, that when I stand up from the table after we're done, I spill my entire file onto the floor.

Several staff members pause on their way out, and one of the newer hires turns back to help me. I think his name is Kenneth?

"I got it," I snap at him, not because I'm irritated at his assistance, but at myself for letting Pierce fuck with my head. My body was enough—does he need access to every part of me?

Kenneth? Keith? hurries from the room, and I finish sweeping the papers into a pile and shove them back into the folder. I'll reorganize them later. Right now, I would kill for a glass of ice water and some fresh air.

I'm almost to the door when I see Pierce. He's leaning against the wall, ankles crossed, watching me as usual. Am I doomed to spend the rest of my life in *Groundhog Day*?

When I'm within feet of escaping, he straightens and nudges the door shut with the toe of a leather loafer. "Not so fast."

I desperately want to run, but I can't. I'm frozen to the spot. He walks over to the large window facing the corridor and flicks the blinds close. My mouth goes bone dry as I watch him.

He turns back to me, then raps his knuckles on the conference table. "I've been envisioning laying you out across this thing for the better part of an hour. I'd really like to see that particular fantasy come to life."

My search for something to say comes up empty. What is it about this man that jumbles every thought in my head and turns every practical bone in my body to dust? We've been friends for years, and it wasn't until we started hating each other's guts that I saw him in anything but a platonic light. I don't want to consider what that says about my psyche.

The single step he takes toward me unleashes the words that have been trapped inside me. "As much as I hate being a disappointment, that fantasy will have to die a slow, painful death." I manage to keep a straight face as I say it, despite the fact that my insides are roiling like a sea during a storm, every nerve standing at full attention.

A tiny smile crosses his very nice mouth—well, mediocre mouth, really—and he comes even closer. "We both know how much you love disappointing me."

Regardless of the fact that he's right, this is one fight I have every intention of winning. "I told you that was a one-time thing." I edge toward the door as though he doesn't make my blood run hot.

"Mmm," he says, then winces. "And yet you seemed particularly tense during the meeting. Seems to me you could use a little stress relief."

I tighten my grip on the folder I'm holding. "Which is why I'm heading to the spa after this."

Pierce closes the distance between us, and once again, I'm unable to move. Reaching out a hand to cup my jaw, he leans in close. "Fuck the spa. I'm much more effective." His voice is to my eardrum what chocolate is to my tongue—smooth, rich, velvety.

At his touch, my eyes flutter closed and goosebumps travel down my spine. I drink in that intoxicating scent. He rubs his nose against the column of my neck, and I shiver. How am I supposed to resist him like this? Maybe once more would purge the desire from my body.

I reconsider his offer, and my eyes fly open. "I'm not having sex on a table," I say, pushing away from him before I can allow him to do whatever he wants to me.

He snags my wrist, stopping me in my tracks. "Why not?"

Turning, I gape at him. "Have you seen it?" I motion toward the huge slab of wood in the middle of the room. "It's hard."

"I'll show you hard." A quick tug plants me back in his arms.

I gasp and stage a resistance, but it's a weak one at best. "Someone might see."

"A great reason to hurry."

"I will never be comfortable on that thing."

"You're not exactly comfortable now, are you?" He shoots a pointed look below my waist. Rude. "Besides, I told you to let me handle the logistics."

"That night was nothing but a very bad decision."

His thumb strokes lazy circles on the inside of my wrist while my brain spins lazy circles in my skull. "Then why haven't I been able to stop thinking about it?"

"Because you have OCD."

He takes the file from my hands and places it on the table before I can object. "Just once more, Maeve."

"I—" My protest dies on my tongue as he once again nuzzles my neck. Is it possible that he knew exactly which scent notes would trigger my pheromones? "Have you always smelled this good?" I say instead.

He chuckles against my skin. "My teenage years were a little rough, but—"

I pinch his side, making him squirm, but he doesn't loosen his hold on me, nor remove his mouth from my collarbone. "Not what I meant."

"You like it?" he murmurs.

Like it? I fucking want to snort the man, and that's not saying anything about what I want him to do to my body. If he can make me feel the way he did a few nights ago, he could smell like a pig farmer for all I care. Actually, I take that back. My libido would shrivel up and blow away if he smelled like that.

"What's it called? Your cologne?" I ask. Getting a bottle for myself would be safer than being around Pierce for my fix.

He hoists me up and sets me on the table, then pushes between my legs. "It's a custom scent."

Of course it is. I want to snap at him for it, but I know that would only reveal the depths of my desire, and right now, those are the only cards I'm still clutching to my chest.

But as it turns out, he takes those away too the second he slides a hand under my black-and-white floral-print dress and finds me more than eager for him. As his fingers make contact with my damp panties, he lifts his head and meets my eyes.

"You want this more than you let on," he says, a smug look on his face that I badly want to smack off.

"That's sweat." Gross, but better than the truth.

"No it's not, Panther." He pushes two fingers inside me, exposing my lie.

I no longer care. My head falls back as I prop myself up on the table. His hand pumps in and out, and a tiny moan slips past my lips. He exerts the perfect amount of pressure, hitting all the right spots, but it's still not enough. I spread my thighs further apart, and he greedily pushes my dress up higher.

"I haven't been able to stop thinking about this," he says, grabbing a condom from his pocket while keeping his other hand busy with me. He holds out the wrapper, and I dutifully tear it with my teeth.

"Well, you're going to have to stop," I say, panting just a bit, "because this is the last time."

"That's what you said last time." Pierce winks as he rolls the condom on. "Now, lie back."

I carefully lower myself onto the table. I will never be able to climax like this, but maybe that will bring him down a peg or two. "Well, this time I mean it."

Pulling his hand out, he lifts my legs and tosses my ankles over his shoulders, zero regard for my knee-high Saint Laurent boots. God, it's like I'm nothing but a doll to him. "We'll see if you still say that after I'm done with you." Then he pushes my panties aside and thrusts into me hard and fast, sending a sharp burst of pleasure through my core.

I gasp as he fills me, spots dotting my vision for a few seconds.

He grasps my hips and uses them as leverage to push in and out of me. I'm flat on my back on the conference table, but I don't even feel it. The only thing I'm aware of is the sensation of Pierce seated deep inside me, rubbing against the walls of my vagina like he owns it.

"Nothing changes," I manage to get out, but it's like my brain doesn't remember what words are.

"Everything changed the second we kissed in that elevator, and you know it," he says, grunting as he picks up the pace.

I shake my head, giving up on verbal communication entirely. As crazy as it is, my core is clenching tightly, and I may have been wrong about not having an orgasm this time. When I say the man is good at this, I'm not kidding.

He reaches for my clit, applying pressure with those expert fingers, and I start to spiral.

"Pierce," I say around a moan.

He responds by thrusting even deeper. "That's it," he murmurs.

When my orgasm hits, I lock my ankles behind his head and cry out. I can feel him pulsing inside me as he releases, and somehow that only increases my pleasure.

Once we've both finished, he gently lowers my legs back down and helps me sit up. Now that my sexual needs have been satiated, I feel completely stupid. Mark this down as one of the dumbest things I've ever done, and don't let me ever repeat it.

"Do you want to do this?" Pierce says, zipping his pants back up.

I frown at him as I hop off the table. "Do what?"

"Hook up. In secret, of course."

"What a ridiculous question." I smooth down the skirt of my A-line dress, but it looks none the worse for wear, even after being crushed against a hard, wooden table.

"Think about it. Sex whenever we want, no strings, no one finds out. You can relax, and I don't need to go through the rigamarole of dates and gifts."

"That's what dating apps are for, idiot."

He sticks his hands in his pockets. "This is much easier. Besides, I already know you're a good fuck."

I want to point out that it's definitely *not* easier, but I trip over the last part of his sentence. "Excuse me?"

"Admit it. We're good together." Grabbing my waist, he pulls me toward him.

"I won't, because we're not," I say, tilting my nose up.

"Come on, let's try it. Any time you want. Text me and I'll come."

I bite my lip as I consider what he's proposing. The day after I went to his flat, I had a million regrets, of course, but I also had one of the best days I've had in a while. The tension didn't stay away for long, though, and by this morning, I was a bundle of nerves again.

Preston is often unavailable for weeks at a time, and even when he is around—he only gives me an orgasm about half the time. The other half, I get tired of waiting and end up faking it, or he comes too early and it kills the mood for both of us. I can't believe I'm saying this, and it pains me to admit it, but Pierce was right about one thing—I hadn't been properly fucked until he came along.

He tugs my lip from between my teeth, then leans forward to take my mouth with his. It starts out sweet and innocent, but the second his tongue swipes across my mouth, it turns greedy and hungry. I wrap my arms around his neck and pull him down further. His hands snake around my waist, trapping me in their wide grip and keeping me from moving.

A knock on the door startles us both, and we break apart just as it opens. One of the senior staff members sticks her head in and blinks in surprise when she sees us. "I'm so sorry." She starts to close it again.

"No," I say, and lunge for the door. "It's fine. Mr. St. James and I were just finishing up our debriefing on the meeting." Then I grab my folder from the table, shoot Pierce a "we're done here" look, and walk out.

I may have lost that round—and had sex on a conference table, of all places—but just because you lose a single battle doesn't mean you've lost the war.

# 18

## "Fire Up the Night" - New Medicine

*Pierce*

I can't tell what Maeve is thinking, because she's locked her thoughts behind that icy mask of hostility she wears to keep people at bay. I've rarely seen her lower it, but every time she does, it hits me like a punch to the gut.

The second someone knocks on the conference room door, I know I've lost her. She shoots me a lethal glare, as if it's my fault we were interrupted, and marches out of the room. I can still picture those tall black boots thrown over my shoulders long after she leaves.

Visions of taking her in a million different ways haunt me wherever I go. I can't enter a room without picturing the way she'd look splayed on the desk or pressed up against the wall. I hit the gym early after work, but even there I imagine fucking her in front of the floor-length mirror.

I don't hear from her for two whole days, which isn't exactly surprising, since I'm under no illusion that she's actually considering my suggestion. But that doesn't mean I'm happy about it. It's not even that I need sex so badly—it's the fact that she thinks she can just ignore me after everything.

She even blew off poker night, blaming the same virus she used to get out of the Tokyo trip. While that may have fooled the rest of the gang, she's not even trying to hide her true reasons for bailing from me, since she was alive and healthy that same afternoon.

But on the third day, after I've fully given up hope that she will ever call, she sends a text. *Are you free tonight?*

Instead of answering her question, I ask one of my own. *Where are you?*

I'm at work, but I turn everything over to my assistant and am taking the elevator to the car park within four minutes of getting Maeve's message.

Her response comes while I'm driving down Twenty-Fifth. *Just got home. Why?*

I'm already halfway to her house, that's why. She's as predictable as the sunrise, and I know her schedule almost as well as my own. Fridays she has lunch downtown with Lux, Walker, and Saylor, before doing a little shopping. She's home by early afternoon to freshen up for dinner at her parents'.

She frowns at me when she opens the door, then glances down at her phone like she's looking for something she missed.

"Hey," I say, pushing my way inside. Rather than allow her to waste precious time telling me to leave, I grab her and kiss her soundly, stopping all arguments before they can form. It only takes seconds for her to relax fully in my arms so I can press her up against the foyer wall.

We don't even make it to the bedroom, at least not the first time. I take her against the wall, and she climaxes like a champ. We get a little further into the house the next time—the living room sofa—and finally, the last time we strip down and do it on the bed.

After her fourth climax—I gave her two on the couch—Maeve lays her head on the pillow and falls asleep. I watch her for a few minutes, but sex makes me ravenous, so I slip out to the kitchen for some food.

While I'm rummaging through the drawers, I come across a small tray filled with keys. Each one is labeled with a name. *Todd, Wesley, Ethan.* There are around two dozen of them, and it takes me a second to realize what I'm looking at. Then it hits me.

These are the duplicate house keys she has made every time she dates a guy, in case she ever needs to break into his flat to do some damage. They've come in handy a few times when she's won the revenge pot during poker, but mother of god—the woman is positively diabolical.

I dump the entire collection of keys into the trash. She won't be needing them, and I don't fancy her having mementos of the stupid-ass blokes who dated her and let her go.

When she wakes up, we have another round in the shower before she rushes around her bedroom, lamenting how she's going to be late to dinner. I hint around about going with her, but she blows me off. Probably a good thing. I wouldn't want anyone—including her—getting ideas about us. Shit like that just makes you weak.

\* \* \*

I expected her to wait a week before calling again, so I'm completely unprepared for the message waiting for me when I check my phone during poker on Tuesday night.

*Bathroom?*

I can't help the way my eyes instantly lift and find her across the table. Things have gotten tight in here now that both Lux and Rhett started bringing their significant others, but there could be a hundred people in this room and I'd still know immediately where Maeve is.

She's in the middle of an argument with Rhett—seriously, those two fight like brother and sister—but she flicks her eyes in my direction as if she can feel my gaze on her. We're meant to be planning another revenge plot on Deirdre Cox, but as you can see, it's not going well.

I don't bother replying to her message, just stand and stretch my arms. "I'm going to fetch fresh drinks," I say, before walking out.

Maeve meets me in the restroom several minutes later, and I finally get the opportunity to set her ass on the vanity and fuck her with our friends in the other room. We're done before anyone gets suspicious, and she wipes a smudge of her lipstick from my neck without a word. I guess that's what we do now—fuck secretly and silently, then go back to our normal lives like nothing's happened.

The trend continues throughout the next two weeks. In addition to both our houses, we make use of a small closet at the Wilson Foundation headquarters, a hotel stairwell during a charity event, the back of a town car, and the bathroom at Heath and Walker's, until I start to lose track of all the places we've debased.

I've let her initiate everything up until this point, afraid she'll be scared off if I send the first text. But now it's been several days since I've seen her, and I'm starting to get antsy. I've gotten used to having sex every day, and going without for more than forty-eight hours is getting uncomfortable.

After pouring myself a glass of bourbon, I send her a text.

**Me:** *Tonight?*

I wait an agonizing ten minutes before she finally replies.

**Maeve**: *Can't tonight. Sorry.*

What the fuck?

**Me**: *What's going on?*

Is she sick? On her period? A thousand possibilities swirl through my head as I wait another eternity for her next message.

**Maeve**: *I'm busy.*

**Me**: *No, you're not. Tell me what's up.*

She sends me the middle finger emoji.

**Me**: *Fine. I'm coming over.*

Her response is instantaneous.

**Maeve**: *No!*

The best way to handle her is to sit back and let her make a mess of things, which is exactly what I intend to do.

**Maeve**: *Do NOT come over.*

**Maeve**: *Promise me.*

**Maeve**: *Pierce.*

**Maeve**: *PIERCE*

If she's really worried, she'll call me if I don't respond.

Except she doesn't. My phone stays quiet. The longer I wait, the tighter my jaw clenches. I know exactly what's going on. She has shown her hand by not calling.

**Me**: *You're with him, aren't you?*

She doesn't reply. I've been sitting on this damn sofa for thirty minutes waiting for her to give me the green light to come over, and this whole time she's been with him. Fucking Preston Ansley.

Yeah, I know I have no right to feel this way, but I'm going to tear that idiot's head from his shoulders anyway. Just watch me.

# 19

## "Getaway Car" - Taylor Swift

*Maeve*

This month's challenge is absolutely absurd. Pierce and I are supposed to fake being in a relationship at tonight's gala and convince at least three people we're in love. I'm positive this was Lux's brainchild. She's been trying to get Pierce and me together for years—as in, *dating*. Can you even fathom the audacity? Hopefully after tonight she'll realize what a preposterous idea that is.

He's picking me up because of said stupid challenge, and I answer the door and step outside when he rings the bell. His eyes widen—in surprise? appreciation? admiration?—as he takes in my outfit, but that's a fitting response considering what I'm wearing: a floor-length, one-sleeve black fitted gown with chandelier earrings that reach my shoulders.

He doesn't say anything for several beats.

"Are we still going?" I ask when the silence grows uncomfortable.

His look turns smoldering. "On second thought, I'd rather stay in." He reaches above my head to push the door open.

I give him a smug smile. "Too late." It's already locked, the alarm activated. He's not getting inside without my permission.

"There's always the car," he growls as he escorts me to the limousine waiting on the street.

True to his word, he has me pinned against the back seat within seconds. We're heading to the Bay River Yacht Club, which is less than ten minutes away—a blessing, since I have no idea how my dress will survive Pierce St. James's ravaging hands. I'm already regretting the updo my stylist spent an hour on.

Thank god for powder rooms.

Our friends are all waiting for us in the ballroom, and considering the giant grins plastered on their faces, I'd wager they're all in on Lux's little plot to throw Pierce and me together. God, if only they knew.

So not only do we need to convince three people here tonight that we're madly in love, but we also need to remind our friends that we hate each other's guts. Because the only thing worse than being in a benefits-only relationship with a man I can't stand would be having my friends find out about said relationship.

Pierce and I separate naturally during the cocktail hour, and it isn't until I look up to find his eyes on me that I remember we're meant to be putting on a humiliating show. His mouth twitches as he turns away, then lifts his hand to his neck as though he's scratching an itch. I know what he's actually doing, and I know that he knows that I know. That is way too much knowing for my liking.

In the car earlier, he clamped his fingers around my throat, much the way he's doing to his own right now. Under the influence of his intoxicating scent and experienced touch, I may have mentioned what a turn-on that is for me. And now the bastard finds this an appropriate time to remind me.

Just wait until I get my hands on that neck myself. He may not find it so humorous.

In the hopes it will keep my mind off Pierce and the heat that's been growing between my thighs since the minute he showed up at my door, I turn to listen to the group of women next to me discussing the queen and prince consort's choice of baby name. I'm on my second glass of champagne and considering a third—seriously, who cares what they name her?—when a hand slides across my lower back and a familiar scent envelops me.

Pierce leans close to whisper in my ear, "Ready for dinner?"

I'm well aware of what he's doing. The winner of tonight's challenge will be the one who looks the most convincing, as determined by our watching friends. He's doing a stellar job of playing his role so far, but he's not the only one who knows how to fake something they don't feel.

Leaning back against him, I say, "Whenever you are, darling."

He lets out a quiet snort. "Don't you dare call me that." His voice is nothing more than a low rumble, too quiet to be heard by the people around us, but just loud enough to make a thrill shoot through my body.

I turn in his arms and adjust his already perfect white bow tie. "Oh, but darling, I know how much you love it."

His grip tightens around my waist, a tiny promise of exactly what he could do to me if he so wished. "Let's go eat." He leads me to our seats, his hand never breaking contact with my body.

Our entire group sits down at the round table. After scooting my chair in, Pierce takes the one next to mine and clamps his right hand on my thigh. I glance down, wondering what the hell he's thinking, but he just gives it a small squeeze and continues his conversation with Heath.

My dress reaches the floor, so it's not as though he can access anything, and my legs are under the table, so it's not as though anyone can see anything. What is he playing at? I start to remove his fingers one by one, but he grabs my hand and tucks it under his.

He keeps it there until the first course is served, and I find I rather miss the weight of it once it's gone. Don't tell the prick, though. His ego is big enough as it is. Besides, he'd read into it, and he doesn't need anything else to hold over my head.

I push back my chair to go to the bathroom after the main course, remembering at the last second that I'm meant to be playing the doting girlfriend. Wrapping my arms around Pierce's neck from behind, I lean in and plant a kiss on his cheek. "Be a good boy while I'm gone."

Lux coos, and I shoot daggers at her with my eyes. I knew she was up to something.

I move to straighten, but Pierce takes hold of my hands and tugs me back down. "Take your panties off while you're in there and stow them in your purse," he murmurs into my ear. "Then we'll see how good I am."

My face is ablaze as I move to the restroom. I debate whether or not I should do as he said, but the thought of what he's planning to do later prompts me to follow through. The car ride was only a tease, and I'm already desperate to sneak away with him.

I've tucked my thong in my bag and am washing my hands when Florence Piccadilly joins me at the sinks. "I had no idea you and Pierce St. James were together!" she says, meeting my gaze in the mirror with her own animated one. "You are just the most gorgeous couple."

I give her a perfunctory smile and reach for the paper towels. "It happened suddenly, but we are crazy about each other," I say through my teeth.

"Oh, I can tell," she gushes. "Be sure to invite me to the wedding."

Score. She will not be receiving an invitation to any wedding of mine, and definitely not one with Pierce. But now that the first person has been convinced that I not only tolerate, but *love*, that pain in the ass, there are only two more fools to go.

I walk back to the table, my steps a little lighter. As I approach, I can see that they've already served dessert. A mini pavlova sits by my spot, dusted with confectioner's sugar and crowned with strawberries.

"I asked them to hold the whipped cream," Pierce says. When I don't respond, he places a hand just above my ass. "Is that okay?"

I nod, because my throat has grown thick. Maybe I shouldn't be surprised that he remembered that I'm sensitive to both gluten and lactose, but I'm stunned. I had no idea he's been paying attention all these years.

I scoot my chair out, but Pierce pulls me down onto his lap instead, then continues a friendly argument with Slate about the merits of solar energy, as though nothing out of the ordinary has happened. As though I'm not sitting on his lap in a room crowded with people we know.

One of his hands snakes up my back to where my dress dips down, revealing a healthy amount of skin, and starts moving in lazy circles. His other arm rests across my legs, his hand once again firmly attached to my thigh.

I'm beginning to suspect he didn't share well as a child.

I clear my throat and glance around the table. I'm met with varying shades of amused expressions. "I'm pleased to announce that Mrs. Piccadilly is convinced Pierce and I are getting married."

Lux grins and claps her hands.

Raising a brow, I say, "You do realize this is all for your little game, right?"

She nods but continues beaming, her face all lit up and glowing.

Fuck me now.

Pierce's hands are still busily moving over my body in a way that would appear casual to an onlooker, but that I know is anything but. The man doesn't do anything that isn't measured and calculated. I've been fucked by him often enough in the past month to know that much.

"Let's go," he whispers.

I pretend not to hear him and laugh at the story Rhett is telling. In truth, I have no idea what he's even saying, distracted as I am by the paths of Pierce's touch.

He tightens his grip on my leg. "Now."

"I haven't even finished my dessert yet," I say, pouting.

"Precisely the course I'd like to start on," he growls into my ear. "Now take a bite, and let's go."

I lean forward and stab my fork into the meringue, then quickly stick it into my mouth.

Pierce takes the utensil from my hand, tosses it onto the table, and shifts me off his lap. "Excuse us," he says to the rest of the table, maneuvering me past our chairs.

I reward him with an elbow to the side, but he just keeps walking, one arm firmly wrapped around my waist, leading me along with him. Apprehension and excitement both take root in my belly as we exit the ballroom.

"Where are we going?" I say once we pass into the main reception area of the yacht club.

He doesn't answer, just steers me down a corridor. We stop in front of a doorway, a little metal plaque hanging over it reading "Cloakroom." My heart rate kicks up a notch.

The attendant looks up from where he's scrolling on his phone. "Name?"

Pierce pulls a large bill from his wallet and hands it to the teen. "Give us twenty minutes?"

The kid's face goes from bored to interested in less than two seconds. "You got it." He can hardly scramble off his stool fast enough as he takes the money.

After he's gone, I move further into the room. "Twenty minutes? It's going to take you that long to finish?"

"On the contrary. I fully intend to give you three orgasms in here." Pierce shuts the door and flips the lock.

"That's 6.67 minutes per."

"I guess we'd better get started then." He closes the distance between us and slides a hand into my hair. "Did you take off your panties like I told you to?"

"Why don't you check for yourself?"

"Careful," he says, a warning in his eyes, "or I'll fuck that smart mouth of yours." He spins me around and presses me against the only wall not lined with coat racks. "Spread your legs."

I open them as wide as my dress will allow, and he takes his time raising the black fabric, slowly uncovering my bare legs inch by inch. "You'd better hurry if you want to be done before he comes back," I say.

Pierce stops, and I glance over my shoulder to find him staring at me, an unamused expression on his face. "On second thought"—he lets the gown drop back down—"I think we'll be needing those sooner rather than later." He rummages in my purse for a few seconds and returns with my discarded panties. "Open up," he commands.

I shake my head and give him an incredulous look. "No way in hell."

He presses the thong against my lips and whispers in my ear, "You don't want anyone to hear you screaming my name, do you? Now open up."

Hesitantly, I part my lips, and he shoves the thin fabric between them. It's not even enough to fill my mouth, let alone gag me, but a shiver runs down my spine all the same.

He continues shimmying up my dress, and I fight the urge to squeeze my thighs together. Without my underwear to soak up moisture, it's been slowly leaking down my legs. Pierce discovers this and lets out a quiet "fuck" while trailing a hand up my inner thigh. When he reaches my apex, he drags his fingers back and forth several times before shoving them inside me.

I press against the wall at the sudden movement, my cry muffled by the panties. I should have expected it—he loves to keep me on my toes—but my desire for him is so strong, all reason seems to fly out the window the moment I know he's about to fuck me hard.

"Are you on birth control?" he rasps as his hand works me over, pumping harder and faster.

I toss him an irritated look between heaving breaths. "Of course." It comes out garbled by the fabric in my mouth.

"Been tested recently?" He switches angles, driving even deeper, and I'm fully relying on the wall to keep me upright now.

I remove the thong and grunt out, "Like clockwork, but I never skip a condom."

"Well, you're about to."

"What are you—"

"Hands above your head."

He shoves the panties back between my lips, then jerks my hips back. After unzipping his pants, he presses his bare tip against my seam. "I want you walking around with my cum trailing down your legs."

An electric thrill races through me, and I pant as I try to maintain some semblance of control when he pushes into me. Using the wall as leverage to push back against him, I expand to take him in deep. He groans and drives in even further. With one hand, he pulls back on my hips, and with the other, he works until he finds my clit under the fabric of my dress.

With his cock inside me from behind and his fingers ministering to me in front, it doesn't take long at all for me to shatter. The underwear was a good call, because I definitely let out a scream as the orgasm tears through me and he continues his relentless pounding.

By the time his release comes, my second orgasm is hovering on the fringes. The feeling of his warm cum pulsing into me is all it takes to tip it over the edge, and we fall together.

Once we've recovered feeling in our limbs, Pierce takes it upon himself to deliver the third orgasm as promised. Between him pushing into me again and gravity doing its job, by the time I've climaxed a final time, liquid is trailing down both of my legs. Normally, I would insist on cleaning up in the restroom, but tonight I don't care.

The cloakroom attendant is nowhere to be seen when we step into the corridor, thank god, and Pierce leads me down the hall with a hand on the small of my back. I'm not sure if it's a conscious action on his part or if he's simply playing the part of gentleman. Either way, I like it more than I should.

I excuse myself to the powder room to freshen up—there's no way in hell I'm returning to the ballroom looking like a recent fuck—and to put a little distance between Pierce and me. The way my heart jolts every time he touches me is highly concerning, and the best thing to do is maintain distance whenever possible.

After fixing my hair and reapplying a fresh coat of lipstick, I return to the corridor and nearly run into Preston. He's wearing a black tuxedo with a white bow tie like most of the men here tonight.

I halt in surprise. "Hi," I say, quickly glancing around to see if it's safe to have a conversation.

He nods down the hall. "Can we talk?"

"Sure." We head away from the bathrooms and the potential of being spotted.

I saw him earlier with his wife, but we haven't had the chance to do more than exchange glances across the room. Dear god, I hope he isn't going to suggest we have sex in the cloakroom, too.

Once we're hidden from the view of anyone coming in and out of the restroom, I turn to face him. "Is this good?"

"Are you seeing him?" he says, ignoring my question. There are frown lines etched into his face, which looks older than I remember. He's only in his midthirties, and I've always found his maturity to be refreshing compared to the ridiculous dipshits I've dated in the past. But tonight, he just looks . . . old.

"Who?" I say.

"St. James." He presses the words out between his teeth.

"What? No. Of course not." I feel a twinge of guilt as Pierce's now dried cum on my legs taunts me.

"Don't lie to me, Maeve. I saw the two of you tonight."

Horror washes over me. Did he somehow see us sneak into the cloakroom? But then I remember the very precarious situation we're in ourselves. "That's rich coming from the guy who came with his *wife*."

Preston narrows his eyes. He hates when I bring her up. "It's not the same, and you know it."

"Do I?" I cross my arms. "You're accusing me of seeing other people, but you're going to take her home and have sex with her, aren't you?"

"We're not— We rarely do that," he says, a tiny hint of remorse flickering across his face. "Besides, this isn't about me and Janie. What is going on with you and Pierce?"

"Nothing." If he can deny what we both know is true, then so can I.

"You were sitting in his *lap*."

Ah, so that's what this is about. Relief courses through my body, and I force a laugh. "That was some ridiculous challenge our friends concocted. It's stupid and doesn't mean anything."

The lines on Preston's face grow deeper as he leans closer. "I saw the way he was looking at you."

I raise a skeptical brow. "And how was that?"

"Like you belonged to him or something."

"Yeah, because he's trying to win the game." Except now I'm curious about this look of Pierce's myself.

"You seemed pretty damn cozy," Preston says, anger lacing his words and face. For the first time during this conversation, I wonder if I'm playing with fire.

"It's not like that." I want to convince him he has nothing to worry about, but the words are eluding me.

"Then what is it like?"

How do I explain that when I'm not even sure myself?

# 20

## "Sick Little Games" - All Time Low

*Pierce*

Maeve's been gone a long time. A lot of women take an eternity in the restroom fixing their makeup, but she isn't most women. She prides herself on efficiency and still manages to look more stunning than all of them put together.

I excuse myself from my conversation with several members of Parliament and go to find her. Without reading too much into it, let's just say I feel better when I know where she's at.

The prime minister's wife is just exiting the women's bathroom when I approach, and I ask her if she's seen Maeve. She hasn't, so I continue my search down the corridor. The offices that line it are all dark, but as I near the end, I hear voices. A brief pause gives me enough time to determine that one of them is Maeve's.

I feel like a bloody idiot intruding on a private conversation when she's clearly fine, but I can't help taking a quick peek around the corner to see who she's talking to. The second I do, I wish I hadn't.

Fists clenched at my sides, I stalk back down the hallway. Here I am, concerned for her well-being, afraid she's hurt or needing something, and she's off having a rendezvous with her lover. Her *other* lover.

I can't believe she went from letting me fuck her against a wall—twice—to sneaking off with him. Maybe she's planning to use the cloakroom again.

What the fuck was she playing at earlier, then? Sitting in my lap, stroking my hair, practically purring in my ear—I mean, I know we were putting on a show, but at least some of that felt real. The way she tightened around my cock right before climaxing certainly did.

This whole thing is a nightmare.

Once I reach the ballroom, I scan the space for a suitable candidate. Blond, good rack, likes to have a good time but is willing to let the guy lead. Spotting a woman who looks like a decent fit, I stroll across the room and introduce myself—an unnecessary tactic, but one that always produces the right effect.

"I know who you are," she laughs, her eyes lingering on my mouth.

Ah yes, baby. This mouth will be all yours soon.

Several minutes later, her glass of champagne is empty, her number is stored in my phone, and she has directions to my flat. Tonight will be a good night—I can feel it.

Things are getting dangerous with Maeve. My completely irrational jealousy proved that much. When you give someone that kind of power over you, it makes you weak. And weakness is not something I can afford to have, not even for Maeve Wilson.

\* \* \*

The ride home is unusually tense, since I still need to give Maeve a lift. Normally, we'd fill the time making out with my hand up her dress, but I turned her down when she tried to straddle me after we climbed into the back seat. I claimed to have a headache, but she's still pissed. Anger rolls off her in giant waves meant to suck me under.

That's fine. She can be mad, because so am I. By sneaking around with him, she's implying he and I are playing the same game. Call me arrogant, but Preston Ansley and I are nowhere near being in the same league.

She's facing the window, arms crossed over her chest, still looking like a dream in that black dress I had the most fun peeling off her earlier. I wonder if my cum is still dried on her legs or if she felt guilty and washed it off in the restroom.

The car slows in front of her house, and she turns to me. "Are you coming inside?"

I glance up from my phone before immediately returning to my screen. "No. I have some things I need to do." Namely a certain blond with legs up to her chin waiting for me outside my flat. If Maeve wants to keep her fuckwit of a boy toy, fine. But she needs to understand that this works both ways.

She hesitates with her hand on the door.

I lift my eyes. "What?"

A frown creeps across her forehead, puckering those lines I know she pays thousands to erase. "What's going on with you?"

"Nothing. I told you, I have a head—"

"A headache, I know. But you've never turned down sex before," she says.

I shrug, as though it's perfectly normal. "First time for everything." Looking down again, I pray she leaves soon before I change my mind and haul her across the seat and into my lap where she belongs.

"What about tomorrow night?" she says, settling back down and opening her planner app. The entire thing is color coordinated and makes mine look like a clumsy schoolboy's.

Tossing my phone aside, I rest my arm on the seat back. While I have no intention of screwing her again tonight, I'm not opposed to spending extra time with her in the car. "I'm actually going to be out of town this weekend." It's a lie, but a necessary one. The flash of jealousy I felt tonight needs to die, and the best way to kill it is to spend time with someone—*anyone*—other than its source.

Her frown deepens. "Oh." She continues staring at her screen for a few more seconds, and I know she's doing her best to recover her composure. She doesn't like losing the upper hand, and it's throwing her off, especially after she lowered her guard with me earlier tonight. "When will you be back?"

"Late. Maybe not until Monday. I'll call you." I will call her, but I'll make her sweat first.

She grabs the handle and pushes the door open. "Have fun." Her tone is sarcastic, and I bite back a smile. I'd love nothing more than to follow her inside and make her regret talking to me that way, but that's exactly the problem.

The door slams shut, and as my driver pulls away from the curb, I try to muster up excitement for the gorgeous woman waiting for me at home. But unfortunately, my brain is still stuck on the raven-haired vixen I left on the sidewalk.

# 21

## "That's So True" - Gracie Abrams

*Maeve*

There are three things you should know about Loretta Donaldson. First, she went under the knife for the first time at fifteen. I'm all for plastic surgery, but god. Give your bones a chance to form first. Second, she can spend hours—and I do mean literal *hours*—talking about the merits of grass-fed beef. Her family is practically ag royalty, and she thinks that gives her some kind of bragging rights. And lastly, her eyebrows are overplucked. I think that speaks for itself.

It's Monday, and I'm currently stuck beside the cow princess at a luncheon. She is knee-deep in an exposition on the health benefits of red meat, either because she failed to notice the salmon nicoise salad in front of me or because she did and took it upon herself to set me on the straight and narrow. I tuned her out the moment I sat down, but she hasn't noticed. The woman does enjoy the sound of her own voice.

"You know," I say, when she pauses long enough to spear a piece of steak—grass fed, to be sure—"you're smarter than people say." Taking a bite of salad, I give her a syrupy smile.

She giggles and playfully rests her hand on my arm. "Oh, Maeve.

You're too sweet."

My eyes widen as I poke at my food. No one has ever accused me of being sweet before.

Leaning in close, she says in a mock whisper, "We should totally get together more often. I love your sense of humor!"

I raise my fork, but something stops me. An instinct, if you will. It takes a few seconds for my brain to recognize what my subconscious did right away. I hate to be wrong, so I tilt my head toward hers to get another whiff. "I'm just a bucket of laughs," I say as I inhale.

I was right.

There is only one bottle of that scent in the world, and it's in Pierce St. James's bathroom. And there are only two ways a woman would smell like that—if she'd sprayed it on herself or had his body pressed against hers long enough for the scent to seep into her pores. I ought to know.

I just spent the entire weekend with my vibrator, because now that Pierce has put me on to sex, it seems I can't go more than twelve hours without an orgasm or two. Preston did sneak over to see me once, but when we tried sex in the shower, he couldn't manage to get the position right, which kills libido in a heartbeat, trust me.

Meanwhile, Pierce was hooking up with Loretta Donaldson? Does the man have no taste whatsoever? Besides, wasn't he out of town?

"What did you do this weekend?" I ask my new BFF.

She laughs again, but there's a definite note of anxiety tingeing it. Interesting. "Just this and that. Nothing super exciting."

People like us don't just putter around our houses—we have staff. So there's no way in hell Loretta had no plans all weekend. I mean, god, even I had a ribbon cutting, a bridal shower, and grabbed brunch with Lux and Walker. If I wasn't already convinced Pierce was sleeping with her, that seals it.

"No traveling?" I ask.

She shakes her head demurely and pushes her steak around her plate. "Nope, just at home. What did you do?"

Loretta isn't the brightest star in the sky, so it's obvious she has no idea what I'm fishing for. I ignore her question and excuse myself to go to the restroom. There's no way I can process all of this while sitting next to my replacement.

Is that what she is? Has Pierce grown tired of me already? Was that why he told me he was going to be out of town all weekend?

Thankfully, the powder room is empty when I slip inside. I rest my palms on the vanity and take several deep breaths. Counting the tiles in the blue-and-green floor mosaic, I focus on what I know.

First, I know that Pierce lied to me Friday night, claiming he was going to be out of town and therefore wouldn't be free to hook up all weekend. Second, I know that, rather than traveling for work, he was here—in the city—fucking Loretta Donaldson. (And honestly, the more I think about it, the more I can see it. She's exactly his type: blond, leggy, brain the size of a pea.)

Third, I know that I was alone all weekend with my vibrator, which doesn't even come close to the real thing, at least not the real thing with Pierce. And lastly, I know that I am pissed. No wonder he turned me down after the gala. He'd probably already made plans with Loretta. What does she have to offer him that I don't, anyway?

I don't return to the table. I don't need to see Loretta's perfectly sculpted face or those perky tits under her dress. I don't need to imagine Pierce putting his hands on her or tilting her face back or pushing into—

God, make it stop. I bolt out of the restaurant and wait for the valet to pull my car around.

The drive back to the Wilson Foundation is a blur. I'm torn between wanting to rip Pierce's head from his shoulders and wanting to crush Loretta beneath the heel of my stilettos. A million things need my attention when I arrive at work, and they thankfully keep me distracted for the rest of the day.

I've finally managed to push all thoughts of Pierce out of my mind when my phone buzzes with a text notification. My heart goes cold when I read the message.

**Pierce**: *Plane just landed. Want me to come over?*

The fucking git. Does he actually think I'm that stupid?

I lay my phone back down on my desk. He may think he holds all the cards in this little situationship of ours, but that's where he's wrong. He should have known from the moment he first suggested hooking up who he was dealing with.

I give it six hours before I text him back, making sure it's late enough that he's likely already in bed. Let him wonder what I've been up to while he was gone. He's not the only one with tricks up his sleeve.

**Me**: *Sorry, just saw this. I can't.*

Remembering what happened the night Preston came over and Pierce threatened to show up, I send a follow-up before he gets any ideas.

**Me**: *I already found someone for tonight. Maybe tomorrow. xx*

It's a lie, of course. Preston would never come over so soon after a previous visit. My only fuck buddy tonight is my trusty vibrator, who should be happy about all of the action it's been receiving the past few days.

With any luck, that text will mess with Pierce's head the way he messed with mine. He forgot two can play this game, but I'll simply have to remind him.

Pierce I'm already working to bring down. His little side piece is next.

# 22

## "Better Than Revenge" - Taylor Swift

*Pierce*

Everyone is here except Maeve, and I can't help but remember a time not too long ago when she was always the first to arrive for poker and would help me carry drinks into the game room. Now, half the time it feels like we're strangers.

I was hoping for a few minutes alone with her when she gets here, but I'm still mixing cocktails when she knocks. Lux rushes to open the door, eager to get her infernal plan underway. Maeve doesn't even spare me a glance as the two of them walk in, and I'm left following her with my eyes like some lovesick teenager.

*Get it together, Pierce.*

I think about her spending the night with Ansley last night, and my gut churns. Leaning against the counter, I take a few seconds to breathe deeply so I don't end up hurling into the rubbish bin. She went hours before responding to my text, long enough that I checked my phone more times than is healthy for a guy in my position. Or anyone, for that matter.

Nausea builds as I think about him in her bed, doing things to her that I should have been doing, getting to witness her falling apart.

Does she say his name when she comes? Does he make her scream? Does she leave scratches on his back the way she does on mine? I wear those marks like a fucking badge of honor, but thinking about him having a matching set makes me see red.

At the poker table, I hand Maeve a charred-pineapple Mezcal smash, but she still won't meet my eyes, preferring to bicker with Rhett over his shirt, which is actually pretty ridiculous: black silk covered in giant bumblebees. She takes the drink from me without letting her fingers brush against mine, a nearly impossible feat with a coupe glass. I glance at her hands for evidence of her tryst last night—a broken nail, some chipped polish—but her manicure is as impeccable as always.

She's wearing a schoolgirl dress with a rounded collar that's meant to look cute, but all I can think about is taking it off her later. She doesn't look at me or say anything, treating me like a fucking server. Something is definitely up, and if she thinks I'm not getting to the bottom of it, she's wrong.

I sit down in the only empty seat—not next to her—and grab the stack of cards from the center of the table. I start shuffling them, mostly to keep my hands occupied. Otherwise they might do something stupid, like yank Maeve into my lap in front of everyone.

Lux clears her throat and claps her hands together. "Before we start playing, we need to announce the winner of this month's challenge."

Maeve looks over at her, and I swear I can feel her eyes wanting to turn to me as if drawn by a magnetic force field, but she resists. "Terrific," she says.

"The winner is . . ." Lux waits for a dramatic beat or a drumroll like a game show host. "Pierce!"

I shoot her a droll look, because how they came up with that one is beyond me.

Apparently, I'm not the only one who's skeptical. "Objection."

Maeve's face resembles a storm cloud.

"This isn't a courtroom, May-eve," Rhett says. The guy must have a death wish.

Her head snaps toward him, eyes blazing with fire. "I want an explanation. We did that challenge together. The only fair outcome is for it to be a tie."

"But that would have been pointless. There has to be a winner," Lux says.

Maeve still hasn't looked at me, and it's painfully obvious she's willing to go to great lengths to avoid doing so. "Then explain to me how he is the winner." She points in my direction but keeps her eyes on Lux.

As if prepared for this, Lux pulls her phone out and reads from her screen. "He fetched you drinks, he whispered in your ear, he kept a hand on your back, he watched you the whole night." She glances up. "Should I keep going?"

Maeve's face turns a new shade of red with each line item. "I sat in his *lap*," she hisses.

Lux nods. "We have that down, but we also noted that Pierce was the one who pulled you into his lap, and he looked more happy about it than you did."

As if she can no longer stop herself, Maeve finally turns her gaze to me, and god help me, I don't even care that she's glowering and looks like she wants to gouge out both my eyes. It feels like I've been underwater for far too long, and looking at her now is like breaking the surface and sucking in as much oxygen as I can handle.

She's gorgeous, her hair tucked behind her ears, her dark eyes sparkling with all the emotion she's holding back. Thin strands of diamonds dangle from her lobes and catch the light every time she moves her head.

I don't even care about fucking her right now—not that I'd pass on the opportunity, don't get me wrong—because I could stare at those eyes all night long. It's been four long days since we've been together, and god, I miss her. You have no idea how deep my regret runs over telling her I'd be out of town for the weekend. All I can think about is how many opportunities I missed because I had my head up my ass, not to mention practically driving her into that fucker's arms. I don't know how long this thing between us will last, but if there's even a chance it will be over sooner rather than later, I need to take advantage of every moment.

"If that's settled," Slate says, "for the next challenge, the two of you will plan a blind date for each other."

It's obvious that it's not settled in Maeve's mind, but this new information distracts her for the moment, and she looks away from me. "Can you repeat that?"

This time she's not alone in her irritation. "What does that prove?" I say. I'm not setting Maeve up on a date with some wanker. I'd rather cut off my middle finger.

Slate shoots us both a warning look, probably concerned we'll start flipping tables. He doesn't need to worry. We do our best sparring verbally and in bed. "The winner is the one who has the most fun on their date," he says.

Now I'm even more confused. "Shouldn't it be the person who arranges the best date?" I ask.

Rhett laughs and leans back in his chair. "Nah, mate. This will be way more entertaining."

The pieces click into place, and I see what they're doing. They know Maeve and me well enough to know we'll try to find the worst possible person for each other. The winner will be the one who not only does the best job feigning their enjoyment, but also sets up a date so bad the other person can't possibly fake their way through it.

It's actually kind of genius. I look up to see what Maeve thinks, and from the diabolical gleam in her eyes, I can tell she agrees with me. I don't even care that she's already plotting my demise in that brilliant brain of hers. I'm just happy she's finally looking at me again. How fucked up is that?

When neither Maeve nor I have any more objections, the game starts. We play poker and plot a revenge scheme most Tuesdays, but after all these years, sometimes it's more fun to sit around and talk. Maeve is still a stickler for tradition, however, so if she has her way, we take someone down every week.

The way she's shifting in her chair and tapping her cards against the table tells me she can't wait to submit her victim tonight. It must be a good one. I haven't seen her this agitated since Walker came home after being gone two years.

Betting moves around the group, and when it's Maeve's turn, she's nearly giddy with excitement as she pushes all of her chips into the center of the table. "Loretta Donaldson," she says.

My forehead creases into a frown. What the hell is she playing at?

Everyone waits for her to drop more info, but she just sits back in her chair, coy smile on that mouth I very much want to taste.

"We're going to need more than that," Lux says. "What's the story?"

"Let me guess," Rhett interjects. "She stole your parking spot." He gives Slate and Lux a knowing look.

"Wrong," Maeve sings. "But she did steal something from me."

I press a thumbnail to my lips as I study her. There is no way in hell this is a coincidence. She's back to ignoring me, which is all I need to confirm my suspicions, although how she figured it out remains a mystery.

Loretta is the woman I took home after the gala. She ended up being decent in bed, so she stayed all weekend, and we fucked our way around the flat, including on this game table. Best of all, she wiped thoughts of Maeve from my mind. Most of them, anyway. I'm still determined to take Maeve on this green baize at some point.

But now Maeve is submitting Loretta as her revenge victim. It has me reeling. We're obviously not exclusive—not with fucking Preston Ansley still hanging around—so is it possible she's . . . jealous? I want to laugh out loud at the thought. Maeve Wilson jealous over the woman I fucked all weekend? Now that is pure gold.

"What'd she steal?" I ask, sipping my drink.

Maeve's eyes snap up to mine, and if looks could kill, I'd be nothing but ash. "Nothing of significance."

"Then why the high stakes?"

A muscle in her jaw jumps, and I want to kiss it. "I just feel like teaching her a lesson." Her smile is so achingly fake, it hurts my teeth to look at it.

The game commences, but I'll be the first to admit it doesn't have my attention. In fact, there's little that does besides Maeve. I keep stealing glances at her, but she's studiously turning her eyes everywhere but in my direction. I'm ready to get up and demand she talk to me when she provides me with the perfect opportunity.

She pushes back her chair and excuses herself. After a minute, I corral the empty glasses and take them back to the kitchen for refills. The second I hear the restroom door open, I bolt into the hall and grab Maeve's arm just as she's coming out.

"Ow!" she says, and swats at me. "What are you doing?"

"We need to talk." I lead her to the kitchen, and you'd think we're headed to the gallows the way she's sulking.

She leans against the counter and crosses her arms. "So talk."

I face her, leaving about two feet of space between us. "Why Loretta?"

"I already told you," she snaps. "It's personal."

"Cut the bullshit, Maeve. We both know what this is about."

"Well if you know everything, then why are we out here?"

Narrowing my eyes, I tilt my head to the side. "I want to know why you're jealous."

"Me?" She points to herself and gives an incredulous laugh. "You think I'm *jealous*?"

I roll my eyes. "Yeah, I do. You submitted her in tonight's pot."

"Why would I be jealous of a blond with fake hair, fake boobs, and a fake nose? God, even her personality is fake." Her voice is climbing, and if we're not quiet, someone will come out here to see what's going on.

I lower mine to just above a whisper. "I know that you know she was here."

This seems to knock the wind out of her sails, but only for a second. A few quick blinks, and then she's recovered. "I don't keep track of who you sleep with. I don't have that much time."

"Cute," I say, scowling. "So why were you jealous?"

"I told you, I wasn't jealous," she hisses.

"And I told you, I don't believe you. What I don't understand is why you care what I do when you're sneaking off to flirt with *Preston*." I hate that guy's name in my mouth.

"What are you talking about?"

"I saw you during the gala."

"We weren't flirting. I was explaining to him about the stupid challenge," she says.

"Seems like an awful lot of words wasted on a dead relationship."

Realization dawns in her eyes, and she taps her chin. "So that's what this is all about. *You* were the jealous one."

I force a laugh. "What do I have to be jealous of? I just fucked a hot girl all weekend."

"And lied about it."

"I thought we needed a little distance."

"But instead of having a conversation, you thought turning me down and lying about it was the way to go?"

I cross my ankles and shrug. "It had the desired effect."

"Oh yeah?" Maeve edges closer, until the tips of her pumps bump against the toes of my shoes. "And how does it feel when the tables are turned, hmm?"

A flicker of unease crawls up my spine. "What's that supposed to mean?"

Her mouth curves into a smug smile. "Just that last night, I did the same thing. Turned you down and lied about it."

I frown at her for several beats before saying, "Why?"

"You were acting like an ass, so I decided to treat you like one."

Bending down until we are nose to nose, I say, "I am five seconds away from fucking you on this countertop."

"That's not going to happen."

"So stay tonight."

She shakes her head. "No."

"Why not?"

"You were the one who said we needed distance."

"And now we've had some."

Her dainty shoulders lift as though we're discussing something banal, like the weather. "No, I think you're right. Things were getting too . . . intense."

I watch her struggle to find the right word to describe us, and through the small crack in her veneer, I catch a glimpse of a side of her few people have ever seen. Maeve's armor is bulletproof steel, but inside, she is sensitive and riddled with fear that she'll come up lacking.

Reaching out to cup her jaw—my favorite place to rest my hand—I say, "Come here."

There's a brief moment when she hesitates, and I think she's about to lean into me, but just then, Rhett appears in the kitchen doorway.

I drop my hand, and Maeve takes a step back.

"There you two are," he says, tossing us both a weird look. "I was afraid I'd find a dead body out here."

"Maeve's helping me with the drinks," I tell him, and gesture to the counter where the empty glasses are still sitting.

If Rhett thinks there's anything going on between us, he doesn't voice it, just turns and heads back to the game room, leaving Maeve and me to make good on our word.

She carries two cocktails at a time, distributing them to our friends the way she used to. It's such a domestic task to do together, and I can't help but imagine what it would be like if this were actually our life. Hosting the people we love together. Brushing up against each other in the kitchen. Defiling every surface in the flat because we can't get enough.

When she returns for the last round of drinks, I place a hand on her wrist. "Stay," I say again. "Please."

She blinks up at me, those huge eyes framed by the most luxurious lashes, and I see the hesitation there, the question of whether I'll hurt her again, if this whole thing will blow up in her face, and if it's worth the risk for temporary physical pleasure.

I know she's going to say no again, and I find myself wishing that love didn't make you weak, that it somehow made you stronger, because if anybody were capable of strengthening me through their love, it would be the woman in front of me.

But unfortunately, that's not the case.

# 23

## "Bad" - The Cab

*Pierce*

It's taken me three days to find the time to get to the Wilson Foundation. I could've made up an excuse sooner, but my schedule has been swamped due to a breakdown of some of our tech, which created a PR shitstorm and a bunch of fires for me to put out. But I'm here now, which means I'll be seeing Maeve in a matter of seconds rather than days.

I can't even explain to you the adrenaline that starts pumping through my blood when I think about it. I haven't seen her since the poker game Tuesday night. She refused to stay afterward, and we've hardly spoken a word to each other since, let alone gotten together.

The lift stops on the fifth floor, and I head down the hall to her office. After rapping on her door with my knuckles, I open it and step inside. She's at her desk, wearing a black tweed dress with white trim around the square neckline and pockets.

Her frown is firmly in place, but a look of surprise crosses her face when she sees me. "What are you doing here?"

While I'd prefer a warmer welcome, at this point, I'll take anything she's dishing out. I hold up the file in my hand. "Dropping off some legal paperwork for HavenNet."

She reclines slightly in her chair. "Shockingly enough, they have something called email. Want me to tell you about it?"

I close the door behind me and approach her. "Not especially, but if it means you'll let me fuck you across your desk, I'm all ears."

She gives an annoyed shake of her head and turns back to her computer. "Not today, Pierce."

I toss the papers onto her desk and place my palms on its smooth wooden surface. "Then when? You've been ignoring me for days."

"Maybe you should call Loretta." She doesn't even look at me when she says it, just keeps her eyes firmly fixed on her screen. That's the first indication that something is wrong. Under normal circumstances, she'd never give up the opportunity to shoot daggers at me with those eyes.

Leaning closer, I say, "I'm not calling Loretta." Why would I want that woman if I can have Maeve instead? The thought is completely absurd.

"Well, don't call me either." Her voice sounds tired, lacking its usual spite.

Taking a minute, I study her. Now that I look more closely, I can see several things that escaped my notice initially. Her eyes are hanging heavy, not flashing with fire. She's moving more slowly than usual—with the speed of a normal person rather than a caffeine-fueled panther. She looks peaked, tired, and a little sad. Is she coming down with something?

I reach across the desk and place my hand on her forehead. She startles and shoots me a look, but I keep it there. No sign of fever. I frown, considering my options. She'll balk if I try to take her to the doctor, but I'm not opposed to using physical force if necessary. Getting her out the door will be a problem, though, because I won't disgrace her like that in front of her employees.

Perching on the edge of the desk, I wait for her to look at me. When she finally does, there's annoyance on her face, along with something else I can't identify. Apprehension, maybe?

"Go away," she says. "Some of us have work to do."

"What's wrong?" I ask, crossing my arms.

"There's an egotistical wanker sitting on my desk."

"Maeve."

"Is busy."

"*Maeve*." The edge in my voice gets her attention, and she turns her chair so she's facing me.

"What do you want, Pierce?"

"I want you to tell me what's wrong."

"Nothing's wrong. I'm fine. You're being weird."

"The sooner you tell me, the sooner I'll be gone."

She clicks her pen off and on rapidly. "Tempting. But calling security would be much faster and more entertaining."

I let out an abrupt laugh. "Those guys love me."

"Well, they get paid by me, so—"

"For the love of god, Maeve, just tell me what's going on."

"I told you—nothing!" She throws the pen, which goes flying across the desk and lands on the floor. "Now will you please go? I have a million things to finish up by the end of the day."

If she thinks I'll be that easily brushed off, she's about to find out differently. Something is causing her anxiety, and for once, I don't think it's me. I pluck her phone from the desk and unlock it.

She sits up abruptly. "How the hell do you know my passcode?"

I scroll until I find her calendar app. "Easy. Most efficient code to type in: 8-5-2-3." After clicking on today's date, I scan through her schedule, and that's when I see it.

*Dinner @ Kenswick House.*

Fuck. I didn't even think about the fact that it's Friday. I know she doesn't particularly enjoy spending time with her family, but is it bad enough to affect her this much?

"Is it the dinner tonight? Is that why you're stressed?" I ask, setting her phone back down.

"Mind your own business."

Like hell I will. Besides, she's my business now. "Why are you dreading it this much?"

She folds her hands on the desk and looks up at me. "This may be hard for you to understand, since you come from the perfect Wesbournian family, but my parents aren't easy to please. From the second I walk in the door to the second I can finally escape, they will barrage me with a litany of all of the ways I'm disappointing them. Their favorite at the moment? The fact that I'm single. Last time, my father asked if I'm a lesbian and planning to disgrace the family."

I shake my head. "That's fucked up, Maeve. I'm sorry."

She shrugs and grabs another pen, starts clicking the life out of it. "Welcome to the Wilson family, where 'fucked up' is served alongside the caviar."

I knew things weren't great at home for her—I mean, her dad, god, what a nightmare—but I had no idea they were this bad. "You aren't single, though. Not really," I say.

She gives me a look that says I should know better. "Are you referring to Preston?"

My fists clench at the sound of his name on her lips, and I force them to uncurl. "Sure. Or me."

She lets out a tiny snort. "You and I are not dating. And Preston and I— It's not like I can tell them about that, can I?"

"So take me."

Her brows pinch together, and the pen-clicking stops. "Take you where?"

"To dinner."

"Absolutely not."

"Why not?" I ask.

She smashes the pen onto the desk, and it's a miracle it doesn't break. "Because my mother would have our wedding planned before we left the house."

I shrug and give her a lopsided smile. "So? That doesn't mean we're engaged."

"Practically! My parents think you hung the moon. If I show up with you, they're going to think I'm finally living up to their expectations."

"Isn't that a good thing?"

"Not when the truth comes out." She rests her head in her hands.

It infuriates me that she's suffering this much anxiety over a meal with her parents. God, she should be looking forward to it, not on the verge of throwing up.

"I'm going," I say. "And I'll keep going until you're actually dating someone." Maybe not the wisest of decisions, because I don't know what I'm going to do if she actually wants to start seeing someone else—break his neck, probably—but for now, what choice do I have? It's not like I can leave her like this.

"No." She shakes her head, but it's less emphatic than before.

"It wasn't a question." I hop off the desk. "I'll pick you up at seven."

# 24

## "The Fate of Ophelia" - Taylor Swift

*Maeve*

I'm in the passenger seat of Pierce's car, and we're on the way to dinner with my parents. Before you can tell me what a terrible idea this is, I assure you, I am well aware. We're heading into a den of vipers, and the guy seems to be genuinely looking forward to it.

I glance sideways at him, not moving my head so he doesn't catch me staring. "You realize the stupidity of what we're about to do, right?"

He removes one hand from the wheel and places it on my thigh, giving it a gentle squeeze. "It'll be fine. We'll fake it like we did at the gala."

My eyes drop to his broad hand, which spans the entire width of my leg. "And look how well that turned out."

He navigates in and out of traffic with the deftness of someone completely at ease with power beneath his fingertips. "Well, you're sure as fuck not sleeping with Ansley tonight, so I'm not too worried."

"You were the one who slept with someone else that night, not me."

His grip tightens on the steering wheel, and I imagine what those fingers would feel like wrapped around my throat as he presses me against a wall.

"You're not going to let that go, are you?" he says, his voice quiet.

"Probably not," I say honestly.

I let the scent of his Aston Martin—of him—fill my nostrils, inhaling deeply only when I'm sure he's distracted by driving. I've ridden in this car plenty of times before, but somehow I missed how good it smells, how smoothly it rides, or how safe I feel with him. Safe, but also like I'm on the brink of danger—a controlled danger.

We arrive at Kenswick House much sooner than desired—sometime in the next century would have been preferable—and my mother greets us at the door. She's wearing a silk gown with a pastel watercolor pattern from an up-and-coming designer.

When she sees Pierce behind me on the stoop, she gasps and claps her hands together. "Pierce St. James! What a surprise."

He has positioned himself so that he can shake the hand she extends while keeping his left one firmly planted on the small of my back. "Mrs. Wilson, it's a pleasure. I hope you don't mind me joining you tonight."

"Absolutely not." She beams at him, then looks at me for the first time. "Although Maeve didn't mention she was seeing anyone." She ushers us into the house before I can set her straight, maybe because she knows it's too much to hope for and doesn't want to hear it. That's fine. I'll let her live with the fantasy a little longer.

While my mother fusses with getting the staff to set an extra place at the table, my father gives Pierce a hearty handshake and a slap on the back. "I don't know what she did to rope you in, but this is the best surprise I've received in a while." It's as if I've delivered a boyfriend to him on a silver platter.

I would pay a million dollars for the floor to open and swallow me up this second. When it doesn't, I catch the attention of a passing server and request a drink. I don't care what it is, as long as it's strong.

Pierce's laugh warms my belly. "No roping needed," he says. "I'm smitten." He reaches for me, and I turn to find his eyes on me, a softness there I don't often see.

Giving him a smile in return, I scoot back to his side, eager for his hands to be on me again. They feel like armor against whatever lies ahead. Obviously, I'm aware none of this is real, but it's nice to imagine having it, even if just for a few moments. Not with Pierce, of course, but someone who looks at me the way he does when he's pretending.

We move into the dining room, and when Pierce sees that they've placed him across the table from me, he asks if he can sit beside me instead. My mother blushes and flutters her hands at the staff, who scramble to do her bidding.

The meal begins, and my father and Pierce quickly descend into conversation. Pierce is smooth where I'm harsh, and my father will always prefer the diplomat to the fire wielder. My mother doesn't do a good job of concealing her delight at seeing the two of us together. She'll probably slip me a list of baby names before the night is over. It doesn't help that Pierce has his hand on my thigh again, splaying his fingers so they cover as much skin as possible.

It's absolutely mortifying, their eagerness to see the two of us together. If they were genuinely interested in my happiness, fine, but we all know that has little to no bearing on their opinion of our supposed match. They're thinking about how the alliance between our two families will benefit them.

While the servers clear our plates for the next course, Pierce gives my leg a reassuring squeeze, sending tingles of pleasure directly to my core. When I look over at him, he gives me a wink, as if reminding me that we've made it through one course already.

My mother keeps glancing at us with tiny smiles, and if my father's grin stretches any wider, his face will split in two. By the time the fish is served, I can't take it anymore.

"Pierce and I aren't dating," I announce, interrupting my father in the middle of his spiel about oil prices. I interlace my fingers with Pierce's, hoping he knows how much I appreciate his willingness to help me out, but I can't do this. I prefer their disappointment.

There's a sadistic pleasure in watching their faces fall, in letting them down once again. At least this time, it's a controlled explosion, one I'm in complete charge of.

Pierce slides his hand from my leg, and for a second, I'm terrified he's going to leave me here with them. But then he drapes it across the back of my chair and says, "We're getting there, though, aren't we, babe?"

I swivel to look at him, but he picks up his wine and takes a sip, oblivious to my confusion or simply choosing to ignore it. What is he playing at?

"They stopped drilling off the southern coast," he says, which captures my father's attention again, and soon they're back in the throes of money talk.

It bothers me that I don't know what he's up to, and I can't exactly ask him. His thumb strokes my bare shoulder, sending shivers down my spine. I finish the food on my plate and lean back. He moves his hand to my neck and rubs the muscles there, and I have to fight to keep from moaning and closing my eyes.

While continuing his conversation with my father—neither my mother nor I attempt to join in—Pierce reaches for the hand resting in my lap. He places it on his own leg and plays with my fingers, his other hand still massaging the tight knots in my neck. It's the kind of touch you expect from someone you're dating—not that I have much experience, because I prefer not to be touched—and I know he's doing it for my parents' sake, but what I can't figure out is why. Why is he trying to convince them we're together?

"How's HavenNet coming along?" my father asks as dessert is placed before us.

I've been dreading this question, but I suppose it's better than being interrogated about my love life, or the lack thereof. It's directed at Pierce, since my dad doesn't speak to women when men are available, but I discover a new reservoir of courage and decide to take the bait. "Good. We're looking at a fall launch, although a hard date hasn't been set yet."

Annoyance crosses my father's face, but I ignore him and tuck into the pastry before me. At least I know my mum always plans her menu with my food sensitivities in mind.

"Why not this spring?" he says, once again addressing Pierce. "We can't wait until fall. Think of all the good it could do before then."

What he means is "think of how many donors might drop out with a delayed launch."

Pierce still has an arm over the back of my chair, using his right hand to spear a bite of his mille-feuille. "By waiting until fall, we're able to rebrand and create an even stronger launch plan than we were initially going to implement."

My dad grunts, then shovels half of his dessert into his mouth. "I thought the plan was to skip a rebrand." His eyes flick to me, one of the first looks he's sent my way all evening, as if he's insinuating I've somehow managed to bring this entire thing down around us.

Pierce's hand comes to rest on my shoulder, gently caressing it and stroking the wisps of hair at my neck with his thumb. "At first I thought that was the way to go, but Maeve's plan is quite brilliant. She only had to show me a few of the things she had in mind for me to be completely on board."

That isn't entirely true. We spent hours going over the plans, him cutting nearly half of them before finally agreeing to a rebrand before we officially launch. But tonight I don't care about the details. He's helping me save face in front of my parents, and that is worth a few white lies.

I'm still not sure *why* he's doing it, though. If he's trying to make a good impression, he could have done that by joining in as they regaled me with a list of all the ways they think I'm screwing up my life.

Pushing my plate back, I recline in my chair, ready for this night to be over.

Pierce leans over and whispers in my ear, "You done?"

I don't know if he means with my dessert or with the night, but I nod in answer to both.

He slides my plate closer to him and breaks off a bite with his fork. My father continues questioning him about his family's companies—why, I don't know, but it's embarrassing—and Pierce takes it all in stride. He finishes the rest of my pastry in three bites, then settles back and continues his neck massage from earlier.

My father motions for the whiskey to be brought, taking great delight when Pierce approves his selection. "Karuizawa 'The Dragon,' aged fifty-two years," he says, puffing his chest out as Pierce takes another sip.

"I love the smoky finish," Pierce says, pretending to be impressed, even though I've seen the same bottle on his own shelf at home. He holds out his glass to me. "Want to try it?"

I take the tumbler from his hand and let a sip of the liquid hit my tongue.

"Maeve's not a whiskey drinker," my dad says with a laugh.

Pierce ignores him, eyes on me as I swallow. "What do you think?" he asks.

"It's good." I nod. "I'll stick to cocktails, though."

He gives me a soft smile and takes the glass back. Returning his hand to my thigh, he plays with the hem of my dress while my father drones on. His fingers slip beneath the fabric, taunting and teasing me with a preview of what's to come after we leave here.

I suddenly want to go even more than I did before.

I'm still confused about Pierce's intentions, but for the first time, I wonder if maybe he was just trying to make tonight bearable for me. Maybe he just wanted me to have a reprieve after everything. It doesn't fit with our vibe of fucking each other while we fuck each other over, but maybe he decided to step out of character. I don't hate it, even if I don't know what to do with it.

The next thirty minutes pass agonizingly slowly, and when Pierce asks softly, "Are you ready to go?"

I nearly bolt out of my seat. Instead, I nod demurely the way I've been trained. "Whenever you are."

He scoots my chair back, then tucks my hand in his while thanking my parents for a wonderful evening. (That one's a stretch.) As they walk us to the door, my mother stops me with a hand on my arm. Pierce doesn't disentangle our fingers.

"I was just thinking," she says, "we should do lunch some time. Maybe do some shopping?"

I give her a skeptical look. My mother and I don't do lunch. We don't "do" anything together. This has nothing to do with wanting to spend time with me and everything to do with her imagining she's about to be planning the wedding of the year.

"Sure," I say. "I'll check my schedule." I won't, because the only thing worse than sitting through this dinner would be planning a wedding with my mother. A wedding to a man who is faking everything about tonight.

Pierce helps me into my coat, and when we finally step out into the cold air, I draw in several large lungfuls.

"That wasn't so bad, was it?" he asks, wrapping an arm around my neck to tug me in close and kissing the top of my head. My parents must still be watching from the front stoop.

"You're right. I could have been served as the suckling pig instead."

He grins as he opens my door, stepping back so I can slide into his sleek Aston Martin. The luxurious scent of it hits me anew, and I recline into the buttery-soft seat with a sigh. Back to safety.

Pierce gets in and pulls the car onto the street, the silence between us almost blissful in contrast to what we just walked out of. As we drive, I find myself lulled into a sense of security I've never experienced before. While dinner was awful, it really was a thousand times better with Pierce there. He was like a lifesaver in the ocean—literally the only thing keeping me from drowning.

"Thank you," I say. "For being there tonight."

He glances over at me, then reaches for my hand and squeezes it. "It was my pleasure."

I stare at our entwined fingers, wondering what all of this means, if there's more going on here than I realized. "Why did you go to such lengths?"

If he has feelings for me that are more than physical, I don't know what I'll do with that information. I do know that, after tonight, I don't hate the thought. In fact, I might actually like it.

He's quiet for so long, I think he isn't going to answer me. When he finally does, I wish he hadn't.

"I figured it was the best way to get you into bed tonight."

## 25

## "Maneater" - Nelly Furtado

*Maeve*

It's taken me a full week to orchestrate tonight's blind date, because after the stunt Pierce pulled at dinner with my parents, I had to completely scrap my original plan and start over. Forget a date with the American heiress with a Southern drawl who'd be sure to get under his skin. No, tonight will require pulling out all the stops.

I momentarily considered hiring a hitwoman to take him out during the meal, but I'm afraid it would be too easy to trace back to me. Besides, it's much more fun to play with your food than to eat it.

Both dates are to take place at The Glasshouse, a rooftop restaurant with floor-to-ceiling windows and panoramic views of the city skyline. I honestly can't think of a better way to spend my Saturday night than watching Pierce St. James squirm through an entire meal.

As obsessed as I was with orchestrating all the details of his evening, I managed to forget about the fact that he has also planned a date for me. Now that I see the man waiting at the host stand, my stomach churns with dread. He's average-looking, if you like faces that are instantly forgettable and impossible to pick out from a crowd. A bit stocky for my tastes, but I'm determined to find something redeemable about this guy before the night is over. After all, the person who has the most fun wins, and tonight's victory will be mine.

"Hello," I say, pasting a giant smile onto my face as I approach. "I'm Maeve."

The man shakes my outstretched hand, lingering too long on the release, and my queasiness level rises. "Austin." His grin reveals even, white teeth, so at least there's that.

We're ushered to our table, and I walk too fast for him to put a hand on my back. He looks like the type who would try, regardless of the fact that we just met.

I spot Heath and Walker as soon as we walk into the dining room. Walker gives me a small wave and an apologetic smile. Rhett and Saylor are sitting at the bar, where they have a view of the whole room. Saylor nudges him when Austin and I walk past, and I shoot them both annoyed looks. Lux and Slate's table is on the far side of the room. Lux grins widely, and I subtly flip her the bird. Slate simply glowers, but that's nothing new.

I don't see Pierce and his date anywhere, which means I'll get to watch them walk in together. Resisting the urge to clap my hands in delight, I take the chair the host has pulled out for me. Our table is set with a bud vase of orchids, sparkling glassware, and polished cutlery.

The sommelier comes to take our wine order. I happen to know that this place carries an exceptional 1945 vintage that isn't listed on the menu, but before I can request a glass, Austin makes a big show of tossing the drink menu onto the table.

"Hey, mate," he says to the server, whose brows flicker ever so slightly. "I'm looking for your most expensive bottle." He inclines his head as though sharing a secret. "I have a date to impress." Then he tosses a wink in my direction.

"MANEATER" - NELLY FURTADO

I can feel my lip curling in disgust, and it's then that I catch a glimpse of Pierce and his date walking into the room. Slapping a sugary smile on my face, I fold my hands together, elbows on the table, and gaze at Austin like he's the universe's blessing to women—a sentiment he evidently shares—and order the nausea to stay put.

"Tell me about yourself, Austin," I say after the sommelier leaves, my voice pitched extra high. My guess is he likes women who squeak.

As he begins regaling me with details of his life I would rather scratch my eyes out than listen to, I distract myself by watching Pierce and the woman I chose for him settle in at their table. He's in a light gray suit with a dark blue shirt and no tie, a maddeningly striking combination. Damn him for choosing something that looks good.

I don't miss the fact that he's taken the chair that gives him a view of our table. Apparently, he fully plans to enjoy tonight's shenanigans as well. His eyes snag on mine, and my heart snags in my chest. There's a challenge in those dark shadows. The thought of it makes me shiver.

Turning my focus to his date, I do a quick appraisal of her appearance. She has dressed exactly the way I hoped she would when I scouted her online. She's wearing some kind of gauzy kimono thing that definitely should be against the restaurant's dress code, a pair of gladiator sandals—disgusting—and gigantic hoop earrings strung with colorful beads. Her long blond hair hangs loose and reaches the seat of her chair.

I hide a smile behind my hand as I return my gaze to Austin.

"Do you own cryptocurrency?" he says, tearing off a hunk of the bread on the table and shoving it into his mouth.

Taking a deep breath, I let it out slowly through my nose. "No, I don't."

"Mm, you should." He gestures with his bread. "Crypto is the future."

I force a smile and take a sip of my wine. It's not terrible, but not nearly as good as the one I wanted. "I'm happy with my own investments, but thanks for the advice." Remembering that all of my friends are watching, I do my best to give him a genuine smile. "I'd love to hear more about it, though."

That ought to keep him busy for the next ten minutes. All I'm required to do is smile and nod occasionally, which allows me plenty of time to watch what's unfolding at the next table.

Pierce must look like he's enjoying himself to the casual observer—one arm resting on the table, body slightly inclined toward his date, head tilted as though he's engaged in whatever she's saying. But the signs of his misery are there if you know where to look. The hand that isn't on the table is on his leg, fingertips white from clutching it so tightly. The smile on his face is as fake as his date's name—Celestia. His right foot is twitching so hard I have to fight the urge to laugh out loud.

As I'm watching, Pierce's eyes suddenly flick over to meet mine. They narrow ever so slightly, and his smile slips. I feel his gaze in my core, and butterflies start flapping their wings in my belly.

Yanking my eyes away, I try to recall something Austin just said. "A broker?"

"Oh, yeah. Are you familiar with what they do?"

I frown in confusion. "Am I familiar with what a broker does?"

"They help clients navigate complex processes—"

"Austin." I reach across the table and tap his hand. "I know what a broker is."

"There are a lot of people who aren't familiar with the world of crypto, and brokers really help them feel at ease," he says, as if I haven't spoken.

I grit my teeth and shoot Pierce another glare, but he isn't looking.

"MANEATER" - NELLY FURTADO

When our server comes to take our orders, I make sure to get mine in before Austin can assume he knows the first thing about what I want. "I have another small request," I say, motioning for the waiter to lean down. "Can you keep that table over there"—I gesture subtly in the direction of Pierce and his date—"supplied with wine all night? It's a special occasion for them, and I want them to have a good time. You can put it on my tab, but let's keep it between us."

The server nods. "Of course, Ms. Wilson."

I extend my drink to Austin. "Cheers." We clink glasses, and I allow my smile to bloom fully the way it wants to. Pierce won't get tipsy—he's always in control of his drinking, and I've never once seen him drunk—but I have it on good authority that his date will get raucous after three glasses.

"Those friends of yours?" Austin asks, but doesn't even wait for me to answer before relaunching into what I'm discovering is his favorite topic—himself.

Holding back a massive eye roll, I watch as the server stops by Pierce's table to refill Celestia's wine glass. Pierce has his phone in his lap, eyes cast down, obviously texting. Rude. I sure hope the others are taking note of the way he's ignoring his date.

Seconds later, my bag vibrates against my leg at the same time he glances up and meets my eyes. I wait until he looks away before reaching for my own phone.

**Pierce**: *How much cryptocurrency have you bought tonight?*

The bastard. I type out a response as quickly as I can to avoid detection.

**Me**: *It actually sounds like a good investment. Thanks for setting us up!*

I stick my phone under my leg, hoping no one noticed the five seconds it took me to reply. Austin certainly didn't. He's still blathering on about his family's money. Doesn't he realize that the first sign of new money is the need to talk about it? God.

Tossing my hair over my shoulder, I drain the contents of my goblet and reach for the bottle.

Austin senses what I'm after and grabs it from my hand. "I'm actually really good at this," he says. "My friends call me a sommelier." He lets out a faux-self-deprecating laugh.

My eyes widen as he refills my glass, then gives an exaggerated twist to the bottle, somehow still managing to dribble liquid down the side. I blink at my wine, which is much fuller than it should be for breathing purposes, before finally picking it up and taking a large gulp. Tonight's drinking will be done in service of intoxication—aka survival—not enjoyment.

Pierce and his date are chatting—or rather, she's talking and he looks like he's on the verge of thrusting his steak knife into his own heart. Maybe it's time to liven things up for them.

I excuse myself from the table and approach the host stand. "Hi," I say, smiling sweetly. "I was wondering if I can place a special request for the band on behalf of a friend."

# 26

## "A Love Like War" - All Time Low ft. Vic Fuentes

*Pierce*

Why the fuck does that glass have to be so thick? There are nearly six inches of it separating us from the outside. If those were normal windows, I could easily break one with my fist and escape this hell. Plummeting from twenty-one stories would definitely do the trick.

But since the only way I'm getting through this night is either by enduring the rest of my date or throwing in the towel, I return my gaze to the woman sitting across from me and pick up my wine. At least there's alcohol.

She's currently in the middle of explaining to me the power of manifestations. She has already shared no less than five different examples to prove her theories, all of which were taken from one form of social media or another.

"Let's take a selfie," she coos, reaching for me.

I grit my teeth and plaster a smile on my face as I incline my head toward hers. We've already taken three, because—and I quote—"her followers expect updates from her every fifteen minutes."

When the server brings our entrees, Celestia won't let me take a bite until she's snapped at least two dozen photos of my beef Wellington. By the time I'm finally allowed to cut into it, my tenderloin is room temperature.

"I've talked so much about me," she says, finishing her third glass of wine. The server keeps refilling it every time he walks by. "I want to hear all about your life."

I flick a look at Maeve, who is sitting several tables over with her finance bro. Biting back a smile at the look of irritation she's struggling to hide, I turn back to my own date, chosen no doubt for her absolute charm.

"There's not much to tell." I spear another bite of cold tenderloin. "I mostly work."

It's the wrong thing to say. Celestia's jaw goes slack, and her eyes look like they might pop out of her head and roll across the table. "That's so unbalanced and unhealthy. It isn't good for your soul to be consumed by your work."

I give her a placating smile while cutting my food with more force than strictly necessary. "My soul is practically a wasteland these days."

"Oh em gee." She grabs her bag from the floor—some macrame thing that looks more like a reusable shopping tote than a purse—and pulls out a set of index cards. "We need to write some affirmations for you."

Pausing with my fork halfway to my mouth, I blink at her. "Some what?"

She doesn't bother looking up, just starts pushing dishes and cutlery to the center of the table to make room for her paraphernalia. "You're going to look into the mirror and recite these every morning when you get up and every night before you go to bed."

Like hell I am.

She starts scribbling some shit on the cards, and I look over at

Maeve. If she smashes her lips together any harder, I'm afraid they might actually burst. Even from over here, I can tell that she's a bundle of nerves. Hopefully, she'll be wound so tightly that she'll let me help her relax tonight.

She turned me down after dinner at her parents', but I deserved that one. I have no clue what prompted me to say what I did. All I know is that she was fucking with my head during the meal—or maybe I was fucking with my own head—and I had to do something. Pushing her away seemed like the only option.

In hindsight, I realize that waiting until after we had sex would have been better for both of us. We haven't slept together since the cloakroom at the gala, and that was over two weeks ago. Other than my weekend with Loretta, I haven't touched anyone else, and it's driving me mad.

Maeve's silky dark green dress drapes over her body, and I imagine taking it off later. Her creamy skin will be luminescent, as always. I can already feel its softness beneath my fingertips.

As though she can sense my eyes on her, Maeve looks over and meets my gaze. Electricity shoots through my core. God, what I wouldn't give to march over there and take her in my arms. Fuck this stupid challenge, fuck keeping our hookups a secret.

"Yoohoo!" My trance is broken by my date waving her hand in front of my face. "Where'd you go?" she asks, her expression animated.

I take a deep breath. "Sorry, just spaced out for a second."

"You looked like you traveled to another realm." Her voice is rife with anticipation.

"Nope. Definitely earthside."

She shakes it off with a jingle of the bangles lining both her arms. "I have your affirmations ready. Want me to read them off for you?"

*I'd rather cut my own throat.*

Fortunately, our server appears before I can voice my thoughts out loud. "Will we be ordering dessert tonight?" he asks, hands crossed in front of his white apron.

I get one of everything from the menu, hoping it will keep Celestia quiet for a while. "Can I also place a special request for the table in the center?"

He leaves with our order, but before my date can continue harassing me about my work-life balance, one of the members of the jazz band on stage steps up to the mic. "This next selection is for the woman in the floral kimono, chosen by the man who hopes he is the love of her life."

Celestia's hands fly to her mouth as she gasps and turns her excited gaze back to me.

I force myself to smile back, vowing to end Maeve later for this.

The band starts up a sultry tune, singing some nonsense about us being written in the stars. Meanwhile, Celestia's eyes fill with tears, and she stares at me through the entire song. I've never been more uncomfortable than I am at this moment, including the time I stood five feet away from a hungry lion on a safari.

As soon as the song ends, Celestia pulls her phone from her bag. I think she's about to force me into another selfie—or worse, a video sharing our "love" with the world—but instead she asks for my birth date. I give it to her, just happy not to be taking another fucking photo, but I realize my mistake as soon as she flips her phone around.

"Oh my god, I just looked up our star charts, and you won't believe this."

Fuck me now. I pull my own phone out and shoot another text to Maeve.

**Me**: *You're dead.*

Celestia continues gushing about how perfectly matched our star charts are—whatever the fuck that means—but I'm focused on Maeve, wanting to see the exact moment she reads my message. It takes less than thirty seconds.

Her eyes flick toward mine as she pulls her phone out, then a small smile tugs at her lips as she looks at the screen. She types something back before returning her full attention to her date.

**Maeve**: *Actually, I'm feeling more alive than ever. Thanks again for a terrific setup! This guy is a keeper. xx*

I frown as apprehension crawls through me. She's joking, right? I know for a fact that he must be annoying the shit out of her. But that doesn't eliminate the trickle of unease I feel as I stare at the two of them.

The server walks into my line of sight and places a bowl of gelato in the center of their table, complete with two spoons. I wipe the corners of my mouth to keep my smile in check. Maeve suddenly looks less happy than she did a few seconds ago.

Celestia is still discussing our star charts, not taking any cues from the fact that I'm not paying the least bit of attention to her ramblings. It's a shit thing for me to do, but I can't keep my eyes off Maeve. I'm desperate to see her facade crack, and I'm certain the dessert will be the thing to push her over the edge.

Her date picks up one of the spoons and swirls it through the creamy gelato. He inhales several bites within the span of a few seconds. When Maeve doesn't join him, he says something to her, and she shakes her head. Her eyes meet mine for the briefest of seconds.

"Let me see your palm," Celestia says, grabbing my hand and flipping it over.

I steel myself against her too-hot touch as she fiddles with it, tracing her fingertips over the lines.

"Ooh," she croons. "There's so much depth here."

From the corner of my eye, I see Maeve stand and excuse herself from the table, presumably for the restroom. I wait a little longer before wresting free from Celestia's grip as gently as possible.

"I need to use the bathroom. I'll be right back." I'm out of my chair before she can blow a kiss or anything equally obnoxious.

The hall outside the restrooms is dark, and I lean against the wall as I wait for Maeve to emerge. A few minutes later, she steps out and startles when she sees me.

"I cannot believe you," she snaps. "*Gelato?*"

I smirk down at her. "I've heard it's the best in the city. I was just trying to help you have more fun."

She moves closer and thrusts a finger against my chest. I'm so overjoyed to have her touching me, I don't give a shit that she's mad. "He wouldn't stop pestering me to try it."

As I knew he would. Guys like that can't handle not making decisions for everyone around them. "Surely you explained that you're lactose intolerant."

"I tried, but then he went on this long tirade about how food intolerances are nothing but a myth." Even in the dark, I can see the sparks flashing in her eyes.

"Hmm," I muse. "Maybe the old boy's right. You sure you're not just making that shit up, Maeve?"

She lets out an exasperated huff as she pokes my chest even harder. "You're fucking unbelievable."

I grab her hand and spin her so she's pressed between me and the wall. She rewards me with a small gasp. God, I've been waiting so long to feel her again. Propping an arm against the wall above her head, I lean down. "Says the woman who set me up with a crazy person."

The corners of her mouth twitch. "I thought you two would have so much in common."

"Like hell you did." I claim her mouth with mine before she can spout off any more rubbish.

She melts beneath me the way she always does, letting me slide my hands down her body to cup her ass. A tiny moan escapes her lips as I yank her against me, my cock hard and ready for action.

"Come home with me." I nuzzle her neck with my nose, peppering it with kisses.

Maeve sucks in a breath as I nibble the sensitive spot beneath her ear. "I thought you and Celestia would be discussing baby names late into the night."

Switching from lips to teeth, I give her a warning bite. "Not funny."

She snorts a laugh. "Either way, Austin has already invited me over. Apparently, he's quite good in the bedr—"

I cut her off with a hand on her throat, pinning her hard against the wall. "He will not be touching you," I hiss into her ear. "Is that clear?"

"If you didn't want me to sleep with him, you shouldn't have chosen him for my date," she purrs.

I swear I see lights flashing behind my eyelids. No way in hell is Maeve going home with that creep. I know she's only saying this to mess with me, and goddamn it, it's working. "No fucking way."

"Calm down," she says. "Why are you acting like a jealous psycho?"

"Because you're mine." It comes out as a growl. I wonder briefly at the urge I have to brand her with my teeth, to show the world she belongs to me. I've never had that desire with anyone else. What's so different about Maeve?

Her pulse skitters beneath my fingertips. "We could slip into the bathroom for a quickie." Two months ago, she would have raised hell if anyone had suggested she have sex in a restroom, especially a public one.

"No," I say, running my lips along her jawline as I tilt her chin up. "It's been too long since I've had you to myself. I'm ready to play."

Her throat bobs as she swallows. "Play?"

"That's right." I chuckle into her ear. "By the end of the night, you're not going to be able to walk without remembering that I've been inside you."

# 27

## "R U Mine?" - Arctic Monkeys

*Maeve*

When I return to the table after my run-in with Pierce outside the restroom, Austin looks peeved. "Sorry about that," I say, sitting down. "There was a long line."

"And I don't suppose you could have waited," he says, rolling his eyes.

"Excuse me?" I've had enough of this guy's bullshit tonight. "And endured more directives to eat the fucking ice cream, even after I told you I was lactose intolerant?"

He has the decency to look a little sheepish, but then it gets lost behind the cockiness. "It's gelato, actually."

"As if I care." I stand up and grab my bag. "This date is over." I stalk toward the exit without looking to see who's watching. Let Austin pick up the tab for this atrocious night.

My driver is waiting for me, thank god, and I sink into the back seat in relief. I cannot imagine a more miserable way to spend an evening.

The text alert on my phone chimes just as we're pulling up to my house. I wait until I'm inside to read it.

**Lux**: *Where'd you go?*
**Me**: *Home.*
**Lux**: *It's not like you to bail. Everything okay? xx*
**Me**: *I wasn't feeling good so I decided to call it a night.*

That's one way to put it. I head to the master en suite and draw a bath.

**Lux**: *That's too bad!! We were going to declare you the winner.*
**Me**: *And you're not going to because . . . ?*

Did Pierce and Celestia end their date with a flourish? Oh god, what if he kissed her?

**Lux**: *Because you forfeited? And both you and your date looked pretty pissed at the end.*

Yeah, because Pierce got under my skin.

**Me**: *Don't be ridiculous. It was obvious I had more fun than Pierce.*

I need this win.

**Lux**: *Oh definitely. That was never a question.*
**Me**: *Then why are you giving this to him?!*
**Lux**: *We're not. He forfeited too.*
**Me**: *What?*
**Lux**: *He walked out right after you did.*

You've got to be kidding me. I'm relieved they didn't declare him the winner, but that victory belonged to me. I endured that date from hell for nothing.

I toss my phone aside and am about to undress for my bath when the doorbell rings. I consider ignoring it, but it will forever bug me not knowing who is here this time of night. Maybe Lux changed her mind and came to tell me in person?

But when I pull up the camera on my phone, it's Pierce standing on my doorstep. The sight of him makes my blood pound, and no, not in the way you're thinking. Forget the bath. I turn off the tap and march to the door. I have things I need to say.

I yank the door open without any intention of letting him inside, but he barges past me anyway. Gasping, I slam the heavy oak door behind me before the chilly night air can creep in after him. It closes with a loud shudder. I press my back against it, trying to put as much distance between Pierce and myself as possible.

"What are you doing here?" I say, crossing my arms over my chest. The dress I'm still wearing from tonight's date is thin and sleeveless. Goosebumps cover every inch of my bare skin despite the fact that the house is toasty and warm.

Pierce tosses his jacket across the emerald-green divan in the front sitting room. With nary a care in the world, he begins rolling up his sleeves.

*Oh fuck.*

"I should think that obvious," he says without looking at me.

I shake my head, a little more fiercely than necessary, but I'm starting to spiral. "Absolutely not."

His eyes dart up to find mine. "Excuse me?"

The man doesn't like to be told no, a thought that pleases me to no end. There are just so many opportunities for upsetting him in that little nugget of knowledge. "You cannot waltz in here and demand sex."

A dry chuckle slips out from between his lips. "I haven't demanded anything."

"There's only one reason you're here, Pierce, and it's not to sell me insurance."

Both sleeves now rolled up to his elbows, he takes several measured steps in my direction. The solid door at my back provides little comfort. "You need a lot more than insurance to relax."

My nostrils flare as I inhale sharply. "Tonight should have been mine," I hiss.

"And?"

"And because of your shenanigans outside the restroom, I lost. *Again.*"

He clicks his tongue in mock sympathy. "Poor baby."

I clench my jaw so hard it trembles. "I hate you."

Closing the distance between us, he leans down and whispers, "I'm well aware." He reaches into my dress for my nipple and twists it—hard.

I gasp and slap him across the face. "How dare you?" I feel heat flooding my cheeks as though I'm the one who just got slapped.

Pierce huffs out a breath, fingers now making love to my tender peak, then studies me through narrowed eyes. The glint lighting his pupils makes me nervous. "Does fighting with me turn you on?" He says it as if he's made some breakthrough discovery.

I open my mouth to reply, but no sound comes out. "No," I manage to splutter, right as his hand reaches beneath my dress and inside my panties, where the evidence of my lie is currently soaking through.

"Oh, fuck," he says, echoing my earlier sentiment, then drives two fingers in, deep and hard.

I cry out and smack him again, but we both feel the rush of moisture releasing onto his hand.

He chuckles into my ear, and it's so dirty it almost brings me to climax right there. "Oh, baby," he says, and laughs again as if he's just discovered the secret to the universe.

I guess he's discovered the secret to mine.

His hand pumps into me faster and faster, causing the strength in my legs to drain away. I slump against the door, Pierce's arm around my waist keeping me upright.

"God, I've been thinking about this every day," he says.

My eyes flutter open, and I meet his gaze. "Why?"

He raises a single brow while the rest of his face remains frozen. "*Why?* Why do you think?"

## "R U MINE?" - ARCTIC MONKEYS

I moan as he curls his fingers inside my pussy, finding new spots of sensitivity. "You could've slept with someone else. Kind of your thing, remember?"

"*Not* my thing," he says with a growl, driving even deeper. "And I didn't want anyone else."

Gasping as my orgasm builds, I cling to his arm. "Wh—why not?"

He slows his movements, leaving his fingers inside me. Their maddening paralysis makes me tighten around him. Not that it does any good. He won't let me climax until he's ready for me to. "I thought we'd already established that." His voice is husky in my ear.

"I mean, I get that you're attracted to me—"

Pierce cuts me off by shoving his fingers in as deep as they'll go. "Attracted to you? You think I'm *attracted* to you?"

I glance down at his cock straining at his trousers. "Kind of hard to hide."

"I'm attracted to half the female population in this city."

My eyes narrow. The nerve of this man. "Wow. Good to know."

"If I was attracted to you, I would have fucked and dumped you long ago."

I push at his hand, which is still under my dress. It doesn't budge. "This conversation is actually killing my libido, so—"

He spins me around and pushes me onto the divan, then lifts me until I'm on all fours, my dress shoved up to my hips. I have just enough time to gasp before he pushes into me from behind, yanking my hair back as he does so.

"Does this feel like 'attraction' to you?" he growls.

I don't know what it feels like. Heaven? Hell? A combination of both? I sink into the velvet cushions of the sofa as he sinks into me. If he's not attracted to me, then what is he? Certainly not repulsed, if the way his cock is currently filling me up is any indication.

"When I tell you to come," he breathes into my ear, "you're going to come."

I groan as he drives in even deeper.

"Have you ever climaxed on command before?"

"No," I rasp out.

He lets out another deep, dirty chuckle. "Oh, this is going to be fun." His hand slides along my hip and settles between my legs, his fingers dancing across my freshly waxed skin.

Panic settles in my chest. "What if I can't?" He's already established that I can't fool him by faking it. What am I supposed to do if I can't come when he tells me to?

He sniffs a laugh, as though I've said something amusing. "You can."

"You can't know that." This conversation is making it hard for me to focus on what we're doing. Anxiety creeps in, and fear claws its way up my throat.

Pierce plants kisses across my shoulders, his stubble tickling my bare skin. "Of course I can."

I envy the confidence in his tone. "How?" I ask, the slight tremble in my voice giving me away.

He pulls back, but keeps his cock buried deep inside me. "I'll help you." His fingers reach around to play with my folds.

I moan as he pinches my clit. "But at the end of the day," I pant, "it's still my job to orgasm."

"No, it's not." He thrusts in further with a grunt. "It's my job to understand your body, to discover what you like, to realize when you're close."

"But—"

"You have to trust me to know your body as well or better than you do."

Picking up the pace, he pounds into me from behind, and I let my head hang, my hair falling around my face like a curtain. I cry out as he moves his thumb over my swollen nub, which only makes him press harder.

"Now, baby," he whispers in my ear. A shiver travels down my spine. "Come for me. Let me feel that pussy clench tight around my cock."

As though I have zero control over my body, it does exactly as he commands, climaxing hard and hot while he continues plunging into me. My cry is loud and guttural, but I don't care. This is by far the best orgasm I've ever had.

"*Maeve.*" As he thrusts in even deeper, I feel his warm cum shooting into me. I squeeze tightly around his pulsing cock, and he moans and buries his face into my neck. "Fuck," he breathes out as we both collapse onto the divan.

*Fuck* is right. Why do I end up giving this man more power over me every time I turn around?

# 28

## "Bring Me to Life" - Evanescence

*Pierce*

I whistle as I walk down the corridor to my office. My assistant, Hillary, looks up as I approach. "Everything okay, Mr. St. James?"

Tossing her a wink, I move toward my door. "Better than okay."

I'm not sure where my good mood came from, but I'm flying high. Maeve and I have been seeing each other nearly every day since that atrocious date night, and I'd be lying if I said it hasn't at least contributed to my feeling lighter. I'm meeting her again tonight, and I'm already counting the hours.

"Before you go," Hillary says, standing up from her desk, and I turn back to face her. "Did you get the memo I sent you earlier?"

I frown, trying to recall the various things I handled this morning. "I'm not sure. What about?"

"Dr. Hewitt called. He was trying to reach you. He heard about HavenNet and was concerned about continuing to fund the Wilson Foundation."

At the mention of Maeve's pride and joy, my nerves go on high alert. "Did you tell him I'd return the call?"

My assistant pulls back slightly. "No. Was I supposed to? I told him we're not affiliated with the Foundation outside of our partnership through HavenNet, and that any of his concerns would need to be directed at them."

I fight the urge to snap at her. Technically, she did the right thing. Luminara Tech has no business interfering in things that don't involve us directly. Not only can we not afford the risk to our own reputation, but we're far too busy creating life-changing technology to worry about small things like a single donor being displeased with a current partner of ours.

But this is Maeve we're talking about. If Dr. Hewitt already called her, she's probably freaking the fuck out right now.

"No, that's fine," I tell Hillary. "I'll handle it from here."

She gives me a surprised look but nods. "Okay."

I walk into my office, already pulling up Hewitt's contact info on my phone.

He answers on the third ring. "Pierce St. James," he says, sounding jovial. "What can I do for you?"

"Sorry to bother you." I take a seat at my desk. "My assistant told me you called earlier about the Wilson Foundation."

"Ah, yes." He clicks his tongue. "You know Lord Wilson is a friend of mine, but I can't help but be concerned about the direction things have taken in the past few years."

"Can I ask what kinds of things we're talking about?" I lean back in my chair as he tells me about various vague insinuations and miscommunications. "I can assure you those were nothing but rumors."

He sighs heavily into the phone. "I'll be honest with you, Pierce. I'm just not comfortable with his daughter leading the organization. She doesn't seem capable."

I press a fist to my mouth to keep from saying what I really want to. Maeve is far more capable than her asshat of a father ever was.

"I know Maeve quite well. We've been friends a long time," I say, although one could argue that what we are now is a far cry from "friends." "She is definitely capable of leading the Foundation."

"I'm just not sure . . ." Hewitt trails off, hesitation still lingering in his voice.

"She's got the most brilliant mind of anyone I've ever met," I say. "Her ability to lead a team, to rally them around a central cause, is remarkable. In the three years she's been at the helm, the Wilson Foundation has doubled its annual donations, which is the only reason we were able to create HavenNet. There were some mishaps there, yes, but none of those were Maeve's fault."

"I'll admit, the HavenNet fiasco has been the main cause for my concern," he says.

"It was a major disaster on all fronts, but Maeve is leading us toward a rebrand and relaunch. The final product will be even better than the original. I don't think you'll have any regrets if you continue your sponsorship."

Hewitt sighs again, then lets out a small chuckle. "Well, lad, I must say, you put up a fine argument for the girl. You sure you're only friends?"

# 29

## "No I'm not in Love" - Tate McRae

*Maeve*

The instant I smell the delicious interior of Pierce's car, I'm reminded of why this is a bad idea. I open my mouth to protest, to tell him I'll call a driver, but he places a hand on my lower back and gently pushes me into the Aston Martin.

"Just get in," he says into my ear.

I obediently slide onto the leather seat and let my muscles relax. He can drop me at home, we'll have time for a quickie, and that will be it.

It's Friday night, and with my father out of town on business, I'm free to hang out with the whole crew. We executed a flawless revenge plot on Saylor's ex-husband, who tried to steal thousands of dollars from her parents. Slate knocked the idiot out, then the guys stuck his head and arms through the first unlocked window they could find in the neighborhood. Meanwhile, Lux called it in as breaking and entering, playing the part of distraught pedestrian perfectly.

All in all, it was a great night.

Pierce puts the car into gear, and I glance down at the gearshift. A pair of cream-colored lace panties hang from it. Before I can remove them, he grabs them and shoves them into the pocket of his trousers.

"Hey," I say. "That's a five-hundred-dollar thong." He took it off me the last time I was in here, and I forgot about it, probably due to the incredible orgasm he gave me in return.

"I'll buy you a dozen more."

My cheeks flush. Is he a trophy guy?

His grip flexes on the steering wheel, grabbing my attention. A desire to have his hands on me rises up as thick veins bulge beneath his taut skin. The way they would feel on my body, caressing me, possessing me, finessing me . . .

As if he can read my thoughts, he reaches over and seizes my thigh. His fingertips just graze my bare leg. He doesn't even try to feel me up, just drives with one hand staking claim to me.

I need something to distract me. Opening the glovebox, I search for something to pick a fight over. It's what we do best, after all. True to form, however, the compartment is neat and tidy, just like the rest of his car, his flat, his closet. God, doesn't the man have any flaws?

Pierce doesn't ask what I'm doing as I continue rifling through it, but I can feel his quiet amusement. Finally, buried at the bottom, I find an old tube of lipstick.

"Use this often?" I ask, holding it up.

"Every day."

I huff and sit back in my seat, turning the stick over. "Which one of your girlfriends wore Chanel in 99 Pirate?" Now I am pissed, no more effort needed. Everyone who's anyone knows that's *my* shade.

"None that I know of," he says, glancing over. "You probably left it in here."

I frown. It's not like me to leave things lying around, especially not in other people's spaces, but this is the second time something of mine has shown up in Pierce's belongings. The scarf seemed like a coincidence, but twice in a row feels . . . I don't know, odd?

"Why didn't you throw it out?" I toss the tube back in the glovebox.

He sighs heavily. "I don't know, Maeve. Probably because I didn't notice it."

I feel a little bad for picking on him, which is strange. Definitely not like me at all. "What you said the other night," I blurt out before my filter can kick in, "what did you mean?"

He cuts me a side glance before hitting his blinker. "You're going to have to be more specific than that."

Heat settles in my cheeks, mingled with regret at bringing up the topic. Who short-circuited my mouth to bypass my brain? "You said it's your job to know my body."

"It is." His hand tightens ever so slightly around my leg. "Don't you agree?"

My brows pinch together as I consider this. "Maybe if we were a couple, but—"

"Aren't we?"

I whip my head to the side to look at him, even though it's too dark to make out much besides his profile. "Of course we're not."

As carefully as you might pet a wild animal, his fingers begin stroking my inner thigh. "In one aspect we are."

"That's beside the point," I say, flustered by his movements. "Even if we were . . . *dating*"—god, what an insane thought—"that wouldn't make it your responsibility."

"Then whose is it?" His touch causes goosebumps to flood every inch of skin below my waist.

"Mine." I overemphasize the word, not because it deserves it, but because I'm on the verge of spiraling. Again. When did that become my default state around this man? "It's my responsibility."

His hand stills, and he turns to look at me, then focuses his attention back on the road. "That's a load of crock."

I gape at him. "I suppose you're the master of sexual etiquette?"

"Practicing it doesn't make you a master," he grumbles.

I shake my head, truly confounded. "No one I've been with has considered my orgasms their responsibility."

"Until me."

"Until you."

"Just because you've only dated wankers before now, doesn't mean they're right," he says.

I can't afford to focus on what he's saying—not when the scent of him is seeping into my pores, when my head is spinning from the way he's touching me—so I pick at the one thing in his sentence that's safe.

"Yes, but we're not dating either."

Rain patters softly against the car windows, blurring the lights of the city as we zip down the streets. A gentle jazz melody oozes from the speakers, the kind you imagine someone dancing to when they're seventy years old and have spent over half their life loving the same person.

Pierce is quiet for so long that I think he's not going to respond. When he does, my heart jumps in surprise. "No, but we could be," he says quietly.

I can't help the abrupt laugh that bursts out of my mouth. "I'm not your type."

His fingers continue their sensual dance on my leg, trailing up and down the sensitive skin of my inner thigh. "What makes you say that?"

Grabbing a hunk of my black hair, I lift it off my shoulder. "I'm the opposite of blond. And my name doesn't end in '-ella.'"

Pierce snorts and keeps his eyes focused on the street. "I don't have a type."

I laugh again, and it sounds a little maniacal. "You are the personification of a guy with a type."

"That's absurd."

"I could open a catalogue and order your girlfriends for the next five years, and you'd have no complaints."

He snaps his fingers. "So that's where you found Celestia."

Rolling my eyes, I shift lower in my seat, allowing our sparring to relax me. "The fact that I knew exactly what kind of woman would most annoy you only proves my point."

A low murmur comes from his chest, but he neither confirms nor denies my statement. My assessment is obviously correct—the guy is as predictable as Monday-morning traffic—but it bothers me a little that he seems to have forgotten the origin of this conversation. Which is concerning. It's not like I want to *date* Pierce.

I'm not waiting for him to offer a rebuttal and prove that I am, in fact, exactly his type. The two of us would never work out as anything other than what we are—frenemies who fuck. And I'm not so insecure that I need to be adored by every person I encounter.

Besides, if he were to say he wanted more, this whole thing would have to end, which would be a travesty, because I've come to quite enjoy our little rendezvous. Everyone knows that when feelings catch in situations like ours, things go south very quickly. So it's for the best that Pierce and I are on the same page about this just being sex.

"Which number in line would you be?" His voice startles me, and I turn away from the rain-streaked window to look at him.

"What?"

"The girlfriends you're ordering for me. Would you be the first or the last?"

I blink several times as my brain scrambles to find words. It seems they've decided to pass through the gray matter after all, except now they've gotten stuck, because I'm incapable of giving him a response.

As if sensing my dilemma, he adds, "We both know Maeve Wilson doesn't do the middle."

I swallow thickly. Several more beats pass before I locate my voice. "I told you, I'm not your—"

"My type. I know." The vehicle swerves as he pulls into a car park and stops.

"Why are we stopping at"—I crane my head to read the sign on the pale-yellow building and scrunch up my face—"Mama C's Pizzeria?"

Pierce doesn't look up, just keeps his eyes on the steering wheel. Without the driving sounds drowning it out, his breathing becomes audible. He's no longer grabbing my leg, both hands now pressing into his own thighs.

I'm about to ask if something is wrong when he speaks, his voice nothing more than a low rumble.

"What if I told you I only dated blonds so I wouldn't accidentally say your name while I was fucking them?"

## 30

"The Archer" - Taylor Swift

*Maeve*

My mouth has gone dry, every word in the English language disappearing from tongue and mind, just like that. Poof.

*What if I told you I only dated blonds so I wouldn't accidentally say your name while I was fucking them?*

Pierce looks at me for the first time since stopping the car, as though he actually expects me to say something after dropping a bomb like that. His eyes catch the light from the pizzeria and do funny things to my chest.

I drop my gaze to my lap. That felt like an unspoken game of chicken, and I just lost. The silence swirls around us, thick and murky, threatening to suck me under, and god, there is nothing I hate more than silence.

"I'd say that's insane," I blurt out.

He coughs out a disbelieving laugh. "Insane."

"Yes, insane."

Shifting in his seat until he's facing me, he lets the full weight of his attention fall on me. "Why would that be insane?"

"Because—"

*Because I don't know how to handle that.*

"Because we can't say things like that to each other," I say in a rush.

He tilts his head to the side, considering me. "Why not?"

"Because we're . . ." I gesture to the space between us. "Because we don't like each other."

"Mmm," he says. "That's not what you implied last night."

"I—" The rest of my words dry up on my tongue.

As he leans closer, his voice lowers even further. "Last night you begged me to never stop playing with you. You said—and I quote—'I will die if you stop.'"

I shoot him a glare, my face hot with embarrassment. "That was the sex talking. It doesn't mean I like you. Or that you get to like me."

Pierce grabs my thigh and jerks me closer to him. "You don't decide what I get to do. If I say I've fantasized about you for years, then that's the truth."

I'm panting, my breath stolen by the intensity in his eyes and voice. "Have you?" I squeak out. "Fantasized about me?"

"Have I fantasized about you," he mutters. Shaking his head, he sniffs a laugh. "Why do you think the sex is so good, hmm?"

It's my turn to shake my head, speechless. How should I know? Sex was always mediocre for me before Pierce and I started hooking up.

"I have a list, you know," he says, as if that explains anything.

"A list."

His tongue darts out and licks his bottom lip. "A list of things I think you'll like."

I keep my eyes on him, but my mind is whirling at two hundred miles an hour. "Things I'll like?" I'm pretty sure I know what he means, but this feels too significant not to verify. "What, like sex stuff?"

Nodding, he shifts and leans his elbow on the center console, putting us less than six inches apart. "Sex and other stuff."

## "THE ARCHER" - TAYLOR SWIFT

I lean back. "Other stuff? Like what?"

A tiny smile plays at the corners of his mouth. "I can't tell you."

"Why not?"

"Because that will ruin it."

Trembling all over, my body feels like it's being wracked by a fever. I'm both hot and cold and can't stop shaking. "I need to see this list."

He laughs and drapes a wrist over the steering wheel. "You're not seeing the list."

"This is all some twisted game to you, isn't it?" I cross my arms over my chest and settle back into my seat. The shaking eases a little. "You're just messing with my head."

A heavy sigh heaves from his chest. "And what would be the point of that?"

Narrowing my eyes, I keep my gaze on him, searching for any sign that he's playing me. There has to be more to this, even if I can't see it. People don't spill secrets like that unless they have ulterior motives. "I don't know what goes on in that screwed-up head of yours," I say.

Pierce exhales and leans his head back. "God, Maeve."

"Is that what this is? Lies so that you can gain the upper hand?"

Several beats of loaded silence pass before he turns slowly. "Not everything is a game."

"It is with us," I shoot back.

His eyes cling to mine, bottomless in the dark car. "Not for me."

He appears so . . . *earnest,* and I think that's what bothers me the most. I'd be more comfortable if he just admitted he's messing with me. Then I'd think up some way to get back at him, and everything would right itself again. But the look on his face—that's not something I know how to handle.

Reaching out a hand, he brushes his fingers across my cheek. It causes me to start, even though he's moving with the speed of molasses and my body is as familiar with his touch as it is with taking a shower.

"Why won't you lower your defenses?" He plucks at my bottom lip with his thumb, letting it spring back before pressing it again.

"I can't," I whisper, tears welling in my eyes out of nowhere. Blinking quickly, I pray they disappear before he notices.

"Not even for me?"

I consider what he's asking, but the risk is too great. Without a defense, there's nothing stopping him from breaking me completely, until I'm as shattered as Humpty Dumpty, unable to ever be put back together. Shaking my head, I sink my teeth into my lip. "I can't." *I'm sorry*, I stop myself from adding just in time.

"I wish you could see that you're safe with me." His gaze focuses on my mouth, and for a second, I think he's going to kiss me, but then he meets my eyes again. "I'm not going to hurt you."

I try to swallow the thick lump in my throat, but it won't budge. "You will," I say softly.

His gaze darkens. "What do I need to do in order for you to believe me?"

"I don't—I don't know." The lump grows even bigger, nearly gagging me now.

"Do I need to fuck you hard and slow until you're begging me to let you climax?"

*Oh god, please no, but also yes.*

"Do I need to take you right here, right now, to prove that you're mine? Hike that dress up around your hips and feast on your pussy like a starving man?"

A tiny whimper escapes my lips, and he growls in response.

"Or maybe I'll leave you like this, wet and swollen for me, so I can take you home and fuck you in ten new places."

"Pierce," I manage, breathless and trying desperately not to pant. My panties are already soaked through, and we're still ten minutes

## "THE ARCHER" - TAYLOR SWIFT

from home.

He moves closer, until his stubble scratches my jaw. "If that's the only way you'll let me have you, I'll take it." Straightening in his seat, he adjusts the crotch of his pants, then puts the car into gear.

I stare at him, mouth agape. He's just going to leave me like this?

But then his hand reaches across the console, and instead of settling on my thigh, it travels up beneath my dress. He mutters a quiet "fuck" when he reaches my drenched panties. "These are going home with me, too."

As he pulls into traffic, he's also pulling back the fabric of my underwear, giving himself access to me. I groan and let my head fall back against the seat as he slides two fingers inside.

"God, I will never get over how tight you are," he says as we stop at a red light. "So ready to swallow my whole hand." He turns his attention to my lap. "Pull up your dress so I can see what I'm doing to you."

I'm more than happy to obey, because it means I get a front-row seat as well, if I can keep my eyes from rolling back in my head. Lifting myself up, I tug the fabric up to my waist, amazed and a little impressed that Pierce keeps pumping into me the whole time.

The light turns green, and he accelerates while keeping an eye on me. "So fucking beautiful," he murmurs. "And all mine."

Scooting down, I give him more room to explore. He takes it greedily, shoving a third finger in to join the other two. I moan as he fills me, then watch as he pulls them out, only to shove them back in a second later. My panties are blocking my view, so I reach down and shimmy them off.

"Good girl. Now you can watch me fuck you." He drives responsibly on the road and recklessly into me, turning to cast a glance at me every few seconds, the streetlamps acting as spotlights for our show. His fingers know exactly what I need, the best spots to hit, and how to curl to bring me to the brink of combustion.

Grabbing his forearm, I encourage him to go faster, deeper, harder. "More, Pierce. I need more."

He complies, but the second I start to tighten around him, he slows down. "No fucking way," he says. "You're not climaxing until I can watch, too."

I let out a frustrated cry and content myself with staring as he wrecks me on the front seat of his car. He slows his movements down until his fingers are doing a sensual dance as they slide over, then between, my folds and finally—blessedly—slip back inside me. Refusing to drive them in all the way, he only goes in a few inches, then pulls out and starts the whole process over.

The smell of my sex fills the car, combining with the scent of Pierce in a seductive way that has me drinking in huge lungfuls of it. Every time he draws back out, my moans punctuate the wet noises his fingers make. This man will be the death of me, I'm sure of it.

We finally turn onto my street, and I've never been so grateful to be home in my life. As soon as the car is in park, Pierce leans over and switches his hands. Sticking the fingers that were just inside me into his mouth, he moans as he sucks them clean.

"You taste like heaven," he says. "Now, let's get you taken care of, baby." After turning on the interior light so he can see better, he slips his free hand behind me, cupping my ass before finding his way to my seam. "Someday, I'm going to fuck this, too."

The thought makes me release moisture into his other hand.

His chuckle is deep and sexy. "You like the sound of that, don't you?"

I squirm as I try to find friction and relief.

"Patience, baby girl. I'll make you come, don't worry." He spreads my folds wide. "Look what I do to you. Look how red you are for me."

## "THE ARCHER" - TAYLOR SWIFT

"Pierce, please," I whisper, so turned on just by looking at myself. "I need you so bad right now."

"Mmm, just the way I like you," he says, bending over to drop a kiss on my lips. Then without warning, he plunges his fingers into me as far as they'll go, keeping my ass locked in place with his other hand. Before I have time to recover, he's driving them in again.

My head lolls back, my eyes closed. I'm so close now, I can taste it.

"Open your eyes and watch me fuck you," he directs.

I blink them open and stare down at where his fingers are relentlessly pounding into me, my flesh pink and raw. Gasping, I clutch his arm tightly as the orgasm takes over.

"Keep your eyes open," he says.

I do, watching as he continues fucking me through the last throes. It's the hottest thing I've ever seen.

When the final shudder subsides, he slowly withdraws his fingers. "Now, let's go inside so I can take care of you the way I fantasize about."

\* \* \*

We have sex twice in the house—once just inside the door, because he says he can't wait any longer, and once in the bedroom, because I'm exhausted. He rolls off me and heads to the bathroom to clean up.

I watch him go, that tight ass bouncing as he walks. "Why didn't you tell me?" I ask, raising my voice so he can hear me through the open door.

"Tell you what?"

Tugging the blankets closer to my chin, I burrow deeper into the bed. "That you wanted this." My heart oddly feels warm, not unlike how my body feels beneath the duvet—cozy and safe.

There's silence from the bathroom, and I think for a second that he didn't hear me. Then his voice comes, low and measured. "Because I knew you didn't see me like that."

My heart pounds as I lie here, a million thoughts spinning through my mind and making it hard to settle on a single one. See him as a sex partner? Or something more?

Pierce walks back in before I can think of a response and climbs onto the bed. He leans down, presses a kiss to my forehead, then slides beneath the comforter.

"What are you doing?" I say, propping myself up on an elbow. "I'm too tired to go again."

"Relax." He tugs me down beside him. "I'm just going to sleep." His arms snake around me, cushioning me against his chest. It doesn't feel bad, just unusual.

"Sleep? What, *here*?" I crane my neck to look up at him.

He doesn't even bother opening his eyes, just pulls me closer. "Mmm," he murmurs into my hair. "Is that okay?"

Is it okay for him to spend the night? We've never slept together. In the three months we've been sneaking around, it's only ever been sex. So why does he want to stay tonight? "I—I don't know if that's a good idea," I stammer.

"Why not? I promise I don't snore."

"Because—" I'm not sure how to put into words the trepidation I'm feeling. Sleepovers are for couples, and we're not a couple. If he's been thinking about me for a long time, what if there are feelings involved? "I just think it could get messy."

He blinks his eyes open and looks at me. "We already made a mess. Don't think it's going to get worse than that."

I flush, thinking of my wet sheets. "You know what I mean."

"I don't, actually." His hand moves up and down my back, the warmth from his palm seeping into my skin. "What are you so scared of?"

*That I'll start to trust you and you'll ruin me.*

"I just don't want you thinking this is anything more than sex," I say to his sculpted chest.

There's the tiniest pause in his movements, but then he continues as though nothing's happened. "You don't need to worry about that," he says quietly. "You don't need to worry about anything. Just go to sleep." Digging a hand into my hair, he buries my face against him.

My nose pressed up against his skin, I'm treated to the unadulterated scent of him. It's like a direct line into my veins, making me heady with desire again. God, the man smells good. "Fine," I mumble. "But only for tonight."

# 31

## "cowboy like me" - Taylor Swift

*Maeve*

My feet are killing me. I made the irresponsible choice to wear a brand-new pair of Manolos without breaking them in first, and now I'm paying the price. I shift from one foot to the other as I listen to Mr. and Mrs. Patel voice enthusiasm over tonight's initiative.

It's the ninth annual Pulse of Hope gala, and the Wilson Foundation is bringing awareness to and raising funds for rare genetic heart conditions. The Patels' son was diagnosed with ARVC several years ago, and they've been among our most generous donors since.

While I'm passionate about the cause, I've been rushing around for hours. Not only am I hosting this event, but several of the party planner's crew came down with a stomach bug last night, leaving us short-staffed. I found myself arranging floral bouquets most of the day.

There's a gentle touch on my elbow, and I turn to find Pierce at my side, holding a French 75. He hands it to me, and before I can even thank him, he's disappeared back into the crowd.

Gratefully, I sip it, letting the alcohol loosen up my muscles. I'm still hours away from being able to go to bed, but this will help me make it to the end of the night.

Pierce and I aren't here together, obviously, but the way my body relaxed when I saw him walk into the ballroom earlier is hard to explain. It felt akin to sinking into my mattress in after a long night—like pure relief.

The Patels murmur their thanks and drift away. I take another sip and glance around the room.

We're in the ballroom of the historic Allerton Hotel, which is an incredible piece of architecture, even if it's in need of some updates. Thick pillars stand guard on the east side, lending the space a Roman look. Intricately carved stone molding lines the ceiling, and the marble floor gleams. Round tables are spaced throughout, holding the floral centerpieces we labored over earlier. The crystal stemware catches the light from the chandeliers dangling above.

Before I can circulate and make sure things are going smoothly, one of our long-time donors approaches. I paste on my biggest and best smile. "Dr. Hewitt," I say. "It's so nice to see you."

"Likewise," he says, lifting his drink to his lips. Hewitt is a short man, but what he lacks in height, he makes up for in his midsection. His tuxedo shirt stretches over his paunch before disappearing into his trousers.

"Thank you for coming tonight. Pulse of Hope wouldn't be possible without generous people like you." I've given this speech so many times, it rolls off my tongue without a thought.

"It's a great cause." He scans the room. "To tell you the truth, I almost didn't come tonight."

Afraid he has the same stomach bug as the missing staff, I take a step back. "Well, I'm grateful you were able to make it."

"I had some concerns, you know." He takes another sip of his whiskey. "After the HavenNet fiasco."

My spine stiffens. What went down with Deirdre and HavenNet

isn't public knowledge, but enough people are aware of it that I'm not too surprised by his words. The mortification from the disaster hasn't worn off, though.

"I wasn't sure it was something you could recover from," Hewitt continues. "I'm still not sure. But I've heard enough to give me the confidence to stick it out a little longer."

Brows knit, I turn to look at him. "What did you hear?" We haven't issued any press releases concerning HavenNet since the initial one after we discovered what Deirdre had done.

He sniffs and takes another drink. After lowering his glass once more, he gives me a knowing look. "Someone spoke very highly of your leadership abilities and your vision for the future. Needless to say, it was enough to keep me on board for the time being."

"Who?" I say before thinking better of it. It's a major faux pas, but I don't care. My curiosity is burning. It couldn't have been either of my parents, unless they were trying to save face for the foundation.

Dr. Hewitt smirks. "Pierce St. James. It seems the man holds quite the opinion of you."

I feel my lips part in surprise, but no words are forthcoming. As if he's served his purpose, Dr. Hewitt walks away, smiling into his wine.

My eyes scan the room for Pierce, something that's becoming a habit. Was he simply trying to retain funding for HavenNet, or was it more than that? I drop my gaze to my glass, now empty, and wonder about the fact that he brought me the exact cocktail I would have ordered for myself. Is it possible he—

"What a fabulous evening," a shrill voice says.

I turn to my left to find Gladys Fairchild nursing what is likely her sixth glass of chardonnay. "Gladys," I murmur, wishing my own drink wasn't gone. "I'm so glad you're here." It's obviously a blatant lie, which you'd know if you'd ever met the woman.

The Fairchilds are old money, but I use that term loosely, since they're more old, less money. The family fortune ran out some seventy years ago, but they've done their best to maintain the same lifestyle as earlier generations. Unfortunately, that has required racking up considerable debts and donating just enough to charity to retain their invitations to these kinds of events. Needless to say, this woman is a thorn in my side. She costs us more than she's worth, contribution-wise.

"Oh, we wouldn't miss it for the world," she gushes. "You know how passionate Patrick is about genetic diseases."

"Yes, of course," I say, nodding. *I think you mean sexually transmitted ones.*

As Gladys drones on and on about her "dear Patrick," who is currently flirting with not one but two other women, I keep an eye out for a passing waiter. The party is winding down, though, and most of them seem preoccupied with collecting empty stemware.

I become aware of a presence behind me, but before I can turn around, a strong hand slides around my waist. My heart leaps into my throat, but my body instinctively knows who it is. Even if I didn't recognize his touch, his scent would have identified him.

"Time to go," Pierce whispers in my ear.

My eyes flutter at the way his breath tickles my neck, and I blink to recover my composure.

Gladys is still talking, flapping her pudgy hands around to convey god only knows what. I haven't exactly been paying attention. Her gaze snags on Pierce, and her eyes light up, even though he is at least thirty years her junior. "Pierce St. James," she croons. "How do you manage to get more and more handsome?"

I glance up to see how he reacts to this, but his face remains as neutral as always, not even a hint of pink in his cheeks. Damn him.

"Mrs. Fairchild," he says. "It's good to see you. If you don't mind,

I need to steal Ms. Wilson away." He increases the pressure on my lower back until I don't have a choice but to go with him, Gladys still sputtering her thanks behind us.

"What are you doing?" I hiss when he directs me to the exit. "I'm not leaving yet."

"Yes, we are." He snags the empty coupe glass from my hand and passes it to a server.

I let out a humorless laugh and stop walking. "You're free to go. *We* are not doing anything."

"Maeve, you're dead on your feet."

Staring up at him, I wonder if my fatigue is obvious to everyone in attendance or only those who have slept with me. Fortunately, that faction is quite small, and at this party, practically nonexistent, with the exception of the man in front of me. "Might I remind you, I'm the hostess, and I need to—"

"Get some sleep," he finishes, then grabs my arm to steer me to the door. "I know."

"Pierce, don't you dare," I snap under my breath, lest anyone overhear us. "I am perfectly capable of making that decision for myself."

"Are you?" He regards me with a raised brow. "Because if I know you, you'll be on your feet another three hours before finally calling it a night."

I lift my nose in the air. "As a matter of fact, I was planning to head home before you came barging in."

"My apologies. Why don't I go fetch Gladys so you can continue your conversation with her."

Shooting him a lethal glare, I march past him toward the double doors.

"That's what I thought," he mutters, following me.

Once we're in the foyer of the hotel and away from the eyes of the gala guests, I whirl around. "While I may be grateful for your little rescue operation back there, I can get home on my own just fine."

"I have no doubt," he says, and crouches in front of me. "But I'm seeing you home all the same." He lifts my left foot and tugs off my shoe.

"What are you doing?" I have to hold on to his shoulders to keep my balance.

He makes quick work of the other heel, then stands up. "I don't know why you do that to yourself."

I gape at him, alternating between his face and the Manolos dangling from his fingertips.

Without giving me a chance to protest, he grabs me beneath my legs and sweeps me into his arms, not an easy feat since I'm wearing my Cynthia Mancroft ballgown in red silk. I gasp at the sudden movement, then exhale as he settles me against his chest. Wrapping my arms around his neck, I hold on tightly, half afraid he'll dump me on the ground as a prank.

"Relax," Pierce murmurs into my ear. "I've got you."

Something stirs in my belly, something warm and fluttery, something altogether foreign. Maybe I shouldn't be surprised by his actions after that revelation the other night, but I am. I relax my grip, letting my head rest against his shoulder as he carries me to his waiting car.

He is strong, and my fear that he'll drop me dissipates as quickly as it came. As he walks, I study his jawline, covered in a thin layer of stubble I've run my hands and mouth over more times than I can count. It's a good jaw, exceptional even, and frames a very nice face. He's looking especially handsome tonight in his tuxedo and white bow tie.

As if he can feel my eyes on him, he casts me a sidelong look. When he catches me staring, a hint of a smile lights his eyes. The gurgling feeling in my stomach intensifies.

Things have felt weird since our conversation in the car the other night. He hasn't confessed to having feelings, exactly, but it feels like skirting the issue at this point. Maybe I should be excited that Pierce St. James seems to want me in more ways than one, but the truth is, I'm terrified.

We reach the car, and the driver opens the door for us. Rather than depositing me inside, Pierce doesn't even loosen his grip, just slides across the seat with me still in his arms. I hope to god no one saw us outside the hotel.

I make a move to crawl off his lap, but he holds me firmly in place and presses my head down on his shoulder. "Try to sleep," he whispers.

Feeling like a child, I do what he says, his arms much more comfortable than you might expect. Not to mention that being this close to him means every breath carries his scent. I snuggle into his neck until my nose is pressed directly against his skin.

When we reach my house, he lifts me once again. He doesn't even set me down once we're inside but continues upstairs to my bedroom. Lowering me onto the bed, he says softly, "Where are your pajamas?"

I point sleepily to the closet, and he wanders off. Sighing, I recline, grateful to be home at last.

Pierce returns and smirks down at my sprawled form. "Okay, Sleeping Beauty. Let's get you ready for bed." He helps me stand and gently removes my dress, which is studded with hundreds of tiny diamonds.

"Thank you for the lingerie," I say, tracing the edge of the lace thong I'm wearing. True to his word, a box of them arrived several days ago. I blush thinking about him choosing them.

"You deserve it." He presses a kiss to my bare shoulder, then expertly removes my strapless bra and unclasps the Amarilla Pearl necklace.

After locking my jewelry in the safe, he tugs a satin slip over my head. My shoes are already off, so he pulls back the comforter and pats the mattress. "In you go."

I crawl to my pillow, and he pulls the blanket up, tucking it under my chin. Behind me, the bed dips, and I realize he's crawled in beside me. "What are you doing?" I murmur, already half-asleep. "We don't sleep together."

"Shhh," he says, spooning me. "We do now."

# 32

## "Rebel Girl" - Bikini Kill

*Maeve*

This time I'm going to win. Call me arrogant, but I've got this month's challenge in the bag. Quite literally, in fact. I shift the CELINE tote higher on my shoulder as I step out of the lift.

I called Pierce's assistant earlier, pretending to have questions about something concerning HavenNet but really just wanting to confirm his schedule. She's too much of a dolt to have suspected anything and played right into my hands. According to her, he'll be in meetings until at least five tonight.

For once, our diabolical friends issued a challenge that is quite inspired. None of that ridiculous fake relationship or blind date rubbish. No, this month Pierce and I are to steal something from each other's flats. The first one to notice what's missing wins.

Now, using the key I had made from a mold—you didn't think I wouldn't collect collateral, did you?—I slip inside his apartment, praying his secretary wasn't feeding me a bunch of lies.

The lights are off, and there's nothing but the hum of the refrigerator breaking the silence. I step inside and carefully shut the door behind me. I don't know why I feel the need to be quiet, since there's no one here, but it seems weird to do things at normal volume when sneaking into someone's house, even if they're not home.

I don't need to take more than a couple steps before I reach my destination. The painting is hanging in the front entrance, its simple gold frame belying its worth. It's much too modern for my tastes, but I happen to know Pierce is very fond of it.

Simone Caldwell's *Emancipation*.

After Walker entered it into the auction several years ago, Pierce paid nearly twice as much as the first time to get it back. The man is positively mad, but then again, I did practically the same thing for the Amarilla Pearl necklace, which, in my defense, is a family heirloom and much prettier than a black-and-white mess of stripes.

I set my bag down and remove the painting from the wall. It's not very large, maybe eighteen inches wide. Settling myself on the floor, I dig through the tools I brought until I find a screwdriver. With the flat tip, I pry off the staples attaching the backing to the frame, being careful to drop each one into my purse.

My heart is racing, and the screwdriver keeps slipping in my sweaty palms. I'm terrified Pierce will come home any minute and find me. Losing this challenge is something I can't afford to do.

Thinking about his reaction doesn't scare me as much as it should, though. The sex afterward would likely be our hottest yet. He would find the entire thing hilarious, and as mad as I should be, I know I'd find myself laughing along with him.

He has the strange ability to relax me. I know he thinks I won't lower my guard around him, but that's not true. I'm more vulnerable with Pierce than I've been with anyone. Ever. The man has even spent the night with me—not once, but twice. He has a weirdly calming presence, and my reaction to it scares me more than getting caught right now. He's dangerous to my mental health.

If I'm not careful, I'm going to lose sight of what's really important—

winning this challenge and getting Pierce out of my life, once and for all.

Once it's loose, removing the artwork is simple. I carefully ease it out and roll it into a tube before sticking it in my bag. Then I grab the painting I had custom made and expedited, unroll it, and place it perfectly inside the frame.

I've never used a staple gun before—who even knew such a thing existed?—so it takes me a few tries to get it to work. Fortunately, Pierce isn't likely to remove the painting from the wall, so he won't see the extra staples in the back.

Once I have the frame reattached, I hang it back on the wall and stand back to inspect it. It's perfect. There's no way to tell it's not the original.

I clean up all evidence of my presence. I didn't even wear perfume, in case the scent lingered after I left. When there isn't a single thing that can point to my having been here, and the fake painting is hanging perfectly straight, I lock the front door behind me and head back to the lift.

This time, I'm definitely going to win.

# 33

## "End Game" - Taylor Swift ft. Ed Sheeran, Future

*Pierce*

It's been a long, shitty day. In fact, it's been an even longer and shittier week. There was a major glitch in one of our main software databases, and we only resolved the issue this afternoon, after the team worked around the clock on it for two days.

Now I collect my mail and head to the lift, eager for a workout. Tension emanates from every muscle in my body. I'm entering the code for the tenth floor when the click of heels on tile sounds from the lobby. Instinctively, I glance up.

While seeing Maeve stalk toward me in a short black dress that I'm already envisioning on the floor of this elevator is the last thing I expect, it's certainly the most welcome. Some of the tension in my body immediately starts draining away. Don't ask me why or how. She just has that effect on me, especially tonight. I haven't seen her for several days thanks to the crazy shit going on at Luminara, which has required me to pull some late nights, and I've missed her more than I thought it possible to miss anyone.

Her expression, however, does not show any signs of her having missed me.

Holding out a hand to keep the doors from closing, I give her a slow grin. "Hello, sunshine."

Her face grows more stormy, if that's even possible, as she joins me in the lift. "Where is it?"

"My cock? It's right here, baby." I reach for the front of my trousers. "But maybe we should wait until we're upstairs—"

"Don't be an imbecile." She swats my hand away, and a thrill shoots through me at the brush of her skin against mine, even if her hackles are sharp enough to scratch. "You know exactly what I mean."

"I don't, actually." I cross my ankles and lean against the wall. I'd much rather be putting my hands and mouth on her, but she's as lovable as a porcupine at the moment.

"My perfume, you asshole." Folding her arms over her chest, Maeve glares at me with a ferocity that only increases my desire to kiss her.

"What perfume?" Obviously I know exactly what she's referring to, but it's more fun to watch her grow devastatingly furious. Besides, if fighting turns her on, I'll be getting lucky soon.

"I had that scent custom made," she says. "So give it back."

"What makes you think I have it?" I snuck into her house yesterday after playing her own key trick on her and swiped the bottle from her bathroom. I expected this confrontation last night or this morning, but she must not have discovered it was missing until tonight.

The lift dings, and we both step off. I keep my strides long as I walk to my flat, but she manages to stay right behind me.

"Because I'm not an idiot. Who else would take it?"

Unlocking the door, I shrug. "A stalker, maybe."

She snorts. "You would have been more subtle spray-painting the side of my house with the words 'Pierce was here.'"

I give her a quizzical look as I swing the door open. "I'll keep that in mind for next time."

"There won't be a next time," she says, barging inside like she lives here, and I can't help wondering what it'd be like if she did. "You didn't even try this time. You had to know I'd miss it right away."

"Actually," I say, holding up my index finger, "you didn't miss it for twenty-four hours."

"Only because—" She stops and shakes her head. "Never mind. You obviously don't care about the challenge, so you won't mind if I sweep the table with you this time."

"I can think of a few other things you can do with me on a table."

Rolling her eyes, she holds out her open palm. "Just give me the bottle."

"Why do you need it this second?" I give her outfit another look as I move closer. She's too dressed up for a night in. "Are you going out?"

"That's none of your business. Now, admit defeat and hand it over."

Narrowing my eyes, I run through the possibilities and land on the only logical one. "Are you seeing that fucker tonight?" My head is starting to pound, and the vein in my temple twitches.

Maeve blinks rapidly, taking a tiny step backward. "Of course not," she says, but the truth is written all over her face. She can't lie to save her life.

"The fuck you're not. You're staying with me." I grab her wrist and yank her toward me.

She gasps as she bumps into my chest. "You don't get to tell me what to do."

I laugh loudly and abruptly. "Like hell I don't." Lowering my nose to her neck, I inhale deeply. Even without her perfume, she smells a million fucking times better than anything else on the planet.

"Just give it back, Pierce," she whispers, all of the fight draining out of her the second my lips are on her throat.

"Not if you're going to wear it for him."

"He's my boyfriend."

I pull back and glare down at her. "He's *married*, Maeve."

"You know what I mean," she grumbles. "We hardly get any time together, and—"

"So then he can wait another night."

"That's not fair. You and I are together much more often than—"

"As it should be."

Her mouth drops open, and I resist the urge to kiss it. "Whatever fantasies you have in your head about the two of us will just have to wait for another night, okay?" she says. "Preston and I have plans."

"Where is he going to take you? You can't go anywhere with him, or someone might see you. You can't even get dinner with the bloke, let alone be seen together in public. That doesn't leave a lot of options, does it?"

A red flush stains Maeve's neck and cheeks, but she doesn't try to correct me. I expected her to at the very least say he's flying her to London or renting a villa on the coast, maybe arranging a private dinner at a club in a nearby town. But she stays silent.

The truth hits me squarely between the eyes. "He's not taking you anywhere, is he? You're all dressed up just for him to come over and what? Make you fake an orgasm?"

She swipes a hand over her cheek, leaving behind a streak of moisture. *Shit.*

"Why the fuck did you say yes?" I ask, lowering my voice. "You can do so much better than that." *You deserve to be treated like a fucking queen.*

"He makes me feel safe." Tilting her chin upward, she looks tiny, frail, and so damn scared, despite her best efforts to the contrary.

This is so fucked up. Why would she feel safer with a married man than with me, especially after everything we've gone through? Especially after I practically confessed to having something closely resembling feelings for her a few weeks ago?

"He makes you feel safe," I mutter. "Are you listening to yourself? He's married to someone else. How does that make you feel anything other than repulsed and angry?"

Her glare turns vicious, all traces of tears and fragility gone. In its place is red-hot fire. "You're the only thing making me repulsed and angry right now."

I step back like she's burned me, and then it hits me. She feels safe, because with Ansley, she knows exactly what to expect. The guy's already proven himself to be a cheater, so she'll never be blindsided by him. She doesn't need to fully trust him, which means she remains in control. She's convinced herself that she's the one making all the calls, that the relationship is on her terms.

"You don't actually believe he'll leave his wife, do you?" I say the words slowly, the realization coming like the parting of clouds, the sun finally breaking through. "And you don't even care."

"Fuck you."

"Okay, then." I reach for her again, but she steps backward and lifts a warning finger.

"Don't you dare."

"Maeve," I say, a new level of pleading in my voice. It feels like a spike has been driven through my heart. She thinks she doesn't deserve better than a cheating bastard, because her whole life she's been told she's not enough. This is her way of preventing her heart from getting broken.

She extends her hand, palm up. "Just give me the perfume, and I'll go."

I consider it for two seconds. If he really made her happy, I'd get out of the fucking way. But he doesn't, even if she's convinced herself otherwise. Then another possibility occurs to me.

Leaning forward, I grab her chin and drag her face up to mine.

"Tell me you didn't come here to fight with me so that you'd be ready for him."

Her eyes widen. I can't tell if that was actually her plan, or if she thought of it as a beneficial side effect. Either way, that's not how this is ending.

"No fucking way," I say, then press my shoulder into her stomach and toss her over my shoulder.

"Put me down!" she shrieks, pummeling her fists into my back. I barely feel a thing.

"Not happening, Panther." I smack her ass, which is bare, thanks to her dress sliding up when I grabbed her. "What the fuck," I hiss as my fingers make contact with skin where her thong should be.

She cries out, not in pain but in anger, so I do it again. Her hands come down even harder, but they might as well be cotton balls for all the damage they're doing.

"Why are you not wearing underwear?" I say, heading to the bedroom. "I bought you an entire box."

"It's not like I was going to wear those, was I?" She punctuates each word with another blow.

I shove two fingers into her drenched pussy and groan. No way in hell is she giving this to another man. If I turn her on, I'm the one who gets to fuck her. I drop her unceremoniously onto the bed, and she lands with a small thump. She scrambles backward, keeping her eyes locked on me but making no move to escape.

As I'm shrugging out of my jacket, I see it. On my shoulder, right where she was a second ago, is a small wet patch. "This was a twenty-thousand-dollar suit." I slip the coat off and inhale the scent of her moisture before tossing it aside. "You just made it priceless."

## 34

## "Call It What You Want" - Taylor Swift

*Maeve*

I rush through my shower, and don't you dare ask me why. I don't normally enjoy turning myself into a waterlogged prune, but tonight I've managed to cut my time under the hot spray to five minutes. If I can keep up this pace, he might still be here when I'm finished.

Wrapping a fluffy white towel around myself, I step onto the plush bathmat. As I'm applying moisturizer to my face and neck, I manage to knock one of my earrings onto the floor. I bend over to pick it up, and my gaze catches on the small rubbish bin under the vanity.

I reach for the only thing inside. Confusion swirls through my mind as I stare at the lavender silicone object in my hand. How did this end up in the trash? I definitely didn't throw it away. It's not like I use it very often, but I certainly didn't toss it during a mad decluttering spree.

Which leaves only one explanation.

Tucking my towel tighter around my chest, I walk to the doorway of my bedroom. Pierce is still here, and at the sight of him, my heart picks up speed. He's lying back against the pillows, reading a book with a bright red cover and wearing a black T-shirt, gray sweatpants, and those obscene glasses. It's completely unfair that he looks this good.

"Why was my vibrator in the trash?" I hold up the toy in question, a little mortified that he evidently found it in my bedside table, but my anger is squashing all other emotions at the moment. How dare he go through my things, let alone have the audacity to dispose of them at will?

He glances up from his reading with a bored expression on his face. "You don't need a fucking vibrator." Then he flips another page as though this conversation is over.

I let out a disbelieving laugh. "I'll be the one to determine that, thanks."

His eyes cut to mine, fingers stilling on the corner of the paper. "Explain to me why you need it."

"Uh—" I start, but the ridiculousness of this situation is making it difficult to form an answer. "Because this is the twenty-first century, and if I choose to masturbate, that is my right."

The book shuts with a soft snap that makes my heart jolt. Pierce swings his legs over the side of the bed and approaches me with the precision of a jungle cat. I consider bolting to the bathroom and locking myself in, but he'll only stay by the door until I come out. I've tried it before.

He stops once he's directly in front of me, close enough that I can smell his stupid fucking cologne and feel the heat of his body against my bare skin. He's still wearing those stupidly sexy glasses, which only infuriates me more. It's like he wears them on purpose whenever he wants to win a fight.

Faster than I can blink, he grabs the vibrator from my hand and tosses it onto the bed behind him. "I've told you before, your orgasms are my responsibility."

I suck in a breath, my brain gravely starved of oxygen. Taking a step back to put some much-needed distance between us, I cross my arms over my chest. "And what if you're in a meeting?"

He laughs humorlessly. "I hate meetings." This is, in fact, the truth, but it does nothing to prove his point.

"You expect me to believe that you'll walk out of a meeting to give me an orgasm?" A short laugh escapes my mouth.

Now it's his turn to fold his arms over his chest, and his biceps strain at the fabric of his shirt sleeves. Again, absolutely unfair. "I'd clear the room and fuck you on the table if that's what you needed."

Images of him doing that exact thing flash through my mind, and I remind myself that I have a fight to win. Now is not the time to imagine Pierce going down on me in a boardroom. "What if it's a really important meeting?" It's a stupid thing to say, but you try arguing with a Greek god in glasses and see what you come up with.

"How is that relevant?" he asks, inclining his head until I can see flecks of gold in his dark eyes.

I shrug, then quickly grab my towel before it can slide off. "I just think that, depending on the importance of the meeting, you might change your mi—"

He bunches the terrycloth in his hand and yanks me against his chest. "Maybe you didn't hear what I said. Every orgasm you need, you will get from me." With his other hand, he tilts my chin up so that I have to meet his eyes. "Understand?"

Swallowing the sudden lump in my throat, I say, "What if—"

But then his mouth is on mine, his tongue pushing into it and stealing all my words. With a quick tug of his wrist, the towel falls off my body and pools onto the floor. Moving my face upward with his hand, he uses the leverage to press even deeper.

His hand travels up my hip and over my side, moving slowly, as though he's touching the softest velvet. When he reaches my breast, he cups it and teases the nipple, which forms a hard peak under his fingers.

I moan into his mouth, and he pinches my nipple.

He pulls back just far enough to ask, "Are we clear?"

I murmur something that sounds like agreement but wouldn't hold up in court.

"Maeve," he warns, moving away from my greedy mouth. "No more vibrator unless I'm the one holding it. You text me any time you need me, and I'll come. Got it?"

God, he's really not going to let this go. "Yes," I say, and hungrily lurch for him. I need his mouth on me, I need his hands on me, I need his body pressing down on me. I need him like you need black Louboutins—eessential, necessary, vital.

I know it's a bad position to be in—dependent on another human being. It will come back to bite me in the ass. But right now, the only ass I'm thinking about is Pierce St. James's, and holy fuck, it is a fine one.

\* \* \*

Several hours of mind-blowing sex later—including one vibrator-induced climax that far surpassed anything I've ever given myself—Pierce and I are brushing our teeth at the double sink. Our gazes snag in the mirror above the vanity, and the moment feels so intimate, so *domestic*. He spits and rinses, then tosses the toothbrush into the holder with a clatter.

I pause midscrub, mouth filled with foam. "What are you doing?"

He wipes his lips with the back of his hand and gives me a skeptical look in the glass. "Putting my toothbrush in the cup?"

"You don't *have* a toothbrush," I say, then rinse the paste from my mouth. He asked for an extra one earlier, but when I gave it to him, it wasn't an invitation to leave it here.

## "CALL IT WHAT YOU WANT" - TAYLOR SWIFT

"I do now." He winks and walks out the door.

I rest my palms on the counter and lean against it for strength. What is happening here? Staring at the blue toothbrush next to my purple one in the holder, I feel a cloud of anxiety press down on me.

I know what happens when you start keeping things at each other's houses. Feelings get involved, and feelings mean messiness. Pierce and I can hardly function like normal human beings under the best of circumstances. Put us both at our worst, and someone's likely to die.

This is supposed to be a benefits-only relationship, but it's starting to feel like a . . . *relationship* relationship.

Should I feel flattered that he evidently wants more than I'm willing to give? Probably. A thousand women would kill to be in my position. Not only is he one of the wealthiest and most powerful people in this country, but I genuinely enjoy spending time with him. At least when he's not making me want to rip his head from his shoulders, so like 5 percent of the time, but that 5 percent is incredible.

But I'm not willing to give him what I know he wants from me. He won't ever be happy with only a piece of me. A man like that never is. They want everything from you—body, mind, soul. And I just can't do that. The only thing I can give is my body. If he wants it, it's his. But if he wants more, he's going to be disappointed.

I grab the latest issue of *Vogue France* and join Pierce on the bed. It's late, but if I go to sleep now, he'll either leave or slip beneath the duvet too, and I'm equally terrified by both prospects. It's completely moronic, but neither option brings me comfort. So I flop down on my stomach and flip through the glossy pages. In truth, I've already read this issue, but if I don't have something to distract me, god only knows what I'll let him do to me.

Seconds later, his fingertips begin tracing the curve of my spine. I'm wearing a backless slip in midnight-blue silk. His attention is back on his book, but his hand casually drifts up and down my back as he reads.

Goosebumps break out across my skin, and I fight the urge to shiver. His touch is electric, and for a brief moment, I let myself imagine what life with him would be like. Would we spend our evenings like this, touching each other like our existence didn't depend on it, brushing past each other in the bathroom, planning our weeks around and with each other?

It's not a bad picture. It's actually quite lovely, if I'm being honest. It's the thought of doing those things with Pierce that sends a bolt of terror through me. He wouldn't allow me to lead, to be in charge. One minute with the guy will tell you as much. And I need control, need it like oxygen. The only reason this situationship has worked so far is because both of us have retained power. If I were to give it up to him—

"I have one more question." His voice startles me, and I look up.

His eyes are still on the book in front of him, so it must not be important. I make a noncommittal sound and return my gaze to the magazine. The way his fingers are traveling over my back has me in a near coma.

"Who did you think of when you used it?"

My hand halts mid page-flip. "What?" I glance over at him, genuinely confused. "When I used what?"

"Your vibrator." He continues stroking my skin, his eyes still glued to his book, although the set of his jaw tells me he's not reading a word. "Did you think of him?"

My blood throbs so violently through my veins, I feel like I might spontaneously combust. We're treading dangerous waters, and it both terrifies and excites me. One wrong move and I'll send us both over the edge, but isn't that the fun of it?

"Who?" I say innocently, and continue poring over the pages of

*Vogue*. I know exactly who he means, just like I know exactly what he's asking. It doesn't mean I'm obligated to answer him.

"You know who," he says through his teeth.

I smirk at the restraint he's obviously exerting as he pretends not to be bothered by this conversation. A conversation he chose to start, I might add. Flipping to a spread of Imaan Hammam, I shake my head and say as nonchalantly as possible, "No, I don't."

His book closes with a snap, and I bite back a smile. "Fuck it, Maeve. Do you think of that lowlife with a wife when you're getting yourself off?" Pierce withdraws his hand from my back, evidently no longer able to concentrate on anything but the subject of my vibrator.

"That really bothered you, didn't it?"

"Yeah, it did. Now answer the question."

I can feel his eyes on me, and I swallow under the weight of that stare. It's my turn to pretend to be absorbed by a publication. "That's none of your business."

"Regardless, I need to know."

Tilting my chin up, I steel myself to meet his eyes, knowing the power they have over me. "Need and want are two very different things. Didn't they teach you that in primary school?" He's still wearing the glasses. Fuck my life. "And for the love of god, can you please take those off?" I add, gesturing at them.

He frowns and adjusts the black frames. "Why?"

"Because they give you an unfair advantage," I snap, without thinking.

Realization dawns on his face like the sunrise, and I immediately kick myself for once again opening my mouth when I should have kept it shut. "An unfair advantage," he muses. "Your entire body is an unfair advantage."

My cheeks heat, and I drop my gaze back to the magazine in my hands.

"Maeve, answer the question." Pierce's warning tone sends a bolt of pleasure to my core. "Do you get off imagining him doing that to you?"

He's not going to let it go. The only way out is through. "No," I say, my voice small.

"Who then?"

God, I should have known that answer wouldn't be enough for him. He always wants more than I can give. "Can't you be satisfied knowing it's not him?" I turn the next page so violently it rips.

"No, I can't. Not until I know who you envision," he says.

"Why? What are you going to do when you find out?" I glare at him. "Hunt him down?"

Pierce's face is as hard as stone, nostrils flaring with everything he's holding back.

"I'm done with this conversation," I say, flipping another page and tearing it, too.

"You're done when I say you're done." He snatches up the magazine. "Who is it, Maeve? Just tell me."

"No."

"Tell me. *Now*."

My breath catches in my throat. Part of me wants to tell him. Another part of me thrills at this game, the one neither of us ever seems to win, but which neither of us can stop playing. "I don't want to."

"Why not?" He tosses the issue of *Vogue* aside, and it hits the floor with a thump.

I swallow again, but the lump in my throat has doubled in size. "I—"

His eyes narrow and grow several shades darker, as if he can sense that I'm considering lying to him. Fuck it. He'll never leave if I don't just tell him the truth.

"Fine. I imagined you. Happy now?"

He doesn't smile or look relieved. Instead, the lines on his face only grow deeper, and the hardness in his eyes increases. He fucking glowers at me.

"Are you—*mad*?" I ask, incredulous. Why is he upset about this? He should be overjoyed. I gave him the answer he wanted, and fortunately for both of us, it also happens to be the truth. There is no one else in the world who can make me come faster than Pierce St. James.

"I'm fucking pissed."

I gape at him, no longer able to suspend my disbelief. "Why? I just told you it was you—"

"Yeah, I know," he says, grabbing my chin. "I'm pissed because those orgasms belonged to me."

# 35

# "Nothing's Gonna Hurt You Baby" - Cigarettes After Sex

*Pierce*

Some of my favorite things in this world are the ones that require extra care, special handling, and white-glove service—rare pieces of art, historical documents and artifacts, and Maeve Wilson.

Pulling up outside her house, I put the car in park and let it idle, watching a well-dressed couple make their way down the sidewalk, him pushing a stroller, her holding the leash of a tiny white dog. I'm several minutes early, and I don't want Maeve to flip out on me.

I know we're on thin ice. I felt it cracking beneath us last week when I insisted on staying over several nights. The toothbrush thing nearly gave her an aneurysm. I thought I was moving slowly, but goddamn it, the woman is so skittish she acts like I'm trying to put a ring on her finger.

Am I? I don't fucking know. I don't think so. It's not like I have a lot of spare time to think about getting married and having kids. God, I'm only twenty-six.

My eyes focus on the couple again. They've stopped at a park bench, and she's bending over the stroller doing something with the kid while he holds the dog. They don't look any older than me, maybe even a little younger.

I'm lucky enough not to have parents who breathe down my neck about shit like that. They'd rather see me build another billion-dollar empire than father a bunch of grandchildren for them.

Obviously I've thought about it before, but only in that vague sense of "that's at least five or ten years down the road." It's been the cause of most of my breakups. They all wanted something long-term, to lock me into something permanent, and I just couldn't do it.

Maybe I wasn't ready yet, or maybe I've just never been with the right person. And I'm not saying Maeve is the right person, but she's sure as hell the only person I want to spend any time with at the moment. Rhett texted me about golfing yesterday, and I found myself first asking Maeve if she was free. It wasn't until after she said she was stuck in a meeting that I responded to him.

Tell me why there's a physical ache in my chest when she's not with me, and sometimes even when she is. We can be laughing and having the best time together, and all of a sudden, I see the blinds close over her eyes. She shuts herself off from me after that, and I'm left wondering how I fucked up this time.

I'm not stupid enough to fall in love. Not with her, not with anyone. My parents didn't do much to raise me—that's what they paid the best nannies in the country for—but there are a few lessons they managed to instill in me. One of them being that love makes you weak.

So before you go thinking that I'm head over heels for Maeve or some stupid shit like that, just know that that's not what this is. I think it's that I've finally met my match. We're both competitive enough to keep each other at our best. I like that. Do you know how hard it is to find someone who is your equal in every way?

I may have caught feelings, but who the fuck can define those anyway? There are plenty of feelings besides love. All I know is that I need that woman more than I need anything else on this earth, and I'll fight anyone who tries to get in my way.

I climb out of the car and approach Maeve's front door, my heart pounding in my chest like a fucking jackhammer. Tonight is essentially a date, whether she wants to admit it or not. It's probably a stupid idea that will backfire, but after she said she felt safer with that fuckwit Preston than she did with me, I knew something needed to change. I may not be able to help her fully relax, but I sure as fuck can make her feel safe.

Knocking on the door, I listen for the click of her heels on the other side. I could go on in—I have a key after all—but that would only rile her up more than necessary. While I enjoy playing with my food before I eat it, I know better than to tease a cobra.

My hands in my pockets like a teenager on his first date, I prop an elbow against the door frame as I wait for Maeve to show up. Maybe if I act nonchalant, my stupid galloping heart will take heed and follow suit.

She opens the door seconds later in a short flared black dress with an off-the-shoulder neckline that leaves her shoulders and collarbones exposed. I swallow loudly and straighten.

"Hey," I say, fighting the urge to take her back inside and do all of the dirty things currently parading through my imagination. "You look incredible."

The look she shoots me is both guarded and apprehensive. "Thanks." She locks the door behind her, then follows me to the car.

Silence surrounds us as we drive, but I know she won't be able to handle it for long. Sure enough, we're still on Twenty-Fifth when she turns from the window to face me. "Where are we going?"

I smile and keep my eyes on the road, something I need to do all night if I want us to arrive in one piece, even if exploring what's beneath her dress sounds more appealing. "It's a surprise."

"I don't like surprises."

"I know," I say. "You'll survive."

Folding her arms over her chest, she lets out an annoyed huff. "That's assuming the surprise isn't you killing me in a back alley somewhere."

"Babe, please." I give her a horrified look. "I have way more class than that. At the very least, I'd do it in the Allerton penthouse suite."

I'm rewarded with a tiny smile that she immediately hides by turning her attention back to the window. We ride in silence for a few more minutes, then she says, "Just tell me, Pierce."

I don't say anything for a few beats, waiting. When she finally looks at me, I hold her gaze. "Why can't you trust me?"

Her hands twist together in her lap, the only indication that she's experiencing anything emotionally, because her face remains stony. "I don't trust anyone but myself."

"I know." Nodding to show her I get it, I merge onto the freeway leading out of the city. "But I want you to be able to trust me, too."

Maeve sighs deeply. "It's nothing against you. I just—"

I reach over and grab her hands, which are still knotting together. "Hey, listen to me. I'm not going to hurt you." Lifting them to my lips, I press a kiss against her skin, which smells of vanilla.

She stops twisting her fingers, but she refuses to meet my eyes. "You can't know that," she says softly.

"And you can't know that I will." Glancing back at the road every other second, I drop her hands and tilt her chin up. I need to see her eyes when I say what I'm going to say next. "You don't have to do everything alone. Let me help you."

Her long lashes brush against her cheeks as she blinks at me. Finally, she says, "Okay."

That single word makes my chest surge with emotion. I desperately want to pull the car over and kiss her madly, because this feels like a breakthrough. But I don't. Baby steps, remember? I can't afford to send her running again.

Instead, I tuck her hand in my own and raise it to my lips once more, needing her scent in my nostrils and her porcelain skin against mine. She gives me a shy smile in return, and I feel as high as a fucking kite.

\* \* \*

Forty-five minutes later, I pull up outside a small gallery. Maeve's fingers are still entwined with my own, a miracle in itself, and she never questioned me about our destination again—miracle number two.

I circle the car and open her door, offering my hand as she climbs out. She takes it without hesitation and doesn't even pull away as we walk to the door. Is this what progress looks like?

We step inside the swanky gallery. Soft jazz music greets us, and black-and-white photographs hang on the exposed brick walls. Tonight's featured artist, Finnegan Sinclair, is someone I've never heard of before—probably because he's still a university student—but I needed a place that was far enough out of the city no one would spot Maeve and me together. Not because I don't want to be seen with her—god, I'd shout it from the rooftops—but because I know she's weird about stuff like that.

A server brings us flutes of champagne on a tray, and Maeve and I clink our glasses together. She keeps her eyes locked on mine as she takes a sip, and I want nothing more than to sink my teeth into her red lips. As if she can read my mind, she gives her left brow a slight cock, her mouth tugging up on the same side.

Pulling her arm through mine, I lead her around the room as we study the photographs. They're exceptional—the kid clearly has talent—but if I'm being honest, only about 10 percent of my attention is on the artwork. The rest is absorbed by the woman at my side, who smells like a dream and looks like a goddess. I can't get her out of my head no matter how hard I try. And before you call me out on it—no, I'm not exactly trying. I'm not a bloody idiot.

"I love this one," Maeve breathes out as she stops in front of a photo of a pier at sunset.

It's black-and-white like all the others, but you can make out the fading sunlight hitting the wooden planks and the water surrounding it. At the end sits a solitary figure, long hair blowing in the breeze. Her face is slightly angled toward the camera, as if she's just said something to the photographer.

"It's beautiful." I brace myself as Maeve pulls away, afraid our perfect night is already drawing to a close, but she's only leaning in for a better look, her hand staying perched in the crook of my elbow. "What do you feel when you look at it?" I ask.

"I feel . . ." She stops, eyes still glued to the picture. "I feel . . . peaceful."

I study her, and then I see it—the softness, the lightness in her face and eyes. "Yeah," I murmur, mesmerized by the change in her features. "Me too."

The gallery owner approaches us, sniffing a potential deal, and strikes up a conversation. "The artist is here, if you'd like to meet him," she says, gesturing to a young man chatting with several people near the entrance.

I look at Maeve, waiting to see what she wants to do. "It's your call, babe." It slips out before I've even registered it. We're not big on pet names—not unless they're being used as a joke—so it hits me out of left field.

She takes it in stride though, blinking once before turning to the owner. "Yeah, sure."

"We'll also take this one," I say, nodding at the photograph.

* * *

"That was . . . really nice," Maeve says as we pull into the underground car park at the Atlantis. "Thank you."

I squint at her and turn off the engine. "Did you just pay me a compliment?"

"What?" She laughs. "I give compliments."

"Yeah, like Scrooge," I say, opening her door.

She socks me playfully in the stomach as we ride the lift up to my floor, and I tug her in close under my arm. If I had to describe what it feels like to be with her, I'd say it feels like home.

Once we're inside the flat, I unwrap the framed photo and hold it out. "Do you want to take this home or should we hang it up here?"

"You really didn't need to buy it, you know."

"I know." I set it against the wall and cup her face, then lean down to give her a long kiss. "I wanted to." I'd buy out the entire gallery if it would make her happy.

She rises on her tiptoes and kisses me again. "Let's put it up here."

I was hoping she'd say that, hoping it will give her even more reason to visit, to feel like she belongs here. "Great," I say, hardly able to tear myself away from her mouth. "But it will have to wait for later. Because I have another surprise for you."

She gives me a droll look. "Pierce, I've seen your cock a thousand times."

Giving her a mock glare, I tweak her nose. "That's the surprise after the surprise."

"I told you, I don't like—"

"And I told you to trust me." I grab her hand, twining our fingers together, because you'll have to kill me before I'm letting this woman go. "Now come with me."

We take the elevator to the rooftop, and Maeve surprisingly refrains from putting me through the Spanish Inquisition on the way up. She just rests her head against my arm, making my insides churn. Is this what people mean when they describe feeling butterflies? It doesn't feel like fucking insects flying around, but it also doesn't feel like anything I've experienced before.

When the doors to the private terrace open, Maeve stifles a tiny gasp. "Is this where you kill me?"

I take her hand and lead her to the small table lit with candles. "Yes, but first let's have some wine. It will help with your crash landing later."

The place is completely decked out. There are twinkle lights everywhere, speakers playing some kind of sappy pop music, and a vase of red roses perched in the center of the table. I hired an event planner to set it up, but I said "date night," not fucking "proposal." Still, Maeve looks a bit in awe, which makes it all worth it.

A server wheels over a cart of plates covered by silver cloches and sets them before us. It's a beautiful night, the sun low in the sky, the air still balmy with residual heat from the day. Across from me, Maeve shivers and rubs her arms. I guess I'm the only one who thinks it's still warm.

I shrug off my jacket and drape it over her shoulders. She protests, but I ignore her, pressing a kiss to her hair before sitting back down. I may not be good at relationships, but I do know how to take care of a woman.

She tucks her hair behind her ear and takes a sip of wine. I wonder if she even knows she's doing it, if she knows I have all her tells memorized like catechism. That one right there means she's slightly embarrassed, and next she's going to say something that's borderline aggressive, because defensiveness is her favorite coping mechanism.

"You didn't have to go to all this trouble to get me into bed," she says, smirking. "You could have just asked."

And the shields are back up.

I reach for her hand across the table, play with her fingers, wait for her to lower those defenses. "I wanted to."

She doesn't know what to do with that. I'll bet that fucker of a boyfriend never does anything like this for her, and the guys she's dated in the past have all been fuckwit university boys who think that beer pong is a recreational sport.

"Maeve." My voice sounds like sandpaper, and I clear my throat, but there's still a lot of emotion clogging it, making it difficult to get anything out without sounding like a kid going through puberty. "Listen, I—"

"I need to use the restroom." She stands up, pulling her hand from mine and tossing her napkin onto her untouched plate. "Excuse me."

And then she's gone, if not from my life, then at least from me. My heart sinks to the bottom of my chest. It feels like all the progress we made tonight just plummeted over the side of the building. Is this a taste of what it'll feel like when she finally walks away from me for good?

Her phone vibrates on the table, the screen lighting up. I glance at it, partly out of habit, mostly out of pure curiosity. Who's texting her while she's with me?

**Preston**: *Hey babe, can I see you tonight? I miss you. xx*

I clench my hands into fists and press them into my thighs. Is this why she shut down just now? Or was it because something fucked up in her brain told her she still can't trust me? Meanwhile, this complete wanker is slipping out behind his wife's back to see Maeve, and she says he makes her feel safe.

Somebody please explain this to me, because from where I'm

standing, it's all going to shit, and there isn't a damn thing I can do about it.

# 36

## "us." - Gracie Abrams ft. Taylor Swift

*Maeve*

It's the beginning of June, and you know what that means. Well, you would if you ran in our circles. Every year, my parents usher in summer with an annual house party. And I know what you're thinking. You're imagining something out of Austen or Brontë, where a group of people spend weeks at the same house in the country hunting and playing cards and promenading around the gardens.

This is nothing like that. Well, it's a little like that, except there is indoor plumbing and everyone goes home after the weekend, thank god.

The party begins on Friday afternoon and lasts until Sunday evening, when everyone makes the trek back to the city. We spend those two and a half days at Belgrave Park, a country estate that's been in the Wilson family for generations.

It's a gothic mansion—huge even by our standards—that takes a ridiculous amount of money to keep up. Built in the eighteenth century, back when men used to play "how big is your dick" by building grander houses than their neighbors, its numerous spires poke at the sky as if they're taunting God Himself. The main section has three stories, but the turrets have up to seven. With thirty-five bedrooms, there's more than enough space for fifty guests to spread out.

A set of gigantic ornate metal gates swing open as our car pulls up. The grounds used to span hundreds of acres, but each generation seems to sell off more and more land to pay for repairs to the house and outbuildings. By the time the property gets passed down to one of my father's children, the gardens will be the size of a postage stamp.

Vivienne's obsessed with the place. I have no idea why, except that my sister is a bit of a head case, which you'd know if you'd ever met her. She prefers the countryside and her horses to the city with its sophistication and parties. Weird, I know, but that's Viv for you. If my father has any sense about him, he'll leave Belgrave Park to her, but more than likely, he'll make me deal with it as a final "fuck you" from the grave.

All of the Wilson children are expected to be in attendance this weekend, because there is nothing my mother loves more than parading her offspring in front of her insipid friends. Fortunately for my sanity, I've managed to wrangle invitations for all of my own friends this year, something neither of my siblings was able to do, which means Viv will practically be living in the stables all weekend and Bash will be doing god only knows what behind his closed bedroom door.

My mother insisted I accompany her to the house early, though for what purpose I can't tell you, since she hired an event planner and enough staff to service an entire hotel, but I'm sure I'm about to find out. I'm nothing if not a dutiful daughter, so I'm riding with her to the Park instead of with my friends.

I will admit, there's something about the country air. It's like it lightens you or something. That's stupid, I know, but I can't explain it. Wildflowers and freshly cut grass may not be my favorite scents in the world, but they do remind me of summer.

As guests start to arrive, I keep my eyes peeled for a familiar vehicle. I'm excited to see everyone, not just *him*, obviously. Usually this weekend is a bore. This year it might actually be fun.

When Heath's Grenadier pulls up in front of the house, I take a steadying breath. Walker and Saylor climb out, and the guys grab the luggage from the back. Pierce isn't with them, and I swallow my disappointment as I greet them. Moments later, Lux's Ferrari purrs up the driveway, Slate behind the wheel. The top is down, and it's immediately apparent that they came alone.

Once everyone's gathered in the front parlor and the staff is bustling the luggage to each of the assigned bedrooms, I glance around and say as nonchalantly as possible, "Where's Pierce?"

"He wanted to drive up by himself," Heath says.

Before I can ask anything else, my mother waves at me from the entrance. Fighting the urge to roll my eyes, I set my drink down on the sideboard and move to the door. "I'll be right back."

Fifteen minutes later, I've helped my mother solve the crisis of dinner placements, which wasn't a crisis at all, but some mock disaster she created in the recesses of that terrifying brain of hers. What does it matter if Freida McIntire sits next to her ex-husband? Maybe the meal would actually be interesting for a change.

I return to the parlor, and before I see him, I know he's here. There's a change in the atmosphere, or maybe my body just responds to his because I've become so familiar with it over the past four months.

Pierce is casually leaning against the fireplace mantle, talking to Saylor and Rhett, but the second his eyes land on me, he stops midsentence. In a light blue sweater, navy trousers, and white sneakers, he looks more relaxed than usual. His gaze wanders lazily over my face, as if he's memorizing it and has all the time in the world.

My cheeks heat under his attention, and I quickly retrieve my now lukewarm glass of Long Island iced tea, draining it in one go. His eyes are still on me—I can feel them as easily as I would his fingertips—but I know he's covering his tracks well. While it may feel like he's staring, it's only because I'm hyperaware of every movement he makes. He won't be careless enough to let anyone catch him looking.

Lux is interrogating Walker about her wedding gown, insisting she let her commission a designer from Paris. I pretend to be listening, but it's hard to focus when the only thing I can think of is Pierce. We've only been together a handful of times since he took me to the art gallery, and that was two weeks ago.

Our date that night was actually kind of wonderful, at least until I realized just how hot the water I'm standing in is. We were having fun, the kind of fun you have with someone you *like*. And I don't like Pierce. I can't even tolerate the guy. Doing those things with him, spending time with him like that—it messed with my head. I haven't been able to stop thinking about him since. I know I need to stop—that this whole fucked-up situation needs to stop—but I don't know how. I don't know how I'll get through shitty days when my dad is yelling at me or my mum is nagging me about still not having found anyone who wants me without knowing I can see Pierce in a matter of hours. He's the rock that's getting me through the storm right now, and I just don't know how to let him go.

I don't *want* to let him go.

"Maeve?" Walker asks, giving me a weird look. "You okay?"

Shaking my head, I try to remember what they were talking about. "What? Yeah, I'm fine."

She doesn't appear convinced. "You were kind of spacing out there for a second."

"I'm just tired." I wave my hand as though it's no big deal, and my eyes catch Pierce's at the same moment. "In fact," I say, hoping his telepathy is working, "I should go see if my mother needs any more help."

I shoot Walker and Lux both apologetic smiles and risk one more glance at Pierce. He raises his tumbler to his lips, giving me a subtle nod.

My heart racing, I slip back through the crowd congregating in the parlor and front hall, hoping Pierce will somehow be able to figure out where I've gone. This is crazy—the chances of getting caught are way too high—but I'm desperate enough to try it anyway.

When did I become so reckless, so willing to abandon everything for a few stolen moments? It's not like me, and that thought alone should stop me in my tracks, but it doesn't.

I don't pause to catch my breath until I'm in the north wing of the house. Sagging against the wall of the corridor, I glance up to find the eyes of some long-forgotten ancestor staring at me from the oil painting hung on the opposite side. His beady black eyes mock me with their all-knowing stare.

Footsteps sound down the hall, and I turn to find Pierce walking toward me. I get the strange urge to run to him and throw myself into his arms. What the hell is wrong with me?

Before my malfunctioning brain can get any ideas, I reach behind me for the closest doorknob. I turn it and stumble into the library, Pierce right behind me.

The second the door is closed, he grabs my face and kisses me deeply. "God, I've missed you," he breathes out. He threads his fingers through my hair and tilts my face up to his.

"No, you're just horny," I say, unwilling to consider the possibility that he might be right, because if he's right about missing me, that introduces all kinds of problems that I don't have the mental bandwidth to deal with right now.

He doesn't say anything, just hikes my dress up and lifts me into his arms. Seconds later, I feel the bookcase at my back, the wooden shelves pressing into me from behind, Pierce pressing into me from in front.

"Are you ready for me, baby?" he asks in a hushed voice laced with restraint.

I can feel his erection against my stomach, hard and throbbing, aching for *me*. For three whole seconds, I allow myself to imagine what if. What if we didn't have to sneak around? What if we could do this whenever we wanted? What if I acknowledged out loud that he's become my safe place?

But I push those thoughts aside and nod. "I'm so ready."

He growls in my ear. "That's good, because I'm about to fuck you so hard the entire house hears you screaming."

\* \* \*

Within ten minutes of entering the library, we're already slipping back out. Pierce did not, in fact, fuck me hard enough for the entire house full of people to hear me, but that had more to do with my determination to stay quiet, not how hard he was slamming into me. If we had been alone— Well, let's just say my voice might be a bit raspy right now.

The hallway is still deserted, so we make our way back to the front of the house, where we hopefully have not been missed. More guests have arrived since we snuck away, and the front hall is teeming with luggage, floral sundresses, and boat shoes.

"God, I've never seen so much seersucker," Pierce says behind me from our vantage point in the corridor.

"It's like Tory Burch threw up in here," I add.

"They'll be six drinks deep within the hour, don't worry." My sister

Vivienne shoots us a bored look as she brushes past us.

I frown, wondering how much she gathered from how close Pierce and I are standing to each other. I can't put more distance between us without stepping out of the dim recesses of the hallway, and right now, that seems worse than staying here. Especially with Pierce's warm strength at my back.

Scanning the room for our friends so we can start our own drinking spree, my eyes land on the last person in the world I expected to be here this weekend. Pierce must see him at the same time I do, because I feel him tense up behind me.

"What the fuck is he doing here?" he says quietly.

We both watch as Preston greets several people with a wide smile, shaking hands and clapping them on the back, ever the diplomat.

"I have no idea," I reply, and it's the truth. If I'd known my mother was planning to invite him, I would have done everything in my power to prevent it. Not because I don't want to see him, but because this is a disaster waiting to happen.

"Don't lie to me." Pierce's voice is a low rumble in my ear. "You helped plan this party."

I turn to gape at him. "Exactly what are you insinuating?"

His eyes have taken on an disinterested look, as if everything about me suddenly bores him. "You expect me to believe this was nothing but a coincidence?"

"You know what?" I say, glaring up at him. "You're right. I wanted to keep my options open this weekend."

He studies me for a few seconds through narrowed eyes. "Yeah? Well, maybe I will too."

"Fuck you," I bite out, hating him more right now than I thought possible after the last few months.

"You just did," he growls, and yanks me flush against him.

"Get your hands off me." I slap my palms uselessly against his chest.

He doesn't release me, only leans in until his lips are hovering right above my ear, his scent making my nose tickle with the need to drink him in. "You say that, but you don't mean it."

I force myself to breathe through my mouth, so as not to add his addictive scent to the list of things I'm fighting against here. "You don't know the first thing about what I mean."

His lips trace the shell of my ear as he says, "Need I remind you that I am intimately acquainted with your sounds? I know which whimper means 'yes, just like that' and which one means 'a little to the left, baby.'"

A shiver runs through me.

"There's very little of your body that hasn't been in my mouth at one point or another, so yeah, I think I can claim to know what you mean. But if you think you can do better than me, go ahead and try." He releases me so suddenly, I stumble backward.

I hold up a warning finger. "Don't you dare patronize me."

"Hey, what's going on?" I glance over to find Heath and Walker watching us, concern etched on their faces.

"Maeve's off her meds." Pierce winces and throws me a look that has me balling my hands into fists at my sides. "Looks like it will be a long weekend."

"I'll show you 'long weekend.'" I lunge for him, but Heath grabs me before I can swing my fist into Pierce's face.

"You're attracting attention," Heath whispers before letting me go.

One look down the hall proves he's right. More than a few curious glances are being thrown our way.

Pierce is biting back a shit-eating grin, and I've never wanted to gouge the eyes out of someone more. I flip him off as I stalk past Walker, who appears unprepared for two of her best friends wanting to kill each other.

I find my mother in the front hall, perfect hostess smile in place, although I have no doubt that internally she's solving no less than three crises that have arisen in the past half hour.

"There you are," she says, placing a hand on my arm as though we're an affectionate family. "Can you show the Hamiltons to their suite?"

I frown at her. "Don't we have staff for that?"

She gives me a glare sandwiched between faux amusement and adoration—the glare's for me, the other two are for the Hamiltons. "They're all busy at the moment."

"I actually need to talk to you," I say, ignoring the couple and motioning for my mother to come with me. The Hamiltons can wait five seconds until one of the busboys can grab their luggage.

Surprisingly, she follows me, but her lips are squashed into a line so flat, I have no doubt she intends to use the opportunity to berate me for my lack of obedience. Now probably isn't a good time to remind her that I'm twenty-six years old and no longer need to march to her commands like an infantry soldier.

"Did you invite the Ansleys?" I say once we're away from listening ears. "I didn't see them on the guest list." There's no way I would have overlooked the name.

She blinks at me in surprise, probably shocked to hear I was paying attention to her little party. "I did, but it was a last-minute thing. The Diedlots canceled, and I didn't want empty chairs at dinner."

"Of course not." I shudder. "The abhorrence."

"Mock me all you want, Maeve Allegra," she warns, "but someday you'll be in my shoes, and then you'll understand the importance of a nicely balanced table. Of course, you'll need to find a man first—"

"Please, Mother." Holding up my hand, I add, "I already have your speech memorized. Save us both the time." I turn away and head for the hall that leads outside. Right now, I'd kill for some fresh air.

The gardens at Belgrave Park are a work of art, as any belonging to a large house should be. Perfectly trimmed hedges, cascading blossoms in all shapes and colors, gleaming stone walks leading to worlds unknown. I fill my lungs with the warm summer air and let Pierce, my mum, and the chaos awaiting us this weekend melt away.

"Maeve?"

I open my eyes and spin around. I didn't realize I wasn't alone.

Preston is leaning against the side of the house near the French doors, an unlit cigarette between his fingers. He's wearing tan trousers and a crisp white shirt that sets off his dark hair. "What are you doing out here?" he asks.

Checking to make sure no one can see us from inside, I move toward him. "I could ask you the same thing."

He holds up the cigarette, one side of his mouth pulling up in that lopsided smile I love.

"Not out here." I gesture around at the garden. "At the house party."

"Ahh." He nods and tucks the cigarette back into his pocket. He hasn't smoked in years, but he told me just holding it brings him a sense of relief. "Your mother invited us?" It sounds like a question, and his passiveness about it only furthers my irritation.

"Why didn't you decline?" I hiss, taking another step closer. He should have known better than to accept. This is playing with fire.

He shakes his head and looks off into the distance, as though the clouds might hold the answer. "Janie was the one who accepted. By the time she mentioned it to me, she'd already spoken to your mum."

I press my fingers to my temples, a migraine building deep within my skull.

"Are you—" He touches my forearm, and his fingers feel warm, almost clammy. "Are you upset?"

"No, I'm not upset," I snap. "I'm freaking out."

"Why?" Deep frown lines are etched across his forehead.

"Because, Preston," I say, swinging my arms around. "You're here with your wife and your mistress. Don't you see any cause for concern in that picture?"

He stares at me for a few beats before answering. "Not really, no."

"Unbelievable," I mutter.

"Hey." Reaching for me, he tugs me into his arms. "I'm just thrilled I get to see you for an entire weekend."

"It's not like we can be together." My words are muffled by the starchy fabric of his shirt.

"Who knows?" he says. "Maybe we'll find the perfect opportunity. I miss you."

"Yeah, maybe," I mumble, but there isn't an ounce of hope in my heart, just a giant vat of anxiety.

# 37

## "Mr. Brightside" - The Killers

*Pierce*

After figuring out which room is mine, I toss my duffel onto the bed with a sigh. This weekend is already off to a fucking great start. Maeve and I hooked up in the library, then within minutes she was yelling at me, all because her weasel of a boyfriend showed up and she didn't appreciate me asking questions.

The old-fashioned I had earlier has done nothing to calm my nerves, and as soon as I unpack my stuff, I'm heading back downstairs to find another drink.

There's a basket on the dresser containing a bottle of vintage red, some artisanal chocolates and snacks, and a folder containing a floor plan of the house, an intricate overview of the grounds and their activities, and a detailed itinerary for the next forty-eight hours. It has Maeve's touch all over it.

I've been assigned one of the east-facing bedrooms, but fortunately, the windows have blackout drapes. I have no intention of getting up before noon, not if it means I have to watch Maeve pine over a fucker who will never leave his wife for her. She claims she didn't have anything to do with him showing up here, and I want to believe her—I really fucking do—but it can't be a coincidence, right?

Walking over to the large arched windows, I remind myself that this party will be over in two days. I've watched Maeve with plenty of guys before; I can handle a single weekend. Besides, they'll have to be discreet with his wife around.

I look out at the grounds, beautifully manicured lawns and gardens of flowers and shrubs stretching in all directions. The hedge maze, topiary walk, and koi pond mentioned in the brochure are visible from here, and below me is the large terrace spanning the back of the house. I'm just about to turn back and unpack my suitcase when a couple on the stone pavement catches my eye. My body registers it before my eyes do, my blood running cold before I've even had a chance to recognize who I'm looking at.

Preston pulls Maeve into his arms—right there in broad daylight—and she goes willingly, just walks into his embrace as if she belongs there. Which, for the record, she doesn't. Anyone with eyes in their head can see that she deserves a million times better than that cheating bastard.

They stand there pressed together, and when they don't pull away after several seconds, I snap the curtains shut and turn toward the bed. Fuck them both. If that's her choice, fine. It's the shittiest one she could possibly make, but if it's what she wants, I won't get in her way. But fuck her if she expects me to believe this wasn't her plan all along.

\* \* \*

Drinks are being served in the drawing room, and I'm relieved to see Slate, Rhett, and Saylor already there when I walk in, each of them holding a glass. After getting a Negroni from the makeshift bar by the fireplace, I join my friends near the windows overlooking the front lawn.

"Ready for this, mate?" Rhett asks, clapping a hand on my shoulder. I toss back my entire drink in one go. "I will be soon."

I've just grabbed a refill and am turning back to rejoin them when I bump into Caroline Hatchett, who is standing behind me. Liquid splashes over the side of my tumbler, and I set it back on the bar to grab some napkins.

"Shit," I say, offering several to her. "I'm so sorry."

Her laugh is slightly high-pitched, and my first thought is of how much it would annoy Maeve. "It's fine." She blots at the droplets on her arm. "No harm, no foul."

Caroline is a tall blond with the kind of face that belongs on magazine covers. In fact, if I remember correctly, she's done some modeling in the past. "I didn't realize you were here," I say. It feels rude to walk away after spilling my drink on her. "Did you come with someone?"

She laughs again, and I get the distinct impression it's something she does often. "No, I'm here alone. What about you?"

"The same." I pick up my glass again, but it's all sticky now. I ignore the prickling sensation I get from that knowledge and take a long sip.

"We'll have to look out for each other," Caroline says, placing a hand on my arm and giving me a conspiratorial look. "During all of the couple-y things."

This isn't a couples retreat, I want to tell her, but I don't, because at that moment, Maeve walks into the room. It takes exactly two beats for her to spot me, and when she does, she shoots me a filthy look. I see the scene through her eyes—Caroline's hand on my arm, residual smiles on both our faces—and I suddenly feel a million times better than I did five minutes ago.

Tearing my gaze from Maeve, I turn to the blond beside me— Maeve's opposite in every way. "Let me introduce you to my friends."

\* \* \*

Spending the evening with Caroline on my arm has the desired effect. Maeve looks pissed enough to blow a gasket. I've been on the receiving end of more glares than ever, and each time I look over to find her scowling at me again, my heart trips over itself. No one said two can't play this game.

Caroline meshes with the rest of our group well—better than I would have expected. Then again, I've never brought a girlfriend around my friends before, so maybe this is normal. I've never had a serious enough relationship to go there.

I'm ordering another round of drinks for Caroline and myself when I smell it: toasted vanilla with smoky afternotes. Biting back a smile, I don't turn, just wait for her to speak.

She doesn't disappoint. She never disappoints. "You sure you should get that martini full strength? Barbie over there seems like a lightweight."

I release the grin and lick my lower lip as I turn to look down at Maeve, who barely reaches my shoulder—a whole head shorter than Caroline. "Nah, she's got a long way to go before she's wasted."

Maeve nods in agreement. "And that's the end goal? Get her wasted?" Without waiting for my response, she adds, "Let me guess—that's the only way she'll sleep with you."

I snort a laugh and accept the glasses from the bartender. "Actually, we're having a great time. We might duck out early."

Her face hardens into stone, that jaw clenching tightly even though she's pretending with all she's worth not to be bothered by our conversation. "She certainly fits the girlfriend mold. Do you think she'll mind if we call her Carolella instead? I'm just not sure we'll be able to remember her name otherwise."

I take a sip of my whiskey before answering, enjoying the way her discomfort grows the longer the silence between us stretches. Years ago, I made the mistake of dating four women in the space of two years whose names ended in "-ella." No one has let me forget it since. And maybe they have a point. I like what I like. Namely, I like to date the opposite of the little vixen standing in front of me.

Leaning down so we're not overheard, I desperately hope that wanker she's fucking is watching us. "You'll get used to it soon enough if things go the way I hope."

It's nothing but a bald-faced lie, but the way Maeve's lip is trembling with the exertion it's taking to keep her emotions in check tells me she's buying every word. Unfortunately, her jealousy doesn't satisfy me as much as I thought it would.

"Great," she says through clenched teeth. "Preston just told me he's filing papers after he gets back to the city." Turning her back to me, she approaches the bar and orders another drink.

As I rejoin everyone else, my heart feels like it's hanging out in my shoes. I have no idea if Maeve's telling the truth or if she's spewing bullshit as fast as I was. What happened to the understanding we had a few days ago, when she finally started to lower her guard and let me in? God, I'd do anything to have that back.

I hand Caroline her drink, and she starts telling a story about something that happened to one of her friends. The others all laugh, so it must be funny, but I can't focus on a word she's saying. My brain has decided now would be the perfect time to torment me with images of Maeve and Preston hooking up.

Who knows how the fuck he plans to sneak away from his wife, but if there's one thing I know, it's that Maeve is the queen of sneaking around. There's a reason she's the cat burglar during our revenge plots. The two of us have been hooking up for nearly five months, and none of our friends have a clue. She's been seeing the cheating dick for over a year without detection, so if anyone can do it, it'll be her.

My stomach churns, and I think I might actually be sick. I know we're not exclusive—fuck, we're not even a *we*—but the thought of her sleeping with that pig, sleeping with anyone who isn't me, sends a giant wave of nausea through me.

I can't do this. I can't watch her leave with him, or stumble upon them in the hallway—or fuck, the library. I can't see him put his hands on her the way he did outside. The fucker doesn't even know how to touch her, that much is obvious. I bet he doesn't ever get rough with her, and Maeve Wilson sure as fuck likes it rough.

Don't worry, I'm not so stupid I don't understand what's happening here. My feelings for her are growing. The problem is, they're growing too fast, and they're not reciprocated. Maybe if she felt the same way, we could figure this shit out. But she's made it abundantly clear she hopes I burn in hell.

Meanwhile, I look like a fucking fool, falling for a woman who doesn't give a shit about me. No, worse—hates me with a passion. I play along with her game, but only because it forces her to pay attention to me. And I love to see that spark light up in her eyes, the one she gets every time she's challenged.

What kind of wanker gets sucked into something like this? I'm bigger than this, better than this. I'm a fucking St. James, for god's sake. It's time to start acting like it. If Maeve prefers a married bastard to me, fine. I wish them many happy fucks.

"Are you okay?" Caroline places her hand on my arm again. She's weaseling herself into a future girlfriend role with the finesse of an expert. It was probably only a matter of time.

I drain the rest of my whiskey and smile at her. "Actually, do you want to get out of here?"

She doesn't say anything, but the blinding smile she gives me speaks louder than any words.

## "MR. BRIGHTSIDE" - THE KILLERS

As I set my empty glass on the sideboard and wave good night to my friends, I'm rewarded by the look of quietly simmering rage on Maeve's face.

# 38

## "Misery Business" - Paramore

*Maeve*

Was it stupid of me to think that Pierce might come to my room last night after everyone else had gone to bed? One hundred percent. Was it stupid of me to be excited by the thought of sneaking him in as if we were teenagers? Definitely. Is it stupid of me to be this insanely jealous of some ho with terrible highlights and legs up to her neck? I don't think I need to answer that.

I know I have no right to be jealous, so stop thinking it. And don't you dare pity me, either. I have no claim on Pierce; we're not exclusive, we're not even together like that. Trust me, I am fully aware of how absolutely ridiculous this situation is. Does that stop me from wanting to destroy both of them? Hell no.

Her, I can actually understand. Who wouldn't take one look at Pierce—currently single and worth billions—and try to lock that down? She needs a better stylist, sure, but I can't blame the woman for trying. She's the exact same prototype as his previous girlfriends: blond, leggy, and gorgeous. This one seems to have more in her head than most of them, but first impressions can be deceiving.

It's him I have a problem with.

Just hours before hooking up with her, he threw a tantrum about Preston being here, accusing me of inviting him so the two of us could sleep together—the most ridiculous idea anyone's ever had. He was clearly jealous, so I know exactly why he took Caroline to his room. Whether I spent the night with Preston or not is beside the point. He did it to get back at me, and if he thinks that makes us even, he's grossly mistaken.

Breakfast is served in the morning room. The blue-and-white toile curtains have been pulled back to let in the sunshine, and it hits the gleaming silverware next to the buffet, making it sparkle. I'm relieved to see Heath and Walker already sitting at one of the tables, nibbling on muffins and strawberries.

After filling my own plate, I join them. I've just sat down when Pierce walks in. Our gazes lock immediately, and I give him a cool stare before turning to Walker.

"Let's talk about the wedding. What are you thinking for flowers?"

She begins explaining her dilemma, choosing between lilies and orchids, but I'm embarrassed to say I'm only half listening. My attention is focused on Pierce, who's now standing at the buffet along the far wall. He looks far too refreshed this morning for my liking. After all the drinks he pounded last night, he should carry at least a hint of a hangover, but the jerk looks crisp and polished in a white polo shirt, dark brown pants, and leather loafers without socks.

Caroline is nowhere to be seen.

He joins us at the table, his china plate loaded with bacon and eggs. After smiling and wishing Heath and Walker a good morning, he looks at me. "Maeve." His voice is as flat as fake champagne.

"Looks like you worked up an appetite last night." I shove another bite of gluten-free muffin into my mouth.

Walker clears her throat nervously. "You two ready for your next challenge?"

Somehow in the chaos of arranging a house party for fifty people, I forgot that we'd agreed to complete the next challenge this weekend. Clenching my fork tighter, I give her a plasticky smile. "I've never been more ready."

Pierce lets out a quiet scoff and takes the seat next to mine. "How could you possibly be ready?" He says it softly enough that I'm the only one who can hear him.

"Unlike you, I got a great night's sleep," I say just as quietly.

Heath and Walker may not be able to hear us, but they can definitely sense the tension. They're doing a good job pretending otherwise, though. He says something that makes her laugh, and she looks up at him with a disgustingly adoring face. Why are people in love so intolerable?

"How would you know how I slept?" Pierce takes a massive bite of his bacon as he waits for my answer.

I roll my eyes. "Please. Where is Barbie anyway?"

He shakes his head, a small smile playing at his lips, and ignores my question. Instead, he turns to Heath and starts talking about doing some riding while we're here.

Grabbing my fork, I press the silver tines into his thigh. After several seconds, he seizes my wrist and locks it in place on top of his leg while continuing his conversation with Heath. He doesn't even bother glancing at me.

"I would kill to see Slate on a horse," Heath says, a huge grin cracking his face in two.

"Maeve would come, wouldn't you?" Pierce asks, finally gracing me with a look.

I scowl at him and try to yank my hand away. "Since when do you like riding?"

He shrugs. He doesn't even have to struggle to restrain me, although

## "MISERY BUSINESS" - PARAMORE

the veins in his wrist are bulging. "I'm always down for a ride." Keeping his eyes on me, he takes a long sip of his coffee.

"I'm well the fuck aware," I snap, and finally manage to free my hand. "Excuse me."

I've only had a few bites of my food, but I can't take another minute at this table, enduring Pierce's goading and my own jealousy. I imagine Caroline Hatchett wrapped in his sheets, maybe wearing the T-shirt he sleeps in, or using his bodywash as she showers. His scent has probably seeped into her pores the way it did into Loretta's, and if it hasn't, it will by the end of the weekend.

Once again, he had a fuck buddy while I was left alone. And this time I didn't even have my vibrator to keep me company, thanks to Captain Prick himself.

I've nearly reached my bedroom when he catches up to me.

"Maeve, wait."

I don't listen, just reach for the doorknob, but he stops me before I can slip inside. His hand on my arm is so warm it practically singes my skin.

"What do you want, Pierce?" Pulling away from his touch, I back up until there's some distance between us. I'm not sure if I'm more liable to throw myself at him or slap him, but I have no interest in finding out.

"What's going on?" he says, his dark brows pulled together.

"Nice try." I turn for the door again.

He jerks it closed before I can open it more than a few inches. "I asked you a question."

"Go to hell."

"Not until you talk to me."

"Is that all it will take?" I turn my face up and flash him a victorious smile. "In that case, please continue."

He sighs and rests his shoulder against the wall, looking down at me with tired eyes. "How long are we going to do this, Maeve?"

Shrugging with my entire face, I say, "I guess until you stop being an asshole."

"Right." Closing his eyes, he massages his temples. "And how was I an asshole this time?"

I bark out a laugh. "Please tell me you're joking."

He opens his eyes and looks at me through his fingers before slowly dragging his hand down over his face. "While you normally wear every single thought on your face, I'm struggling to pinpoint the exact cause of your anger this morning."

My face heats as if sunburned. "You can't expect me to believe that, not after you paraded her in front of me for hours last night."

He blinks at me, his tongue in his cheek. Finally, he says, "Who?"

I roll my head up to look at the ceiling, hoping I'll find the answers to his stupidity in the intricate molding. I don't. "You're being obtuse, and my patience is wearing thin," I say.

"Your patience is always thin."

"Well, right now it's see-through."

"Terrific." He scuffs the toe of his sneaker against the gleaming hardwood floor. "Is this about Caroline?"

Gasping in shock and delight, I clap my hands together, garnering a look from a couple heading for the staircase. "Ding, ding, ding!" I sing out, ignoring them. "Job well done, Pierce." I grab his arm and shake it like a game show host.

He shrugs me off. "You're making a scene." His eyes flick down the corridor.

"I'm about to make an even bigger scene if you don't get your head out of your ass."

He pins me with a hard gaze that makes me swallow. "You're the one who's making a big deal out of nothing."

"*Nothing*? Really?" I cross my arms and glare up at him. "That's the way you want to play this?"

"Why are you so mad about Caroline?" he asks, returning my scowl with a nasty one of his own.

"Because—" I start, then stop. Anything I say will point to jealousy, and it's not like I'm going to admit that out loud. God, I'm not a masochist. "Because I was under the impression that you were going to spend the night with *me*."

His face turns incredulous. "I would have," he says slowly, "but you brought your own fuckboy."

I rear back. "What? Are you talking about—" After pausing to catch my breath, I continue, my voice lowered in case anyone is walking down the hallway. "About Preston?"

Pierce lets out a deep sigh and rolls his eyes. "No, the prime minister. Obviously I'm talking about that dickhead."

It's my turn to look incredulous. "He came with his bloody *wife*. Did you think we were going to have a threesome?"

He runs his hand through his hair before spreading both arms wide. "What was I supposed to think after you invited him here?"

"I told you, I had nothing to do with that," I hiss. I was angry before, but now I'm fuming. Why the fuck would he think I was going to sleep with Preston while his wife snored down the hall? I'm not suicidal.

"I saw you outside," Pierce bites out. "After the library."

My mind whirls as I try to piece this all together. Pierce saw Preston and me on the terrace, but we weren't doing anything. We may have hugged, but it was hardly sexual. So he hits on Caroline Hatchett to—what? Make me jealous?

"I haven't even seen him since then," I say, wishing I had the ability to scorch the man in front of me with my eyes alone. I can already picture smoke billowing from beneath his shoes.

Pierce blinks in surprise. "So you didn't see him last night?"

"I just told you," I snap. "He was with *her* last night." For some reason, the thought of Preston having sex with his wife doesn't repulse me the way thinking about Pierce with Caroline does.

"Oh." Pierce sags against the wall and stares at the floor. "Caroline and I didn't have sex either."

His words hit my chest with a jolt, and I jerk my head upright. "But I saw you two—"

"I just walked her to her room. Nothing happened."

*Nothing happened.*

All morning he let me believe they spent the entire night together. For god's sake, I was picturing her in his *clothes*. "Did you kiss her?" I blurt out, my brain apparently malfunctioning. I don't actually want to know the answer to that. Maybe I'm a masochist after all.

He lets out a soft chuckle. "No, Maeve, we didn't kiss." Taking a step toward me, a spark lights his eyes, changing his face into what I've come to recognize as *dangerous Pierce*. He tucks a strand of hair behind my ear, and I forget how to breathe. Tilting my chin up, he leans down and says, "I'm saving all my kisses for you."

## 39

## "Out of the Woods" - Taylor Swift

*Maeve*

If anyone ever dares you to venture into the forest surrounding Belgrave Park, say no. Actually, if anyone ever dares you to go into any forest anywhere, say no. They're nothing but a cesspool of danger.

As I swat away the branch currently trying to kill me, Pierce looks back over his shoulder. "You okay?"

I return his concerned look with a scowl. "Tell me we're nearly there."

He sighs and continues walking down the path leading deeper into the woods. "How am I supposed to know how much further? This is your property."

"By that logic, you're intimately acquainted with quite a few properties," I grumble, trudging after him.

"The only thing in this general vicinity I'm intimately acquainted with is you." He says it so quietly, I almost miss it. In fact, I'm not even sure he meant for me to hear it in the first place.

We're on a "treasure hunt," which is code for "something Lux thought was funny and cute but which I'm definitely going to kill her for later." The first five clues were hidden in the house or gardens, but the last one drove us into the forest, with its towering pines, scurrying animals, and disgusting scent of decay.

"It's not that bad," Pierce said when I voiced my thoughts out loud earlier.

"Says the guy probably deciding where he'll bury my body."

Our mission at the moment is to find a hollow tree, and judging by the number of trees in this place in general, it looks like we'll be here for the rest of the year.

"I'm going to murder Lux," I say, stopping to catch my breath.

They fortunately allowed me to change shoes before we started, but it's not like I packed my bags with wandering through the wilderness like a mad person in mind. Saylor offered to let me wear her boots, but they were two sizes too big, and lifting that much extra weight with my feet seemed like a bad idea. I settled on my Miu Miu slingback ballerinas, not because they seemed practical, but because they were the only flats I brought with me.

Reaching down, I dislodge the millionth pine needle from beneath my heel.

"Want a piggyback ride?" Pierce asks, coming back to stand beside me.

Shooting him a glare, I march past him up the trail. I know I have no right to be upset with him—it's not like this ridiculous challenge was his idea, after all—but I guess I'm still a little hot about the Caroline Hatchett thing. If he'd just asked me, I would've told him there's no way in hell Preston and I were hooking up last night.

I hear him coming up behind me on the path, and I feel a little bad about how I've been treating him, as though everything that's happened is his fault. In reality, I'm much more responsible than I'd like to admit. I may not have invited Preston here, but if the situation were reversed and Pierce's girlfriend showed up—well, let's just say, both of their lives would be pretty fucking miserable right now, and that's assuming she'd still be alive.

Turning around to offer him an attempt at an apology, I miss the giant tree root sticking out of the ground with the sole purpose of tripping me up. My limbs go sprawling in every direction as I tumble to the ground.

"Shit," Pierce says. "Are you okay?" He crouches beside me and places a hand on the back of my head.

"Ow," I moan. Everything hurts.

"Can you move?"

"Just leave me here to die," I mumble into the ground, which is covered in a layer of leaves in various states of decomposition.

"I'm so glad you're not going to be dramatic about this," he says, wrapping both arms around me. "Come on. I've got you."

I have no choice but to stand when he lifts me, although I let out a wail loud enough to scare off any animal who thinks I look like easy prey right now.

"Can you put weight on your leg?" His touch on my knee is gentle, and I glance down to see what he's looking at.

An angry red scrape streaks up my calf, and a small trickle of blood runs down to my ankle. I quickly look away before I get woozy.

"Maeve?" Pierce looks at me expectantly. "Unfortunately, I don't have anything to clean up the blood with, but I'll carry you if you want."

I shake my head. The last thing I need is to be cradled against Pierce's chest like some kind of baby. His scent would torment me the whole way back. "I'll be fine," I say, standing upright. It hurts, but it's not intolerable, unlike this bloody mission we're on.

"I think we should head back and get that taken care of." He motions to my wound.

"Not until we find the clue." We've come this far, and it has to be close.

I turn in a circle, hoping a hollow tree will magically appear. Then I see it. The exact tree that tripped me has an opening about four feet tall. Inside, on the ground, is a paper airplane. I snatch it up and read aloud.

"'You've come this far together, but the journey's not yet over. Your final clue can be found near the nectar of the clover. Great job on the teamwork, but it's time to say goodbye. Race to the finish, give it your best try.'"

"Which one of them wrote these things, do you think?" Pierce says, kicking at the dirt.

"My money's on Walker." I shove the paper into the pocket I'm fortunate enough to have on my dress—a dress that was white this morning but is now smudged with all manner of dirt and debris. I squint up at Pierce. "Well, I guess we're on our own now." The thought makes my stomach churn with nausea.

He shakes his head, the expression on his face letting me know I'm ridiculous. "I'm not letting you fend for yourself out here."

"I'll be fine." I'm not exactly confident it's the truth, but I'm pretty sure I'll at least survive. We can't be that far from the house.

"Maybe, but I'm not taking any chances." Pierce extends his hand, palm up. "Come on."

I look from it to his face, considering my choices. Running ahead of him back up the path isn't an option, not when my leg is starting to throb with pain. If I accept his help back, I can always ditch him at the last minute and find the final clue on my own.

He wiggles his thumb, wanting me to hurry, and I make up my mind. Ignoring his hand, I push past him and start retracing our steps on the trail. His footsteps make a soft squishing noise as he follows me.

The sun is starting to set, taking its warmth with it. It must be at least ten degrees colder here under the shade of the tall trees.

I rub my hands over my bare arms and speed up my steps. The sundress seemed like a good idea when I thought I'd be spending the day playing croquet or watching the guys make fools of themselves shooting clay pigeons.

"Maeve, wait," Pierce says behind me.

I'm reluctant to slow down now that I'm finally starting to warm up a bit, but I turn back to see what he wants. He drags his light gray sweater over his head, and the white shirt he's wearing underneath it rises up just enough to reveal a sliver of his toned stomach. Mouth watering, I quickly avert my eyes.

Holding the sweater out to me, he says, "Here. Put this on."

I open my mouth to object, but before I can, he clears the distance between us and tugs it over my head. His scent immediately envelops me. Keeping my eyes locked on him, I don't say anything as he helps me into the sleeves, then pulls it down and lifts my hair out of the collar.

"Thank you," I whisper.

His hand lingers in my hair, letting it slide through his fingers. "How's the leg?"

"Hurts."

"Want me to kiss it better?" Mischief dances in his eyes.

I remember what he said earlier about saving all his kisses for me. Talk about confusing. I swallow the sudden urge to seal my mouth to his. "I'm good."

He turns back to the path leading to the house. "We should keep going. It's getting late."

This time when he holds out his hand, I slip mine into it and let him lead the way. When I'm confident he's facing forward and can't see me in his peripheral vision, I lift the cuff of his sweater to my nose and drink in his scent. It's been muffled out here—nature trying to out-scent him—so getting a direct hit is the exact rejuvenation I need.

I pick up the pace until I'm beside Pierce, his fingers still clutching mine. "Why didn't you sleep with her? With Caroline?"

His eyes go wide as he turns to look at me. After blinking a few times, he turns his attention back to navigating. He scrambles over a fallen log, then lifts me across it. I do my best to ignore the way his hands feel on my waist, firm and strong and so warm.

I've given up on getting an answer from him and am just about to press him again when he speaks. "I didn't want to."

"Why not? She's hot." It's a stretch for me, calling a woman hot, but that's how most straight men would see her—a prized trophy to bang and brag about.

"She is." He shrugs, leaving his sentence hanging in the air unfinished.

I'm dying to know what else he might say, but I don't have the nerve to find out. We've got a good thing going here. I don't want to jeopardize that.

Pierce keeps his eyes on the ground, brow furrowed. "Maeve—"

I don't find out what he's going to say, because at that moment, I catch my foot on a small root and almost plummet face-first again but for Pierce's hand keeping me balanced. Leave it to the woods to make me feel like a fucking giraffe trying to do ballet. A glance at my leg shows a thicker stream of blood running down my shin than before, dripping into my shoe. My head spins, and I lift a hand to my forehead to steady myself.

"Please let me carry you." He stops walking and looks at me.

"I'm okay."

"I want to."

When I open my eyes, he's bending down to scoop me into his arms. I suck in a breath as he picks me up and cradles me against his chest. Letting myself relax, I trace the collar of his shirt. A thrill goes through me when he swallows, making his Adam's apple bob.

I didn't realize how much I was slowing Pierce down before with my thousand-dollar slingbacks and Frankensteinian injury (which had better not scar). Now that he's carrying me, his strides are eating up the ground. We're back at the house in no time, and when he goes to set me down, a tiny pang of regret echoes through my chest.

"In case anyone sees," he says, as if he owes me an explanation.

"Yeah, of course." I brush my dress down and hope no one lays eyes on this travesty before I have a chance to get cleaned up and change. Pierce's cashmere sweater covers most of the grime, but that would be even harder to explain.

"You all good?" He squats down to inspect my leg. "Looks like it's stopped bleeding."

Fortunately, the grounds seem to be deserted, probably because it's dinnertime. Pierce shoves his hands in his pockets as we head to the back terrace. Right before we round the corner of the house, he stops and pulls something out.

"I almost forgot. You dropped this when you fell." He holds out the necklace I was wearing earlier. "Actually, let me just—" Moving behind me, he rests the gold chain against my collarbone and fastens the clasp.

I touch the miniature charm—a diamond-studded heart—and try not to shiver as his fingers brush the back of my neck.

"There," he says, spinning me around and admiring his work. "Now let's get you cleaned up."

We begin to climb the terrace steps, only to stop short at the sight of my sister and a boy next to the shrubbery where Preston and I met yesterday. The shadows shift, and I see that it's Cassian Cordero with her. At first glance I thought it was Sebastian, but Cass's skin is brown, and he's not wearing Bash's blinding smile.

"What are you two doing out here?" I say.

Viv gives my injury and the oversized sweater a pointed look. "I could ask you the same thing."

My cheeks heat, but fortunately it's too dark for anyone to see. I don't need to be embarrassed, though. Pierce St. James is the catch of the decade. My sister, on the other hand, is sneaking around with the help. Cassian might be Bash's best friend, but he's also the estate manager's son. If our parents caught wind of this—

"We should get you inside," Pierce says before I can warn Viv about the huge mistake she's making.

I allow him to steer me into the house while casting one last look over my shoulder. Viv and Cass have disappeared back into the shadows, and I can't help wondering if that was really what it looked like. Maybe they were just waiting on Bash. Vivienne would never throw her future away over a moody bad boy who has more tattoos than dollars.

Since everyone—except those two—is at dinner, Pierce and I make it upstairs without running into anyone else. He tugs me into the en suite attached to his bedroom.

"Sit," he orders, and squats in front of the cabinet.

I sit down on the lid of the toilet seat, grateful to be able to rest my limbs. Walking in the forest is no joke, and I don't recommend it if you value your body. "God, I can't believe I nearly died."

Pierce emerges with a first aid kit and a devilish smirk. "Narrowly escaped with your life."

I watch as he gathers supplies on the vanity, his fingers moving dexterously, unwinding the bandages and opening disinfectant wipes.

"You're not going to slap me if I use this, are you?" He holds a wipe several inches from the cut and looks up at me with a cocked brow.

"Don't be ridiculous. I'm not a baby."

His grin is hidden by his bowed head as he gently tends to my wound, but I can feel him smiling, the way you can hear it in someone's voice over the phone. It feels like sunshine on my skin. It's warm enough to distract me from the pain as he disinfects the cut.

After sticking the last bandage into place, he stands up. "You'll just have to wear pants the rest of the weekend."

I stare at him in horror. "What are you talking about? I don't *own* pants."

He flicks his tongue over his lower lip. "That's unfortunate. We still have a challenge to finish."

Apprehension fills my veins. I don't want to traverse the stairs again, especially not if dinner is over. There might be people milling about, or worse—my mother.

Pierce must sense my unease, because he says, "What if I go grab the clue, and we'll say we both found it?"

I frown. "Then this whole thing will have been pointless."

He helps me to my feet and leads me to the bedroom. "Okay, then we'll say you found it."

"Hilarious."

"I was being serious." With his hands on my shoulders, he guides me backward until my knees hit the bed. "Get comfortable, and I'll be right back."

"Where are you going?"

"To the kitchen."

"The kitchen."

"Yes." He drags out the word, his hand on the doorknob. "We need food and the next clue."

I pull the crumpled paper airplane from my pocket and toss it onto the bed. "Honey." *Nectar of the clover.* "How do I know you'll actually return with it and not just go claim the victory for yourself?"

He winks before opening the door. "I guess you'll just have to trust me."

## 40

## "Paper Crown" - Alec Benjamin

*Pierce*

Maeve looks genuinely surprised when I return with the final clue, which stings a bit. What do I need to do to finally earn her trust? She'll lower her walls for brief moments, but as soon as she feels the slightest bit threatened, they lock back into place.

I hand her the plate I scavenged from the kitchen. "Lux was asking about you."

Maeve flicks her dark eyes up at me before taking a bite of halibut. "What did you tell her?"

"That you were probably in the shower and going to bed right after." Sitting down beside her on the sofa, I keep my hands busy with my own food so I don't haul her into my lap.

She must have slipped back to her room while I was gone, because she's no longer wearing the dress she had on earlier. Instead, she's in tiny floral-print pajamas. The straps of her camisole are as thin as thread, and if she stands up, I doubt her shorts will cover her ass.

It's not the fact that she changed that gets me—it's that she came back to my room afterward.

We eat our food mostly in silence, nothing but the clink of our forks against the dinnerware echoing through the room. I wonder if she wishes she were downstairs with everyone else, if she wishes she were with *him* instead of me.

Maeve doesn't usually tolerate prolonged periods of silence. They make her highly uncomfortable, and she fills them at the first opportunity. The fact that she's not doing that now can only mean one of two things: either she's pissed and on the verge of erupting, or she's relaxed enough that she can sit here with me without saying a word.

I hope to god it's the latter.

She sticks the last bite of fish into her mouth, and I hold out my hand for her empty plate. Stacking it with mine, I set both of them on the floor. I'll take them down later. I'm not risking someone stopping me downstairs, or worse, Maeve running off while I'm gone.

I sink back into the sofa and let out a deep breath. "Who knew strolling through the woods would be so exhausting?"

"That was no stroll," she says, lifting her legs and placing them in my lap. "That was a bloody quest."

Running my hands down her calves, careful to avoid her injury, I sniff a laugh. "You wouldn't survive thirty minutes out there on your own."

"Obviously." A shudder runs through her body. "Why would anyone want bragging rights to that?" She pulls her phone out and starts tapping at the screen.

I use the opportunity to study her without her freaking out. Other than the scrape on her leg, the only evidence of our escapades today is the small bit of color on her cheeks and the tiny scratch on her forehead. I press my thumb to it. "Does this hurt?"

She lifts her eyes distractedly before immediately dropping them back down. "No."

Her legs are as smooth as butter, and I drag my hands all the way down to her ankles. I've touched her body a thousand times, but it's nearly always been in a sexual context, at least more recently. But this is nice, sitting here with her like this, like—fuck, like a *couple*.

Taking her foot in my hand, I begin massaging it. After a few seconds, Maeve tilts her head back against the arm of the sofa and moans. "That feels incredible."

I watch her as I work her tender muscles. She's so fucking beautiful, it hurts to look at her. There's a physical ache in my chest as I consider the gulf that still lies between us—a gulf she has no desire to bridge.

What will it take to win her heart? I don't even care whether this is love or not. If it is, screw it. I just know I want it all, and I want it with her. Call it love, call it lust, call it fucking unicorns and rainbows. I don't give a shit.

I just want her.

"Can I ask you something?" I say.

Her eyes are closed, head still resting on the sofa. "That depends."

"On?"

"On whether I want to answer or not."

"I brought you the final clue."

Several beats pass before she squints at me with one eye. "Fine."

I switch to rubbing her other foot. "Have you ever been in love?"

Her muscles tense immediately, and she lifts her head to look at me. A tiny crater forms between her brows. "Why?"

"I was just curious."

"No." She sighs and flops backward again. "Have you?"

"Maybe," I say quietly. "Just once."

Bolting upright, she gapes at me. "With who?"

I smile sheepishly and hold on to her legs to keep them from tumbling from my lap. "No one you'd know."

"Liar!" She socks me in the arm. "I know everyone you've dated."

I let myself get lost in her eyes for just a second. "I never said it was someone I dated."

"I want details."

"Well, you're not getting them." I carefully lower her legs to the floor. It's time to get this train back onto a track I can control.

"You're so unfair," she says.

I shift forward and rest my elbows on my knees. "I've been called worse. Mostly by you." I glance over my shoulder to let her know I'm teasing.

She shifts until she's right beside me, then leans her head on my shoulder.

I freeze. I can't fucking move. Maeve has her head resting in the crook of my neck, and I feel like a teenage boy who's never kissed anyone before.

She reaches for my hand and threads our fingers together. Her palm is so tiny that mine swallows it up, hiding it from view. "Why do you stay?" she whispers.

Blood starts working its way through my veins again, and I take a steadying breath. "Stay where?"

"With me."

Fuck my life. "Why wouldn't I stay with you?" My voice sounds scratchy.

She strokes my arm with her free hand. "No one else ever does."

I move my head to look at her, but she has hers tucked so closely against me that her face is hidden. "That's their loss."

She doesn't say anything. I wish I could wrap my arms around her, but she's clutching my hand so tightly I wouldn't dream of prying her off.

"Maeve?" I murmur into her hair. "You believe me, don't you?"

The laugh that slips past her lips borders on hysterical. "Of course."

"Oh, baby." Screw what she wants. I'm more worried about what she needs. Shifting her into my lap, I wrap my arm around her and tug her as close as I possibly can. She doesn't even put up a fight.

"I keep waiting for you to leave," she says against my shirt.

I squeeze her even tighter. "I'm not going anywhere."

She brings her hand up and rests it against my chest. Nothing in the world has ever made me feel like more of a man than that small gesture. "I want to trust you. I really do." Her voice is tiny and hesitant.

"Shhh. I know."

"There was a teacher." Her fingers tremble against my shirt. "When I was in primary school."

I wait for her to continue, afraid that if I say a word, she'll clam up.

"I was ten. He was—well, it doesn't matter how old he was. He was my teacher." Her whole body is shaking now, and I wish there was a way I could wrap her within myself, hide her from whatever demons are chasing her.

I'm terrified of what she's about to tell me. Whatever it is, judging by the way she is shattering in my arms, I know it can't be good. Inhaling a measured breath through my nose, I remind myself to stay calm.

"He took a special interest in me. That's what my mother called it. 'A special interest in our special girl,' she'd say." Bitterness coats Maeve's words. "He used to 'tutor' me. I wasn't struggling in school, but I didn't know any better. If an adult said something back then, I believed them."

My heart is pounding so hard, I have no doubt she can hear it. I have to fight to keep my hands flat on her back, because all they want to do is clench into fists.

"It didn't take me long to realize the tutoring had little to do with my schoolwork and more to do with—" Her voice breaks, and I cradle her jaw in my hand.

"I'm right here," I tell her. "I've got you."

She sniffs. "He made me do these horrible, atrocious things to him. And when I told my parents, they said we couldn't afford the scandal."

My vision has gone red. Blood no longer runs through my veins, just fury. I'm going to find this sorry excuse of a human and make him pay for what he did to my girl. "What happened to him?" I ask in as measured of a tone as I can manage, which isn't very.

I can feel the faint shrug of her shoulders against me, and she says, "I don't know. I'm guessing he's still teaching. It was my last year of primary, so I moved to the Academy after that."

"He'll be lucky to be alive once I'm through with him," I growl.

"Pierce, please don't," she says, once again placing her hand on my chest. "That's not why I told you."

All this time, all these years of getting revenge for the stupidest shit, and she doesn't want me to go after the one guy who deserves to die? We'll see about that.

Things make a lot more sense now, though. The way she has to be in control all the time. The way she never opens up, never lets anyone in. Her skittishness when it comes to sex. Her goddamn fortress of an exterior.

When you've been violated like that, you deserve a fucking fortress.

"Maeve," I say quietly.

She nuzzles closer, and my heart bleeds pain and joy in the same gush.

"Earlier, you asked who I was in love with." I wait for her to say something, but she stays quiet. I gather my courage, ready to show her that someone is ready to fight for her, that she is worth fighting for. "It's you. I think I'm in love with you."

When she still doesn't say anything, I crane my neck to see her face. Her eyes are closed, her lips slightly parted.

She's fallen asleep in my arms.

# 41

## "if u think i'm pretty" - Artemas

*Maeve*

I don't often have bad ideas, but I seem to be on a roll recently. Today's plan might just take the cake, however.

Pierce is standing in my living room, unbuttoning his shirt. He's already discarded his suit jacket on the sofa behind him. His eyes fix onto mine, and the smile on his face is pure arrogance. A tiny jolt of desire rushes through my core.

But before you go getting any ideas, I should probably add that he's surrounded by seven women who are all currently three glasses of pinot noir into their afternoon. An easel, a blank canvas, and a paint palette waits in front of each one of them.

When my cousin Benita asked me to be her maid of honor, it wasn't because we're close. It was because she knew I would throw her the best bridal shower and bachelorette party. And considering the way she's currently drooling over Pierce, I'd say she is congratulating herself on her choice.

Pierce undoes the last button and moves his hands behind his back to strip off his sleeves. I've seen him do it a hundred times, but for some reason, in front of all these women, I see it with fresh eyes.

The muscles in his chest ripple with the movement, and everyone catcalls—with the exception of yours truly—as the shirt falls to the floor, leaving that delicious torso of his on display.

"Oh my god," Giselle Wheeler says. "It is real?" Giggling, she moves to the center of the circle and runs her manicured hand over Pierce's skin, which is smooth, tight, and golden.

Laughter rings throughout the room.

Frowning at Giselle, I call out, "Okay, let's get started on these paintings."

They make a half-hearted attempt to follow my instructions, every eye still glued to our model. He ignores them and reaches for the zipper of his pants, keeping his gaze fixed on mine. I expect to see mockery there, but instead it's something softer. Sympathy? Or, god forbid, pity?

I blink quickly and turn away, breaking eye contact. The house party at Belgrave Park was two weeks ago, and the two of us have hardly spoken since—not because he hasn't tried, but because I can hardly stand to face him after the things I told him.

It was an amateur move, one I only made because I was shaken up by the events of the day. Hell, I barely escaped with my life in those woods. At the time, he seemed trustworthy, and I was just so bloody tired of carrying everything myself. I told him those things because in the moment, I trusted him. In the moment, I forgot what we are to each other—competitors.

So I made the worst mistake of all: I showed the competition my weakness. Weakness that he now has the ability to weaponize against me. He hasn't done anything yet, but I'm preparing myself for it. He would be a fool not to, and Pierce St. James is anything but a fool.

After turning in the final treasure hunt clue—which Pierce surprisingly kept his word about and let me claim—we were given our next challenge. The note read, *Choose your weapon! You must each choose an activity to complete together. The first one to bail or complain out loud loses.*

I'll admit, this one had me a little excited. There were so many things I knew Pierce would hate to do—a yoga class, a craft project, a guided therapy session—but I needed the perfect activity to break him. When I remembered Benita's upcoming bachelorette party, it was like the clouds parted and the angels started singing.

It all feels a little less angelic as I watch Pierce slide his pants down over his hips before releasing them in a puddle at his feet. He slowly steps out of them, much to the glee of his audience, another cocky smile spreading across his face.

He is enjoying this way too much.

"Does everyone have their paints?" I ask, walking behind each easel to inspect the supplies. I don't look at Pierce. I don't need to. I'm intimately acquainted with those muscled thighs of his, those sculpted calves, everything covered in a light layer of soft hair.

"Forget the painting," Fiona says. "Can we get a dance instead?"

There's a chorus of tittering laughter as the others wholeheartedly agree.

I aim a glare at the back of Fiona's head. The whole point of this was to humiliate Pierce, and yet I seem to be the only one not enjoying myself.

Forcing a chuckle, I return to my own easel. "Unfortunately, Mr. St. James has only been contracted for two hours of modeling." Our eyes meet above my canvas, and there's a knowing twinkle in his eyes.

The bastard knows exactly how to ruin me.

I should have remembered that when we were at Belgrave Park. He will do anything to win, including sabotaging me. If I care at all about beating him at this challenge, I have to keep my eye on the prize.

I tilt my chin and don't back down from his gaze. "Okay, Pierce. I think we're ready."

Instead of flushing or looking embarrassed, he just nods and drops his black Calvin Kleins with the flourish of a French model. Several quiet gasps float from behind the easels as we all take in his considerable length. Even when it's not erect, his cock is quite impressive. A faint line of hair trails down from his navel, and I know exactly how soft it is.

Realizing I've been staring along with everyone else, I jerk my gaze up, only for it to collide with Pierce's once again. He tilts his head to the side, giving me a small mocking smile. My cheeks immediately burst into flames.

"Can you turn to the side just a bit?" I ask. "The lighting is hitting you all wrong from this angle." It's nothing but a lie, but I need to do something to regain control of this situation.

Once he's shifted his position slightly, we all pick up our brushes and start painting. After an hour, I glance around at the other canvases, but it seems nobody is spending much time with their art. They're all much too interested in ogling the model.

My irritation blossoms, especially when I look up to find Pierce's eyes on me. It's like he thinks he can get me to bail on my own activity. The absolute audacity of the man.

Soon our two hours are up, and I don't think I've ever felt so much relief coursing through my body before. I toss my paintbrush aside and begin gathering the supplies. The women take far too long saying thank you to Pierce, who is still undressed, save for his boxer briefs.

After the last one has gone, shutting the door behind her, I sink onto the sofa and shut my eyes. "God, what a nightmare."

I can feel him smirking at me from where he's still standing in the middle of the room. "You're not the one who was naked."

"Why are you still here?" I say, opening my eyes. "You can leave now."

"I'm not going anywhere."

My mouth turns dry as I watch him watching me. I recognize that smoldering look. It means I'm five minutes away from getting fucked in a corner somewhere, *hard*. Sitting up, I force a laugh. "It's my house."

He ignores me and moves closer to the couch. "Do you know how difficult it was not to spring a semi? Or fuck, a full-blown hard-on?" Pressing his palms into the cushions on either side of me, he leans down. "I just spent two hours thinking about my grandma so I wouldn't think about what I was going to do to you afterward."

I swallow as a thrill races up my spine.

Abruptly, he pushes off the sofa and straightens. "Take off your clothes."

I'm feeling devious, so I shake my head. "I don't think so."

"That wasn't a request."

"All the same, I prefer not to be naked in my own living room."

Pierce's movements are as quick as a snake's. One second he's standing across from me, and the next he's pulled me upright against him, his erection pressing into my stomach. "When I tell you to do something, you do it."

I gasp, then let out a breathy exhale. "And if I don't?"

"Then I drag out your orgasm."

A slow smile spreads across my lips as I consider the implications of what he's saying. "That sounds even more fun."

"Oh, I don't mean for another five minutes. I can play with you for hours, Maeve Wilson." He twists my arm, bringing me even closer so he can grab my chin. "In fact, that's exactly what I'm going to do."

# 42

## "Jump Then Fall" - Taylor Swift

*Pierce*

I couldn't have asked for a better day. The sun is shining, and there's a perfect amount of cloud coverage. A gentle breeze is blowing just enough to keep it from feeling hot.

When Lux issued this month's challenge, I knew immediately what I wanted to do. Maeve is terrified of heights, but this isn't about scaring her and claiming victory for myself. I don't give a fuck about the game anymore. All I care about is ensuring that she remains mine for the rest of eternity.

Ever since the party at her family's estate, she's been pulling back. I'm guessing it has to do with what she told me about her teacher, but I'm terrified it has to do with Preston, terrified that she's thinking about breaking things off between us in order to be with him.

Her dark green Bentley convertible pulls up on the tarmac with the top down. My heart ricochets around my chest as I wait for her to get out. When she finally does, I can't help the grin that spreads over my face.

"I thought you didn't own pants," I say.

She stops just short of me, wearing a dark red sports bra and black leggings that hug her figure in all the right places, tempting me to ditch my plans for the morning and run my hands all over her. Huge sunglasses cover her eyes. "I do yoga, dumbass."

I shake my head and lower my aviators. Today will be fun. Maybe not as fun as her making me the nude model for a bunch of horny women, but fun in a different way.

"You could have told me we were flying today." She points at the small plane parked behind us. "I definitely don't need spandex for that."

I stride over to the gear piled on the asphalt and return with a jumpsuit. "Actually," I say, handing it to her, "you need it for this."

Maeve fingers the nylon material with disdain. "This is synthetic."

"Precisely. It will protect you from the wind." I slip my feet into the legs of my own suit and pull it up.

"It's hardly windy out here, and I'm fine," she says. As if on cue, the breeze lifts her hair and gently blows it across her face.

I squint up at the sky. "You're fine here, but you won't be thirteen thousand feet up there."

Her entire body freezes, her alarm bells clearly ringing. "You've got to be fucking kidding me."

"I'm not kidding, but I'm happy to fuck you first." Flashing her a grin, I pull up my zipper.

"Pierce, I'm serious." She shoves her black suit at me. "I'm not doing this."

"You sure? That's an automatic forfeit."

Her face turns ten shades of red as I waggle my eyebrows at her. I knew she'd never agree to this any other way. The only thing that will get her into that plane is the competition. She hates losing more than she hates heights.

At least that's what I'm banking on.

"I cannot jump from a plane," she says, her voice small.

"That's okay. I'll do the jumping for both of us."

She doesn't seem to take much comfort from the thought.

"Hey," I say, placing my hands on her shoulders so she'll look up at me. "I wouldn't take you up if it wasn't safe. Do you trust me?"

She pushes her sunglasses onto her head, revealing eyes wide with fear. I can read the hesitation there, her questioning how to respond, and I know that whatever she says next will be the truth. Her swallow is audible. "Yes," she says quietly.

My heart soars like a plane on the jump run. "Good." I lean down and drop a kiss on her lips. "Then let's get you suited up."

She reluctantly dons the jumpsuit. "I look like an idiot," she mutters as she yanks up the zipper.

"A very hot idiot." I pull her hair back and gather it into a quick braid, tying the end with a rubber band I grabbed for this reason.

She smooths her hand over it and gives me a questioning look. "How do you know how to do that?"

Instead of answering, I toss her a wink and grab her hand. "Come on, let's go."

It's been months since I've been up, and I can't wait. Having Maeve with me will only make the experience that much better. At least that's my thinking until we take off and I see her face lose all of its color the higher the plane ascends. She looks terrified out of her mind.

"Hey." I cup her face in my palms. "We don't have to do this."

She drops her eyes down to her lap. "And then you'll tell everyone I forfeited."

"I won't. I swear. No one has to know you didn't jump."

I can see the wheels turning in her head. She's probably wondering what I stand to gain by lying for her. The truth is, nothing. I would give up this whole game if I thought I'd still have her after it ended. But I'm too scared she'll cut me out afterward to risk it.

"No, I'll do it," she says softly, even though her hands are trembling. I wrap both of them between mine. "All you have to do is trust me. I'll be with you the entire time, okay?"

"Believe me, the fact that if I die, you die is the only thing giving me hope." She gives me a coy look, and my heart pounds with the need to make her mine.

When the altitude is right, the private instructor I hired helps strap us together. As the door opens, I place my hands on Maeve's hips. "I've got you," I murmur into her neck.

And then we're free-falling.

Maeve screams, and I laugh, not at her but from the sheer exhilaration of plummeting thousands of feet to the ground. It's one of the most incredible experiences I've ever had, and sharing it with her is absolute bliss.

After a few seconds, she quiets. I can sense her body relaxing beneath mine as we continue falling. Then it's time to deploy the canopy, and there's a slight tug as it slows our descent.

"Are you good?" I yell over the rush of the wind.

She nods, her hands clutching the straps of the harness.

Within minutes we're landing, the parachute collapsing behind us in the drop zone. I release the buckles, and she stumbles away from me, resting her hands on her knees.

I detach my gear and drop it onto the ground before approaching her. Stroking her back, I wait for her heart rate to decrease. When she finally realizes I'm there, she collapses into my arms.

"Hey," I say, catching her. "You were amazing."

Her heart is still pounding furiously—I can feel it—and her body is trembling. She doesn't say anything, so I tuck her in close, resting my chin on top of her head, where it belongs. I squeeze her tight, wishing I could weld her to me and never let go. In the space of a few short months, she's become the most important thing in the world to me.

Sensing her pulling back, I slide my hands down to her waist and wait for her to meet my eyes. We've both removed our goggles, and her cheeks are slightly windburned. She looks like a dream.

Maeve lets out a shaky breath. "That was the most terrifying thing I've ever done."

"Worse than letting Rhett drive your car?"

Making a conciliatory face, she says, "Okay, second most terrifying."

"Was it at least a little bit fun?" I ask, scrunching up my nose.

She blows a tiny raspberry. "Fun might be a stretch. I can't believe I'm still alive."

Tucking a strand of hair behind her ear, I gaze down at her. She's the most beautiful thing I've ever seen. "I don't know," I murmur. "I think this might be heaven."

## 43

## "Colour My Heart" - Charlotte OC

*Maeve*

There are a few moments in life that define us. They reveal who we truly are underneath, what's rotting inside our core—or flourishing, if we're lucky. They tell us all we need to know about ourselves.

The call comes at three in the morning. I've only been asleep for a few hours, and my voice sounds groggy when I answer the phone. I don't even look at the name on the screen, just mumble hello and hope whoever it is has a damn good reason for waking me up.

You'd think I would know. I should know. People don't call at three in the morning to chat. They don't call to tell you they're engaged or that their husband is a cheating asshole. They sure as hell don't call to gossip.

There's only one reason they call, and it's never a good one.

Subconsciously, I know this, but I'm still too foggy from sleep to prepare myself for the worst. But the second my mother's voice sounds through the line, the last particle of grogginess vanishes.

"Mum, what's wrong?" I say, sitting up straight. I can't even make out what she's saying through the sobbing on the other end.

My mother doesn't cry. She certainly doesn't sob. People think

Italians are passionate and full of life, but my father has trained all of that out of her. At least he *had*, but it turns out some moments have the power to undo even thirty years of instruction.

"It's Bash," she wails, and my blood runs cold.

"What's happened?" I'm already out of bed, fumbling for the light switch and grabbing the nearest piece of clothing I can find.

Through the jumble of words, I make out the name of a hospital. I disconnect the call after assuring her I'm on my way. My mind whirls, imagining my baby brother on a hospital gurney, bloody, unconscious, or worse. What if he's dead?

Nausea floods my stomach, and I run to the bathroom to vomit. When I'm done heaving, I wipe my mouth and brush my teeth. The mirror reveals just how terrible I look—matted hair, bleary eyes, no makeup. But for once in my life, I don't care.

After throwing a few things into my bag, I head to the hospital, praying that Bash is okay but preparing myself for the worst.

In the car, I make the call without a second thought. It feels like the most natural thing in the world.

"Maeve?" Pierce's voice is full of gravel, and I know I've woken him. I also know he won't care. "What's wrong?"

"Bash was in an accident," I say, doing a better job than my mother at keeping my emotions in check, although the gigantic lump in my throat from unshed tears makes it difficult to form words without breaking down.

"Where are you?"

"Frederick Memorial," I say as the hospital comes into view ahead of me.

"I'm on my way." Pierce ends the call, and I drop my phone into my purse, desperate to get to my family, but also dreading this with all of my heart.

As the automatic door swish open, I squint against the bright lights of the lobby. Seriously, has anyone ever thought of making hospitals a little less hostile? Maybe some mood lighting, a soothing playlist, furniture that doesn't look like it was ordered from a catalog? Evidently, they've never heard of ambiance.

After receiving Bash's room number from the receptionist, I ride the lift to the eighth floor, praying he will still be alive when I get there, that this isn't the thing that destroys my family for good.

\* \* \*

Vivienne and I are sitting on a vinyl sofa in the waiting area while our mother paces the length of the room. My father is somewhere in the building, probably making demands of the staff and reminding them of how many millions the Foundation has donated to this place over the years.

They haven't let me in to see Bash yet, and I'm not sure if I want to go even when I'm allowed. I want to remember him the way he's always been—magnetic, charming, devious—not strapped to a bed with tubes sticking out of his arms and face. I don't know if I can handle seeing my baby brother like that.

Viv reaches for my hand, and I remind myself that this must be even harder for her than it is for me. Not only is Bash her twin, but she was the one who found him after the accident, the one who had to call our parents and tell them. I want to ask her what happened, but I can't make her relive it, not now. The only thing I know, which I suspected the second my mother called, is that street racing was involved.

I squeeze Vivienne's hand between mine, conveying bravery I don't feel. "Where's Cassian?" Considering his proximity to the accident, my money is on him being who Bash was racing. With his father being the estate manager at Belgrave Park, it is only natural that

Cassian and the twins have become inseparable over the years.

My sister shrugs, looking delicate and pale in the black hoodie that's swallowing her up, which probably belongs to Cass. While I'm not excited by the prospect of her spending time with someone who will likely wind up in prison, he did stay with both her and Bash after the accident.

"I think he went to find coffee," she says.

I'm on the verge of pointing out the coffee maker on the other side of the room when I hear footsteps in the hall. Hoping it might be a doctor, I turn and see Pierce approaching instead, and suddenly everything inside me shifts. I feel relief flood my nervous system, like a kid who has just located their parent after being lost at the grocery store.

My feet are carrying me down the tiled corridor before I even realize I've left my chair. Pierce opens his arms to catch me, and the second I'm in them, the world finally—blessedly—stops spinning.

His chest is warm and solid, his scent clean and masculine. He wraps himself around me, as if by doing so, he can take away all of the pain and hurt.

Several minutes pass as he holds me. Around us, nurses are scurrying back and forth, their trainers squeaking on the smooth floor. It feels like watching pedestrians in the rain while you're safe and dry inside a car.

Finally, I ease my grip on his torso slightly.

He strokes my hair, his palm big enough to cup the entire back of my head. "How is he?" he says softly.

Pressing my face into his T-shirt, I sniff. "He's still unconscious. The doctor said—" My voice breaks, and I fight to regain control. "He said they're going to do surgery as soon as he's stable."

"Fuck," Pierce mutters under his breath. "How are you holding up?" He tilts my chin up so he can inspect my face.

"I'm okay." I swipe at the fresh tears trailing down my cheeks, slightly embarrassed to have him see me this way, but at the same time caring a whole lot less than I would if it were anyone else. "I'm okay now."

How can I put into words that I wasn't okay until he got here, that even just calling him soothed some of the anxiety in my heart? How do I explain the way I want to stay in his embrace forever, or that the thought of him leaving makes dread well up in my stomach? I've never felt this way before, and it terrifies the hell out of me to be feeling it now, to be feeling it with *him*.

## 44

## "Control" - Halsey

*Maeve*

"You can go in," the doctor says, "but only two at a time."

I've never understood why they say that. What's going to happen if there are three people in the room? Spontaneous combustion?

My parents look at Viv and me and nod, gesturing that we should go see him first. I clutch my sister's arm, needing her strength as much as she needs mine. We follow the doctor to Bash's room, and my heart feels like it could bust through a brick wall, it's pounding so hard.

We hesitate outside the door for just a moment, then Viv grabs my arm and turns to me. "We have to do this," she says, her voice urgent.

I let her drag me into the room, even though everything within me is screaming for me to run. They've pulled a sheet over his head, and my heart plummets to my toes, no longer pounding, no longer even beating.

Viv lowers the sheet, and I'm about to call out to her to stop, to tell her that I don't want to see him like this, but she moves too quickly. I see his dark hair first, and then the fabric reveals his face. Only it's not Bash lying there—it's Pierce.

A guttural wail tears from my throat, and Viv catches me just before I hit the floor. I try to shut my eyes, to prevent this image from searing itself into my memory, but it's too late. His pale face, his lifeless eyes, his unmoving body—they're already there, erasing all the memories I had of him before, replacing all of the good—

Heart thumping, I bolt upright in bed. I glance around, looking for the monitors and tubes, but I'm not at the hospital at all. I'm in my bedroom, and the sun is peeking through the amethyst velvet drapes. It must be afternoon already.

Refusing to let myself sink back into my pillows—I can't risk the dream returning—I head to the bathroom for a shower. My pajamas are sticking to my body. I've never sweated so much in my life. After turning the spray as hot as I can tolerate it, I step beneath it, letting the water scorch the pain of that dream away.

Bash is still in a coma, but the doctor said his vitals are looking good. Pierce waited for me while Viv and I went in to see our brother. When our ten minutes were up, he wrapped me in his arms again and promised everything would be okay.

The crazy thing is that I actually believed him.

I squirt shampoo into my hand and massage it into my scalp. Every time I close my eyes, I can still see the haunting picture of Pierce lying dead in that bed. It doesn't take much imagination to figure out why my brain chose to play such a horrible trick on me.

I should be freaking out right now. My brother is in a coma after nearly dying in a car accident, and I'm okay. I didn't think I could have received worse news than learning that one of my siblings is fighting for his life. But I was wrong.

If it had been Pierce—

I cover my mouth with a sudsy hand to muffle my cry. Tears are streaming down my face, and I let the water wash them away. I have to get ahold of myself. Bash is going to be fine, and Pierce is more than fine. But my brain won't stop playing what-ifs.

What if it had been Pierce instead? What if it's Pierce next time? A sharp, stabbing pain—like someone has shoved a hot poker into my lungs—surges through my chest. I press my hand against the stone wall of the shower to keep from collapsing onto the floor.

I've never felt like this before. I love my brother and sister, but this feels different. If Pierce were dead, I'd want to be dead too. I need him like my blood needs oxygen. When did he become necessary to my survival?

You don't need to tell me the danger of this situation. I'm fully aware.

I love him. I'm *in* love with him. Do you have any idea how fucking terrifying that is? Being in love with someone means they own a piece of your heart—or if you're really unlucky, all of it. The minute you give your heart away, you give them the power to hurt you.

It's not like I didn't sense this coming. I knew he was doing something to me, that the way I felt about him was changing the more time we spent together. It's like when the weather app predicts rain, but you have your heart set on a picnic, so you convince yourself the forecast is wrong.

I thought it would be fine. I wanted him more than I wanted to be safe. I thought I could have my cake and eat it too.

As the water rinses the lather from my hair, I try to convince myself that everything will be okay. That Pierce and I will figure this out. That we'll work something out that doesn't put my heart at risk. That we'll be good—happy even.

But even as I think it, I know it's not true. Things were fine with us before my feelings decided to get involved, and now I'm not sure how to go back to what we were. Just the thought of seeing him again makes my heart ache with need. I need to regain command of the situation, or else my entire life will spiral out of control. I can't afford to let that happen.

Wrapping a towel around my body and another around my hair, I start applying moisturizer. Even the simple act of doing my skincare routine brings a semblance of peace to my heart. This is all going to work out. I just have to find a way to stay in control.

My phone rings from the bedroom and startles me so bad, I drop the jar of face cream. It shatters on the floor, spraying ivory-colored lotion all over the tile. For several seconds, I stand in front of the mirror, immobile as my phone continues trilling with an incoming call. My mind is racing, going a million directions at once, none of them good.

Is it about Bash? Has he taken a turn for the worse? Has someone else been hurt? What if Pierce—

I cut off those thoughts and take a deep breath. Staring at my reflection, I straighten my shoulders. "Nothing bad has happened. You're going to go in there and answer the call."

Carefully avoiding shards of glass, I walk to the bedroom to retrieve my cell from the nightstand. It's stopped ringing, but I see that I have a missed call from Preston. Relief comes so fast, I have to sit down on the bed as I call him back.

He answers on the first ring. Just hearing his voice slows my heart rate. "Hey, sweetheart," he says. "I need to tell you something."

I squeeze my eyes shut, unwilling to face more bad news. "Okay." I haven't even told him about Bash, because my dad wants to keep the whole thing under wraps until he can sell the right story to the press. He's an asshole like that, even managing to buy off the hospital, no doubt thanks to his insanely large donations over the years.

Preston takes a deep breath and exhales through the phone. "Janie found out. About us."

It takes me several beats to process this, and when I do, I want to shout "thank god," because I'm getting sick and tired of being the other woman. I've even considered letting her know myself so that the two of them will finally get divorced, since he has yet to make a move in that direction.

But I don't tell him any of those things. "Oh no," I say, forcing sympathy into my voice.

"Yeah." I can picture him running his hand through his hair. "She's filing for divorce."

I've been asking him for this exact thing almost since the beginning, because I hate the stigma of an affair, even if the sneaking around has been pretty hot. If he's not going to take matters into his own hands, then let his wife, for fuck's sake.

"How did she find out?" I ask.

"She found my burner phone. She doesn't know who I'm seeing, though, and I didn't tell her."

This is an unexpected blessing. "I'm sorry."

"Well, actually," he says, his tone lightening, "this means we can finally be together."

My head spins. Is that what it means? Do I even *want* to be with him? Maybe it's not about what I want but what I need. And right now, that's regaining some semblance of control. If everything around me is falling apart, maybe this is exactly what I need to feel safe again.

"It's about time." I force a laugh and clutch the phone tighter. "It's been a year and a half."

"I know, baby. I'm sorry. I just didn't want to hurt her, you know?"

"Yeah, I know," I say soothingly. "But it's all going to be okay."

"I hope so." There's another big sigh. "Can you come stay with me? She kicked me out, so I'm at the Allerton."

My thoughts immediately fly to Bash, who's lying in a hospital bed, waiting for surgery. I can't tell Preston anything yet, thanks to my bloody father, but at least he didn't suggest leaving the country together. "Yeah, I can do that. I'll be there in a few hours."

After we hang up, I get to work packing an overnight bag. I'll stop at the hospital and see how my brother is doing on my way to Preston's hotel.

I know you're wondering how I could choose him over Pierce, but that's because you don't know Preston the way I do. He's a good guy. Sure, he doesn't always make the right choices, but who does? The two of us are good together. He allows me the control I need in order to function.

What Pierce and I have scares me. What we have together is like dynamite. One stray spark and the entire thing will blow up in our faces. Preston is more like a flint. You have to work hard to get the flame going, but at least there's no chance of an explosion.

There are some things in life more important than love—like safety. My heart craves something secure, something I can count on. Pierce may be doing and saying all of the right things right now, but what about tomorrow? What about next week or next year? He's volatile. Together, we're dangerous.

The chance of getting burned is just too high with him. And I can't take the risk.

I zip the suitcase shut and set it on the floor, then reach for my phone charger beside the bed. I'm winding it up when there's a sound from the hallway. Fear shoots through my veins as I look for the nearest weapon.

But when Pierce appears in the doorway of my bedroom, I realize the weapon I need isn't something I can hold in my hands.

## 45

## "You're Losing Me" - Taylor Swift

**Maeve**

"What are you doing here?" I stumble against my suitcase as I take a step backward.

Pierce glances at it as he moves into the room. "I thought you might need support."

"You should go." My pulse is a skittering insect beneath my skin. I need him to leave. I don't have the energy to resist him if he stays.

His steps are muffled by the carpet, but I feel each of them resonating through my bones. "Is that what you want?"

"You shouldn't be here." It doesn't answer anything, but it's my last line of defense. If I don't send him away, if I let him break through a single wall, everything will blow up.

"You're sad." It's all he says, because we both know the rest by heart. *You're sad, and I'm the only one who can make you feel better.*

The words to drive him away are on the tip of my tongue. I can taste their sharp metallic flavor. *I don't need you.* I open my mouth to push them out, but they won't come.

Pierce reads my intention along with my inability to follow through. He reads it all, the way he always has. One look, and he sees into the darkest, dirtiest parts of my soul.

I hate him for it.

I love him for it.

He takes another step closer, eliminating the distance between us. Before I can force a word out, his hands are threading through my hair. His thumbs sweep across my cheeks, causing stupid tears to well up in my eyes. "Say it," he whispers.

I want to. I really do. If I tell him that I need him, that I love him, I know what happens next. He will make my heart soar for the clouds. I'll experience happiness like never before. But the problem with soaring is that you always have to come down, and I'm too scared that this parachute is faulty.

So I don't say it. Instead, I push against his chest. "Let me go, Pierce."

An ominous chill envelops me as he drops his hands and takes a step back. "Where are you going?" he says, nudging my luggage with his toe. His tone is icy.

"The hospital." I waited only a split second before replying, but it was too long.

"Bullshit." He crosses his arms over his chest. "Tell me the truth."

I push past him into the bathroom and start adding cosmetics to my bag. "I am." It may not be the whole truth, but it's not a lie either.

"You expect me to believe you need three different hand creams in order to spend the night at the hospital?" He's followed me into the room, and I'm reminded again of why the two of us would never work.

Shooting him a glare, I reach for my toothpaste. Sharp pain pulses through my foot, and I look down to find a shard from the broken cream jar embedded in my heel. "Ow," I moan, leaning against the vanity.

Pierce is immediately on his knees beside me. "Hand me a pair of tweezers, and I'll pull it out."

I give them to him and scrunch my eyes together as he removes the glass. A minute later, he has my foot bandaged and good as new.

"Why am I always tending to your wounds in the bathroom?" he asks, running his hands up my bare calves.

I long to sink into his touch, to let him take me one last time. But if I do, it will only be that much harder to leave when it's over. Filling my lungs with courage, I back away from him. "I need to go."

He moves to block the doorway. "Not until you tell me where you're going."

"Pierce, I don't have time for this." I sigh and try to sidestep him, careful not to put my full weight on my injured foot, but he's faster than I am.

His hands snake around my waist, holding me in front of him. "I know you're not traveling until you know Bash is okay."

I hate that he knows me this well. At the same time, it's comforting to know that there is at least one person in the world who understands exactly how I tick. Comforting, and absolutely terrifying.

"I told you," I say, breathing through my mouth so his scent holds no power over me. "I'm going to see him."

A low growl comes from Pierce's chest. "Which *he* are we talking about?"

Dropping his gaze, I make a last-ditch effort to move from his arms. Surprisingly, he lets me go. Slightly off-balance, I stumble to the bedroom to pack up the last of my things.

"Maeve." A warning pings in his voice, sounding the alarm, alerting me that I need to seek shelter immediately, that the storm in the vicinity is dangerous. He's still blocking the door between the bathroom and the bedroom, the light behind him making it hard to see his features clearly.

I know there's only one thing I can do, only one thing I can say, to make him stop chasing me. One thing that will drive him away for good. No matter how much I like dancing in this thunderstorm, it's time to get to a safe place.

"Preston is getting a divorce." There's a note of confidence in my voice that I don't feel, not even for a second, but my acting must be pretty good, because Pierce's face falters just slightly in the dim light. I force myself to press on. "Which means this thing between us is over."

"No." The word rings out, slamming into my chest with the force of a bullet.

Fortunately, it also has the power to bring me to my senses. "Yes," I snap. "It's not your decision to make."

"The fuck it's not." He strides across the room until he's standing directly in front of me. "Tell me this is your idea of a sick joke."

Rolling my eyes, I hoist my duffel over my shoulder. "You're right. Obviously I'm only joking, because who wouldn't choose you if given the chance?"

With a jerk of his thumb, he lifts the bag off me. "We're not talking about anyone else. Just me and you."

"Well, this conversation is getting boring."

He leans down until his voice hums in my ear. "That's not what you said when I had your ankles around my neck."

I close my eyes against the flash of memories threatening to assail me if I give in. "Listen," I say, looking at him so he can see that I'm serious. "This was fun. But we both knew it was a temporary thing—"

"*Fun?*" he interrupts, and a vein in his jaw ticks. "That's what you call what we had? Fun?"

"I—" The words won't come, because he's right. It was so much more than fun, but if I admit that, I'll have to admit exactly what he means to me, and I can't do that. I can't give him that power. So I swallow the fear clogging my throat and whisper, "You know there's no future for us."

He reaches out and cups the side of my face. My eyes flutter shut of their own accord, my head leaning into his touch.

"Only because you won't let there be," he says softly.

I blink my eyes open, staring at him, wondering if he's right. If things were different—if *I* were different—would we have a chance? A future? "I'm sorry. I just can't."

"Why not?"

"Pierce," I say, a plea in my tone. Why does he have to make this so much harder than it needs to be? "You know I'm right. We can't even stand each other most days." But even as I say the words, they ring as hollow as the inside of a church bell. Because he doesn't feel like my rival anymore, the guy I love to hate, my nemesis and the bane of my existence.

He feels like my . . . everything. And that's a thousand times more dangerous.

"Are you fucking kidding me?" he breathes. "I can't stand to be away from you." The hand on my face tightens, his fingers threading their way into my hair. "You're the only thing I think about. I literally count the minutes until I can see you again."

It's only the lust talking. It has to be. Anything else is too lethal to consider. And if it's just lust— "You'll find someone else in no time," I say, my voice breaking at the thought of him putting those hands on anyone else. "I'm sure Loretta or Carol—"

"I don't *want* anyone else. I want you." His lips crash into mine, and I taste the desperation there, the way he fully intends to claim me for himself, to force me to admit the truth standing between us.

I'm as eager for him as always, but the voice of reason in the back of my head cuts through the fog of desire, reminding me of what I need to do. Pulling away, I take a deep breath, more to fortify myself than anything else. "Just let me go, Pierce."

My words shock him. I can see their impact, the way his face changes, the expression melting off until there's nothing but cold stoicism left. Instead of saying anything, he simply drops his hands and takes a step back. He tosses my bag at my feet. "Fine. Go. Just admit one thing first."

I lift my eyes, not because I want that connection, but because I'm powerless to resist his magnetism.

"You don't love him. You just love who you think you are with him." There's a hint of challenge in Pierce's voice as he folds his arms.

I let out a scoff and drop my gaze. Fuck him. Grabbing my duffel and swinging it over my shoulder once more, I vow that nothing he might do or say will stop me from walking through that door. The handle of my suitcase makes a loud pop as I extend it.

"We both know the only reason you're choosing him over me is because you can control him," he says.

Setting my purse on top of the luggage, I glare at him. "I couldn't make him leave his wife, could I?"

Pierce's laugh is sharp, cutting through my flesh and right to my heart. "The guy is a bastard. He doesn't deserve you."

"I suppose you think you do."

It's a cruel thing to say, but that's what we do, isn't it? We know each other so well that we can pinpoint the exact place to strike—the point of greatest damage—which is why we've always been best at hurting each other.

"No," he says simply, hanging his head. "I know I don't."

It's the last thing I expected to hear, and I frown. He's going off script, and that makes me more nervous than if we were hurling insults at each other. At least then I'd know how to prepare.

There isn't anything left to talk about. I've made up my mind, and he can't stop me. Wheeling my suitcase by the handle, I head for the door.

## "YOU'RE LOSING ME" - TAYLOR SWIFT

At first I think he's going to let me go without another fight, and I can't decide if I'm relieved or disappointed. But then I hear his footsteps on the stairs behind me. My driver must have been waiting for at least thirty minutes already, and it looks like he'll have to wait a few more.

I turn to face Pierce, knowing it's a bad decision, but unable to stop it all the same. It's like looking at a car wreck. You don't want to, but you can't help it.

My breath goes ragged in my chest when our eyes catch, like steak on a dull blade, because I know that he's hearing all of the words I'm not saying—can't say—and I wonder if it's possible for someone to know you better than you know yourself, as if they've studied your molecules under a microscope and can anticipate every action you'll take, every thought you'll have, before you do.

He does. He always has.

"I love you. If you walk out that door, you're going to rip my fucking heart out of my chest and take it with you," he says.

"Pierce." It comes out as a whimper, and it's the only thing I can say. Anything else will destroy me completely.

"Stay, baby." He falls to his knees in my foyer, his heart laid bare before me, his face a crumpled mess. "Stay with me."

My heart tears in half as I look at him begging me for something I can't give him. I let out a hiccuping sob before I do the hardest thing I've ever done and open the door. "I can't. I'm sorry."

## 46

## "Burn Me Beautiful" - Shadow Beloved

*Pierce*

I glance up when I hear a knock on my office door. My assistant sticks her head around the corner and gives me a bright smile.

"I'm going to head home unless there's something else you need from me," she says.

It's only then that I realize what time it is. "No, I'm just wrapping a few things up," I tell her. "Have a good weekend."

She nods and begins to leave, but at the last second, she pops her head back in the door. "You really should go home, too." Her lower lip finds its way between her teeth. "You've put in some long hours this week."

I take a deep breath to keep from snapping, telling her that I'm the fucking CEO, and sometimes that means working late. She's only looking out for me. Instead, I flash her a cardboard smile. "I will. Thanks, Hillary."

As the door closes behind her, I let my head fall in my hands. She's not wrong—I've worked some ridiculous hours this week—but what she doesn't know is that it's the only thing keeping me sane right now.

I can't go home without being assailed by memories of Maeve—pressing her up against the door, the kitchen counter, the walls of my flat; lingering traces of her scent in my sheets even after they've been washed, that fucking photograph I bought for her that's still hanging in my living room. The random things I've found lying around since she left: a hair tie, some French hand cream, a pair of panties, her favorite wine.

She's fucking everywhere, and until I can do an exorcism, it's just easier not to go home.

When she walked out that door, it felt like the Demogorgon reached into my chest and plucked out my heart before dragging me into the Upside Down. The shock that, after everything, she still chose that fucking prick took a while to wear off.

I've tried to tell myself in the days since that if that's who she's chosen to be with, she's clearly not worth it, but that doesn't work either, because I'm well the fuck aware of what I've lost. I've been with a lot of women, and none of them compare to her. I am Orpheus, and she is Eurydice. I would pay any price to get her back, except she doesn't want to return.

Pressing my fingers into my eyes, I take several long breaths, letting her out of my system. It won't work for long—she always finds a way to return—but it will get me through the next five minutes.

I finish up the project I'm working on and head to my car. It's Friday night, and I don't have a thing planned. Normally, I'd hit a club with some of the guys or ask a girl I've hooked up with to come over, but nothing sounds like fun. Not anymore.

From the beginning, I should've known this was what she'd do, but I got too cocky. I thought I could finally change her, make her want me the way I've always wanted her. And it worked for a while. But she was never going to be mine. Not when she never learned to trust me.

I'm supposed to host poker night in a few days. How the fuck am I supposed to sit at the game table with her and pretend everything's fine, pretend that we didn't have sex on the green baize—I finally convinced her to do that—that she didn't kick me between the teeth when she left? Pretend that she didn't tuck my heart into her bags the night she walked out the door? How am I supposed to pretend that it's not killing me that she's with him and not me?

I lie awake at night, imagining his hands on her, and I know it's stupid to torture myself like that. Believe me, I know. But it's like picking at a scab. You don't want it to bleed, but you can't stop.

I wonder if she still fakes her orgasms for him, or if the wanker has somehow figured out how to bring her to climax on his own. What kind of dipshit doesn't know how to pleasure a woman? That should be an exam you have to pass to graduate to manhood.

Pulling out of the car park, I head to my flat at the Atlantis. Rush hour traffic is already over, although there are plenty of people downtown for dinner and drinks. Maybe I should stop somewhere and get hammered. It might help soothe the black hole in my chest.

Ultimately, I decide to just keep going. I have a stocked liquor cabinet at home. I can get smashed there if I want to.

But when the lights in my flat flicker on, I'm hit with the lingering notes of Maeve's perfume—that toasty vanilla I'd recognize anywhere. It's there and gone in a flash, fast enough that I must have imagined it. It happens sometimes, like her scent is caught in the walls of this place and the right amount of air movement at the right time causes it to release.

She's not here. I know that much. I've fallen into that trap too often this week already—searching each room, looking for evidence that she's been by—but I always come up empty and feeling like an even bigger fool than before. Now that she's gone, it's like my brain has decided it's time to remind me of just how much I've lost.

After tossing my keys in the bowl on the foyer table, I run my hand through my hair. I can't do this. I need to get wasted and forget about her, even if just for one night. And fuck that—I need her out of my life for good. If she shows up for poker night once a week, I'll never get her scent out of here. There's no way in hell I'll stand a chance of getting over her if she's constantly in front of me.

There's only one thing I can do.

\* \* \*

Everyone is here, which means that not only do I have some pretty great friends who are willing to give up their Friday night at the last minute, but also that I must have sounded pretty fucking miserable on the phone for them to drop everything and meet me at Dorian's.

The speakeasy is a staple in circles like ours, complete with black-and-white tile, chrome accents, and art deco lighting. Their whiskey menu is extensive, and I order a 1946 Macallan single malt before settling into the black velvet booth, which is actually large enough to fit our entire group. Well, our entire group minus one.

It takes roughly two minutes of catch-up and placing drink orders for anyone to notice.

"Where's Maeve?" Lux asks, glancing around the table. "She's never late."

"She, uh—" I tilt my tumbler back for a small sip while gathering my thoughts. "She had a family dinner tonight and couldn't make it."

It's a lie, of course, because I didn't call her, but that won't matter once I tell them why they're all here.

I haven't talked to her since the night she left to be with Preston. Can't stomach the thought of hearing her voice and knowing she no longer belongs to me in even the smallest way. Of wondering if he's in the room with her, or if she snuck out because she's ashamed to be talking to me.

Conversation buzzes around the table, but I don't hear much of what's being said. I'm still trying to figure out how to tell them what I need to. I never expected it to be this hard.

Walker grins at something Heath whispers in her ear. Lux and Rhett are bickering over something stupid, while Saylor and Slate look on with amusement and annoyance, respectively. Things feel unbalanced without Maeve here, but maybe I'm the one who's throwing things off. If she were here, she'd have the entire table roped into a conversation. By the time we'd finished our drinks, she'd have planned an entire trip to the Maldives.

She would hate to miss out on tonight, but I hope when she finds out, she'll understand why I did it. It's the only way forward. I know how much this challenge means to her, how much these friends mean to her. They're important to me too, but they're essential for her. She doesn't let enough people in, so it's crucial she keep the ones she's chosen to open up to.

I only wish she'd let me stay on that list, too.

Clearing my throat, I glance around at these people who are as close as family to me. This is the last time we'll sit here like this, because after tonight, nothing will ever be the same. "I asked you all here because there's something I need to tell you."

All six pairs of eyes settle on me, and I can read the questions there. The atmosphere has shifted, as though everyone's waiting for the other shoe to drop.

"Don't tell me you're moving to Canada, mate," Rhett says, leaning forward. "I've heard some crazy shit."

I smile down at my glass. "No, I'm not moving to Canada."

"What's going on, Pierce?" Lux asks. She's twirling a set of gold bracelets around her wrist, and I have a flashback to the time when she was dating that asshole Carter. Thank fuck that bastard got what he deserved.

"I need to forfeit the challenge." I toss back the rest of my scotch and motion for the server to bring another.

Silence greets my announcement, as I expected. It's quickly followed by a barrage of voices speaking over each other, demanding to know what I mean.

I hold up my hand. "I've given it a lot of thought, and it will be better this way."

Lux and Walker share a look.

"Is this about Maeve?" Lux says.

Fortunately, I was anticipating this question, so I've come prepared. "Partially," I say. "I know you were all hoping for a reconciliation, but that's not going to be possible. Maeve and I are never going to see eye to eye." *At least on the issue of whether we belong together or not.*

"Does she know you're doing this?" Walker is staring at me, her brows pinched together.

I drop my eyes and scratch at a scuff on the table. "We're not on speaking terms at the moment."

"Fuck, man," Rhett mutters. "That's nothing unusual. There has to be a better solution."

"There isn't." Slapping my hands on my thighs, I lean back in my seat to show them that I'm fine. If I can handle this, so can they. "Besides, we'll still get together, right? Outside of poker and revenge?"

"It won't be the same," he says.

I agree—it won't be. I don't want to walk away from my friends, but if only one of us can stay in the group, it should be her. "You good with hosting poker nights?" I direct this question at Heath and Walker, since they already do on a semiregular basis.

Heath frowns and takes a sip of his craft beer. "Why don't we try to work something out with Maeve instead? None of us want you to just walk away."

"You know how she can be." I run a hand through my hair, pushing back against the memories threatening to suck me under. "Let's just let her have things her way."

"Maybe after she sees how much the group sucks without you, she'll change her mind," Lux offers.

I flash her a sad smile, but I already know that won't happen. Whether Maeve decides to throw out our stupid feud or not, I can't come back. Not like this. Not knowing she'll never give us a chance. "Yeah, maybe," I say softly.

"You realize if you just show up, there's nothing she can do, right?" Slate pipes up for the first time, forearms resting on the table. "She's like five foot nothing. Any one of us can take her."

Lux elbows him in the ribs, but he keeps his eyes fixed on me. "I mean it. Say the word, and we'll put her in her place," he says.

The guy's dead serious, but that's the last thing I want. I clap a hand on his shoulder. "Thanks, mate, but I really think it's better this way. I'll still come around, at least whenever she's not there."

The faces around the table look dejected, eyes lifeless. It pains me to do this to them, but it's only a matter of time until they forget how things used to be. I mean, look at how easily we assimilated Walker back into our group after she came back, not to mention Saylor and Slate.

"Fucking terrific," Rhett says. "Mom and Dad are getting divorced and taking turns with us on the weekends."

Lux's eyes meet those of each person in the group before finally resting on me. "Are you sure there's nothing we can do to change your mind? You really want to do it like this?"

I force a chuckle, because I can't believe we're still having this conversation. When I ran through this scenario in my head earlier, they accepted my answer with hardly any pushback. Now it feels like we're spinning in circles. "Yes, I'm sure."

"Maeve's going to shit a brick when she finds out," Rhett says, popping a toothpick in his mouth. "She's going to want to win the old-fashioned way."

She'll be pissed, but she'll get over it. My guess is she'll be more relieved to have me out of her life than anything. "Nah," I say. "A win is a win."

"You still on for our Thursday tee time?" he asks.

"Wouldn't miss it," I assure him. No risk of running into Maeve on the golf course, at least.

"You'll still come to the wedding, right?" Walker says.

I give her a mock frown. "It'll take a lot more than a tiny hellcat to keep me from the wedding."

"That's good, because I was planning to ask you to be my best man," Heath says.

Holding up my drink in a toast, I say, "I'd be honored, mate."

"Yo, what am I?" Rhett throws up his hands. "Chopped liver?"

Heath chuckles and shakes his head. "Walker told me not to ask you."

Rhett's mouth falls open as he looks at Walker. "Walker. Baby. On what grounds?"

Beside him, Saylor rolls her eyes and does a poor job of hiding her smile.

"I'm sorry, Rhett." Walker bites the side of her mouth to keep her grin in check. "It's the bachelor party more than anything. I still have nightmares about that catsuit—"

"Unbelievable." He throws his hands in the air in mock defeat. "I make one questionable judgment, and you all won't let me forget about it for the rest of eternity."

"Questionable?" Lux says, eyebrows high. "Try 'fatally scarring.'"

Laughter rings out around the table, Rhett's included.

"Nah, man, you're fine," he says to Heath. "I'll be too busy with my girl, anyway." He grabs Saylor and drags her into his lap, making her brown skin turn rosy.

There's a chorus of groans, and it hits me how much I'm going to miss this, how much I'll miss them. We'll still see each other, but it won't be the same, no matter what I said tonight. In some ways, it really does feel like a divorce, Maeve and I alternating nights and weekends so we don't have to cross paths.

But fuck it—no matter how much it hurts, there isn't a thing in the world I wouldn't do for her.

## 47

"Haunted" - Taylor Swift

*Maeve*

I have nothing to wear tonight. Seriously, have you seen the inside of my closet? Not a single thing will work. At least I had a hair appointment today, because trust me, good hair covers a multitude of sins.

Flipping through the hangers, I frown at dress after dress. Many of them I've worn before, which means they're obviously out of the question. I need to pull together a donation, but decluttering my closet hasn't been at the top of my list of priorities recently.

Bash is still in the hospital, still in a coma, and there's nothing I can do about it. There can't be a worse feeling in the world than having your hands tied when all you want to do is help.

I've spent most nights this past week and a half with Preston at his hotel, but when I'm not there, I'm waiting at the hospital. Viv is there every time I go, and my heart breaks watching her. She's completely lost without her brother, and the dark circles growing under her eyes aren't doing her any favors. Last night, I convinced her to go home and sleep in a real bed. She only agreed because I promised to stay with Bash until morning.

Tonight though, I'm ready to have a little fun, to think about something other than the fact that I may never see my brother grinning and making highly inappropriate jokes again. Heath and Walker are hosting poker night, and I'd be lying if I said I'm not relieved. Being in Pierce's flat would have brought back too many memories. I'll have to get used to it eventually, but my emotions are haywire enough at the moment without adding fuel to the fire.

I shove a group of dresses aside on the rack to give myself more room to look through options. Finally, I find one that looks promising. The tags are still attached, and I remember being super excited when I spotted it in the store, before apparently sticking it in my closet and forgetting all about it.

As I carry it to my bed, the crumpled heap of discarded clothes already on top of the duvet mocks me. Let's pretend that I haven't already tried on two dozen options, okay? Sometimes it takes a while to find the perfect one.

After putting the dress on, I stand in front of the mirror to make the final call. It's a black-and-white flared minidress with off-the-shoulder puff sleeves and a sweetheart neckline. The waist is cinched, and the bright white sets off my olive-toned skin nicely. I smooth my hands over the fabric of the skirt, loving the way it rustles against my touch.

I think we have a winner.

Grabbing a pair of nude pumps—which do wonders to lengthen my legs—and a pearl necklace, I can confirm that tonight's outfit looks completely snatched. Some might say it's overkill for playing cards, but believe me when I tell you that you can never go wrong looking perfect.

I've hired a car to drive me to the creepy Gothic manor Heath and Walker bought several years ago. I have no idea why they want to live on the south side of town. It's completely suburban, but they seem happy, in spite of being surrounded by toddlers and Target mums.

In the back seat, my hands knot together in my lap, much the way my gut is doing. I've been dreading this moment all week, but it's unavoidable. *He's* unavoidable. As much as my stomach churns at the thought of seeing him again, this is something I have to do. I made my choice—I can't back down now.

I skipped poker last week. No one expects you to play games when your brother has just been in an accident. But coming up with a different excuse for tonight would only have raised questions I have no desire to answer.

Lifting my chin, I take a deep breath and try to infuse myself with courage. It won't be that bad. Pierce and I have been on much worse terms in the past. We weren't anything to each other anyway, so it wasn't even a real break-up, even if it felt more real than any of the ones I've had in the past.

By some miracle, we've managed to avoid running into each other since that night, which might not seem that impressive, but considering how often Luminara Tech and the Wilson Foundation are crossing paths these days, not to mention us having the same circle of friends, it's actually pretty surprising. Then again, I've been holed up surrounded by fluorescent lights and antiseptic for the past ten days.

Pierce never texted or called, not that I expected him to. His pride runs as deep as mine does, but I was hoping he might check up on Bash. Only so I wouldn't have to be the one to make the first move, obviously. No such luck, though. He didn't come by the hospital or even send flowers.

Before you can tell me this is my fault, let me assure you—I'm well aware. You may not understand my choice, but trust me when I say I made the right one. Pierce and I aren't good together, okay? He—

The car hits a pothole, and I slam back onto my seat, hard. "God," I say to the driver. "Did you even try to avoid that one?"

He shoots me an apologetic look in the mirror. "Sorry."

I roll my eyes and return my gaze to the window. Typically, Pierce offers me a ride when we head out of the city. I must have made a comment once about hating to drive, because he's been doing it for years.

Something tells me that tradition is now dead.

By the time we pull up the driveway to Heath and Walker's house, my heart is pounding like that of an alcoholic in withdrawal. Pierce's black Aston Martin isn't here yet, and I can't decide if I want to arrive before him or not. I open the car door with sweaty palms, already wishing I had tried to use the brother card again this week. Nausea threatens to make me sick, no doubt helped along by the fact that I haven't eaten anything all day.

I tuck my bag more firmly under my arm and make my way to the front porch. Before I can knock, Walker swings it open and pulls me into her arms. She smells like vanilla and peaches, probably from mixing cocktails.

"How is he?" she asks, still clinging to me.

I blink and am about to stammer out something about how I don't know, then I realize she's asking about Bash. "Um, he's still unconscious."

She releases me slowly and gives me a sad smile. "I still can't believe it." She visited the hospital with Heath and Lux a few days ago, reminding me of just how great it is to have friends that are as close as family. If I don't win this challenge, I'll face the very real possibility of losing them forever.

"I guess we should have expected it, given how many times my mother tried to warn him," I say. Bash has always been reckless. The more dangerous an activity is, the more appeal it holds for him. It's actually a miracle he hasn't suffered anything more serious than a broken bone or a concussion before now.

Walker steps back to let me inside, where the rest of the gang is waiting. After giving everyone the latest update on Sebastian and accepting some kind of tropical drink from Heath, complete with a little striped umbrella, we make our way to the back deck, where the poker table awaits.

Pierce still hasn't shown, but he must have told them he's running late, because no one seems to be watching or waiting for him. I want to ask but bite my tongue. There's no need to draw attention to the fact that I've noticed his absence. Better to play it cool than to raise unnecessary questions.

Several times, I think I hear wheels on the gravel outside, and my body tightens as I wait for him to make his appearance, but he never does. When we've been playing for half an hour, I can't help it any longer. I straighten in my chair, careful to keep my cards hidden from Saylor, who's sitting beside me.

"Where's Pierce, anyway?" I say it as casually as possible—I'm a cool cucumber—while inside my heart is still beating 150 miles an hour.

The chatter around the table dies. They all glance at each other, while studiously avoiding looking at me. Saylor shifts in her chair and wipes a trail of condensation off her glass, the gold ring on her thumb glinting in the waning sunlight. Walker is biting the side of her lip, and Rhett is suddenly more interested in his cards than he was ten seconds ago. Heath and Slate are exchanging some kind of nonverbal communication across the table with their eyes.

"What's going on?" I say, an edge finding its way into my voice. "What aren't you telling me?" Because it's apparent now that they all know something I don't.

Lux is twisting her bracelets so fast, I fear for them. After glancing at Slate and getting a subtle nod in return, she turns to me and says,

"He's not coming."

I furrow my brows, taking in everyone around the table. "Okay." Dragging out the word, I add, "So why are you all acting like guilty teenagers?"

She just looks at me, and I can't read her expression, which is aggravating, because she's usually an open book. It's like she's at a loss for words, and that never happens. Like, ever.

"Spit it out, Lux," I snap, without meaning to. If I was on edge before, I'm teetering on the brink of a precipice now. Whatever they have to say had better get said in the next two minutes.

"He's not coming back. Ever," she blurts out.

Six sets of eyes find their way to my face. The expressions I find there are a mixed bag—sad, resigned, accusatory, worried.

"I don't understand," I say, sitting back in my seat before I fall out of it. "What do you mean, he's not coming back?"

Slate clears his throat and props his arm on the back of Lux's chair. "He forfeited the challenge. You win, Maeve." Definitely accusation in his eyes. "Congratulations."

My mind spins like a merry-go-round. He forfeited? What the actual fuck? I scan for a single smile to let me know this is all some big joke, but there isn't the slightest trace of humor to be found, not even on Rhett's face. They are dead serious.

"But—" I start, but I have no idea how to end that sentence. But he can't do that? But I don't want him to leave? But I still need him in my life?

Rhett tosses his cards on the table and folds his arms. "We tried to talk him out of it, but he was insistent. Said it was the only way."

That's impossible. We could have worked something out. We still had months until the challenge was over. There's no way he thought he was going to lose already.

Quiet conversation picks up again, although no one seems to have

## "HAUNTED" - TAYLOR SWIFT

any interest in resuming the game. I stare at my cocktail, which is growing warm in the summer air. I've barely touched it, and the thought of doing so now makes me physically ill.

"Excuse me," I murmur, to no one in particular, before picking up my bag and heading inside.

I have no clear intentions—I just know I have to go somewhere I can process all of this alone. Wandering down a dark corridor, I open the door at the end and step into a huge library lined with floor-to-ceiling bookcases. There are arched windows on the north side and a worn leather sofa in the middle. It's so Walker, I smile without thinking.

As I sink into the couch, anger courses through me like a wildfire blaze. It burns hot, igniting every single inch of me, even my toes, so I kick off my shoes and scowl at the bookcase in front of me.

Why the hell did Pierce string me along this entire time—*months*—if he was just going to bail halfway through? I went fucking *skydiving* for this challenge. I endured the worst date in the history of humanity. I had to be his assistant for twenty-four hours when there are a million other things I could have been doing.

And now I find out it was all for nothing? He couldn't even let me win fair and square. No, he just had to make a show of being the bigger person by pulling out. Now everyone is upset at me, and I didn't even know he was planning to do this.

Before I can think better of it, I grab my phone from my bag and call him. I don't have a clue what I'm going to say. *I'm sorry, please come back?* Turns out, I don't need a plan, because it rings ten times before his voicemail picks up.

"Hey, it's Pierce. Leave a message."

Just the sound of his voice sends a hot poker through my lungs. I gasp for breath and end the call. As soon as it disconnects, I try again. He still doesn't answer.

"Fuck." I toss the phone aside, then immediately pick it up again and send a text.

*Call me. We need to talk.*

I stare at the screen for five minutes, watching as the clock ticks, but the text remains unread. Unbelievable.

Falling back against the soft leather, I let my eyes glass over. I didn't know it would be like this. I didn't know he was going to just disappear. If I had known—

But as soon as I think it, I stop myself. I would have what? Changed my mind? Turned Preston down? Stayed with Pierce when he begged me?

No, this was only ever going to end one way, and we all knew it. There isn't room in this friend group for both him and me. One of us was always going to have to walk away. I'm sure glad it's not me, but did I really want it to be him?

I guess I hadn't actually considered the implications of our agreement, not really. Certainly not recently. It's like I thought we'd stay suspended in time—maintaining a relationship of sorts, even if it wasn't sexual, bickering and fighting because it's what we do best. Never once did I stop to think about what it would feel like once he was out of my life for good.

And now that he is, it feels like the most important part of me has stopped working, the life support turned off with a click as my vitality slowly drains away.

I brush my hands across my skirt, and a new wave of anger surges through me. I chose this dress for him, spent hours looking for the perfect one—one I knew he'd appreciate. I imagined his hands on the small of my waist, pulling me in close and inhaling the perfume I always apply behind my earlobe. It was a false fantasy, because I knew he wouldn't, but I expected to read the desire in his eyes anyway, had imagined us sharing a look as we both pictured what the other would want.

It's ridiculous, I know. I'm with Preston now, and Pierce and I are nothing more than a side note. We were never more than that, even when we were together. He's probably found a new Ella already, a tall blond in a push-up bra and stilettos, trying to sound intelligent while wondering what she can do to lock down Pierce St. James for life.

The thought makes my already nauseous stomach fill with bile. Is that where he is tonight? Is he treating her to dinner before he takes her back to his flat and fucks her on his kitchen counter? Is he even thinking about me at all, knowing I've found out about his decision tonight? He didn't even have the decency to tell me himself, just left his dirty work to our friends.

For a second, I thought he was developing feelings for me, but it turns out that was all a joke too. You don't fall for someone, then leave them on the side of the road to fend for themselves. Nothing will be the same with him gone, and he knows it. He knew what he was doing when he walked away, and he still did it.

And you know what? I'm glad he's gone. I'm glad I kept him at arms' length, because this is exactly what I was afraid of. I knew he'd try to wound me, so I did what I had to in order to protect myself.

So then why does it still hurt so bad?

## 48

"Ruin" - Shawn Mendes

*Two Months Later*

*Pierce*

This fucker is going down, and I can't wait to watch. The sun is just starting to peek over the horizon when the first cruiser pulls up outside the two-story Tudor with its stone facade and dark trim. It's quickly followed by a second and third.

"Showtime," I murmur, and take another sip of my coffee.

I'm parked across the street in an inconspicuous silver rental. My own car would have attracted too much attention in this neighborhood. While its residents are definitely upper middle class, not even professors with tenure drive Aston Martins. Much better to blend in with a BMW.

It takes several minutes for the officers to gather outside the arched wooden door, but once they're all assembled, a burly one steps forward and pounds on it. I can hear his muffled "Police!" even through my car window.

I picture what's going on inside the house. Likely the man inside has been woken by the banging and is currently scrambling to put on a robe and slippers. He's probably wondering what's going on, why his sleep is being interrupted on a quiet Wednesday morning in the middle of August.

He's about to find out it's much more than his sleep being interrupted.

It took me two days to narrow down the list of possible names by cross-referencing it with dates. Mr. Edward Carrow, primary school teacher at Langford Day Academy. He's worked there for eighteen years, but he'll never teach another class again.

The door opens, and it's hard to see his features, but that's okay, because I've spent the past few months memorizing them from pictures I found online. At fifty-one, he hasn't let himself go the way a lot of men his age do. Still as rail thin as he was at twenty-five, the only signs of aging are his thinning hair and the deepening creases around his eyes.

Building a case against him was harder than I thought it would be. His reputation among parents is one a lot of teachers would kill for. They described him as soft-spoken, dedicated, and kind to a fault. The most common thing I heard was that he has a way of making children feel seen.

My gut turns sour at the thought, and I set my to-go mug back in the cup holder.

The police officer leads Carrow onto the front stoop—the fucker *is* wearing a terrycloth robe—then slaps a pair of handcuffs on his wrists. I expected to feel more satisfaction at seeing him led away, but a white-hot rage is burning through me so intensely that my hands are shaking.

I want to charge over there and pummel the man into the ground, to not stop until his face is a bloody mess, until he's crying and begging for mercy, and not even then. I want to drag his thin ass frame into the street and drive over it with my car. I want him dead, his body cold and lifeless. Scum like that doesn't deserve to walk the earth. He may be facing some form of justice, but it won't be enough. It'll never be enough for what he did to my girl.

Blood drains from my knuckles as I clench the steering wheel. Carrow is ushered into the back of a squad car, and I derive a tiny bit of pleasure from watching the officer shove him inside roughly enough that he hits his head on the frame. It seems I'm not the only one who wants this bastard to pay for his crimes.

It took a while to track down his other victims. After asking Lux to break into the school's records, we were able to access a list of Carrow's students. But since they were all under the age of eleven when they came in contact with him, it wasn't as easy as sending an email.

Using the list Lux produced, I cross-referenced the names against social media profiles, the society pages, and my own contacts. Some of them I recognized, of course, and those are the ones I reached out to first, under the guise of being an investigative journalist who was given a tip about potential abuse at Langford Day.

I quickly discovered that Carrow's tastes ran rather singular. All of the men I contacted had only good things to say about the teacher.

"He was a quirky old chap but really good at helping me with math."

"Carrow? Nah, he wasn't abusive. That had to have been Sherer. He was terrible."

The responses from the women were a little different—not necessarily incriminating, but they contained undertones of something more sinister.

"Carrow never laid a hand on me, but my best friend said he could be inappropriate."

"He always gave me the creeps."

It took hours of phone calls and emails to finally track down five victims of Carrow's who were willing to come forward with their testimony. When I asked why they had never spoken up before, they all said the same thing—they'd either been scared, or when they'd tried, no one had listened to them.

From there, I was able to put together a case file and submit it to the police, still using the story about being an investigative journalist as my cover. One of the detectives owed me a favor and kept me in the loop, which is where I got the tip about this morning's arrest.

I watch the police cruiser pull away from the curb, Carrow in the back, and wonder if Maeve will see the news, if she'll even care. I wonder if she'll remember our conversation at Belgrave Park, when she buried her face in my chest and told me her deepest, darkest secret, the one she's carried alone all these years, because when she tried to tell the people who should have protected her, they let her down.

Pulling back onto the street, I make my way home. There's time for a workout before I need to be at the office, but even after an hour in the gym and a shower, I'll probably still end up going in early. Building a case against Carrow has been the only thing keeping me grounded these past two months, and now that it's in the hands of the law, I'll have time to pour myself back into Luminara Tech.

Without something to occupy my mind, it doesn't take long for thoughts of Maeve to come surging back in, threatening to suck me down into the undertow. We haven't talked since she left that day. It's been two months and four days. I've become a bit of a recluse, simply because I know she attends nearly every event on the social calendar.

It's not that I don't want to see her—fuck, I want to see her more than anything. But I know what seeing her would do to me. Shoving a knife into my own chest would be less painful, especially if she's with *him*.

She called me the night they broke the news to her at Heath and

Walker's. I was working late, trying to figure out which teacher at Langford Day had hurt her. When her name and picture popped up on my screen, it took every ounce of willpower I possessed to let it ring through.

It would have been so easy to answer, to listen to her voice, even if she was calling to yell at me—which, let's be honest, she probably was. Despite what I told the others, I'm well aware that Maeve likes to win on her own merits. If she feels like you've given her a victory, it's worse than if she'd lost.

The text came several minutes later, asking me to call her. I didn't, of course, because I'm not a fool. She doesn't want me? Fine. Then she's not getting me.

She eventually stopped trying to contact me altogether, and as I glance at the dark screen of my phone on the seat beside me, I remind myself that it's for the best. He's what she wants. I want her to be happy, and if it takes being with Ansley to make that happen, then I'm going to paste a smile on my face and pretend to be happy for her.

No one promised it would be easy.

## 49

## "The Way I Loved You" - Taylor Swift

*Maeve*

"You're not nervous, are you?" Preston asks as we walk up the stone path to the entrance of Kenswick House. He has my hand tucked in the crook of his arm and gives it a reassuring pat.

I let out a humorless laugh. "Yeah, a little."

Pulling me to a stop on the sidewalk, he looks down at me with that boyish smile. "You have nothing to worry about. Everything will be fine." He bends over and drops a kiss on my lips. "I'm great with parents."

Cocking a brow, I say, "Is that supposed to be comforting? Exactly how many parents have you met?"

His laugh is tinged with embarrassment. "Not that many, but you're missing the point."

"And what is the point?"

Preston and I have been together for a year and a half, but it is only now that I'm introducing him to my family. With Bash finally out of the hospital, it feels like the right time. And while I'm excited at the prospect of ending my mother's harassment about me still being single, I'm terrified it will only transition into bullying to get married. From there, it will be a constant barrage of requests for grandchildren.

I'm not ready for any of that. I'm not sure I'm even ready for this.

"The point is," Preston says, tugging me close, "that you love me, so they'll have to, too."

I take a deep breath and decide to refrain from informing him that my parents haven't received that memo. Me loving something seems to have the opposite effect on them. Not only that, but there's a prickling sensation at the back of my mind, nagging me. Is what I feel for Preston love? It's certainly not the same thing that made my chest ache and tied my stomach in knots when I was with Pierce. It's not the butterflies and fireworks they talk about in books and movies.

But while I may not experience the giddiness of love with Preston, it may surprise you to learn that love is a verb, not just a noun. I'm *choosing* to love him. We're a great match.

Reaching up, I adjust his collar and tie, then smooth my hands over the front panels of his linen jacket. "Of course they'll love you," I say, more for my own sake than his.

While I'm sure my mother will initially be overjoyed to see me with a man—any man—I have a feeling her relief will be short-lived when she realizes who Preston is. He's not poor by any means, but his family is firmly upper middle class. With his political career, he's made some excellent connections, though. And besides, with the two of us working together, he's likely to become prime minister before he's even forty.

As we climb the steps, both of my parents open the door—something my father never does. It's possible Bash's accident changed something in him, but it's more likely that he's as curious to see who I'm bringing to dinner as my mother is.

In the most blatantly obvious way possible—seriously, a fire truck would have been more subtle—they scan Preston from head to toe. As a glimmer of recognition lights my mother's eyes, my stomach sinks. This can't be good. If she knows him, it can only be because of—

"Aren't you Janie Ansley's husband?" she says, loud enough for the neighbors half a mile away to hear.

Preston turns the color of a tomato, and I squeeze his arm. I guess hoping for her forgetfulness to strike tonight was too much of a stretch.

"Ignore her," I say under my breath. To my mother, I say, "Can we not do this out here?" When she doesn't say anything, just keeps staring at Preston, I add, "Please?"

She brushes her gaze across me as she turns for the house without another word.

"I thought you were bringing Pierce," my father says, still frowning at Preston. He's probably scanning his mental Rolodex for the last name Ansley. There's no way he met Preston at his own house party. The man doesn't speak to people "beneath" him unless he's placing a drink order.

Beside me, Preston stiffens. "Pierce?" He casts me a sidelong look.

"It's a long story," I mutter, and pull him into the house. "Good to see you too, Dad."

My father steps aside so we can enter but doesn't offer his hand to my boyfriend. Nothing too surprising there, though, since he judges every new connection based on what it can do for him, and he's likely already decided that he doesn't stand to benefit a thing from the man standing next to me.

As soon as we're inside, my mother's hand is on my arm. "We need to talk," she says.

I give Preston an apologetic look as she pulls me into the dining room, leaving him behind with my father, who will, at the very least, have the good manners to offer him a drink.

"What, Mother?" I say, shaking her hand off as soon as we're in private. "You're being incredibly rude."

She gapes at me like I've said something shocking. "*I'm* being rude? What about you?"

I smash my brows together. "I've literally just arrived."

"You told me you were bringing a guest."

Blinking as I wait for the punchline, I realize there isn't one. "Yeah." I jerk my thumb over my shoulder. "I did. My boyfriend."

Pinching her lips into a flat line, she huffs through her nose. "Last time you brought someone to family dinner, it was Pierce."

I can't help the eye roll—it's too overwhelming. "That was months ago," I hiss as a server enters with a sushi tower. There are already two of them placed in the center of the table, each holding six layers of rolls. "God, how many people are coming tonight?"

Without bothering to glance at the spread, my mother says, "It's your brother's favorite. And don't think you can distract me from the real reason I pulled you in here."

Bash may love sushi, but she could have put a box of cereal at his spot and he would have annihilated it. This is complete overkill, a move she probably played because she thought it would impress my date. If Pierce were here, he certainly wouldn't let her efforts go unappreciated, but Preston won't even know that he's meant to be impressed.

"And what's the real reason, Mother? I thought it was to berate my choice of date."

A flush climbs her neck and settles in her cheeks. "He's married, Maeve." Keeping her voice low so the servers don't overhear, she casts a quick glance around the room before continuing. "Your reputation will never recover from this."

I allow a laugh I don't feel to escape my chest. "Does it matter if I love him or he treats me well? Do you even care if I'm happy?"

"Are you?" she asks, a look of sincerity crossing her face—the first one I've seen in ages. "Happy?"

Lifting my chin, I don't drop her gaze. "Blissfully."

Before she can say anything to that, my father's voice booms from the doorway. "Let's eat."

I turn to look for Preston, and he walks in behind my dad, carrying a tumbler of whiskey and looking relatively unharmed. As I flick a bit of lint from his shoulder, I ask, "Was he nice to you?"

He shrugs and lets that youthful smile cross his face. "I don't think he'll be calling me for a round of golf or skeets any time soon, but we got on."

I search his eyes for any sign that he's lying to me but don't find one. Leading him to the table, I realize that Vivienne slipped into the room while we were talking and is already seated. Bash's spot next to her is empty, but that's nothing new.

Preston pulls out my chair, then takes the one next to me. I shoot him a look that I hope conveys everything I'm feeling—apprehension, anxiety, nausea—and he returns it with a smile before turning to my father at the head of the table and asking about the stock market.

It's a wise tactic, even if the execution was a little sloppy, but he'll figure it out eventually. At least that's the reassurance I'm clinging to tonight. Lifting my wine glass to my lips, I take a sip, meeting my sister's gaze across the table. She mirrors the gesture, her eyes giving nothing away, but I've known her long enough to be able to read all of her thoughts anyway.

Viv and I have never been close, but since Bash's accident, we've been pulled together by some invisible string. The slight quirk of her lips tells me she's amused by this situation, but the steadiness of her gaze means she's also curious about Preston and me.

The dining room doors open, and Sebastian sails into the room wearing a smile the size of a watermelon slice. The three-inch scar running through his eyebrow is the only reminder of his accident. He doesn't have any memories of that night, and I'm not sure if that's a blessing or a curse. I still don't have all of the details myself, but I do know that, given how much our father got involved afterward, they're hiding something.

"Mother." Sebastian stops to drop a kiss on her head the way he always does, but she stays rigid in her chair, her lips somehow even more pinched as she receives a peck from her favorite child. "Father." Bash gives him a mock salute before flopping into his chair next to Vivienne. "Sisters," he says, looking between Viv and me before his eyes land on Preston. "And who is this?"

I fill my lungs with air, because it buys me several seconds to keep my exasperation from boiling over. If I have to hear one more disparaging remark about my choice of date, I'm not sticking around.

"This is Preston Ansley," I say. "My boyfriend."

Bash whistles and picks up his wine. "A boyfriend. Congrats, Maeve. Didn't realize you were into the age-gap thing." He jerks in his seat from what I can only guess was a kick from Vivienne.

My father clears his throat. "Let's eat."

I stare daggers at my brother from across the table, but he only smiles back, already planning a million ways to ruin my evening. The devious look in his eyes makes his intentions all too clear.

Bash plucks a piece of sushi from the tower in front of him and pops it into his mouth. He gives Mum a thumbs-up, then turns back to Preston and me. Directing my gaze heavenward, I say a prayer for the restraint necessary to keep from adding a few more scars to his face.

"So, Preston," Bash says, lifting another roll with his chopsticks. "Do you have any kids? Grandkids?"

I choke on my wine and set my goblet back down before I spill it.

Preston gives me a small pat on the back before turning to Bash with a chuckle. "No, no kids."

I glare at my brother, but he pretends to be oblivious. I'm beginning to wish he'd stayed in that coma after all.

He woke up twelve days after the accident. I'll never forget receiving that call. I had just gotten out of the shower, and when Viv told me he was awake, I sank to the floor of the bathroom and sobbed. I'd been terrified he'd never come out of it.

After my tears subsided, I reached for my phone again, a single thought on my mind. I needed to tell Pierce. He would want to know. But as my thumb pressed the call symbol next to his name, it all came crashing back—the way I'd left him, finding out he forfeited the challenge, him ignoring all of my calls and texts, realizing he might never speak to me again.

I ended the call before it connected and dressed in a daze. Only once I was on my way to the hospital did I let Preston and Walker know. Preston offered to come with me, but I knew that would only lead to questions from my family—questions I was in no position to answer at the moment. Walker assured me she'd let everyone else know, and from the way she said it, I knew she was including Pierce.

My friends haven't met Preston yet, at least not as my boyfriend. They've known that we're seeing each other for the better part of our relationship, and they've made their disapproval clear. But when I remember how we all moved past the drama in Heath and Walker's relationship, and accepted Slate and Saylor into our group, it gives me hope that they'll eventually come around.

I can't handle the thought of any other outcome. I've already lost Pierce; I can't lose them, too.

Glancing sideways, I assess how Preston is faring beneath my brother's interrogation. He seems to be holding his ground, but I notice that he's only taken a few bites so far. I wonder if he's feeling as nauseous as I am.

I reach over and place my hand on his leg, giving him a reassuring squeeze. He smiles at me and rests his own hand on top of mine.

We may not be perfect, but we're good together. That much is obvious to anyone with eyes in their head, whether my family wants to admit it or not. I may crave their approval, but I don't need it. I don't even need my friends' approval, even though it means the world to me.

I may still struggle with control, but one thing I've learned this year is that you can't control other people's opinion of you. You can do everything in your power to ensure they think well of you, but at the end of the day, it's still up to them to make their own judgment.

If my family doesn't approve of Preston and me together, who cares? I'm a grown-ass woman who can make her own decisions. And as I turn my hand palm up on Preston's leg, I decide to give up on trying to control what they think about me. All that matters is the two of us.

# 50

## "exile" - Taylor Swift ft. Bon Iver

*Pierce*

I've never wished I could skip forward in time more than I do right now. As I tighten the bow tie around my neck, my reflection mocks me, proving just how little sleep I've been getting by highlighting the dark circles under my eyes—the exhaustion I can't hide, no matter how hard I try. Not that I've tried very hard. The only thing I've put any actual effort into lately is forgetting, and tonight, even that will be impossible.

My fingers dive into my hair before I remember that it's already styled. Fuck it. Who cares if it looks like a mess? I rearrange the strands as best I can, then take a deep breath and head for the door. May as well rip off the fucking bandage.

The car ride to the Wesbourne Botanical Gardens passes much faster than preferred. I briefly consider asking my driver to circle the block a few times but realize that will only delay the inevitable, so I refrain. At some point, I'm going to have to get out and go inside, even if I'd rather watch while someone carves out my entrails with a dull knife.

As the limo slows in front of the entrance, where paparazzi flank both sides of the red carpet that has been laid out, my heart picks up speed. And even though I've been telling myself this whole time that it's from dread, I have to admit that a tiny amount of the adrenaline comes from anticipation, too.

It's been too long since I've been at an event like this. Without a girlfriend nagging me to take her places, it's been easier to avoid them all together. I've asked Hillary to decline the invitations on my behalf, and other than a raised brow the first few times, she hasn't mentioned anything. I know she thinks I work too much, but the truth is, if I wasn't working, I'd be doing something much worse. At least this way I'm contributing to society.

My car pulls to a stop in front of the red carpet, and I wait as the driver rounds to open my door. I button my tuxedo jacket as I get out, pasting a smile on my face and waving at the nearest reporters. The lights from the cameras are blinding, but I keep my grin in place as I approach the entrance.

Voices call out from both sides of the carpeted walk.

"Are you attending alone tonight, Mr. St. James?"

"Can you share about the effect Solace Link will have on the climate?"

"Is this the start of future collaborations between Luminara Tech and the Wilson Foundation?"

I ignore them all while keeping the smile on my face from slipping. You get good at this kind of thing when you do it every week. Even though it's been several months since I've attended an event, it's comforting to know I haven't gotten too rusty.

Right before the double glass doors, I stop and turn so the photographers can get their shots. Kind of wish there was also a sniper in the crowd, taking aim at my heart. No such luck, though. After thirty seconds, I give one last wave before walking inside.

The lobby has been minimally decorated for tonight, because the event itself is taking inside the conservatory, located behind the main building. Small clusters of people linger around the fringes of the room, but I refuse to let myself scan them and instead head for the doors leading out back.

A brick path lined with fairy lights takes me to the conservatory, which is lit up like a beacon in the night, a soft glow spilling out of its glass walls and roof. We're far enough from the heart of the city that you can actually see a few stars studding the sky.

I slow to the pace of the people walking ahead of me. I'm certainly in no hurry to get inside. The longer I can keep to the shadows, the better. Unfortunately, even turtles eventually reach their destination, and I'm soon crossing the threshold into the venue, which has been transformed into a wonderland for tonight's gala.

Tropical orchids hang from the ceiling, suspended in bloom, while guests in black tie mingle below, sipping champagne and murmuring softly. Several small reflecting pools dot the room, flickering candles and lotus blooms floating on their surfaces. The waitstaff are wearing silver-toned uniforms, giving them the appearance of water as they ripple through the crowd with trays of cocktails and citrus-glazed hors d'oeuvres.

I gratefully accept a glass from a server and toss it back in one go. It's going to take about five more of those to reach the point where I stop caring. May as well get started.

Before I can move to find another drink, a hand claps me on the shoulder.

"Pierce," a booming voice says, and I turn to find Lord Wilson wearing a grin the size of England. "You ready for this?"

*Fuck no.* He means my speech, which is written and ready to go on my phone—not the source of the dread currently pooled in the pit of my stomach. "As ready as I'll ever be," I say, with a smile I don't mean in the slightest.

Another tray of cocktails passes, and I snag one, replacing it with my empty glass. They really should have made these stronger. I force myself to go slower this time, given the man standing next to me.

"I'm confident you'll make us all proud." He clinks his flute against mine, and the tinkling sound evaporates into the noise of the crowd. Leaning in, he lowers his voice to what I assume is meant to be a whisper, but it is still about five decibels above most people's. "Just between us, I was hoping we'd be making an announcement of a different sort tonight."

I raise my brows is genuine confusion. "Were you hoping for a different outcome for Solace Link? I wasn't aware."

We've spent the entire summer rebranding our collaborative project. What was previously HavenNet is now Solace Link, with a renewed and revised mission and an even tighter marketing campaign behind it.

The rebrand wasn't just cosmetic, either. Our team is committed to more transparency, equality, and deeper engagement with the communities we're hoping to serve—refugee camps, natural disaster zones, and war-torn regions—than ever before. If Lord Wilson isn't happy with the project, this is the first I'm hearing of it.

He still has his arm slung around me as if we're old pals—we're definitely not—and he throws his head back to laugh at what he mistook for a joke. "No, the project's fine, now that we finally have something to show our donors. I was referring to something of a more . . . *personal* nature."

Trepidation creeps in, turns a few times in my chest, and settles itself down for a nice nap. Mixing business with pleasure was one of the worst mistakes I ever made, and I'll be dead before I ever do it again.

"I'm afraid I don't know what you mean," I murmur, raising my glass to my lips. I'm beginning to regret not bringing a date to this thing. Even Celestia would have been a nice distraction right now.

"She scared you off, didn't she?" His hand jostles my shoulder, and I move my drink before I spill it on my suit.

It doesn't even matter that he didn't say her name. Not saying it creates a vacuum in my brain—one it's eager to fill, chanting it until my blood itself is pulsing to the cadence of it.

"She always does that. Never grateful for what she's got right in front of her." Shaking his head, Lord Wilson finally removes his arm and throws his cocktail back.

My body feels as rigid as a robot's, but I can't let him talk about Maeve like that. She's his daughter, for fuck's sake, not that he deserves to lay a single claim to her. "We were never more than friends," I say. "It had nothing to do with her."

I can tell he has more to say on the subject, but I choose that moment to walk away, because I'd rather slam my hand in a car door repeatedly than stick around and listen to it.

\* \* \*

I'm in the middle of giving my speech when I finally see her. She's standing near the front, and at first she's just another face in the crowd. But my body knows, and I find my eyes traveling back to her, words becoming foreign entities to my tongue as my heart takes off like a MiG-25.

She's wearing a dress that must have been designed by God Himself—a dark fitted gown that flares at the bottom like a mermaid's tail. It's covered in a gold floral pattern—appropriately chosen with tonight's venue in mind, I'm sure—and the fabric looks like it would collapse if I crushed it between my hands. Her black hair is swept back and softly pinned up at the base of her neck. Gold earrings in the shape of leaves dangle from her ears.

Fuck my life. She's so gorgeous, it's physically painful to look at her.

I force my eyes back to my phone, but it's too late. I've lost my place, thanks to Maeve's face double-crossing my mind. Picking a general location in my notes to restart from, I continue speaking, but my heart's no longer in it. It feels like I can't breathe, like I'm choking on the very air providing oxygen to my lungs.

Five blessedly short minutes later, I've thanked everyone for coming, for their support and generosity, and wished them a good time tonight. Technically, I'm supposed to stick around to schmooze our biggest donors, but I have no doubt the rest of the executive team can handle it if I slink off to a back corner somewhere. I've had all the social interaction I can handle after being sucker-punched in the gut.

Climbing down the steps from the stage with the intention of grabbing another drink, my eyes find Maeve again in the sea of people, as if they're magnets and she's the north pole. She's turned away from me, revealing the fact that the back of her dress dips down to her waist, that creamy skin on display for all to see. I even spy the freckle near her right hip that I've kissed more times than I can count.

When someone bumps into me, then excuses themself, I realize I'm staring. I turn my head to the side, pretending to be lost in thought, but a second later, my eyes are straying back to her. She's holding a glass of champagne in her hand, occasionally lifting it to those red lips and making her slender throat bob as she swallows.

I don't even notice him standing next to her—that's how forgettable he is—until he slips his arm around her, his hand resting on the small of her back. Which is bare. He is literally touching my girl's bare skin, and there's nothing I can do about it.

My head starts to throb. She should be on my arm, not Preston fucking Ansley's. The prick doesn't deserve her pinkie toe, let alone every inch of her. Just a few months ago, he was wearing another woman's ring, and now he's putting his hands on Maeve like he owns her. Like she's lucky to be with him.

Clenching my fists, I go in search of a stronger cocktail. Whatever elderflower shit they're serving won't get me nearly as drunk as I need to be if I am to endure this night.

Armed with a whiskey neat I sweet-talked the bartender into pouring me, I head for the front lobby. It was mostly deserted when I arrived, and I'm hoping it will still be that way. I've got about three more hours of this shit before I can go home.

Turns out I'm in luck. Not only are there only a few stragglers in the reception area, but there's a suede sofa tucked against a wall that is calling my name. I'm not going to sleep—although that sounds pretty good right now—but I need to sit down. I feel like I've been whacked in the chest with a sledgehammer.

I sink into the soft cushions with a sigh and lean back, shutting my eyes. Above me, the air-conditioning purrs, the sound occasionally punctuated by the door to the powder rooms closing or someone softly speaking to a companion.

Just when I start to think I might doze off after all, a voice cuts through everything, like a glass shard through skin.

"Pierce?"

Blinking my eyes open, I sit upright. There she is, standing less than five feet from me, her perfume floating toward me like a siren's song on the breeze. "Hey." I grind my molars together and down the rest of my whiskey before wincing at the burn.

Her dress rustles as she moves closer, and I wish she wouldn't. I wish she'd go back to him so I don't have to see her, don't have to hear her or smell her or think about her. I keep my eyes glued to the tiled floor.

"Are you okay?" Maeve asks softly.

She's never spoken to me like this before—this quietly, this gently. Is it the result of being with him exclusively, or something else? Has she changed that much in the past two and a half months?

I give her a short and humorless laugh without looking up. "Yep, just fine."

Without asking if it's okay, she takes the seat beside me, sending my heart careening over the side of the Grand Canyon and smashing into a thousand pieces at the bottom. Her bare arm brushes against my jacket, and I suck in a breath between my teeth.

I bolt to my feet, desperate to put space between us before I grab her and force her to admit she cares. But the fact is, I thought she cared, and now I don't know anymore. If she did, she wouldn't have left.

She frowns at me, the old Maeve settling into her face. Pushing to her feet—she still only reaches my shoulder—she folds her arms. "You're not acting fine."

"What do you want me to say? That I'm pissed?" I bend over to set down my glass before I throw it across the room. "Okay. I'm pissed."

"What for?"

This time I laugh for real. "You're hilarious."

"Forgive me for trying to understand."

"Fuck understanding." I lean down so she can smell the alcohol on my breath. Maybe then she'll go running back to where she came from. "You're here for what you can't get from him."

The smack comes without warning. Her mouth forms a tiny O the second her palm connects with my cheek. It stings, but I relish it. It gives me something to feel besides this excruciating clawing desire to get out of my own body.

"How dare you," she hisses, but there's less venom in her voice than usual. It seems that slap drained something from her and gave it to me instead.

"How dare I?" I taunt her. "I did nothing."

"The day you do nothing will be the day hell freezes over."

"Hope you've RSVP'd."

Her glare turns lethal, bringing a smirk to my lips. I haven't had this much fun in months.

"What is wrong with you?"

"Wrong with *me*?" I shove a finger against my chest. "You're the one who walked away."

"It was time," she says, but her voice lacks conviction. "We both knew it."

Too bad for her, I don't care. It's too little, too late. If she's here to apologize, she's barking up the wrong tree. "Quit assuming anything about me."

Genuine hurt crosses her face, and a flash of pain tears through my chest. "Pierce," she begins, but I cut her off by holding up my hand. I've seen this movie before. The ending sucks.

"Don't."

She twists her hands together in front of her, her delicate gold bracelet catching the light from the chandelier above us. "I don't understand why you're so upset."

I take a step toward her, because my body physically can't handle the distance between us. If she's in the room, I need to be next to her. Why do you think I've stayed away for so long?

"Tell me you're not serious," I say.

She swallows audibly, and I know I'm making her nervous. Good. Let her squirm. She's had me under her thumb long enough. She nods, lifting her chin the way she does when she's trying to regain control. "I am."

"I would have given up everything for you. Every goddamn thing. If you had asked me for the sun, I would've found a way to get it for you." The words come out strained. "You had me on my fucking *knees*, Maeve."

Her lips part as she inhales sharply, and my eyes immediately land on them, drawn there like a moth to a flame. My mouth aches to crash into hers, to claim it, to remind her of exactly what she walked away from. But I don't let it. I wouldn't even if she begged me to. Because whatever was once between us has been hacked to pieces by the hatchet she keeps in her tiny little bag.

"But don't worry," I say, breathing out the words so that they brush against the shell of her ear. "It won't ever happen again."

When she's good and speechless, I reach down and retrieve my empty glass from the floor. Holding it out to her in a mock toast, I throw her a scornful wink and walk away.

It sickens me to do it, because I know it's going to hurt her, but I don't have the power to resist. Fuck this bullshit. Maybe I should consider relocating to Canada after all. At the very least, I could look into doing some traveling—anything that takes me out of her orbit more often.

Because one thing is as clear as the crystal tumbler I'm holding. I will never give my heart to a woman again.

# 51

## "The Scientist" - Coldplay

*Maeve*

I'm looking for the fan remote in the nightstand drawer when I find the ring. Preston likes to crank up the speed of the fan after I get up in the morning, turning it so high anything not tied down is liable to take off across the room.

He moved in a few weeks ago, after Janie got the house in the divorce. It just made sense, even if adjusting to a roommate has been more difficult than I thought it'd be. No matter how many times I tell him, he still can't manage to put his damn socks in the laundry hamper, and I've watched him use my favorite mug for the very last time. Every time I jump him about it, he smiles as if he's being funny and says, "I like this one better."

*Yeah, so do I*, I always want to snap back, but refrain. But if he does it one more time, that's it. I'm fighting for my cup. This is *my* house.

Preston finally got out of bed a few minutes ago and is currently in the shower. I can hear him singing off-key, probably into my shampoo bottle. Rolling my eyes, I continue rifling through the drawer, then freeze when my fingers close around a box that feels way too familiar, considering I've never seen it before.

I pull it out and move to the bed so I can sit down.

It's small, square-shaped, and covered in black velvet. You and I both know what this is. They don't sell normal jewelry in boxes like this.

Prying open the lid, I prepare myself to gasp, but a tiny whimper comes out instead the second I see the ring. Halo setting, thick white-gold band, at least three carats. It looks like it's a J or K on the GIA scale—not yellow exactly, but far from icy. Definitely SI clarity—it's busy inside, as if it's holding a little storm.

I snap the box shut again, hiding the ring from view. If I had to guess, I'd say he didn't choose it himself. It looks exactly like something a shop assistant would try to upsell.

Shoving the box back inside the drawer, I stand up and blow out a breath. The ring itself isn't the problem. Easy enough to get it exchanged. The problem is how he's planning to propose.

Preston may be a lot of things, but a planner is not one of them. At least not when it comes to his personal life. Even though we're officially a couple now, I organize all of our dates, and he comes along for the ride. So how is he going to pull off a proposal?

The best thing I can do is plan the perfect night and hope he takes the hint.

I glance down at the nail I broke yesterday during a meeting that did not go particularly well. It was a fresh manicure, too, but this gives me an excuse to get a new one. I certainly don't want emerald nails in the photos. They would distract from the ring.

After scheduling nail and hair appointments for this afternoon—god, it's nice to be well-connected enough to get last-minute bookings at the best salons—I mentally scroll through the possible restaurant options while scrambling some eggs for my almost-fiancé's breakfast. We'll need something with privacy, of course, but well-lit enough that the pictures aren't grainy. A discreet staff is a must, since I'll need to give them a heads-up so they can have a bottle of champagne chilled.

By the time Preston joins me in the kitchen, his eggs are perfectly cooked, and I have the perfect place picked out.

"Hey, babe," he says, kissing my cheek and smelling suspiciously like my French conditioner.

"Good morning." I give him a bright smile with his plated breakfast. "I was thinking."

Preston settles himself on a barstool and raises a brow. "Uh-oh."

"Why don't we do dinner at Sauvage tomorrow night?"

"Sauvage?" he asks around a bite of eggs. "Isn't that the place with ice sculptures on the tables?"

"It is," I say, a little surprised he's been there.

"Janie and I went there for our anniversary once."

My heart plummets. At least I'm finding out now and not after the fact. We can't get engaged at a place he's taken his wife. Although that will severely limit our options. "Okay." I square my shoulders and wipe some crumbs from the counter with a dish cloth. "We can go somewhere else, then."

"No." Shaking his head, he takes a long drink of water. "Sauvage sounds good."

I frown at his bent head. Sauvage does *not* sound good, at least not for my proposal. "Preston," I snap, and he quickly looks up. "I don't want to go somewhere you took her."

His eyes widen, and he looks genuinely surprised. "Janie and I went to a lot of places over the years."

"Just forget it," I say, and pick up my phone. "I'll find something else."

He shrugs and returns to his food, happy to let me have whatever I want. See what a gem I'll be marrying?

\* \* \*

We end up going to Élan instead. Atmosphere-wise, it's not quite as good as Sauvage would have been, but at least it's not tainted with memories of Preston and his ex-wife. God, I still don't want to think about how narrowly we avoided that one.

Right before we left, I made up some excuse about needing to grab something from the bedroom. He waited for me in the foyer while I checked the nightstand drawer. The ring box was gone. That can only mean one thing—showtime.

I know you're thinking that realistically the ring could be in a lot of places—hidden somewhere else, taken in for resizing, returned for god knows what reason. But you don't know Preston like I do. He's a simple man with simple intentions. If he's planning to propose to me, he's going to do it in the most straightforward way possible.

I've given him the perfect setup. All he needs to do is take advantage.

We've finished our first four courses—I highly recommend the rosé champagne lobster medallions—and are waiting on our dessert. I wanted to get the *sphère de chocolat etoilée*, which I swear is handcrafted by angels before being delivered to earth, but when I mentioned it to Preston, he said he'd rather share the *nuage de citron et lavande*. I wanted to point out that there is no need to share anything, we could each get our own, but I remembered his financial situation just in time. He's got enough traditionalism in him not to let me pay for our meal, even if his job doesn't pay enough to afford places like this very often.

Especially not with the payments he must have taken on for the ring in his pocket.

Thinking of it reminds me why we're here in the first place. I don't know if he's forgotten or if he's just waiting for the perfect moment, but every man needs a gentle push now and then, right?

I reach my hands across the table for his. He takes them and smiles at me, his brown hair flopping across his forehead, making him look younger than thirty-five.

"I can't believe we can finally do things like this," I say, glancing around the restaurant.

It's late in the evening, so most patrons have cleared out, leaving the perfect atmosphere for an intimate moment.

"It's incredible." He strokes the back of my hand with his thumb.

It happens suddenly, the way most flashbacks do. One second I'm looking down at our joined hands, and the next, I'm seeing Pierce's fingers wrapped around mine, his thumb the one brushing against my skin, except his touch causes goosebumps to break out up and down my arms.

I shake my head, clearing those traitorous thoughts away. Of course my self-sabotaging brain would remind me of Pierce on the night of my engagement.

Giving Preston an encouraging smile, I say, "I don't want to do this with anyone else. You're it for me."

"You're it for me too, Maeve." He tightens his hands around mine. "In fact, there's something I want to ask you."

*Here we go.*

My pulse picks up speed as he reaches into his pocket and withdraws the same box I found yesterday. I take a deep breath to calm my racing nerves. So far, everything is going according to plan. I just wish it wasn't all so damn exhausting.

Out of the corner of my eye, I see the server approaching us with the lemon chiffon cake. I glance up, meeting his eyes, and give him a subtle nod. He retreats to the kitchen, presumably to get the champagne.

Preston pops open the box. My gasp of surprise is perfectly executed—What? I only practiced half a dozen times—and I free one of my hands to cover my mouth as I stare at the ring. It catches the light, and you can hardly see its flaws from here.

"Maeve Wilson, will you marry me?"

The look of expectancy on Preston's face is exactly how I pictured it—everything is exactly how I pictured it. My French manicure is flawless, I'm wearing a black Dior dress with a pearl-edged square neckline I just picked up today, the restaurant receives full marks for both food and atmosphere, and there's a handsome man smiling at me from across the table, asking me to spend the rest of my life with him.

And that's when it hits me.

I spent so much time thinking about the proposal, I never stopped to think about the question itself.

# 52

## "champagne problems" - Taylor Swift

*Maeve*

The cork releases from the bottle with a small pop, and I toss the corkscrew aside and grab a goblet. With my free hand, I tap the phone icon next to Vivienne's photo.

She picks up after two rings. In the background, I can hear the voices of several other girls chatting.

"Hey, Maeve," she says, and I mentally applaud her for not including a single ounce of shock or even surprise into her voice. You'd never know from hearing her just now that we're not the kind of sisters who talk on the phone every week. Or, rather, at all.

We've grown closer since Bash's accident, though, and she's the only person I want to talk to after everything that happened tonight.

"Is this a bad time?" I ask, sipping my wine. "I can call back."

"No, it's fine. Sutton and Marlowe are just talking about boys anyway." The voices grow quieter, as if Viv is walking into a different room. "What's up?"

I bolster my courage with a long swallow of alcohol before telling her. "Preston proposed to me tonight."

There are exactly three beats of silence—I count—before she speaks.

"That's— Wow. That's great, Maeve. Congratulations."

There's something you should know about Viv. She doesn't say a lot, but when she does, she says exactly what's on her mind. Her tongue is as sharp as her riding skills, and believe me, I've been on the receiving end of it more than once. She's no fool, so don't even think of trying to slip something past her, because you won't win. Trust me.

I clear my throat as I pour another glug of red into my glass. Her response worries me, because she isn't Preston's biggest fan, and she's made no secret of that fact. Of course, she's not anyone's biggest fan, except maybe Bash's, but that's purely biological. So why is she congratulating me?

"I said no." The wine burns my throat as I chug it, wishing now I had opted for something stronger.

"You said no? Why?"

Sighing as I sink down onto a barstool, I twirl my glass and watch the liquid slosh up the sides. "Why do you think?"

"Because he's a dick who probably thinks pineapple on pizza is the hill to die on?"

Ah, there's the real Viv. I let out a laugh. "I knew you hated him."

"I don't hate him. I just think the two of you together makes as much sense as a chocolate teapot."

"Well, rest assured, I turned him down *and* broke up with him." I fold my arms on the cool countertop and rest my forehead on them.

"Fuck," she mutters. "How did that go?"

"As well as you can imagine with a guy whose cock is the size of a pencil but who thinks it's a marvel of humankind."

Viv snorts. "How do you feel?"

I take a minute to consider this, something I haven't done since it happened. "Honestly, I just feel relieved," I tell her. "Being with him was so exhausting. I had to do everything for him."

She says nothing.

"What? Are you still there?"

"Obviously, stupid," she says. "But how is that different from every other relationship you've ever been in?"

Shifting so I'm upright in my seat, I take another swig before responding. "What do you mean?"

She sighs as if I've said something especially exasperating. "You've always done everything for every single guy you've dated."

"That's absolutely not true."

"Prove it. Name one man you've had a healthy relationship with where you weren't acting like his mother."

I frown as I flip back through my mental catalogue of past boyfriends. I know what you're thinking, and you can knock it off. There haven't been that many, and she's wrong. "I can't—"

"Exactly my point."

"You didn't let me finish." I roll my eyes and drain the contents of my glass. "I can't dissect every relationship just like that."

"There's no need. I've already done it for you."

Without intending to, I laugh out loud. "You're acting way too big for your britches."

"And you've been watching too much Audrey again. You do realize no one says *britches* anymore, right?"

I shrug and refill my goblet. "I do."

"Well, stop," Viv orders. "So we've established that you create codependent relationships with men who need mothers, not girlfriends. What are you going to do about it?"

There's a loud *ting* as I set my glass down a little too hard. "We haven't established anything."

"I'm still waiting for you to give me a single name."

I'm so desperate to prove her wrong, to prove I'm capable of having a healthy relationship, that it slips out before I'm even aware it's on my tongue, its journey eased by all of the wine I've consumed, no doubt.

"Pierce."

"Pierce," she parrots back, as if I've gone hard of hearing in my twenty-six years.

I realize my mistake thirty seconds too late. "Never mind," I say into my drink.

"Are we talking about Pierce St. James?"

"We're not talking about anyone," I say. I stand up, but my legs have gone a bit wobbly, so I sit back down before they can send me to the floor. "I actually need to go."

"Oh, no," she says, and I'm beginning to regret calling her in the first place. Why didn't I try Walker or Lux? They would have been much more sympathetic. "We're definitely dissecting this."

"Viv," I whine into the phone. "Forget I said it. That was the wine talking."

"I didn't even know you and Pierce dated," she says, completely ignoring me.

"We didn't." Glutton, meet punishment. "Not really."

And then I tell her everything.

Well, not *everything*, of course. She's still a sheltered twenty-year-old, for god's sake. But enough that at the end of it, she says "fuck" and I say "yeah" and there's this moment of silence where neither of us says anything because what is there to say when you've fucked everything up and have just admitted out loud for the first time that you'll never get it back?

"You love him," she finally breathes. "Like, *love* him."

"No, I don't," I scoff. "It was all sexual."

"Maeve."

"Viv."

"You pushed him away because you didn't want to give up control.

But letting him be in charge made you happy. You get that, don't you?"

She's my sister, and I love her, even if I want to strangle her right now, so I give her question thought before I answer it. Was I happy with Pierce?

Memories flash through my mind like a movie montage—dinner with my family, the gallery, the woods, upstairs afterward, skydiving. They're intermingled with plenty of bad ones—him ruining my meeting, him sleeping with Loretta and flirting with Caroline, those stupid blind dates, Bash's accident, the arguments—so many arguments. But even during the bad moments, I felt more alive in his presence than out of it.

He may have fought me for control, but every time I gave it to him, I felt safe. Protected. Cherished. He never let me down or made me regret my decision. I did that to myself. Every time I realized I'd given up control, I fought to regain it, not because Pierce had proven unreliable, but because others in my past had.

"Maeve?" Viv's voice breaks through my thoughts.

"Yeah." I swipe at my nose. "I'm just thinking."

"Maybe you should tell him what you're thinking."

The last time I saw Pierce, the night of the gala, I thought my heart was going to explode. It had been over two months, and my eyes were devouring him on that stage. Even though I have no doubt his speech was incredible, I didn't hear a word of it. I knew he was avoiding me, but when I came out of the ladies' room and saw him on that divan, I was drawn to him by a magnetic force field I've never been able to explain.

Of course, I proceeded to screw it all up as usual, and if I'm being honest, watching him walk away that night was fifty times harder than watching Preston drive away tonight, even knowing he wouldn't be back.

I pour the remainder of the wine into my glass and set the bottle back down. "I can't."

"Why not?" Viv asks, because when you're twenty, everything is just so fucking easy.

"Because he doesn't ever want to see me again."

## 53

## "I Hate That It's True" - Dean Lewis

*Pierce*

The plane touches down on the private airstrip in Belize, and I feel my heart grow physically lighter. Palm trees flash past the windows, signaling that we have entered paradise. We're here for Heath's bachelor party, and I plan to let myself go this time. I can practically taste the margaritas already.

Rhett stands up from his seat, stretches, and claps me on the shoulder. "No thinking about work for the next four days, mate."

I ignore him and stick my phone in the pocket of my laptop bag. While I have brought my computer, it's for emergencies only—namely, times I need a distraction even a tropical paradise can't provide.

What he doesn't know, which I intend to keep that way, is that work isn't the biggest threat to us having fun together. That would be a certain five-foot drama queen with black hair, and she's not even here.

Before the gala, I was doing fine. Okay, fine might be a stretch, but I was surviving, helped along by my mission to bring down Mr. Carrow for what he did to her. Since the gala, however—since seeing her up close, talking to her, smelling her perfume, fighting with her—my head's been a fucking circus, and she's the ringmaster.

I can't fall asleep without thinking about her. She invades my dreams, waking me frequently during the night. She's there every time I'm grabbing a coffee or taking the elevator or choosing a tie. I can't even shower without remembering how it felt to press her against the cool tiles, her skin supple and slick beneath my hands. I need this break like I need oxygen.

"Hey." Heath stops next to my seat, his thumb tucked beneath the strap of the bag on his shoulder. "You good?"

I force a big grin and stand to join him. "I will be once we locate the booze."

He gives me a sideways smile before following Rhett and Slate to the door of the plane. "Let's go then."

*** 

The next few days pass in a blur of sun, sand, and rum as we celebrate Heath's upcoming nuptials. We're staying at a private island resort, and each villa has its own dock and personal staff. It's the perfect place to unwind and let everything plaguing me back home slip away. Beneath the palm trees swaying in the gentle breeze, it's almost possible to forget that I'll be seeing her in just a few days.

Until Rhett brings it up, of course.

"You gonna be okay, seeing Maeve at the wedding?" he asks.

We're sitting under a cabana on the beach, legs stretched in front of us, a pitcher of margaritas on the table—more tequila than anything else. Our flight leaves in the morning, and if I'm being honest, I'm not ready to go back. Work doesn't hold the same appeal it used to, even if it's the only thing keeping me afloat right now.

Rhett kicks my foot, reminding me he asked a question, one I'd rather swallow a gallon of seawater than answer. I open my eyes and shoot him a look, not bothering to lift my head from the back of the lounger I'm reclining in.

Heath and Slate's eyes feel heavy on me, because apparently the entire world wants to know how Pierce and Maeve will handle being in the same room after all this time. None of them know about the gala, it seems.

"Of course I'll be okay." I take a sip of my drink, but the ice has all melted, leaving it lukewarm and watered down.

"That's good." Rhett nods, but I can tell he's not about to let it go yet. "It just seemed like maybe there was something between you guys."

I narrow my gaze. "There is something. It's called 'hate.'"

Heath chuckles from the other side of the cabana. "Yeah, okay."

Pinning him with a look, I say, "What's your problem?"

He holds up his hands, but his smile hasn't entirely disappeared. "Nothing, man. I just think you might be a little delusional."

"What makes you say that?" I keep my tone as cool as possible, but I'm starting to feel uncomfortably hot despite the canvas umbrella over our heads.

Heath shares a glance with Rhett and Slate that makes me shift upright in my chair. "Come on, Pierce," he says, dangling his hands between his knees. "Anyone can see that the two of you have a vibe."

My brows bunch together as I look at him, trying to figure out what we did that gave us away. How much do they all know?

Rhett laughs and slaps me on the shoulder. "Relax, mate. It's cool. Why do you think we came up with the challenge in the first place?"

I toss back the rest of my cocktail and set the glass on the table. "This is fucked up."

"I think you're the one who's fucked up," Slate says, lifting a beer to his lips. He's shirtless like the rest of us, but in addition to a set of abs that must have taken years to refine, he's also sporting a chest covered in tattoos.

Shaking my head, I turn my gaze to where the waves are lapping at the shore. I had been doing so well not thinking about her, but now the memories are crashing back like breakers against rock.

I can still smell her perfume when I close my eyes, still picture the way her face heats when she gets mad, still hear the tiny gasp she makes when I grab her hair. Something aches in my chest, and I'm starting to regret ever coming on this trip. I thought it would help me forget, but now the echoes of her are louder than ever.

When she left, I didn't just lose the woman I loved. I lost my best friend. And being around the rest of our friends has only driven that truth home.

"You like her, don't you?" Heath's voice is quiet.

I keep my eyes on the ocean as I consider my reply. Do I tell them the truth? They already suspect it. Proving them right won't change anything, but maybe they can act as a buffer between us at the wedding. Although with Maeve as the maid of honor and me the best man, I'm not sure there's anything that can prevent the destruction that's about to happen.

Taking a deep breath, I pinch the corners of my eyes with my thumb and index finger. "Unfortunately, it's a lot worse than that."

"I knew it," Rhett exclaims. I shoot him a glare, and he coughs to cover his glee but does a piss-poor job of it.

I force the words out before I can change my mind. "I love her."

"Why is that unfortunate?" Slate asks.

The rest of us give him a look.

"Have you *met* Maeve?" Rhett says. "God, it'd be like trying to bed a wildcat."

"Okay, I'm done with this conversation." I push to my feet, but Rhett yanks on my arm.

"Come on, mate. I was only joking. You have our sympathies."

I roll my eyes and sink back onto my lounger. "Fuck your sympathy. I'd rather have your beer."

Slate tosses me a bottle from the cooler next to him. "Have you guys fucked?"

Twisting off the cap, I smirk and shake my head. "Fucking seems to be the only thing we're good at."

Rhett whistles, but I ignore him.

"Turns out, I'm not what she wants. So"—I take a long swig—"here's to forgetting."

Heath drags a finger through the sand at his feet. "That's bullshit. You guys would be good together if you both pulled your heads out of your asses long enough."

"Hear, hear," Rhett chimes in.

"Try telling her that," I mutter.

"So she dumped you? We didn't even know you were together," Rhett says.

I scratch at the label on my drink. "She didn't want anyone to know."

"Fuck," Heath whispers.

*You don't know the half of it.*

"Sounds like she was scared," Slate says.

"Among a lot of other things." I lift the bottle to my lips again and take another long swallow. It's already half-gone, but it's going to take a lot more than beer to make me forget.

"So what happened?" Heath asks. I imagine him relaying this entire conversation to Walker when we get home tomorrow, and I wonder if Maeve has told her anything about us.

I shrug and realize I'm still carrying a mountain of tension in my shoulders. "The usual. She freaked out and left. Went exclusive with Ansley." The last of my beer goes down smooth and cold.

Slate hands me another one. "You go after her?"

"Fuck no." I shake my head and drop the bottle cap in the sand. "I'm not a complete idiot."

Several beats of silence pass, until I finally scan their faces.

"You think I should have gone after her?" I say, incredulous. "She made me look like a fool."

Heath runs a hand through his hair, pushing it off his forehead. "What if it's what she wanted?"

I know what he's doing, but I don't need him projecting his own relationship onto mine. Maeve and I are not him and Walker. "It doesn't matter. I'm better off without her anyway."

"Dude, you've been depressed as shit for months," Rhett says, backhanding my knee. "You should make your move."

I shake my head. "Love makes you weak, and I'm sick of it."

Heath coughs, and I realize what I've just said may have come off as offensive. We're here celebrating his upcoming wedding, after all.

"Sorry, mate. I didn't mean—"

He cuts me off with a wave. "I don't think it's love that makes you weak. It's giving up on the person you love."

I don't even bother fighting the frown etching itself onto my forehead. I didn't give up. I fought like hell.

"How did you feel when you were with her?" Slate asks.

My gaze drops to the white sand as if it can provide the answer to his question. "Good," I finally say. "Happy." *Like I was on top of the fucking world.*

"Like you're high?" Rhett prompts, and I toss him an annoyed look over my shoulder.

I've never taken half the shit he has, so how the hell am I supposed to answer that? "I guess?"

"Does she make you a better version of yourself?" Heath asks.

"What is this, the fucking Spanish Inquisition?" I'm half-joking, because I know they're just trying to help. "Yeah, she did." *Of course she did.*

The memories come, and I'm powerless to stop them. I'm nothing but a small sailboat, caught in a storm too far from shore.

Making her laugh, and the absolute bliss that came with knowing that I was the one who caused it. Tugging her close to my side and feeling like the luckiest bastard in the world with her on my arm. Listening to her on the verge of tears and vowing to myself that I'd do anything possible to keep her from ever being hurt again. Carrying her in my arms, the heat of her body against mine like a slice of heaven on earth.

I never thought I'd experience something like this. I always saw myself in a marriage like my parents'—a mutually beneficial partnership with someone who was little more than an asset. Love was never part of the equation.

But Maeve had to go and fuck it all up. She couldn't be content with just my body; she had to feed on my heart as well. If I'd been stronger, if I'd kept my feelings out of it—

"Then that's worth fighting for," Slate says.

I glance up. I almost forgot I'm not alone. "I did fight." I was on my fucking knees for that woman, and she still left.

"No, man." Heath shakes his head. "You pulled back to protect yourself."

"Fuck you," I say. "You don't know what I did."

"You pulled out of the challenge." Rhett points his bottle at me. "You let her have it so you wouldn't have to see her anymore."

I scoff and kick at the sand. "What should I have done instead, wise one?"

"Stuck around. Showed her what she was missing," Slate offers.

Maybe they're right. Who the fuck knows? I thought I was doing the right thing by staying away. I thought it was what she wanted, but maybe a part of me was also trying to keep from getting my heart ripped out again.

"It's too late anyway. She made her choice." Tipping my head back, I drain the last of my drink before setting the empty bottle in the sand.

Rhett laughs. "Who, Preston?"

I give him a look that says *obviously* and catch the fresh beer Slate tosses me.

"They broke up, man," Rhett says. "You didn't know?"

The world spins faster as I process this.

"Apparently he proposed, and she turned him down, then broke up with him," he adds.

Sinking back in my seat, I sip my drink without a word. Maeve isn't with that bastard anymore? I can't tell if I'm relieved or pissed by this revelation. She told me they were endgame. I have so many questions, but one screams louder than all the others.

Why the fuck didn't she come back to me?

## 54

## "Cold As You" - Taylor Swift

*Maeve*

This could have been me. I scan the Italian cliffside where Heath and Walker's wedding will take place. It looks absolutely incredible, even if I'd personally prefer a downtown wedding at St. John's Cathedral.

If I hadn't come to my senses when Preston proposed, I might now be planning my own nuptials for next summer. Initially, I thought I might have regrets, but so far that hasn't happened.

Preston felt like a safe option because he never had the power to break me. Turns out, I didn't have the power to hurt him either. Less than two weeks after I declined his proposal, he was photographed having dinner with a twenty-two-year-old brunette. I guess some things never change.

I met his ex-wife for lunch a few days ago and apologized for the affair. She was just as miserable as ever—slipping in no less than three mentions of her relation to Queen Celia—but the truth is, I fucked up her marriage, and no matter how intolerable she might be, it was a terrible thing to do.

My apology must have softened her, because she told me Preston was a cad who cheated on her before they even got married. I longed to ask her why she married him, then, but I think I understand. When you believe you don't deserve better, it's hard not to jump at the first person to show interest.

"It looks amazing," Walker says, sidling up next to me and pulling my attention back to the setup for the wedding.

Together we gaze at the reception area, which has been transformed over the past twenty-four hours. Set in the villa's garden and lit with chandeliers hanging from the tree branches, the space overflows with luxury and vintage charm. Each table boasts its own unique centerpiece consisting of first edition books and an exotic floral arrangement. The place cards are custom bookmarks tied with silk ribbons. On the back of each chair is a cashmere blanket to help fight off the October chill if needed.

Persian rugs, antique furniture, and velvet throws are sprinkled around the garden, where guests will lounge during the cocktail hour. A small stage is set up in the back corner for the jazz band playing after the ceremony.

"It's not too late to take it all back to the city," I tease.

As soon as Walker told me she wanted to get married on the Amalfi Coast, I knew it was the perfect spot. A city wedding would have felt stifling for both her and Heath. They want as little press coverage as possible.

"I think I'd rather jump off the cliff," she says with a half smile. She tucks her arm into mine, and we head toward the private house that is housing most of the guests for the weekend.

Built over two hundred years ago, Villa Fiorita was recently renovated and now boasts every modern convenience—a good thing, because there's no way I could have survived three days without my Dyson Airwrap.

The house is situated at the top of the cliffs, providing incredible views of the Tyrrhenian Sea, its deep-blue waters a striking contrast to the white-bleached rocks bordering it. It's paradise, pure and simple.

At least until *he* shows up. But I'm refusing to think about that. It was the entire reason I pushed for Walker, Lux, and me to arrive a day early. The flight may only have been a few hours long, but I can't think of anything worse than being stuck in an aircraft forty thousand feet above sea level with someone who hates you.

And he's made it obvious he does. As much as I don't want to admit it, I can't really blame him. Everything he said at the gala was true. He was more vulnerable the night I left than I've ever seen him before, and I still chose to walk away. In hindsight, I realize exactly how stupid I was, but at the time, I didn't think I had a choice. I thought my survival depended on staying away from the one person with the power to destroy me.

None of that matters now, though. Pierce has made his opinion of me very clear. He even went so far as to skip the rehearsal last night, making up some excuse about a work emergency keeping him late, but I know the truth. He wants to spend as little time with me as possible.

Heath's cousin escorted me during the practice run down the aisle, and all I could think about was how painful it's going to be holding Pierce's arm during the actual wedding and pretend I'm okay. The best thing—the *only* thing—I can do is act as though he no longer exists. Not because I want to punish him, but because it's the only way I'll manage to survive. My heart may be aching for the sight of him, but my head knows the spiral that will begin the second I see him.

Walker and I join the other bridesmaids in the bridal chamber to get ready for the day. Lux is wearing a gown the color of sea glass, Heath's sister Camilla's dress is the perfect shade of dark teal, and my own is a deep navy blue. Together, they stunningly set off Walker's vintage-style gown of cream silk and lace.

I catch my reflection in the mirror as one of the stylists gets to work on my hair, curling it and tucking it into a low chignon. Before my thoughts can wander back to *him*, the hairdresser tugs a little too hard on the heat wand.

"Ow," I say, pressing a hand to my head. "I can't afford to lose a hunk of hair today."

Her eyes widen as she murmurs her apology.

Lux gives me a look from the chair next to mine, but I ignore her, reaching for the perfume on the vanity in front of me. My movements are miscalculated, thanks to trying to hold still for the stylist, and the glass bottle topples over. "Damn," I say, reaching for it before anything can spill out.

"God, Maeve," Lux says. "Relax."

I dab scent onto my neck and wrists. "I am relaxed."

Her brows pull together as she gives me a skeptical look. "And I'm pregnant."

I drop the bottle in surprise. "You're *what*?"

She covers her mouth with her hand. "Oh my god, chill. I was kidding."

I brush the hairdresser aside before she can scalp me and bend over to pick up the perfume. "Why would you say something like that?"

"I was trying to prove a point. I guess it backfired."

"You guess correctly," I grumble, then turn back to the mirror, snapping my fingers for the stylist to get started again.

She approaches me cautiously, as if she's afraid I'll break her hands, which I might if she's not careful.

"Are you nervous about seeing him?" Lux says.

I can feel her eyes on me in the reflection, but I don't meet them, working instead on applying my lipstick. "Who?"

Her chair squeaks as she swivels toward me. "You can quit pretending. You know exactly who I'm talking about."

I form an O with my mouth and finish tinting my lips crimson. Only when I'm done do I turn my head to look at Lux, carefully so as not to startle my mouse of a hairdresser. "Let's say, for the sake of argument, that I don't."

"This isn't a game, Maeve." Lux leans back in her chair, inclining her head as she studies me. "We're on your side."

I pop the cap back on the lipstick tube and set it on the table. "Great. I'm glad to hear it."

"But we're on his side, too."

My gaze swings back to her before I can stop it. "That's not—"

"Don't." She holds up her hand. "We're friends with both of you. And all of us are tired of taking sides. This weekend would be a great time for the two of you to make up. It would be the perfect gift for Heath and Walker."

Pain punctures a hole in the center of my chest, emotions spilling out as I consider what she's saying. They must all think this is my fault, that I'm the one who told Pierce to stay away. And I guess, in a sense, it is. If I hadn't been terrified out of my mind, if I hadn't walked away that night—

"I don't know what you want me to do." My voice comes out hushed and raw, and I clear my throat.

"Tell him you're sorry. That you want things to go back to the way they used to be."

Tears gathering at the corners of my eyes, I shake my head, forgetting about my hair and probably messing it up entirely. "It's too late. He doesn't want anything to do with me."

\* \* \*

By a stroke of luck, I still haven't seen Pierce. The bridesmaids are due to start walking down the aisle any minute, and so far, the two of us have managed to avoid each other entirely. Not exactly easy as best man and maid of honor, but we made it work.

He hasn't texted me since the night I left him, and I haven't texted him since realizing he has no intention of responding. For all I know, he's blocked my number. All wedding-party communication has been done via other people. Even when I was planning the itinerary for this weekend, I never had the need to send him a solo email. And everyone knows that group threads don't count.

But the second Cami and Lux have made their way down the aisle and my turn is next, my stomach roils and my brain starts chanting about what a terrible idea this was. Avoiding Pierce seemed great in theory, but that means my first glimpse of him will be in front of a hundred people, all of them privy to whatever emotions decide to display themselves on my face.

I walk toward the floral arch near the cliffside, its coastal grasses, white orchids, and sea holly gently waving in the breeze. The guests are arranged in a semicircle facing the ocean, which is providing both a majestic view and a serenade for the service.

My heels make quiet clicking noises on the cobblestone path leading to the wooden platform aisle, erected over the natural terrain to protect the wild landscape. The notes of a cello accompany the music of the sea, the two merging into a sound more perfect for Heath and Walker's day than any symphony ever written.

Only when I step onto the wooden planks do I look up to where the minister is waiting, hands clasped in front of him. Heath is standing beside him in a custom linen tuxedo several shades darker than Walker's dress, a shy smile on his face as he waits for his bride.

I tighten my grip on my bouquet, which mimics the florals in the arch behind the wedding party. Finally, when my heart feels like it will pound right out of my chest, I let my eyes move to the right of Heath.

And there he is. So handsome he makes my breath catch in my throat. Four months of pure air, and I still crave the smoke.

His navy tuxedo matches my dress, as if the gods needed one more thing to mock me with. Gone is his five o'clock shadow, and instead his jaw is sharp and clean-shaven. His hair is perfectly styled, and I can't tell for certain from this far, but I think it might be just a tad longer than the last time I saw it.

We haven't had a civil conversation in nearly half a year. He hasn't been in my bed for just as long, and the last time we were together in any sense of the word was before Bash's accident.

Part of me wondered if the rift between us would be big enough that he'd miss his best friends' wedding over it. I'm relieved to see that it's not, but a part of me mourns the fact that I don't have that kind of effect on him. It's stupid, I know, but if you're not the main character of your own story, when will you be?

Pierce's eyes are on me—they feel like hot coals against my skin—but the moment I meet his gaze, he drops it. There's a subtle shifting in his shoulders as he readjusts himself, keeping his eyes firmly fixed on something over my shoulder. Walker, no doubt.

The pain of his rejection shouldn't sting after all this time, but it still does, especially in light of the fact that a hundred pairs of eyes are glued to me right now. It wouldn't take a genius to deduce the source of the red shame crawling up my neck.

Tattooing how he feels about me across his forehead would have been more subtle.

## 55

## "The Black Dog" - Taylor Swift

*Maeve*

The ceremony is simple and sweet, exactly what I would have pictured. After the minister pronounces them husband and wife, Heath swings Walker backward for a long kiss that garners enthusiastic cheering from the crowd. When he finally lifts her back up, Walker's face is flushed with both embarrassment and pleasure.

They walk down the aisle hand in hand, and I don't even bother tempering my smile. While I might not have been their biggest cheerleader when they first got back together, the past few years have proven just how good they are for each other.

I'm still grinning after them when I notice the wedding planner at the back of the crowd gesturing to me. Blinking, it takes me a second to realize that Pierce is waiting to escort me down the aisle. With my heart somewhere down near my toes, I step toward him, keeping my eyes averted from his, even though I can feel them boring into my skull.

He holds his elbow several inches from his body for me to take, and I rest my fingertips on the soft linen of his jacket. The heat of his arm seeps through the thin fabric, bleeding into my hand until I want to snatch it back.

At a nod from the wedding planner, we make our way down the narrow boardwalk that splits the semicircle of guests in half. *Pretend he's someone else*, I tell myself. Heath's cousin or some random guy I've never met before—literally anyone other than the man who currently holds my heart in his hands with no more care than a gum wrapper.

About halfway down the aisle, my heel catches on a wooden plank, pitching me forward. I don't even have time to fear smashing my nose before Pierce's strong hands are wrapping around my arms.

"God, what is it with you and nature?" he says quietly as he straightens me back up.

I don't want to think about the sensations that course through my body at his touch. Even though he would have done the same thing for any woman he was escorting, my fucked-up heart is doing its damndest to convince me his instincts are heightened when it comes to me.

"You okay?" he murmurs as we once again begin our walk.

The sound of his voice, low and sultry, sends tremors through my bones. I give a shaky nod, not trusting my voice right now.

We make it to the back without another word or incident, and the second we're past the last row of wedding guests, I drop his arm, not because I don't want to go on touching him for the rest of the night, but because I don't think I can handle one more display of rejection from him.

They say he who feels less holds the power, and I have never felt the truth of that statement more than in this moment.

\* \* \*

The time between the ceremony and reception passes in a blur. Heath and Walker greet their guests, and then we spend an hour having formal photos taken of the wedding party. Fortunately, most of those are done with the bridesmaids on one side and the groomsmen on the other, meaning Pierce and I can continue pretending we are strangers who mean nothing to each other.

Every once in a while, it feels like his eyes are on me, but whenever I look up, his gaze is somewhere else, leaving me with the sickening knowledge that I'm just imagining things. The second we're released so the photographer can get shots of the bride and groom alone, I realize exactly how vivid my imagination has been.

The entire bridal party has congregated at the edge of the reception area, sipping cocktails and talking quietly as we wait on Heath and Walker. I've just accepted a French 75 from the bartender when a long-legged blond walks into our midst and throws her arms around Pierce.

If I'd been hit with a wrecking ball, it would have hurt less.

He greets her with a smile, his large hands settling themselves on her waist as if they belong there. And by all appearances, they do. She's a carbon copy of all the other Ellas he's dated. Her tiny little dress covers just enough of her ass to be considered acceptable.

Nausea starts a boycott in me, threatening to empty the contents of my already mostly empty stomach. I set my drink down on the bar before I spill it and shove my shaky hands into the folds of my dress.

Is this what it felt like when he saw me with Preston? Then again, he was so angry at me by that point that I probably meant nothing. There's no way he experienced this searing pain. It feels like something has clawed its way into my ribcage and is pulling it apart piece by piece.

I'm still staring at them, because I'm a sucker for punishment (well, that and a shock victim), when Pierce lifts his eyes, causing his gaze to collide with mine. The contact causes a physical jolt to my system.

## "THE BLACK DOG" - TAYLOR SWIFT

He drops his hands from the woman in his arms without breaking eye contact with me. There isn't even the faintest hint of humor or goodwill in his face, but at least he isn't glaring at me.

No longer able to stare at him, I turn away, grabbing my drink before leaving the garden.

I don't pay any mind to where I'm going. I just need to get away. How am I supposed to watch him fawn all over another woman all night? It was bad enough seeing him flirt with Caroline, but at least she just happened to be there. He *invited* this girl. And not just on a date—to his best friends' wedding.

I wonder if he knows about Preston and me. It was in the tabloids, but Pierce wouldn't be caught dead reading those. Even if he did, I doubt he'd care. He made it very clear I blew the only chance I had with him—a regret I'll have to live with for the rest of my life.

My phone pings from the pocket of my gown, and I fish it out. Apparently I forgot to silence it before the wedding. There's a text notification from my sister on my screen.

**Viv**: *Have you spoken to Pierce yet?*

Suddenly, I want nothing more than to talk to someone about this, and since Vivienne is the only one who knows the depths of my feelings for Pierce, she's the perfect candidate. The only problem is that she's back home in Wesbourne, while I'm stuck in Italy for the weekend with Pierce and his sidepiece.

I settle for texting my sister back.

**Me**: *No. He brought a date.*

**Viv**: *Fuckkkk*

Having someone else acknowledge exactly how messed up this situation is only makes the gravity of it that much stronger. This is it. Pierce and I are officially over. He wouldn't have brought a date if he didn't want to send that message loud and clear.

**Me**: *Yeah. It's fine though. I'm going to drink a bunch of vodka and*

*sleep most of tomorrow.*
**Viv**: *Sounds like a terrific plan.*
**Me**: *I know.*
**Viv**: *I was being sarcastic.*

I find a small stone bench tucked between a few apple trees losing their leaves and take a seat. It feels cool, even through the fabric of my dress, and the temperature is only going to keep dropping tonight.

**Viv**: *You should still talk to him.*
**Me**: *And say what exactly?*

That I'm sorry? That I broke up with Preston and would he like to give us another shot? That—god forbid—I'm in love with him? All so he can throw it back in my face, then retreat back to someone who is my opposite in every way? No thanks.

**Viv**: *The truth.*
**Me**: *He doesn't want to hear it, trust me.*
**Viv**: *You have no way of knowing that unless you try it.*
**Me**: *Do you hate me?*
**Viv**: *Depends on the day.*
**Me**: *I can't do it, Viv.*
**Viv**: *Of course you can. You're the strongest person I know.*

I might have been flattered by her statement under normal circumstances, but right now I only feel the weight of that assessment, and it does nothing to bolster my courage.

**Me**: *And if he rejects me again?*
**Viv**: *He's never actually rejected you before.*
**Me**: *Sure feels like it.*
**Viv**: *Feelings aren't everything.*
**Me**: *How old are you again?*
**Viv**: *Just do it, Maeve. Channel your inner Nike.*
**Me**: *I'm going to pretend you didn't just say that.*
**Viv**: *If that makes you feel better.*

## "THE BLACK DOG" - TAYLOR SWIFT

**Me**: *The only thing that would make me feel better is five shots and an Audrey marathon.*

**Viv**: *Tell him and if he rejects you, I'll fly out and watch all the Audrey movies with you that you want.*

**Me**: *You hate Audrey.*

**Viv**: *Turns out, today is a day I love you so...*

**Me**: *What about the vodka?*

**Viv**: *I have full faith in your ability to swipe a bottle from the bar.*

I sigh and gaze out over the sea. The waves are rolling as the tide comes in, lapping against the cliffs below like they're having a marital spat. Heath and Walker are probably done with photos by now, which means it's time for the reception to start.

The ache in my chest hasn't dulled since I slipped away. If anything, it's grown in size and intensity. The thought of seeing Pierce again—of seeing them together—makes me confident the only thing passing my lips tonight will be alcohol. Even thoughts of the oyster bar I was looking forward to make me want to hurl.

I don't want to continue like this. Anything sounds better than walking around with a gaping hole in my chest. Even confessing my love and having him tell me there's no chance for us must be better than not knowing. At least then I'd be able to talk to him one last time, something the masochist in me can't resist.

I type out another message to Viv, then watch for the bubbles to appear as she responds.

**Me**: *I honestly don't know what I'll do if he says he wants nothing to do with me. He's said it before and I deserve it, but that doesn't make it any easier to hear.*

**Viv**: *Be honest. Tell him how you feel and that you're sorry. His response is out of your control.*

Sniffing, I wipe at tears I didn't even know were falling.

**Me**: *Okay.*

**Me**: *May want to get that plane ticket booked.*
**Viv**: *I'll wait. ;)*

## 56

## "end game" - Cat Burns

*Maeve*

When I return to the party, the chandeliers are all lit and gently swinging from the branches overhead. Soft jazz surrounds us, the garden walls creating great acoustics, according to Rhett. Servers dressed in black-and-white uniforms mill about, carrying bottles of champagne and ice water.

Lux is on my left, chatting with Cami. I haven't been the best company since we sat down. Or all weekend really. On my right, Walker leans toward Heath to whisper something in his ear. Hopefully, my lack of enthusiasm hasn't tainted her happiness. I avert my eyes before they can move past Heath and land on his best man.

Instead, I scan the crowd before us as I sip my wine. In just a few minutes, I need to give my maid of honor toast. I've given dozens of speeches over the years, so why are my hands clammy and my goblet shaking? Is it because Pierce is here or because of my conversation with Vivienne? I promised her I'd talk to him, but now that he's mere feet away from me, every ounce of courage I possessed has taken flight and plunged itself into the Mediterranean.

I wasn't kidding when I said I don't know what I'll do if he rejects me again. I also wasn't kidding about not being able to eat anything. I've managed to get down a single cracker, and that was only to help absorb some of the alcohol the servers keep topping my glass off with.

Anxiety courses through me, and I focus on the fact that, in two hours, this will all be over and I can put it behind me. Viv will be on her way to Italy by morning, and the two of us can stay for a week, watching Audrey movies, wandering the streets of nearby villages, and flirting with Italian men.

Behind me, the wedding planner leans down to whisper in my ear. "Time for your toast. You're going to do great!"

I nod and take a deep breath before getting to my feet. My heels are killing me, and I wish I had kicked them off before standing, but it's too late now. Besides, without them, I look like a child next to any full-grown adult.

Tugging the thick linen stationery from my pocket, I run over the lines in my mind again. The notes were more of a precaution, since I memorized the whole thing, but now I'm grateful for them. There's something about looking at a sea of eyes that makes you forget every word in your head.

I spent hours crafting this speech, and I'm proud of it. I even hired an editor to ensure it's perfect. Maybe nobody remembers the wedding toasts, but that's no reason to slack.

Someone hands me a mic, and the guests quiet as they realize I'm about to speak. I angle my body toward the happy couple, wishing with all my might that Pierce would vanish into thin air so that I could do this without him clouding my brain.

He's right over Heath's shoulder, and my eyes badly want to land on him. I have no doubt he's looking at me, just like everyone else, but the minute I meet his gaze, he'll lower it. *Message received*, I want to tell him. *You hate me. I get it. You don't need to rub it in.*

After softly clearing my throat, I raise the microphone and begin. "I've known Heath and Walker for what feels like my whole life but has really only been about twelve years. In all of that time, I've never seen them happier than when they are together."

I glance up from the sheet in my hands and give them both a sweet smile. They beam back at me before exchanging a knowing look with each other. *This is their day*, I remind myself. *No one else matters.*

"They've had some rough patches, but I think that's made their love even stronger. Through it all, they stood by each other's side. Even when the rest of us thought they were crazy."

"Hear, hear," Rhett says, and several chuckles float from the audience.

I shoot him a look, wondering if he's about to make a scene, but he only tosses me a wink and sips his champagne. I have every intention of bringing my gaze back to the paper in my hands, but my eyes have a mind of their own. Defying my wishes, they flit to Pierce's face like a butterfly to a flower.

As expected, he's watching me. Everyone in the garden is watching me right now, but at this moment, all of that melts away, and there's only him.

My heart lets out a keening wail as our eyes lock. Why didn't I recognize what I had while I had it? Because of my stupidity, I'll never get it back. In a year or two, we'll be at his wedding, but it won't be me beside him at a table like this. It will be a stunning blond with long legs and a gentle tongue, someone who does as she's told, who doesn't fight for control in every situation like a dictator. Who knows if I'll even be invited—not that I'd go if I was. I'd rather rip my heart out, bit by bloody bit, than watch Pierce marry someone else.

I feel my face crumple, and even though I know everyone can see it, I can't do anything to stop it. Tucking my lips between my teeth,

I fight to regain my composure, but it's gone. Jumped over the cliff and nowhere to be found.

My head swims from all the wine I've had on an empty stomach. The best thing—the smart thing—to do would be to hand the mic to Lux and leave while I still have a little dignity left. Heath and Walker would understand, and Lux would do a great job filling in for me.

But there's no way I'll ever find the courage to say what I need to say to Pierce after this. It's now or never.

I rip my gaze from his, and you can almost hear the sound of it tearing as I do. Scanning the paper in my hands one last time, I make up my mind, then toss it onto the table. "I used to think you'd know you're with the right person if you were able to control your emotions and not get carried away. If things didn't get messy. I thought if I could just stay in control, I'd be okay."

Now I have to force myself to look at him. My eyes would rather be anywhere else, those traitors. But if I don't look at him, I'm terrified he won't understand that I'm speaking to him, that this is the only thing I have left to offer him, and I know it's not enough—it'll never be enough. But I can't live with myself if I don't at least try.

He's still looking at me, and I tell myself that's something, at least. He could have chosen to stare at the table or even excuse himself. But his gaze is still fixed firmly on my face, even if there isn't a hint of a smile on that mouth I love so much.

"But I realized that when you truly love someone, you trust them. It doesn't mean they won't ever let you down, but it does mean you're committed to working things out when they do."

Pierce's expression hasn't changed, but he hasn't looked away either. That has to be a good sign, right? I keep those dark eyes as my focal point as I continue, my voice getting clogged with tears.

"Love is about releasing control, not retaining it. It's about embracing vulnerability. It isn't until you can fully relax with another person that you discover true love." I suck in a long breath as I finally turn back to the bride and groom. "While I made the biggest mistake of my life and chased away the only man I've ever truly loved, I'm thrilled Heath and Walker were smarter than me. To the happy couple."

I raise my glass to them, and the rest of the guests follow suit. Walker has tears in her eyes and squeezes my hand as I sit back down. I don't have the courage to look at Pierce again. I just pass the mic to Walker so she can hand it off to the best man.

A quiet hush falls over the garden, almost as if everyone is holding their breath, like the moment right before the curtain goes up and the play starts. Pierce gets to his feet. I don't look at him—*can't* look at him—not with my flaming face and broken heart. What happens next is up to him. The ball is fully in his court now.

It's scary, vulnerability. It feels a lot like that moment right before we fell out of the plane. Your heart is in your throat and your head is in the clouds and you can't think of anything except for the next few seconds in front of you and hope and pray you make it out alive. You have no idea what will happen next—you just have to trust the person you're strapped to.

He didn't let me down then, but I have no idea if he will today.

The paper in his pocket is also crisp—I can hear it snap as he pulls it out. While his speech is grammatically correct and polished—I'm sure his assistant helped with that—it lacks heart. A robot could have written it. Heck, a robot could be reading it, given his lack of inflection.

Within sixty seconds, it's over. I didn't look at him the entire time, so I can't confirm, but my instincts are telling me he kept his eyes on the page for the duration. Anyone looking in from the outside might assume he's just shy, but I know better.

He's as screwed up as I am. We just express it differently.

There's a definite air of disappointment in the crowd. Anyone with eyes in their head should be able to put two and two together. After my embarrassing display during my walk down the aisle, followed by what was practically a confession of love during my speech, it's obvious what's going on between Pierce and me.

He's as stoic as ever, lifting his glass to the newlyweds, pretending he didn't blatantly ignore me, and now we're all forced to avoid the elephant in the room. What did I expect, that he'd get up and declare his undying love for me? I'm such a fool.

After he takes his seat, I let my gaze slide down the table, not looking at him, just in his direction. I see his hand flex as he reaches for his champagne flute. It takes little to no imagination to remember exactly the way it felt clamped on my thigh or wrapped around my throat.

Reality slaps me in the face like a childhood bully. *You'll never feel those hands on you again.*

Somewhere in the carved-out hole that used to be my chest, a dull ache grows in intensity until it reaches the point where I have to clutch it with my hand to keep from crying out. I never knew it could hurt so bad. Why doesn't anyone warn you about this?

"You okay, babe?" Lux asks, pinning me with a look of concern.

Pushing back my chair, I shake my head. "I'm fine. Just need some fresh air."

"When you're feeling better, we need to talk about that toast," she says as I walk away.

I lied. I'm not fine. And given Pierce's apathy, I'm not sure I'll ever be fine again.

## 57

## "The Great War" - Taylor Swift

*Maeve*

A chilly wind whips up from the ocean, wrapping its cool fingers around me as I walk onto the massive terrace extending from the back of the house. It's made of large slabs of stone, probably taken from the very hills surrounding us a century ago. A low wall is the only thing standing between me and a sheer drop onto the jagged cliffs below.

I take a step back before the view gives me vertigo and focus on the waves instead. It's colder here, away from the heaters set up around the perimeter of the garden, but it feels better. Makes me feel alive. For a minute there, I thought I might suffocate.

I'm hidden from the wedding party still going on on the other side of the villa, although the music floats over on the breeze, punctuated every so often by laughter. After sucking in several large lungfuls of air, I consider my situation.

I did it. I gave up control; I told Pierce how I feel. I passed the ball squarely to him. He opted not to play, but isn't that part of being vulnerable? If we knew how the other person would respond, there wouldn't be any risk involved.

The relief from my honesty feels surprisingly good. Not good enough to fill the massive crater in the center of my chest, but it's enough to numb the pain slightly. I do wish I had grabbed a bottle of champagne, though. That would help even more with the numbing.

Footsteps sound behind me, and I quickly brush away the tears drying on my cheeks. I may have chosen to put myself out there, but that doesn't mean anyone needs to watch me fall apart. Turning, I expect to find Lux on a mission to drag me back in time for the cake cutting.

But it's not Lux.

Everything around me stills as I watch him approach. The sounds of the sea and the music fade away until the only thing left is the loud *thump-thump-thump* of my heart. The chill in the air intensifies, leaving my skin as numb as my chest.

Hanging lanterns dot the perimeter of the terrace, casting a warm glow on Pierce's face, and I already know that this image will be joining the thousands of others that have taken to haunting me as I try to fall asleep at night.

Each of his steps is measured, and I'm not sure if it's because he's afraid I'll bolt or because he's questioning his decision to come. I focus on his suit, which looks as crisp as it did when he walked me down the aisle. He's still wearing his jacket, even though the other guys discarded theirs ages ago, but I don't need to see it to know that underneath, his white shirt is stretching taut over the muscles in his shoulders and arms.

My mouth has gone dry—I couldn't say anything if I wanted to—and my brain has decided to take a vacation. A million thoughts swirl through my head. Why is he here? What does he want? How badly is this going to hurt? But I can't speak a single one of them. All I can do is wait for him to come closer and say something.

He stops, leaving enough space between us for a grand fucking piano.

As much as I want to, I can't seem to tear my gaze from his face. There are new lines on it, giving him an aged look that by some miracle only makes him more handsome. His eyes carry sadness, though, and I wonder if it's possible that we've both been in hell in the past four months.

"You forgot something," he says, reaching into his pocket and pulling out a piece of paper.

I spare my discarded speech a single glance before turning my gaze back to his face.

After a few beats, he tilts his head slightly and takes one more step in my direction. "You're not going to say anything?"

My tongue feels thick in my mouth. "I said everything there was to say." The voice that comes out sounds like a stranger's.

Pierce's mouth pulls to the side as he nods. "Okay." It sounds so final, like a gavel hitting the block, like the big black THE END on the last page of a manuscript.

Something falls in my chest—a remaining piece of rock that held on when everything else plunged into the ocean? This is it then. He didn't come here to talk about my speech. He didn't come looking for me because he had things he wanted to say. He's leaving. He's leaving me because I screwed up and realized the truth too late. I guess he just wanted to rub it in my face one last time.

Do you know what heartbreak tastes like? Metallic and slightly sweet, a little like blood, which might explain why so many people seek it out.

Every part of me wants to lash out, to berate him for causing me pain, to inflict as much damage on his heart as he's inflicted on mine. But all of those same parts also want to call out, to beg him to forgive me, to plead with him for another chance.

So I say nothing.

Because releasing control and trusting someone means allowing them to make their own decisions without manipulating them into doing what you want.

Pierce turns slowly on his heel to head back to the house, a pensive look on his face, but stops before actually reaching the door he came through minutes ago. I watch him as he hesitates, my eyes on those broad shoulders in his tuxedo, wishing I had appreciated them more while they were still mine to touch.

"Did you mean it?" His voice is quiet but still manages to pierce the night air and what's left of my heart.

It takes me several seconds to gather my wits enough to form a response, long enough that he angles his body so he can see me. "The speech?" I say, unsure of what he's asking.

Waves crash against the rocks below, sending up a spray that I imagine hitting my skin, cold and biting.

"Yes," he responds in a measured tone.

Emotion clogs my throat, and I raise my fist to my lips as I do my best to clear it before answering him. The taste of metal is still in my mouth, and I suspect it will be there for a long time to come. This isn't the kind of wound you recover from in a week.

I consider lying to him, telling him it wasn't true, that I just wanted to see what he would do if I said those things. At least then I'd be able to walk out of here with a modicum of pride left. But I don't. Maybe it's because of the emotional wreckage that is my heart, or because I've finally had to face the consequences of my own actions, but either way, I can only be honest with him from here on out.

"I did." My voice wobbles, but I force the words out.

I'm not sure what I expect—for him to nod again and walk away? Or maybe say "it was good knowing you" and give me one of those heartbreaking forehead kisses before he leaves my life for good?

He doesn't do either of those things, though, and if there's one thing I've learned, it's that the second you try to predict someone's actions, they'll do the complete opposite.

His movements slow, Pierce turns back around until he's facing me again. The pensive expression is gone, replaced by a blankness that doesn't allow me a single glimpse into his mind. I have no idea what he's thinking or feeling right now, and it makes me nervous. I keep my feet grounded, though, determined to trust him no matter what.

Every single step he takes toward me feels like an artificial heartbeat, echoing through my chest and emphasizing the emptiness of it. Only when he's close enough to touch does he stop and look down at me, letting the paper in his hands drift to the ground. My fingers long to reach out and feel his stubble, already growing back after his prewedding shave.

"And who were you referring to?" he asks in a low tone that makes my core throb with need. "When you said you lost the only guy you've ever truly loved?"

I swallow the lump of emotion barricading my throat. "I thought that would be obvious."

Pierce shifts, bringing us even closer, close enough I can smell his cologne, and that alone nearly wrecks me, but he doesn't lay a hand on me. "I thought a lot of things were obvious, and I was wrong. So I'm going to need you to spell it out for me."

Moisture blurs my vision, and I quickly blink it away. How could there be any mistaking what I meant? Unless he knows about my breakup and thinks I was referring to Preston. "You," I whisper, praying for courage. "I was talking about you."

"Maeve," he growls, and something leaps in my belly. "If you're playing with me . . ." He doesn't need to finish the sentence. His tone says it all.

I shake my head, desperate to move to the part where he's touching me again, if that part's ever coming. "I'm not." My breath comes out ragged, as if I've just run up a hill. "I meant it."

Instead of kissing me the way I need him to, he considers me, probably looking for evidence of a lie in my face. He won't find one, because nothing I've ever said before has been truer.

I push on, needing him to believe me. "I was an idiot. I was scared out of my fucking mind, Pierce. I thought—" My voice breaks as I recall the haunting fear that plagued me every time I thought about how deep my feelings for him ran. "I thought you would hurt me, that I would be safer with someone I didn't really care about."

"What changed?" He still hasn't touched me, hasn't shown any evidence that he's willing to give me another chance. Nothing except for a tiny softening of his eyes. Still, it gives me hope.

Sniffing, I brush at the tears dampening my eyelashes. I need to pull myself together. "Moment of clarity, I guess," I say quietly. "And my sister."

His brows flicker down in confusion. "What does Vivienne have to do with anything?"

I rub my bare arms. The night air is causing gooseflesh to break out all over my skin. "She made me confront some of the things I was avoiding. Namely, how I feel about you."

Before I've even stopped speaking, Pierce has shrugged out of his jacket and draped it over my shoulders. "She's always been intuitive," he says, tugging the lapels together over my chest. His words may be about Viv, but from the way his voice lowers and his hands slow, I know every syllable is for me.

I remind myself to breathe as his fingers skim the fabric of my dress.

"Maeve." This time, it sounds like he's physically in pain as he says it. He shoves a hand into his dark hair, ruining his hairstyle but also making it better. Less polished, more bedroom Pierce, and my knees wobble like a baby deer's. "I wish I had fought harder for you."

Shaking my head as tears continue forming at the corners of my eyes, I say, "I don't know that it would have changed things." Back then, I was convinced that anything with Pierce would lead to epic destruction.

"I lost four months with you," he growls, yanking me against him with a quick tug of my waist. "Don't think I'm going to forget about that very easily."

I gasp as our bodies collide, sending jolts of pleasure vibrating through my every bone and nerve ending. "What about your date?" I almost forgot about the stunning blond. She wasn't sitting next to him at dinner, but that doesn't mean anything.

A glint of amusement lights his eyes before he leans down and runs his lips over the column of my neck. "You mean my cousin Tiffany?"

I'm unclear on what oxygen is at this moment, let alone words strung together into sentences, but I manage to say, "You brought your cousin as your date?"

His teeth gently bite my jaw. "Not a date. She begged to be my plus-one. Last I saw her, she was flirting with a guy with hair bigger than his portfolio." Pierce drops kisses over the spot he bit. "Jealous?"

"Of course not," I say breathlessly. "But I am wondering what took you so long."

He pulls back, a frown deepening the lines on his forehead. "For what?"

As the wind picks up, I grab both lapels of the jacket to keep it from blowing open. "Come on. I gave you the perfect opportunity to make a romantic gesture after my toast."

His left brow rises as he looks down at me. "You took me completely by surprise. I only found out a few days ago that you broke up with that wanker. Besides," he adds, "I waited four fucking months. You could wait a few minutes."

"But you still haven't kissed me," I point out. "I'm getting tired of waiting."

His mouth tightens as he grabs my waist again and pulls me flush against his chest, leaning to growl into my ear, "I will kiss you when I'm damn well ready, and not a moment before."

Moisture rushes again, further south this time, while my mouth goes as dry as the Sahara.

"If I kiss you," he continues, his breath a feather against my ear, "that's it. You're mine. Do you understand?"

My throat makes a tiny gasping sound as I nod.

"I need to hear you say it, Panther."

"I'm yours."

He nuzzles my neck in approval. "Good girl. But it's not enough."

I cry out as he pulls back. My only consolation is that he doesn't go far.

"Sex isn't enough for me," he says, all traces of humor washed from his face. "I want all of you. Body, mind, and soul."

I slide my hands up his chest and curl them around his neck. I knew he'd demand everything, and for the first time, I'm ready to give it. "They're all yours. Forever."

He doesn't take the bait, doesn't wrap those big hands around me, doesn't smile. "You can't fuck with my heart any longer, Maeve."

Cradling his face with one hand, I tug him down to me. "I swear to you that I'm fully in. You and me, forever."

When his lips finally capture mine, they're cool from the night air and firm with intention. I gasp at the contact, hardly able to believe that he's kissing me after I thought I'd lost him forever. He takes the parting of my lips as an invitation to dive in and claim what's his, what's been his all along but I was too much of a fool to recognize.

He tastes like champagne and spicy, sweet cinnamon rolls. He smells like finely aged whiskey and midnight picnics under the stars.

He feels like a warm cup of tea and being curled up on the couch watching old movies.

Tears sting the back of my eyelids as I let him pull me even closer. He lifts my feet off the ground so I'm closer to his height, then groans as I swipe my tongue across his. How could I have come so close to never doing this again?

We stay like this for what feels like an eternity. When he finally sets me down, the breeze whips around us with its icy fingers, as if it's trying to rip us apart. I gaze up at Pierce, determined to stare at his gorgeous face every chance I get.

"I love you," he says, rubbing a thumb across my cheek. "Anything that tries to hurt you will have to get through me first."

A burst of pleasure erupts in my heart, and for the first time, I understand why people in love are so maddening. To know there's another person in the world who will do anything for you—it's kind of magical.

"I love you, too," I whisper.

Those perfect lips of his lift at the corners, gracing me with one of my favorite views of all time—Pierce St. James smirking at me. "I guess this means I won, then."

My back stiffens, my hand freezing in place on his chest. "What are you talking about?"

He shrugs, still leaning in close, that smirk growing wider by the second. "The challenge. I won."

Unease crawls up my spine. "No, you forfeited," I say, dragging the words out as if he's a preschooler, because he's starting to sound like one.

The smirk transforms into a full-blown grin. "That depends on which challenge we're talking about."

My thoughts race a million miles an hour. "Explain."

"I wanted you." He shrugs as if he's talking about the weather. "I did what I had to to win."

"Are you kidding me?" I drop both hands and push away from him, needing space to clear my head.

"Don't be mad." He reaches for me, but I slip away.

Pressing my fingertips to my temples, I try to focus on what he's saying.

"I knew you didn't see me that way, so I made it my mission to change that," he says. "Why are you mad?"

"Because—" I start, but emotion clogs my throat. "Because I didn't even know we were playing. You didn't give me a chance."

"Of course I did." A sad smile tugs at the corners of his mouth. "You pushed me away so many times, it's actually a miracle I didn't give up."

"Why didn't you?" I croak.

"Why do you think, Maeve? I wanted to win."

"But you forfe—"

"Not the game. *You.*" He slips his hands inside the jacket I'm wearing, which smells so much like him it's making me woozy, and holds my waist.

"Well, congratulations. You just lost me again." I spin out of his grasp and head for the door.

"I don't think so." He grabs my wrist and yanks me back against him. "You said forever. You can't just leave every time you get mad at me." He tugs me close, his warmth seeping through our clothes and into my skin.

"Let me go," I say, bucking against the arms pinning me against his chest.

"Absolutely not. Besides, my plan worked."

"Your plans are shit."

His minty breath hovers just above the shell of my ear as he murmurs, "They got me the girl of my dreams, didn't they?" He traces the curve of it with his tongue. "We've always been endgame, and you know it."

My legs are growing weak, and I'm so fucking tired of resisting him, but goddamn, the man makes me so mad. "Do you ever think of anyone besides yourself?" I snap.

"Yes," he says, before leaning down and slipping his hand beneath my dress. "I was thinking of you, too."

Done resisting, I let out a strangled groan as his palm travels up my thigh. "How's that, exactly?"

"I knew the fastest way to get you wet was to fight with you." Two fingers slip past my panties as I let out an involuntary gasp. "Looks like that plan worked too."

## 58

## "Clarity" - Zedd ft. Foxes

*Several Months Later*

Maeve

God, I hate waiting, especially for a lift—a situation only made worse by having to wait with Pierce St. James. I shoot him a sidelong glare as we both face the door. I'm holding Mrs. Rodriguez's cinnamon latte and my own coffee, while trying to keep my bag from slipping off my shoulder. He's got a bag that smells like it contains croissants. His other hand is tucked in the pocket of his gray dress pants, and from the smirk he's proudly sporting, I know he can feel my eyes on him.

I huff out through my nose, determined not to lose the fight this time. "Are you following me?"

He presses a palm to his chest as if he can't believe I've asked something so insulting. "While I would follow your ass all over the globe under normal circumstances, Maeve, on this particular occasion, we both just happen to be headed in the same direction."

It's a load of crock, and he knows that I know that.

HavenNet—rebranded as Solace Link—launched nearly a month

ago, so while Luminara's teams have been busy with troubleshooting, the Wilson Foundation has been dealing with PR issues as they pop up. Something we firmly have in hand, and yet here we are.

"I told you I can handle this," I hiss as we wait for the slowest elevator in the world.

He shifts closer and says in a lowered voice, "You also needed an hour to de-stress last night. Forgive me for wanting to look out for you."

I know you're probably thinking something along the lines of "aw, how sweet," but let me assure you, Pierce is being anything but sweet right now. He's close enough that I can smell his cologne—which I'm sure he's aware of—and he's wearing those stupid-ass glasses that make me weak at the knees—something I *know* he's aware of.

The man doesn't play fair.

"Go back to your tech toys, Pierce."

"You are my toy," he says, in the voice he's supposed to reserve for the bedroom but never does because he's absolute bollocks at following our agreements.

My pulse picks up speed, but I ignore it. "I'm seconds away from reporting you to HR."

"I don't work here, remember?" he purrs.

"Asshole." I press the call button again, even though it's still lit up, then a few more times for good measure.

"Maybe if you smash it, it'll come."

I whirl toward him, my finger raised. "You—"

The elevator dings, and the doors swoosh open. Pierce makes a big show of letting me get on first. I pin him with a dirty scowl, because otherwise, I'd be grinning like a fucking idiot. Why does he have to be equal parts infuriating and sexy as hell?

He steps on after me, then hits the button for the fifth floor. The doors close as the scent of hot coffee, fresh pastries, and Pierce St.

James fill the car. It's like my kryptonite, and I steel my spine with resistance. I skipped breakfast, but there's no way Pierce knows that. He left before I was even out of bed this morning, kissing me on his way out the door.

Now I know what his plans were.

I glare at the bag of croissants in his hand. "I'm not eating those."

He glances at it, then sets it on the floor. "Good. They're not for you." Before I can say anything in response, he reaches for the emergency break and pulls it.

"What are you doing?"

His movements are swift. After setting my coffee cups beside the pastries, he removes my purse from my shoulder and places it down as well.

Apprehension floods my system as I watch him—my default state, but I'm working on it—but it's quickly drowned out by anticipation, because this is Pierce we're talking about, and as much as he might irritate the life out of me, I love him, and I trust him explicitly.

When both of our hands are empty, he gives me a look that screams "predator." I have time for a single inhale before his mouth is on mine, claiming it as if there was any doubt who it belongs to. He grabs both my wrists and pins them above my head just like he did the last time we did this.

When Pierce kisses me, the rest of the world goes black. I know everyone says things like that, but it's never been true for me before. The only thing I can focus on is the way his lips pluck at me, the way his tongue pushes into my mouth, the way he's tasting me and sucking me and licking me.

How can I stay mad at someone who kisses me like I'm something incredible to be savored?

He pulls back, panting. "Do you know how long this particular fantasy has haunted me?"

## "CLARITY" - ZEDD FT. FOXES

I gasp for breath, fighting the simultaneous urges to drag him back down and to slap him. "Is your memory slipping already? We've done this before." My voice sounds raspy, likely due to me being without oxygen for what felt like two whole minutes.

"We may have kissed, but we've never done this in here before." He punctuates his words by slipping his hand under my dress, finding me wet and ready for him. His eyes flutter shut. "Fuck, Maeve."

I moan and let my head fall back against the wall as he begins exploring inside my panties. His fingers slide over my folds, making me see stars over and over.

"Please, Pierce," I whisper.

He groans in response but doesn't push them inside, just continues tormenting my clit. I've learned by now that he enjoys taking me just past the point of desperation. The secret is not to let him see how it affects me so that he'll give me more in an effort to garner a response.

I fight to regain my composure, faking boredom as he strokes my nub again and again. If I thought I could, I'd attempt a yawn, but it's taking all my self-control just to keep from crying out at this point.

I feel his teeth on my neck, a surefire way to make me crumble, but I do my damn best to stay upright.

Seconds later, I feel him smiling against my skin. "You little vixen," he says with a chuckle. "So you want to play, do you?"

Leaving me no time for a response, he whirls me around until I'm facing the elevator wall. He slaps my hands above my head, and I understand the unspoken order—*keep them up*. When I'm in a position he approves of, he trails a finger down my bare arm.

I shiver, no longer interested in trying to fool him.

"Oh, are you done manipulating me?" he asks, like the cocky bastard he is. "In that case, I guess the real fun can begin."

My heart races a thousand miles a minute, and I press my thighs together in anticipation.

He yanks my hips backward, making my palms slide down the wall. "Grab the rail," he orders.

I wrap my hands around the cold metal bar circling the elevator. It feels like a lifeline, and I'm grateful to have something secure to hold on to.

He walks me back a few more steps, until I'm doing a halfway lift in an elevator, my arms straight out in front of me, the love of my life standing behind me. "Good girl," he says. "Now let's see how wet you are for me."

A whimper slips past my lips as his fingers slip past my other lips. The burning sensation is almost too much to bear, and I buck my hips, seeking more.

"Not yet, baby," he soothes. "I want you dripping all over this disgusting carpet before I take you."

I don't spare a thought for the people who are probably waiting on this elevator or what they'll think when we finally tumble out of it. The only thing I'm aware of is the way my legs are turning to jelly from Pierce's hands.

Finally, he decides to bless me with a single finger inside. The thrust is sudden and deep, and he's in as far as he can go, reaching that spot no other man has even attempted to.

I cry out, not caring if anyone can hear me, not even caring if there are cameras in this damn lift. Let them watch. Let them see what this man does to me.

With one warm hand on my stomach, Pierce uses the other to push several fingers in and out of me. His cock is pressed against my hip, and I can feel just how much he wants me. Another release comes when I imagine him finally burying himself inside me.

The sounds of my arousal fill the car, accompanied every so often by Pierce's murmured approval.

"Please," I plead. "I need you, Pierce."

Groaning, he gives two more thrusts before withdrawing his fingers, then with his hands, he nudges my legs further apart. He tosses my skirt up, leaving my backside exposed to him. "God, I envisioned doing this the minute I saw you this morning. This fucking dress."

He's referring to my black A-line flared minidress, and it might be the only thing I'll wear from now on. Cool air hits my bottom, but only for a second, as Pierce smacks it away, making me cry out in shock.

He tugs my thong to the side, revealing my seam, which causes a guttural groan to come from his chest. Using his throbbing cock, he traces it, and it takes every ounce of self-control I possess to not press back against him.

Spreading me even further apart, until it feels like I'll split, he nudges his tip inside. "Fuck, baby. You're so slick and hot and wet. I'm going to go so fucking deep."

I tremble, knowing he means every word. "Please, Pierce. Please."

That proves to be his undoing. With one swift movement, he thrusts inside and, true to his word, buries himself as far in as is humanly possible.

A cry rips from my throat as he fills me to the brim, then pulls back just enough to drive back inside, hard and fast. I grip the handrail and push back to take him again and again. He moves his hand from my hip to my clit, exerting just enough pressure to make me detonate. As pleasure floods my body, my knees threaten to buckle, but Pierce holds me upright. Seconds later, he follows with his own climax, his body shuddering against mine as he releases.

We collapse, spent—me against the wall, him against me. After we've both caught our breath and adjusted our clothes, we pick up our things, and Pierce pushes the button to resume the elevator.

Something occurs to me as the lift groans back to life. "Do you think that's why it was so late earlier?" The thought of someone else doing what we just did in here makes me want to vomit.

"An interesting thought," he says. "Who knows?"

The bell dings, and the doors swish open, revealing Mrs. Rodriguez's cheerful smile. I cast a sidelong look at Pierce before racing out of the lift, determined to reach her with the coffee before he can offer up his croissants.

## 59

## "You Are in Love" - Taylor Swift

*Pierce*

"Can you hand me the marshmallow vodka?" I ask Maeve.

She barely glances at the bottles next to her before grabbing one and passing it to me.

"That's the marshmallow syrup."

"Well, how am I supposed to know the difference?" She sets it back down with a pout.

I bite back my smile and reach around her for the alcohol. "No worries, Panther. I've got it."

She leans back against the counter. "What are you making tonight?"

"Toasted marshmallow espresso martinis," I say, measuring shots into the mixing glass.

She's playing hostess tonight, as she has many times, and I swear it will never get old. She looks like a dream in that tiny floral-print dress, waist cinched, legs lengthened by four-inch heels. One of these days, I'm going to make her mine in every sense of the word.

I already have the perfect ring—four-carat Asscher-cut solitaire on a thin yellow gold band studded with pavé diamonds. The diamond itself dates back to the eighteenth century, and I bought it several months ago when it went up for auction at Sotheby's. I had it set in a custom band at Harry Winston and just picked it up last week.

I wanted nothing more than to give it to Maeve the second I left the jeweler's, but it has to be perfect. She deserves that much. Besides, if I rush things, I only risk scaring her. She's finally starting to trust me, and I'm not going to do anything to jeopardize that.

But you'd better believe I will be asking her when the time is right.

"What?" Her brows knit together as she looks at me, and I realize I've been staring.

"Nothing." I tug her into my arms, then bend her backward for a long kiss. She tastes like the marshmallow she snuck earlier, and I want to take her to the bedroom more than I want oxygen.

Unfortunately, the doorbell rings before I can enact any of the dozen fantasies filling my mind.

"If we ignore them, do you think they'll go away?" I murmur into Maeve's neck, which she's spritzed with that custom perfume she knows drives me nuts.

She presses her palms against my chest, but there's no strength there, because she wants this as badly as I do. "They'd never forgive us." Her teeth sink into her lower lip, painted red like the forbidden apple in the Garden of Eden.

"They've all been in our shoes," I say, nipping at her earlobe as the bell rings again. "Pretty sure they'd understand."

The chime sounds once more, and I raise Maeve back up to standing.

"That would be Lux," she says, rolling her eyes, then straightening her dress and moving to the door. When she opens in, Lux and Co. flood into my flat the way they do every Tuesday night.

Rhett is the last one inside, and he slaps me on the back as I finish garnishing the last of the cocktails with toasted marshmallows. "Hope we didn't interrupt anything," he says, wearing a giant-ass grin on his

## "YOU ARE IN LOVE" - TAYLOR SWIFT

face that completely contradicts his words.

"Fuck off." I shake his hand off with a smile of my own. There will be plenty of time to divest Maeve of her clothes later.

In the game room, I pass drinks to everyone around the table.

"What is this, Pierce?" Walker asks. "It's actually delicious."

"Praise be," Lux says, before taking a sip. "Wow, you weren't kidding. This is amazing."

I shoot them both a droll look and take a seat. "Thanks for the vote of confidence, ladies."

"Remember when he made that jalapeño one for Walker's welcome home and she nearly seared her tongue off?" Rhett says with a laugh.

"Okay, in my defense," I say, "I forgot she doesn't like spicy things."

"I think that was our diabolical queen's doing." Lux gives Maeve a pointed look.

Maeve turns red as she scans the group. "I'll admit it was a bitch move, and that was years ago! Besides, I apologized to Walker."

Walker nods and holds up her glass to Maeve. "She did. Water under the bridge."

Saylor leans over to Rhett and whispers, "You'll have to tell me the story later."

I shuffle the cards and begin dealing as everyone submits their grievance antes. It's all bogus stuff—an idiot catcalling Lux while Slate was walking right beside her, Rhett being offered unsolicited advice, someone cutting ahead of Heath in line, Maeve being left on read in a text thread—and we never go after people for this shit, but it's a tradition, and if there's one thing my girl loves, it's tradition.

"Did Briar get into Oxford, then?" Maeve asks Lux and Slate.

"She never applied," Slate says.

"Oh, is she trying for an Ivy instead? Or Cambridge? I bet she'd do terrific there."

Slate shakes his head and looks at his cards. "She's staying in

Wesbourne for school."

Maeve frowns as the wheels in her head turn. I know she can't fathom why anyone would choose not to try to get into one of the top universities in the world, but she's doing better at keeping some of her thoughts to herself.

I lift a hand to hide my smile.

"Was that her decision or yours?" Maeve asks. Well, her filter is still a work in progress.

Slate pins her with a dark gaze. The man is as protective of his sister as he is of his girlfriend. "We made the decision together."

I can tell Maeve wants to say more, but I put my hand on her thigh and give it a small squeeze.

She deflates and leans back in her chair.

"Good girl," I murmur into her ear as I reach to flip over the cards in the flop.

The game continues as everyone jokes and fucks around, and I can't believe how close I came to losing this forever. Thank God it all worked out, because I can't imagine my life without these people. Those few months away from everyone were hell.

Rhett folds and leans back in his chair, hands clasped behind his head. "Hey Maeve, you still have that hot-air balloon?"

She glares at him. "No. Pierce took care of it months ago."

I tuck my lips between my teeth and study my cards.

Rhett snorts, causing Maeve to swivel her head in my direction. "What?" she says.

I shake my head, keeping my eyes away from her. One look and I'll crumble.

She tosses her cards onto the table and turns her entire body toward me. "What aren't you telling me, Pierce St. James?"

"Here we go," Rhett says, a definitive note of glee in his voice.

"I'll get the popcorn," Heath deadpans.

I flip them both off.

"Pierce."

I can read every note in Maeve's voice, that beautiful voice I love and hate simultaneously. She's sending me a warning, but we both know she doesn't have a leg to stand on. Her hand slides up my thigh and comes to rest on my crotch.

Except that one. I shift in my seat, but she only increases the pressure.

"What happened to the hot-air balloon?" she croons.

"It's handled." I place my own hand on top of hers, but she ignores it and uses the heel of her palm to slowly begin rubbing one out. Any other time I'd simply sit back and watch her, but all six of our friends have their eyes glued to us right now.

"Where is it?"

Wrapping my fingers around her wrist to halt her movements, I finally meet her gaze. "It's still in the basement."

Deep furrows form on her brow as she tries to snatch her hand away. "It's *what*?"

I sigh and lean my arms against the table before she can get any other ideas. "You would've discovered it a long time ago if you weren't so terrified of the dark."

"I specifically asked you to get rid of it. Not doing so means you didn't complete the challenge. That's a direct violation." She turns to the rest of the group for support.

"Maeve, he already forfeited," Lux says.

My girl's face turns red, and I long to reach over and slip a finger into her panties. She must be soaked by now.

"Listen," I say, sliding an arm around her rigid shoulders and tugging her close to me, "we can fight about this later. Right now, we should plan our revenge on Deirdre Cox once and for all."

A chorus of agreement sounds around the table, then everyone waits to see what Maeve will say. No matter how many people we add to our group, she will always be our fearless leader. Except when it comes to dogs and the dark, but don't tell her I mentioned that.

"Okay." Maeve nods, but the look she sends me out of the corner of her eye tells me we'll be revisiting this conversation after everyone leaves, and I can't wait. I'll give her two minutes to yell at me before I fuck her long and hard, all night long.

It takes us an hour to come up with a plot for taking revenge on Deirdre, one that will hopefully work out better than the last one. Ms. Cox is planning a huge party—the witch isn't subtle in the least—in spite of the fact that she didn't win the hot-air balloon of her dreams. We're planning to gift it to her anonymously, but instead of it being her crowning glory, when the balloon is inflated at the party, it will reveal the words *Deirdre: Patron Saint of Greed* painted across it for every guest to see.

It's taken months, but we've finally managed to gather enough evidence to have her arrested. She pulled the same trick on another nonprofit earlier this year, and I've been in contact with them ever since, pooling our data. The only thing left is to play all our cards at the right time.

"Detective Richards still owes me a favor," I say. "He has arranged for the arrest to be made during the party."

I can feel Maeve staring at me. "Who is Detective Richards?"

"An old contact." Tossing her a casual smile, I continue shuffling the cards. She never found out about Mr. Carrow, and it's better to keep it that way. It would only dredge up old memories that are better left buried.

"I can get us all invites," Lux says. "That way we can all watch this bitch burn."

"I say we torch the balloon while we're at it," Maeve mutters.

"Hear, hear," Walker agrees.

"I don't know, babe," I say, nudging Maeve with my knee. "I was kind of thinking it would be a nice way to commemorate the beginning of our relationship."

Her glare cuts like a knife, but her phone rings before she can fire back a retort. Concern immediately replaces the irritation on her face when she sees the screen. "It's Viv," she says. "She'd never call on a Tuesday night unless it was important."

"Take it." I pat her leg reassuringly. I'm glad she's grown close with her sister. Vivienne is one of the most level-headed people I know, and Maeve needs family members she can trust. Ever since Bash's accident, she's become terrified she's going to lose one of them.

"I'll be right back." She stands and walks out of the room, phone already pressed to her ear.

The chatter around the table has died down, our cheerful camaraderie replaced by a thick unease as we wait to see what's wrong.

Walker places her hand on my arm. "I'm sure everything's okay," she says, but we all know those are empty words. The last time Maeve got a call like this, her brother had nearly died in an accident.

Maeve returns several minutes later, her face fighting for composure. Her eyes find mine, and I stand up and move toward her. Whatever has happened, we'll get through it together. We've already been to hell and back. Nothing could be worse than nearly losing her for good.

* * *

Two hours later, I close the door behind the last of our friends and turn to Maeve. "What did Vivienne want earlier? You looked a little shook up," I say, pulling her into my arms.

She shakes her head. "I'm not really sure. She was worried about something Dad did after Bash's accident. I got the sense he was up to something back then, but Viv didn't want to tell me what it was."

I frown. "That doesn't sound like her."

"I know." She bites her lip. "Whatever it is has her feeling guilty."

"If your father's involved, I imagine she has good reason to."

Maeve buries her nose in my chest. "I don't want to think about my family right now."

"What would you like to think about then?" I brush my lips against the shell of her ear, and she shivers.

"I thought maybe you could help me relax," she says, lifting her face to me.

"Maeve Allegra Wilson, are you propositioning me for sex?"

She grins. "What are you going to do about it if I am?"

"If you have to ask that, I clearly have some work to do." I grab her hand to lead her to the bedroom, but the painting in the foyer catches my attention. It's my favorite, *Emancipation* by Simone Caldwell. I hung it right inside my door so I can see it every time I come home, so I've literally looked at it hundreds of times. Tonight though, something feels off.

Maeve tugs on my hand, but I stop in front of the abstract lines. "Hang on," I say, studying the canvas.

"What's wrong?" She returns to my side and stares at it with me.

"There was a tiny mark on this painting when I got it. The gallery said it happened during transit."

"And?"

"And it's not there anymore." I squint at the painting and try to remember the last time I saw the small scratch, but I haven't looked closely at this particular piece in months.

"Okay, well, that's a good thing, right?" Maeve reaches for the top button of my shirt. "Now are you going to take me to the bedroom and do all those things you promised earlier?"

"Maeve, you don't get it," I say, placing my hand over hers. "If that mark is gone, that means this one's a forgery."

She huffs out an impatient sigh. "Or it means that fate decided to reward you for being so sexy. Besides, that painting is ugly."

My frown deepens as I look down at her. Her tone is too flippant. The Maeve I know would already be three feet deep in a revenge plot over this. "What aren't you telling me?" I take a step back and watch her face.

She turns red, as I knew she would. "I don't know what you're talking about." Lifting her chin, she takes a step backward.

My mind whirls over the past six months and lands on one particular challenge—the only one she won, because I didn't give a fuck anymore and stole her perfume.

It drove me crazy that I couldn't figure out what she'd taken from my place, and I tore apart my flat, trying to discover what was missing. After several days, I convinced myself she must have taken a dust bunny from beneath the sofa, because everything else was exactly where it should've been.

"Where's my painting, Maeve?" I move toward her, and she retreats another foot.

"I don't have your stupid painting," she says.

"You'd better have it, because that one's fake." I point at the wall while keeping my eyes trained on her.

She watches me for several seconds, chest heaving. She looks like a deer caught in the headlights. I read the indecision on her face right before she darts down the hall.

Grinning, I give her a tiny head start, then bolt after her. With her short legs, I'll catch her before she reaches the bedroom. And when I do, there's going to be hell to pay.

* * *

**Need more Pierce & Maeve?** Download Pierce's proposal chapter for free at jessicajude.com/jokers-endgame-bonus

Thank you for reading *Joker's Endgame*! If you enjoyed this book, it would mean the world to me if you left a review, even if it's short. Reviews are like tips for authors, and every one helps!

If you're in a reading slump after that or just want more of the same, you might want to try my debut novel, Thrones We Steal, or the first book in this series, Ace of Betrayal, if you haven't read Heath and Walker's story yet!

xoxo Jess

P.S. Want to discuss my books, dissect Easter eggs, and spiral with other like-minded readers? Join my exclusive reader groups on Facebook and Discord. We'd love to see you there!

Join my email list to be notified when new books launch and to receive more exclusive bonus content! Visit jessicajude.com/newsletter to sign up.

Signed copies and book swag are available at jessicajude.com/shop

# Up Next...

Want more from the world of Wesbourne? A new series is launching fall 2026 and some of your favorite Hand of Revenge characters will be back, along with a brand new cast!

**Flare (Embers of Us #1)**
*coming September 15th*

**Pre-order your copy today!**

# Acknowledgments

To Jesus Christ, who paid the ultimate price for me, despite how often I screw up.

To Curtis, who is the ultimate book boyfriend but who I'm lucky enough to call "husband."

To my family, who I would give up everything in the world for, including ice cream and Gossip Girl.

To Jenny de Pierre, my brilliant editor. Thank you for hiding your smirk whenever I write "pantry" instead of "panty."

To Haya in Designs for the gorgeous covers of the Hand of Revenge series. (This one's my favorite.)

To Rumaisa for creating art of Maeve and Pierce that still leaves me weak at the knees. You're so incredibly talented.

To my VIP gang who helped create the perfect playlist for our two scheming control freaks: Kayla Bautista, Paige Miller, Iris Wallace, Thaiyah Sharell, Kerri Mrozinski, Christiana Camacho, Amanda Richard, Grace Dringenburg, Catrina Reagan-Spalding, Robin Frum, Leslie McBride, Maxi, Twisted Bookworm, Caya, Julie Pesik, Katie Bessire, Laquita Agwiak, Danyele Henson, Ashiki Welch, Macy Fleetwood, Angela Green-Carter, Ashley Coons, and Emily Hall.

To my dedicated readers, who devour my books much faster than I can write them—thank you for loving Maeve and Pierce from book one and for having faith in me as you waited for their story.

And to you, dear reader, for picking up this book and giving it a chance. Authors get all the hype, but you're the real hero. Thank you

## ACKNOWLEDGMENTS

for reading!

# Also by Jessica Jude

**Hand of Revenge series**
*Ace of Betrayal*
*Queen of Vengeance*
*King of Obsession*

*They're rich. They're reckless. They're out for revenge.*
A group of wealthy Gen Zers plays poker to determine the victims of their weekly revenge plots. What they don't bargain on? Falling in love with the people who could destroy them.

**Thrones We Steal Trilogy**
*Thrones We Steal*
*Castles We Storm*
*Crowns We Save*

Apparently, I'm the rightful queen of Wesbourne. On paper, it sounds like a fairy tale. Money. Power. Fame. And the chance to make a difference in the country I adore. All I have to do is give up the life I've built and the man I love.
Oh, and one other small thing. I'll have to marry the crown prince. Yes, he's gorgeous and charming and his voice makes your body sing. Everyone thinks I'm crazy for hesitating. But they don't know him like I do. They don't know that he destroyed me last time.

# About the Author

Jessica Jude loves nothing better than sending her characters on an emotional roller coaster of love, angst, and drama, but in reality her life is very ordinary, drama-free, and probably boring to anyone watching. (Which would be weird. And creepy.)

She married her high school sweetheart at nineteen. Being an author is a dream she's had since she was six years old and wrote her first book, which was ten pages long, about a girl named Mary getting lost in the woods. (It was never published, but good news: Mary was eventually rescued.) When she's not writing, she's reading, reading about writing, or eating ice cream. In another life, she would live in England in a sprawling manor house with hidden passages and secret stairways, but for now, she's content with her old brick farmhouse in the Midwestern United States.

Still a fan? Here are some ways you can ~~stalk~~ stay connected!
  jessicajude.com/newsletter
  Instagram @JessicaJudeBooks
  Threads @JessicaJudeBooks
  TikTok @JessicaJudeBooks

# Discussion Questions

1. Why do you think Maeve felt such a need to control everything in her life?
2. How did you feel about her affair with Preston? What do you think drove her to maintain the relationship?
3. Why do you think Pierce waited so long to pursue Maeve?
4. Do you think Maeve and Pierce would've found their way to each other if it hadn't been for their friends' interference?
5. Share your thoughts on a benefits-only relationship. Can it be healthy or does it always end in heartache?
6. Do you think the friends made the right choice in agreeing to the challenge? Why or why not?
7. What scene in Joker's Endgame made the biggest emotional impact on you and why?
8. What quote or moment haunts you?

www.ingramcontent.com/pod-product-compliance
Lightning Source LLC
LaVergne TN
LVHW091654070526
838199LV00050B/2174